HARRY'S QUEST

A NOVEL in FIVE PARTS

A. B. PATTERSON

Published by A. B. Patterson 2018
PO Box A1364
Sydney South
NSW 1235
Australia

First Printing 2018

Cover design by Sailor Studio
www.sailorstudio.com.au

Back cover photographs from iStock
Logo design by Stephen Hill at Dylunio

A catalogue record for this
book is available from the
National Library of Australia

ISBN: 978-0-9923273-2-3 (paperback)

Also available as an ebook:
ISBN: 978-0-9923273-3-0

Published with assistance of Publicious P/L
www.publicious.com.au

To justice ...
And may every dog have its day.

Also by A. B. Patterson

Novels:
Harry's World

Short Stories:
'Little Rich Street Girl'
(Published in *Switchblade* – Issue # 3 – Special Edition)

'White Powder, Black Leather, Grey Badges'
(Published in *Switchblade* – Issue # 4)

'Wankers'
(Forthcoming in *Switchblade* – Issue # 8)

Contents

Contents

About the Author

A. B. Patterson is an Australian writer who knows first-hand about corruption, power, crime and sex. He was a Detective Sergeant in the WA Police, working in paedophilia and vice, and later a Chief Investigator with the NSW Independent Commission Against Corruption.

His multiple award-winning debut novel, *Harry's World*, introduced the jaded and flawed PI Harry Kenmare. He has also had short stories published in the USA. His hard-boiled, gritty, and noir writing style has been likened to that of Raymond Chandler and Ken Bruen.

Harry's Quest is the sizzling second novel in the PI Harry Kenmare series.

www.abpatterson.com.au

Author's Foreword

I've had a huge amount of fun writing *Harry's Quest*, and crafting the ongoing adventures for my flawed hero, PI Harry Kenmare, and his friends. My sincerest hope is that you will have just as much fun reading this sequel to *Harry's World*.

If you are a fan of the first novel, and have been waiting patiently to see what Harry does next, then please accept my apologies for keeping you in suspense. I promise the next one won't take as long.

I certainly got feedback from readers after the first Harry Kenmare book to say how much they had grown to like Harry, and how keen they were to see what his future held. I hope this second outing for him will satisfy you, those readers, at least for now!

And, especially with my overseas readers in mind, I have again included a Glossary to assist with the Australian colloquialisms and the ever-pervasive acronyms that modern society seems to thrive on. I've had mixed feedback on whether to put the Glossary at the front or the back of the book. The majority came down for the back, so that's where you'll find it. But I did want to highlight it before you start your reading adventure, in case you want to peruse it first.

Please enjoy!
Cheers, Andrew

A. B. Patterson
Sydney, November 2018

PART 1

HARRY'S TRAINS

She wasn't too much of a lady to arrange herself appealingly in the chair, and dramatize the plea. There was a chance she wasn't a lady at all.

- Ross Macdonald

But now and then, a woman walks up, full blossom, a woman just bursting out of her dress…a sex creature, a curse, the end of it all. I looked up and there she was, down at the end of the bar.

- Charles Bukowski

– 1 –

The cartilage gave way with a light crunching sound as Harry tightened his hands around the man's throat. It felt like crushing the ribcage of a chicken carcass.

The man's eyes were defiant no longer, as if he realized the end was near. There was no more air coming in.

He still tried to struggle, his last effort, but Harry's knee was on his chest and a hundred kilograms of fury and hatred rendered any movement impossible.

The eyes started to fade.

Harry squeezed all the harder. Between gritted teeth he hissed, 'This is for my Orla, you fucking animal.'

There was a faint flicker of terrorized recognition in the fading eyes, and then it expired. The eyeballs rolled slightly and the man's body went limp.

A flash of light and Harry saw Orla's angelic face.

'Daddy! Daddy!'

Harry sat up with a shout, his head dripping with sweat. Before he could focus, two breasts enveloped his face and delicate arms cradled the back of his head. Tanya's blonde tresses cascaded around him as she hugged him tight and kissed his forehead.

'It's okay, my Mr PI, it's okay.'

Harry's breathing started to slow. As always when he felt the press of Tanya's body to him, he considered it nothing short of a miracle that this gorgeous nineteen-year-old nymphette was content on sharing the bed of a slightly balding and slightly fattening forty-six-year-old private eye. And one who loved the booze and fast women, with plenty of variety in the lust department. Life worked in strange ways, but he sure as hell wasn't complaining.

'Oh, Divine One.'

'Same dream again, Harry?'

'Yes, babe. I got the prick and then Orla appeared.'

'And we will get him, Harry, or them.'

'Yeah.'

Harry closed his eyes and breathed in the residual fragrance of Tanya's perfume, the Guerlain Insolence she always wore. She'd taken to spraying a touch in her cleavage before the nights she spent with him, usually one or two a week, as he loved to bury his face between her full breasts. Usually it was during their passionate sex, but it served just as well for the moments of consolation she gave Harry as well.

'Do you want to get up?' she asked.

Harry raised his face and kissed her lightly on the lips. 'I'm not sure I feel too randy just at the moment, Divine One.'

Tanya stuck her tongue out. 'I didn't mean that, Mr Stud. You've got a one-track mind.'

'Hard not to with you, babe.'

'And don't forget it. I figured you probably wouldn't be able to sleep again and the sun is coming up.'

Harry turned and looked at the eastern amber glow seeping in around the blinds. His apartment windows were closed tight to keep out the cold August air as well as Sydney's endless noise.

Tanya put her finger on his chin and turned his head back towards her. 'And, Mr PI, we have a big day in *our* office, don't we?'

Harry grinned at her. He thought back to that evening two months back when Tanya had comforted him through his desolation at having had shocking news about Orla's rape and murder eleven years ago. It was during that evening of emotional turmoil that he'd agreed to take on Tanya and her twin sister, Sasha, part-time to see if they liked the sleuthing trade.

'Oh, yeah, that's right. It's Monday and it's day one of Kenmare and Associates.'

'Exactly. Finally, after two months. Can't wait to improve your office. Sash and I will change your life, Harry.'

'You already have, babe, I can't begin to explain.' Harry reflected that his own mental health had taken quite a lift with having focus and people to care for in his life.

Since the decision with the girls, he'd organized probationary PI licences for them and readied them to start. This new direction, along with their fashion design apprenticeships with his friend, Tessa Hurst, and associated modelling work, meant that their days in the brothel where he'd met them were now history.

'Maybe you can try the explanation over dinner tonight. And before your mate Liam arrives and it all turns liquid.'

'Liquid dinner? Us?' Harry laughed. He put his hands gently on either side of Tanya's face. 'Thank you, Tanya.'

He touched the tip of his nose against hers and lingered there, looking straight into her pale blue eyes.

'And thank you, Harry,' whispered Tanya. 'Sash and I are so happy to be out of the parlour.'

They kissed.

'Okay, I'm going for a shower and you, boss, can make me coffee and toast.'

'At your service, babe.'

Tanya stood up from Harry's lap, passed her pussy millimetres in front of Harry's now upturned face and stepped off the bed.

Harry groaned. 'Fuck me. I wouldn't be dead for quids.'

'Well, don't get too trashed at dinner tonight and then we can screw all night long. Or as long as your stamina lasts.' She blew him a kiss and sauntered to the bathroom, exaggerating the sway of her taut buttocks as she went.

As Tanya disappeared from view, and Harry felt his erection starting, he found himself thinking of Tessa again. She was rather more in his age bracket, but still gorgeous and an animal in the sack. He'd enjoyed her bedroom attentions twice, but he'd last seen her in June. He'd called her two days ago, on her fortieth birthday, hoping to tickle her fancy. Alas, she was too busy with work and promised him a raincheck. Ah well, Harry, it's not as if you've been experiencing a drought between the sheets. He pictured Tanya's derrière again. He then stood up awkwardly and headed for the kitchen.

— 2 —

By lunchtime, Harry was having difficulty recognizing his own office. It felt like returning to a previous home after many years: sort of the same, but intangibly different. He was standing in the corner sipping a takeaway coffee trying to take it all in. He felt a mixture of amazement and confusion, like a schoolboy in a changing room full of curvaceous cheerleaders. He was delighted to have his new assistants, but equally he was perturbed by the huge change. His office, as grotty as it had been in his single-operator style, was his second home. And he wasn't going to be able to treat it quite the same way again. Still, having two beautiful young women, the divine Roberts twins, in there half the week would certainly make sitting at his desk infinitely more pleasurable.

His old timber desk had been pushed back half a metre towards the window, and an hour previously two beefy, perhaps steroid-assisted, removalists had, with much grunting, heaved another old, solid timber desk up the two flights of stairs and into the office. The newcomer now resided at right angles to Harry's workbench, the corners touching.

Harry had expected the twins to pick something brand new and uber-cool for their shared workstation. He'd half anticipated having to assemble some modern flat-pack contraption.

But Tanya and Sasha had said they wanted their desk and chairs to blend in with his. So, whilst it was longer, to accommodate two seats behind it, its dark and slightly battered timber nestled up amicably to his.

That, however, was where the homage to yesteryear began and ended. On the couch against the wall were stacked sleek white Apple boxes. Oblivious to Harry's protestations about expenses, the twins had insisted on an iMac each, as well as laptops and iPads.

Harry's other sometime offsider, PI Trevor Matson, was becoming more of a regular feature in Harry's business now, given Trev's huge expertise on all things technical and computing. Hence Trev was coming over shortly to set everything up, Harry having figured that what would take him several hours to tackle, and probably stuff up, would be half an hour's work for Trev's nimble, technical paws. Trev had also offered to give the beautiful apprentice sleuths lessons in all the surveillance and technical side of the gumshoe business. Harry had passed this offer on and it had been eagerly accepted. Harry recalled the chat in his office the previous week.

Tanya had said, 'Cool, it'll be good to see Trev again. Plus I think it's good for you to have an offsider like Trev around the place.'

'And he'll be a great teacher,' Sasha added. 'Trev rocks, seriously. And he keeps himself in shape, Harry. Maybe some of that could rub off on you.'

'Yeah, righto. You two really like Trev, don't you?' teased Harry.

'He's lovely to us and he never leers,' replied Sasha.

Harry threw in, 'I don't leer, Divine Ones.' He paused. 'Do I?'

'No, Mr PI. But then you don't need to, you've shagged both of us,' Tanya reminded him.

He reddened slightly.

'Anyway, moving right along. I'll have to tell Trev to concentrate on the equipment in here and not the staff.'

'Yeah, whatever. I don't think you need worry about that,' said Sasha.

Harry took another swig of coffee as he returned from his reverie. Aside from the computing gear, modernity had also crashed the scene with four large framed prints on the walls. Two were by Ken Done and two by Nicholas Girling, their depictions of Sydney magnificently colourful, but in a rather different range of hues than Harry was used to seeing in the darker haunts of modern Port Jackson. Harry had put his foot down about ditching the old TV set and the radio, despite Tanya's taunts about retro not always being a valid defence. He'd responded that he'd happily die old school, thank you very much. He had, however, agreed to a small drinks cabinet, since the office libations were clearly going to have to be expanded from his solitary bottle of Jameson that loitered in his bottom desk drawer, like some dark sentinel of Middle Earth. And then three tasteful, not to mention expensive, colourful glass vases, red, green and purple, had arrived to keep Harry's chunky cobalt blue glass ashtray company. He was keeping his fingers crossed that some new clients emerged to reinvigorate his bank balance.

It was at that moment that Harry heard a key in the door and in bounced the gorgeous twins, their faces radiating enthusiasm and happiness. Sasha was carrying a plastic bag with a bottle shop logo on it and Tanya's arms were laden with flowers. Clearly the empty status of the vases was about to change.

Harry couldn't help but smile and revel in the sight. His nose was going to have to adjust to competing Guerlain and Gaultier fragrances in the one room. And not the bedroom at the Scarlet Boudoir where he'd been outfoxed by these two sirens a year ago. He was going to have to start wearing his Fahrenheit every day, just so Tanya's Insolence and Sasha's Classique would have some rivalry from Dior. Plus he needed to show that sophistication and style could emanate from his desk as well. After all, he was the boss of this outfit.

'Bloody hell, girls. With all these, the florist must have been able to close up for the day.'

'Mr PI, it's not every day you get to welcome two beautiful new associates into your office,' said Tanya.

'Or should we say *our* office?' added Sasha, blowing Harry a kiss.

'I think I need a bloody drink already.'

'And on that subject, Mr PI, we need to get a bar fridge in here. There's room for one in the corner behind the door,' said Tanya.

Harry frowned. 'I've never needed one yet.'

Sasha added, 'We're not going to sit here drinking whiskey with you. We need cold soda water for our vodka, and white wine chilled and ready for when the mood takes us.'

'And bubbles,' added Tanya.

'Aye, aye.' Harry touched his forehead with a salute.

The twins set about arranging the flowers in the new vases: bold and brash orange tiger lilies for the coffee table, buttery and sleek yellow roses on the new desk, and tall and imposing blue irises on top of the squat filing cabinet.

Harry sat nodding in approval, still contemplating a drink. He'd always loved flowers and plants. Some of his best childhood times had been holidays spent at an aunt's rose nursery. And then he'd made a colourful little garden for Orla when she'd turned six. He cherished the memories of playing with her and the flowers.

As Harry momentarily drifted into the past, the buzzer sounded three times in quick succession. It was Trev's signature ring. Harry made a mental note to get another spare key cut and then pressed the release button on his desk.

Trev, also an ex-cop-turned-PI, walked in. He was only two years younger than Harry, but rather slimmer and fitter, and an identical 180 centimetres in height. He was lugging a couple of large, black, rigid plastic cases. He grinned at the scene before him. 'Kenmare and Associates, I presume?'

'Smart-arse,' replied Harry.

'Hi, Trev,' said the twins in unison.

Trev was still grinning at Harry. 'Now, mate, just some wardrobe shopping for you and it's a whole new world.'

Tanya jumped in. 'Don't worry, Trev, we've got new suits on the list of priorities.'

Harry shook his head. 'Yeah, funny ha-ha. Firstly, I hate wearing them. Secondly, there's nothing wrong with my old detective outfits if I need a suit.'

Tanya groaned. 'Bit tight around the middle these days, Mr PI.'

'Or maybe you're hoping safari suits will come back in,' said Sasha.

'Go to buggery,' replied Harry.

They all laughed.

'I'll get to it,' said Trev, heading for the Apple shop on the couch. He started unpacking the first iMac. Sasha went over to help whilst Tanya finished the flowers.

Harry's mobile phone rang.

'G'day, Tom.'

Trev looked over at him.

'Cool. See you in a few minutes.'

He put the phone down on his desk and turned to Trev. 'Tom Strong's coming over. Wants to give me an update on Orla's case.'

'Who's he?' asked Sasha.

'The federal cop in charge of the reopened case file. The state police left the file as a cold case ages ago, but when that fucking Commander Lowe was taken down by the Feds, they started a new task force with the state boys. Here's hoping for a result after all these years.'

'Yep, fingers crossed,' said Trev.

'Do you want us to go out?' asked Tanya.

'No, no, stay. He knows Trev already and it'd be good for him to meet you two, now it's Kenmare and Associates.' Harry over-stressed the last word. 'He'll be here in a few minutes.'

It was less than ten, and the buzzer sounded. The bulky physique beyond the frosted glass was clearly Federal Agent Tom Strong, and Harry pressed the door release. Tom ambled in, looking around at the people and activity. He stretched out his hand to Trev, who was nearest the door.

'Trevor Matson, how's things?'

'All good, Tom. Great to see you.'

Tom kept moving and Harry stood up. They shook hands over the desk.

'Tom, allow me to introduce my two new assistants. Ms Roberts of the Tanya variety, and Ms Roberts of the Sasha variety.'

Tom shook their hands.

He turned to Harry. 'Mate, you never cease to amaze me.'

'You're no orphan there,' came in as an aside from Trev.

Tom plonked himself in the chair in front of Harry's desk and placed a folder onto his lap. Harry sat down again.

'Business good, Harry?'

'Pretty steady, Tom. It's always up and down in this game, but it's paying the bills. Mind you, I need some new clients to pay for these two young ladies.' Harry smiled at the girls, then looked back at Tom.

'Harry, I wanted to give you an update in person on how we're going with Orla's investigation. Less said over the phone, you know.'

'Yep. Much appreciated, Tom. I trust you guys are doing your best, you know that. And the local boys chucked it in the cold case cupboard years ago.'

'We're keeping it open now for the child porn connections, being in our jurisdiction. So, we might be able to get the pricks, even if the original homicide file has been dormant with the locals. And they haven't been exactly too enthusiastic on our supposed joint task force.'

Harry grimaced. 'Yeah, I can imagine. Pricks. Don't think the hierarchy was keen to do anything for me after I got kicked out for belting that ped.'

'You're probably right. Mate, the other reason I wanted to come over personally to was to let you know that I'm retiring.'

'What? When did you decide this?' asked Harry, stunned.

'I've been thinking about it for a while. Even the Feds aren't the police force they used to be. Need to be more interested in politics and game-playing than catching crooks, just like the state forces. I've had a gutful, and I'm eligible for my pension, so it's time to go. There's a whole lot of fishing to be done, mate.' Tom smiled.

'It'll be their loss, Tom, but you enjoy it, mate. Who's taking over from you?'

'One of the new breed, alas. She loves her career trajectory, and hates doing investigations. So, she's going places. But I don't think Orla's case will have anywhere near the same momentum. All the more reason to come and brief you in person.' He tapped the file. 'So this will be my last update, Harry. Obviously I can't give you too much detail. Confidentiality, et cetera. You know the drill.'

'Yeah, of course.'

'Why don't we go and have a coffee and we can chat?'

'We can chat freely here, Tom. You know Trev. And I'd trust the divine Roberts sisters with my life.'

'Of course. But I really do need a coffee. C'mon, my shout, mate.'

'Can you bring me one back?' asked Trev. 'I'm busting for a caffeine fix.'

'Mate, come down as well,' said Tom.

Harry and Tom both stood up.

Harry asked the twins if they wanted a coffee bringing back.

'No, thanks. But we'll stay here in case any customers come calling,' said Tanya.

'And we'll keep them entranced until you get back,' added Sasha.

'You do that, 'cos we need some serious revenue to pay for all this,' replied Harry. 'You are two expensive young ladies.'

'And we're worth every cent of it,' replied Tanya.

'Yeah, yeah,' said Harry.

The three men walked out of the office.

Sasha pulled an iPad out of its box, placing it on her half of the long desk.

'Sis, I'm glad that Harry's been working more with Trev. I think he needs more company than he's been used to.'

'Yeah, an offsider who's not called Jameson. And one he hasn't had sex with.'

Sasha chuckled. 'Harry doesn't have a clue about Trev, does he?'

'Don't think so,' replied Tanya. 'And I've never heard Trev talk about his private life.'

'You thought about dropping a hint or anything?'

'No. Look that's for Trev to handle if he wants to. Anyway, Harry sure as hell wouldn't have a problem with it.'

'Yeah, he's definitely cool like that,' replied Sasha. She looked over at Harry's desk.

'Hey, Tom left that file here.' Sasha walked over and picked up the plain manila folder with an Australian Federal Police badge printed on it.

Tanya came around the desk.

Sasha opened the file and started leafing through the papers. 'It's the Orla investigation. Names, addresses, ugly mug shot photos,' she said. 'Do you think he meant to leave it?'

'Don't know. Although I'm sure he was tapping it when he gave me a funny look as he got up to leave,' said Tanya. 'But this could be a good day one as private detectives, Sis.'

Sasha looked at her. 'Shit, Tan, it's a bloody police file.'

'Yeah, I know, but Tom doesn't need to find out.'

'Yeah, I guess. And Harry would want us to, wouldn't he?'

'As sure as death, taxes, and Harry liking pussy,' said Tanya. 'You keep an ear on the corridor, and I'll do the fastest photocopy job in history.'

Sasha moved over to the door and Tanya took the file over to the small printer-cum-copier. She undid the file fasteners and pulled out the bundle of about fifty pages.

She put a batch into the document feeder and pressed the copy button. The machine emitted a nasty little beep and a red light came on.

'Fuck! The feeder's not working. Harry and his old equipment.'

'Do them one sheet at a time then, Sis, but hurry.'

Tanya started the laborious process of lifting the lid, sliding a page onto the platen and pressing the button.

After twenty-three pages, the machine repeated its nasty protest noise.

'What now?' asked Sasha.

'Oh, for fuck's sake,' said Tanya. 'Now it's out of paper.'

She looked around the printer, but couldn't see any supplies. 'Where the hell does he keep it?'

Sasha moved quickly away from the door and over to the wall with the filing cabinet, a small cupboard, and the new drinks cabinet. She started searching whilst Tanya went over to Harry's desk and began rummaging through the drawers.

'Found it,' called Sasha, pulling a ream of A4 out of the cupboard. She gave it to Tanya, who quickly reloaded the machine and continued copying.

Twenty minutes later, and less than five minutes after the copier had done its last run, the three guys walked back into the office. The AFP file was sitting on the edge of Harry's desk, exactly as Tom had left it. A bundle of papers, still slightly warm from the copier, were skulking in a drawer beneath the twins' desk. If anyone had looked closely, they would have seen tiny beads of sweat on the girls' foreheads.

Harry shook Tom's hand. 'Thanks for all your work, Tom. And keep us posted on your send-off, we'd love to buy you a few drinks, mate.'

'That's for sure,' said Trev. 'Haven't been to a coppers' piss-up for years. Not since I got kicked out, too.'

Tom laughed. 'You pair of reprobates. Anyway, it's been a pleasure and I'll stay in touch.'

He glanced around him.

'Ah, there's my bloody file. Middle-aged forgetfulness. I'll start having trouble with my name next.'

He picked up the file, and grinned at Tanya and Sasha, who were both trying to seem nonchalant. Tom winked at them, and a hint of redness appeared on their faces. 'Enjoy the PI business, ladies, you're with a couple of good men here.'

Tom bade farewell to them all and left.

'What did he say?' asked Tanya.

'Not much in the way of specifics, but he said they were following some strong leads,' replied Harry. 'He does need to be careful with what he says, even if we are mates. He said he was just giving me a summary of what they had in their case file.'

'Yeah. He needs to be more careful with his files, too,' said Sasha.

Tanya pointed to where the AFP file had been sitting on the desk. 'Yeah, careless Mr Policeman.'

Trev started smiling. Harry looked at him, and then it dawned on him.

'You didn't, did you?' asked Harry.

Tanya pulled the wad of pages from the desk drawer. Harry looked at her, then at Sasha, then back to Tanya.

Trev chipped in first. 'Looks like the Kenmare associates have scored high distinctions on their first day.'

'Damned right,' said Harry. 'I could kiss you both. In fact, I'm going to.' He walked over to the girls and gave them both a hug and a kiss.

'Perhaps we should have a drink and then I'll have a look at the file,' said Harry. 'I think I'll need a drink before I read this.'

He pulled the bottle of Jameson and the Cavan crystal glasses out of his bottom drawer. 'Girls, until we get the fridge sorted out it'll have to be whiskey, I'm afraid. But it is Irish.'

Sasha snorted and leant down to her own bottom drawer. A bottle of Grey Goose vodka emerged. 'It came with the flowers.'

Trev laughed. 'They just keep passing with flying colours.'

Harry poured two Jamesons and two vodkas.

They had a quick drink, and toasted the new Kenmare team.

Trev downed the last of his whiskey and turned to Harry. 'Brother, I'll take the ladies out to my van and start their training. We'll leave you in peace with the file.'

'Cheers, mate, appreciate it. See you a bit later. Study hard, girls.'

'Yeah, yeah,' said Tanya. 'Oh, by the way, a new client called just before you came back. Here.' She handed Harry a slip of paper. Trev and the twins headed out.

Harry sat down again. He looked at the note from Tanya. Then he poured himself another drink and picked up the sheaf of papers.

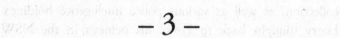

– 3 –

The prospective new client was an interesting one. Harry couldn't for a minute fathom why a lead organizer from the Train, Bus & Ferry Union would want his services. But no doubt all would be revealed in twenty minutes when one Barry Stoddart of the TBFU arrived. Harry hoped he would be rather more punctual than the services provided by his union's members on Sydney's public transport.

It was well into the afternoon and without any lunch, but Harry's hunger was for something far more primal than food, or pussy. He was sitting behind his desk, elbows planted and his fingertips together, thumbs under his chin. He was staring at the bundle of AFP file papers pushed forward on his desk.

Harry had read through it all twice since Trev had taken the twins off an hour earlier to show them the intricacies of his surveillance van and devices. He was mulling over the names, locations and other details in the police investigation.

As he stared at the papers, he conjured up visions of standing over three paedophiles as they knelt in front of shallow graves. Then he held his .38 Special against each perverted head in turn and pulled the trigger.

The interim analysis from the file concluded there were three offenders who had abducted and killed Orla. The analysis was based on the video that the Feds had found amongst former Commander Mervyn Lowe's depraved collection, as well as various police intelligence holdings. Harry thought back to Lowe, his nemesis in the NSW Police who had effectively ended his police career. Sure, Harry punching a paedophile in custody hadn't exactly been a good career move, but Lowe had taken the opportunity to further himself by shafting Harry, as well as others along the way. And then Lowe's underage proclivities had finally come out, and he'd met his fate in remand prison. That was karma, thought Harry, remembering the juicy news details of Lowe being decapitated by another inmate.

The description of the video footage was referred to in the analysis, but the cited appendix document with the gruesome details was missing. Harry knew from what Tom Strong had previously told him that Lowe wasn't on the video, but one of his associates was. And when Tom had shown Harry a snippet of the video, a couple of months back, it was only a frame of Orla, enough to identify her, and that was all. However, the video description in the file detailed three suspects.

Harry wondered if Tom had left the file on purpose, but hadn't wanted him reading the account of what was so awful to contemplate. Harry was torn between wanting to know exactly what happened to little Orla and preferring not to taint his memory of her with the full, disgusting truth. What was in the file, however, was everything needed to hunt the scum down.

The three offenders were still alive, according to the AFP checks so far. The first was Bernhard Schwarz, a now forty-year-old convicted paedophile. He was believed to still be in

NSW, moving between addresses in Sydney and Newcastle. The second was Herbert Farr, now thirty-nine years old, and serving time in Victoria, for child sex offences, of course. Offender number three was Reggie Wheeler, now fifty, and according to a recent Interpol intelligence report, living it up in Vientiane. Poor bloody Laotian kids had even less chance than the Aussie ones, thought Harry. In fact, all three suspects had prior molestation and child porn convictions. Harry frowned as he thought about the revolving doors of the justice system, constantly regurgitating known predators back onto the streets to destroy more lives.

Apart from the monsters who had taken Orla, the file also detailed a number of associates, linked to these three through the various videos found, and the subsequent AFP analysis work. It came as no surprise to Harry that there were several associates in positions of trust and authority.

Harry's mind reverted to wanting to know exactly what these scum did to his little girl. He decided right then that he would do absolutely anything, without any limitations. His little Orla deserved no less dedication to the task.

He was starting to jot things in a fresh notebook when the buzzer sounded. He pressed his intercom.

'Good afternoon.'

A broad Australian accent replied, 'I've got an appointment. Barry Stoddart.'

The voice was deep and rough, with a two-packet-a-day harshness. The bugger was early, something Harry had not expected. He pressed the door release.

'Come in.'

He slid the copied AFP file into a drawer as the door opened.

A short, stocky man in his early fifties walked in. He had a purposeful stride, and led with his chest and chin. Yep, certainly looks like a union organizer, thought Harry. The guy was wearing black Blundstone boots, somewhat grimy jeans, and a blue King Gee polo shirt. Harry couldn't see if the belt, if there was one, matched the boot colour, as an impressive beer gut flowed like magma over the waistline. Harry felt rather slimmer than he had when he got dressed this morning.

The man advanced to the desk and held out his hand.

'Barry Stoddart, mate. Lead Organizer with the TBFU.'

Harry picked up a fresh scent of beer, over the top of rather less fresh sweat. He shook his hand.

'Harry Kenmare. Pleased to meet you.'

Stoddart sat down without invitation, looked around the room, then at Harry.

'Never seen a private dick's office before.'

'Nothing special, as you can see.'

'Yeah. Where's the secretary girlie I spoke to?'

'Out.'

Harry decided not to correct Stoddart. He reckoned he was the type who expected a female to be a secretary, and didn't want to pull him out of his comfort zone when business was still a possibility. You could never have too much cash flow in the PI game.

'So what can I do for you, Barry?'

'Mate, you probably won't believe me, but we got a real stinker of a corruption problem at head office.'

Harry looked at him and fought down half a dozen competing one-liners about union leaders, Labor Party politicians, and corruption being the axis of power for one half of the political charade in Australia.

'Try me.'

'So you've heard about the new train project?'

'Who hasn't? The politicians haven't stopped banging on about it for months.'

'Well, there's some serious dodgy shit going down.'

Harry frowned at him. 'How so? The tender process has been very public in the media. I thought that it was pretty well sorted and some Chinese mob was looking good for the contract.'

'Yeah, the Red Dragon Railway Consortium. Another kick in the nuts for Aussie workers.'

Harry nodded. When it came to manufacturing jobs disappearing overseas, he did have a few patriotic juices. 'No argument from me on that one.'

'Fuckin' disgrace. Not why I'm here, but.'

'I'd guessed you weren't here to have a drink and call me "comrade", either, so go on.' Harry didn't savour the idea of having a drink with Stoddart, so he didn't offer one.

'Mind if I smoke, mate?'

'Feel free, Barry.' Harry indicated the blue ashtray.

Stoddart lit up, drew back hard, and exhaled as he resumed talking. 'The new train design was done by First State Transit. Bastards did away with the guards' compartments. No fuckin' consultation with us. We've got fifteen hundred members who are guards. Fuckers in management reckon we don't need them these days. A "redundant function" they call it.'

'So are guards needed?' This seemed like a logical question to Harry.

'Not the point, mate. It's jobs.'

And my fucking taxes pay people like you, fumed Harry. He kept his disdain to himself. But he had to have a little dig; it was in his Celtic DNA. 'So I guess the union wouldn't be too keen on seeing the new European driverless trains here, then?'

'Over our dead bodies, mate. Never happen here.'

No, thought Harry, this country would always remain a backwater in certain respects: a 1950s time capsule lying on a sun-soaked beach and calling that living in paradise. His sarcasm had clearly soared above Stoddart's grey matter, but it had given Harry a minor tickle of satisfaction, so it wasn't entirely wasted.

'So, Barry, what exactly is the problem I might be able to help with?'

'Mate, there's some serious fuckin' money changing hands over this deal. Those Chinks are big time greasing palms in senior management. And they call themselves communists. They're just as bad as the capitalist wankers.'

Harry tried not to look too bored with the Politics 101 sermon.

'So what's your interest?'

'Mate, it's fuckin' wrong.'

Harry wasn't going to be taken in by any façade of integrity.

'I'm assuming the union has taken on First State Transit over the guard compartments?'

'Fuckin' oath, mate. We're going hard.'

'So, are you getting the compartments or not?'

'All up in the air still. Our State Secretary has made the demands on management and I hear through the grapevine they've talked to the Chinamen as well.'

Harry was a little confused. 'What, your union guys? With the Chinese directly?'

'That's the word, mate.'

'Okay, but I still don't see why you're interested in any pay-offs to First State Transit, as long as you get your compartments. Where's the corruption at your head office you mentioned?'

'Mate, our top blokes are getting paid off, too. Word is.'

'So, you're telling me that we've got a three-way bribery deal – management, union, and Chinese train company.'

'Exactly, mate.'

Harry smelt jealousy, or union power plays, or both. 'So, what's your beef then?' Harry wanted to suggest maybe Stoddart had missed out on the quids, but thought better of it, despite his Irish genes. This was still a potential customer, although he couldn't yet see how.

'Because we reckon our members will get sold out and our bosses will take off into the sunset with the cash. Meanwhile fifteen hundred guards will be on the dole.'

'Not much comrade solidarity up top then?' taunted Harry.

Stoddart snorted, but said nothing. Harry lit a smoke.

'Barry, why not just take it all to ICAC? They'd love this one.' Harry thought of all the times he'd so thoroughly enjoyed watching the public proceedings of the Independent Commission Against Corruption bringing down high-flyers.

'Problem is, mate, everything I've told you is just what we've heard. Nothing solid to take to ICAC, or the cops.'

'Ah, so hence you need a PI to find something solid?'

'Exactly, mate.'

Harry could taste incoming revenue. 'Okay. Now, first things first. My fees. Not sure what work will be involved yet, but I'll need a retainer up front, before we look at anything. Ten grand, and then I'll invoice weekly.'

'Yeah, no worries. I can get the ten large to you this arvo. Cash okay?'

'Naturally.' Harry wondered where ten grand in moolah would suddenly materialize from. Stoddart must have read that thought.

'It's clean dosh, mate. We've a fighting fund for special occasions. And no invoices, mate, we don't want any paperwork. It'll be in readies so there's no trail the bosses can see leading to a private dick.'

Tax-free was Harry's first thought. He cast his eye over the twins' desk and computer gear and considered it would be paid for rather swiftly now. 'Yeah, sensible in the circumstances. How soon do you want me to start?'

'Soon as, mate. They're meeting Thursday evening, we hear.'

'Barry, all this stuff you are hearing, do I get to talk to your source, or sources, directly?'

'Not a chance, mate. The source'd dry up faster than the last beer in Alice Springs.'

'Fair enough, just needed to ask. So, this meeting, what's the go?'

'Private boat on the harbour. Our two top people, the two top bosses from First State Transit, and the Chinamen. Plus sack loads of cash, bucket-loads of booze, strippers and hookers.'

Harry looked at him, his cigarette paused halfway to his mouth. 'What?'

'Fuckin' dead-set serious, mate.'

'Definitely hookers?' queried Harry.

'Damned bloody right, mate. All booked and ready to screw, from what we hear.'

Harry drew hard on his smoke and looked at the unionist. He thought that Stoddart seemed to know rather a lot. But then, there wasn't much honour amongst the corrupt, so who knew exactly how involved Stoddart was.

Harry stubbed out his cigarette, and reminded himself that business was exactly that, and in due course the ICAC could sort out who needed to go down for corruption. His brief was simply to gather evidence, and the hooker angle could definitely be worked to advantage. If there was one industry Harry knew as well as investigation, it was commercial sex.

'All right, Barry, sounds just like my sort of job. Let's do it. I can get all the rest of the details when you come back with the retainer later on.'

'Bewdy. See you in a couple of hours.'

Stoddart stood up, shook Harry's hand, and walked out of the office.

Harry opened his bottom drawer, pulled out the Jameson and poured himself a large one. His thoughts drifted back to Orla and avenging her.

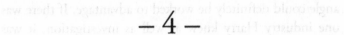

The pads on Harry's right thumb and index finger were dark grey as he reached to pick up his crystal tumbler of Jameson. Stoddart had been back and gone again, leaving a white cotton bank bag of used twenty-dollar notes. Harry had just finished counting the money, hence his grimy fingers. There was a good reason, he mused, that it was dubbed 'filthy lucre'. He recalled reading an article about the bacterial population of an average banknote. Of course, the irony was that the really wealthy never had to touch the physical item itself. That's what underlings were for. Stoddart hadn't hung around and Harry didn't want to offend a client by checking the ten grand in front of him, as tempting as that had been.

Stoddart had simply said, 'Good luck, comrade, we're counting on you.'

In Harry's view, the closest he'd like to come to being a 'comrade' would be shoving a copy of *Das Kapital* fair square up Stoddart's rectum, hardback edition, of course. But again he'd restrained himself, leaving it at, 'I'll be in touch.' After all, he did need to get his hands dirty to pay the bills.

Meantime, Harry had put in calls to two of his more colourful contacts.

The red bundles of twenties were still sitting on his blotter when he heard a key in the door and in walked Tanya, Sasha and Trev.

'Ah, Divine Ones. How did the first training session go?'

'Very cool truck and gear,' said Sasha. 'But a lot more to this gig than on TV.'

'Not to mention a really cool teacher,' added Tanya, touching Trev's arm.

'These ladies are bloody naturals, Harry,' said Trev. 'I'll have them up to speed on all the cameras and listening devices by the end of the week.'

'It's going to need to be a bit sooner,' smiled Harry, waving his hand over the $10,000.

'We could do some serious shopping with that lot,' said Tanya gazing at the piled money on the desk.

'You're certainly going to be earning some of it this week. The union guy was a genuine punter, as you can see. This is just the retainer. Plenty more to come. Let's have a drink and I'll fill you in. Then we could head for an early dinner at the Emerald Bar, if you're up for it.'

The girls each got a vodka and then sat down behind their shared desk. Trev took the Jameson Harry handed him and sat in the client chair, taking out his cigarettes and lighting one.

Sasha spoke. 'Harry, before you start, just to let you know I can't make dinner, sorry.'

Harry looked quizzically at her.

Tanya poked Sasha in the ribs and taunted, 'Sash's got a hot date!'

Both the guys harmonized with 'Ooooh!'

Sasha blushed slightly and smiled. 'You can all piss off.'

The next 'Ooooh' was louder.

'Just as long as it's not another freak sleazoid from your Facebook fan club,' said Trev.

'No way,' replied Sasha. 'I met him through Tessa's studio. He's a display designer.'

'You enjoy yourself, Sasha,' said Harry, 'but make sure he knows that he gets to meet me if he does anything wrong by you. And I'll teach him how to eat his own testicles, raw.'

Trev sniggered into his whiskey. 'Mmm, gonad sashimi.'

'Ooh, that's our tough Mr PI,' teased Tanya.

'You better believe it,' responded Harry.

Sasha looked up, towards Harry. 'Thank you, Mr PI. But I won't actually spell it out quite like that. I might want a second date.'

Harry smiled and nodded once at her. 'Just saying.'

'Harry, what exactly did you guys do to that creep at the pub?' asked Tanya.

'Never you mind. He never bothered Sasha again, so it's all history now.'

'Let's just say the arsehole will never look at a toilet bowl in quite the same way again,' added Trev.

Harry shook his head, savouring the memory of half drowning Sasha's stalker in the pub toilets.

'Okay, enough. Down to business, which includes all of us earning a living. And me paying for all your new gear,' he said, waving at the twins' desk.

Harry proceeded to recount the meeting with Stoddart, in all its details. He lit a cigarette when he'd finished and poured another drink.

Trev then reached for the bottle. 'Nice job, Harry. And a good earner, by the time the bill is finessed and polished.'

'Yep. And once we've got the evidence of the meeting, we can just package it all up and hand the whole lot over. No loose ends to follow up. ICAC will sort it out after that.'

'We've got to cover the meeting, though,' said Trev.

'True, and I've been thinking it through.'

Tanya interjected, 'I can't believe this shit goes on at such high levels on this scale. Do they really think they can get away with it?'

Harry sighed. 'Yes, and the sad, dirty reality is that often they do. And so there are always new candidates eagerly lining up to give it a go.'

'But these wankers are all on fricking huge salaries as it is,' said Sasha. 'Can people really be so greedy?'

'Bloody oath,' said Harry, 'especially the government and public service ones. Snouts into the golden trough of public money, and anything extra, and all gorging themselves stupid.'

'And they're supposed to be serving us,' spat Trev.

'Anyway,' said Harry, 'that's life, and the best we can do is help bring them down. Whilst getting paid for it, of course.' He took a mouthful of his whiskey and continued. 'Now, we need to cover this meeting on the boat on Thursday evening. That's where it'll all happen.'

Tanya jumped in. 'I hope the plan doesn't involve us having to screw any of these arseholes. Does it, Harry?'

The twins looked at each other with disgust on their faces.

'Babe, only figuratively. And in that sense we're all going to be in on it. One huge corruption-busting orgy.'

'So, what's the plan, mate?' asked Trev.

'Right. We know, or at least the drum is, that hookers are going to be available on the boat. So, someone is providing the girls. I've got a call into Miss Andromeda. She'll be able to find out who's got the gig. Then we join in the party.'

Sasha laughed. 'What, you two as bow-tie cocktail waiters?'

Tanya giggled. 'Now there's an image.'

'No, but you're getting warm.' He was still grinning at them.

The girls stopped laughing and looked at him.

'You two as topless waitresses, supposedly thrown in as a bonus to the deal. And somehow wired for sound. Which is your department, Trev.'

'Harry, we're cool with being topless, no worries,' said Tanya, glancing at her sister, who nodded. 'But what if the arseholes decide we're hotter than the hookers and want to fuck us as well?'

'Thought of that, don't you worry. There'll be a body-guard, a massive gentleman, going onto the boat with you precisely to make sure that all the various job descriptions for the evening are respected. And a bodyguard of my choosing.'

Harry looked over at Trev. 'I've put in a call. Think Zanza, mate. Remember Club Mammary?'

'Nice touch, I like that. You girls will be totally safe, you should see this guy.'

The twins looked at each other again, and then turned back to Harry, both nodding.

'And for your info, girls, Zanza doesn't talk. He can't. Had his tongue cut out in the Congo in their civil war. That's where he's from.'

'Poor bloke,' said Tanya.

'Yeah, but at least he's alive,' said Harry. 'And he'll be the best bodyguard you could ever have.'

'Oh, yeah. Huge and muscled,' added Trev.

'Good looking?' asked Sasha.

Trev smiled. 'Oh, yes.'

'Cool,' murmured Sasha.

'Okay,' said Tanya, 'we're good for that. But how are we going to wear a wire in a G string or bikini bottom?'

'Already coming together in here,' said Trev, tapping the side of his head.

'And as you no doubt appreciate after the last few hours, when it comes to the technical devices of our trade, there's not much that our Mr Matson here can't achieve.'

Sasha looked at her watch. 'Shit, I need to fly. Don't want to be late for my date.'

'Exactly,' chipped in Harry. 'If he's any sort of decent bloke he'll expect punctuality.'

'Harry, shut up,' said Tanya. 'When you're a hot chick, you can get away with late.' She kissed Sasha. 'Enjoy, Sis, and text me.'

'Will do. See ya.' She waved as she left the office.

Harry bundled up the cash on his desk. 'Right, let's get this locked away and get going.'

He also pulled the duplicated AFP file out of its drawer.

'We've got some work to do on this, too.' Harry looked momentarily distant, then smiled at them both. 'I'm going to start a hunt, for vengeance. The cops are losing interest again, it would seem, so I'm going to make the most of Tom's absentmindedness with the file. Orla needs justice, or at least the memory of her does.'

'Yeah, count me in, brother. Going to enjoy that work,' added Trev. 'A very worthwhile pursuit indeed.'

Harry opened the safe and put the money and file inside, then shut the door and spun the combination wheel.

Tanya pointed at the safe and said, 'So, come on, Harry, what's in it? I didn't exactly get a chance to read it as well as copy it.'

'Yes, babe, great effort. I love initiative, and I owe you both big time for that.'

'So, what's the plan, Mr PI? I'm on the team now so I want to know when I'm going to see some action.'

'Short version is there are three suspects to be hunted down, at least that's what the cops have pieced together from the video they found. I need to hear confessions from these fucking animals, make sure they're the ones who took my Orla. Then I'll execute them. Justice done.'

'So, who are they?' asked Tanya.

'All convicted paedophiles, according to Tom,' said Trev. 'Fuckers should never be let out of prison the first time. Should let them rot in hell, forever.'

'Yeah,' said Harry through gritted teeth. 'If these bastards had been kept inside for their earlier crimes, my Orla would still be here.'

'Names, addresses?' said Tanya.

'One of them, a Bernhard Schwarz, aged forty, is supposed to be around Sydney and sometimes the Hunter Valley. There's an address in Vaucluse. The other two aren't around, it seems. One, a Herbert Farr, aged thirty-nine, is confirmed as currently in Ararat Prison in Victoria, for molesting a child in Melbourne a couple of years ago. The other is apparently in Laos and has been for years. One Reggie Wheeler, aged fifty now. So, team, we'll get out tomorrow and start work on Schwarz, since he's the only local candidate available to us.'

'Excellent,' said Trev as he drained his glass.

'Certainly not dull around here, is it?' said Tanya.

'Strap yourself in, babe, Kenmare and Associates are in for a few big weeks, if not months. Now, back to current priorities, the pub. Let's go. After this momentous day, I need serious liquid sustenance.'

'Well, not too much, Mr PI,' chided Tanya. 'Not if you're to do your duty tonight.'

'Oh, please, spare me,' said Trev.

Harry laughed. 'Well, Trev, introducing you to my favourite watering hole is way overdue. Especially now that we're a team. The Emerald Bar is my beloved home away from home.'

'Yeah, except for the beds of various ladies and several local brothels,' said Tanya. 'And I'd know, Mr PI.'

'Oh, bugger off, the pair of you.'

Harry held open the main door of the Emerald Bar and Tanya walked in followed by Trev. Inside, Harry went up to the main bar, behind which the manager was drying a pint glass.

'Old Harry. Good to see you.' An outstretched hand followed the Irish brogue.

Harry reciprocated. 'G'day, Shaun. This is Trevor, his first visit here. And you've met Tanya before.'

'Of course,' said Shaun, smiling at Tanya. He then shook hands with Trev. 'Always good to welcome an Emerald Bar virgin; I promise it won't hurt too much.'

They all laughed.

Harry ordered drinks.

'His Eminence here already?'

'In the garden,' said Shaun.

When they had their two whiskies and a vodka, Harry led the other two out the back to the beer garden.

Liam Doolan, known as the pub's Irish Eminence, was sitting up the back corner, a half-drunk pint of Guinness on the table and a newspaper in his hands. He looked up as the newcomers approached. He put the paper down and stood up.

'Harry, my man, how are you? And you, young lady, so good to see you again.' He kissed Tanya on the cheek first. Then Harry introduced him to Trev.

'Harry's mentioned you many times. Pleased to finally meet the man.'

'Likewise,' said Trev. 'Think you'll be seeing a lot more of me, now that Harry and I are doing a fair bit of work together.'

They all sat down around the table.

The big silver-haired Irishman took a deep swig of his stout. 'So how's the shamus business? Apart, that is, from having not one but two incomparably beautiful assistants.'

'Pretty lively, right now,' answered Harry.

He then, in a lowered voice, gave Liam a brief overview of the union assignment.

Liam chuckled. 'How the bastard wankers never change.'

'I still can't believe the greed,' added Tanya.

Liam looked at her in an almost grandfatherly way. 'My lovely young lady.' He took her hand gently in his large paw. 'I know you've already seen too much of the dark side of life for your tender age, but alas there is a lot more. It was Einstein who said, "Three great forces rule the world: stupidity, fear, and greed." And that great man wasn't in the business of spouting bullshit.'

'No wonder I drink,' chipped in Harry. 'And on that optimistic note, let's order some bloody food. I want one of the magnificent steaks they do here, plus a couple of bottles of red.'

'I'll love you and leave you,' said Liam, downing his dregs. 'Have someone I need to go and see at the Gaelic Club.'

'No worries, Your Eminence. I'll catch you soon,' said Harry, as Liam got up to move off.

Trev was perusing the menu. 'Nice looking tucker here, mate.'

'Oh, shit yes,' said Harry. 'Can't beat it. So, let's eat well, indulge a little, and discuss our first day of hunting tomorrow.'

'Cool,' said Trev. 'And I'll do a few checks of online resources overnight to see what I can find of interest. Meantime, this lamb rump is looking good. That'll do me.'

'Yeah, I was looking at that, too,' said Tanya. 'But I think I'm going to go for the wild mushroom risotto.'

'Oh, great choice, babe,' said Harry. 'One of my favourites. I'll go and order.'

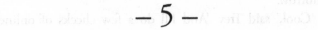

Harry came to the next morning in his dark bedroom, a slight glow of light impinging from under the bathroom door. He blinked, rubbed his eyes, and took a gulp of water from the glass on the bedside table. He inhaled slowly through his nostrils. He was sure of the distinct scent of Tanya's pussy, but it was only his own face. There was also a slight residual metallic tang of blood somewhere around the back of his mouth or sinuses. He frowned, then grinned. If one had to get a nosebleed, then what better way than from a beautiful, sexy woman riding his face?

Tanya had gone at it last night as if she had been breaking in a brumby, and had banged down hard on Harry's nose as she arrived at her third orgasm of their post-dinner tryst, and the second on his face. His first, deep inside her, had been splendid and well and truly enough, given the limitations of age and alcohol. Tanya's wet and highly vocal trinity had tested another limitation: the neighbours' after-midnight patience, as evidenced by the pummelling on the intervening wall. Ah, the joys of apartment living, he thought. Mind you, he could sympathize. He'd been on the receiving end of the carnal cacophony on plenty of occasions. And there was nothing worse than listening to others doing it when you weren't getting any. Nice to have the shoe on the other foot these days.

Harry picked up his iPhone and checked the time: 5.22 a.m., eight minutes before the alarm setting. Always the way. Waking up before the alarm was a throwback to Harry's detective days, and the imperative to be on time for all those early-morning raids. All these years later he couldn't shake the habit. He flicked on the lamp and swung his legs out of the bed.

Tanya walked back in from the bathroom, with wet hair, wearing knickers and a bra. 'Morning, handsome.'

'Good morning, Divine One, although I could do with some more shut-eye.'

She walked over to Harry and bent down to kiss him on the lips. 'My, we do smell like a rutting polecat, don't we?' She smiled.

Harry stood up. 'Polecat PI at your service, *Mademoiselle.*'

'Coffee?'

'Yes, please,' said Harry. 'I'll hop in the shower. Trev said six thirty, and he'll be early. He usually is.'

At six fifteen, Trev messaged to say he was parked in the side street opposite the apartment building. Harry, now deodorized and dressed in jeans and polo shirt, swallowed the last of his coffee. He picked up his keys, a fleecy top, and a small backpack. He looked over at Tanya, who was in cargo pants, a loose T-shirt, and a leather jacket. Her still-damp hair was tied back in a ponytail.

'Let's go, Ms Roberts. Your first operational day on the PI job.'

'Cool. I've been hanging for this.'

They left the apartment building, crossing over Macarthur Street. Harry could see Trev's VW Transporter parked about fifty metres along McKee Street. They walked briskly towards the van.

Harry slowed slightly as he passed a young red-flowering ironbark tree in full bloom, reaching to brush one of the flower heads with his fingers. The scarlet tufts emerging from the small gumnuts always reminded him of the cover of a May Gibbs book he'd had as a young boy. He still had a handful of his childhood books, this one included, with its Australian trees and flowers. He'd passed it down to Orla, and she enjoyed it until she was snatched away. His thoughts turned back to the imminent hunt.

He slid open the side door of the van and followed Tanya inside the vehicle, closing the door behind them. Trev greeted them and Harry climbed into the front passenger seat. Trev started the engine and they headed for the cross-city tunnel to travel east, into the dawn. They emerged onto New South Head Road a few minutes later and continued east, towards one of the more moneyed of Sydney's elite enclaves, Vaucluse.

The sun was rising over the Pacific now, battling to hurdle the long bank of dark storm-driven clouds out on the horizon. The effect was a cascade of amber, saffron and vermillion shafts of light, like flames spouting forth from a dragon arising out of the endless ocean. All three sleuths reached for their sunglasses as the raging ball of flame threw its first leg over the cloudbank, sending a horizontal blast of light through the van's windscreen. The morning peak hour had yet to start, so they arrived at Tivoli Avenue in only twenty minutes. Trev turned the van into the street and drove slowly along it. Harry was scanning the house numbers on the harbour side of the street.

'There it is, and that's his blue Volvo in the drive. It was listed in the file.'

'Sweet,' said Trev. 'I'll turn around and we can prop over there near the one being renovated. Shouldn't look too out of place, at a casual glance, anyway.'

Trev did a U-turn at the end of the street, cruised back down the way they'd come, and parked behind a large builder's skip about fifty metres short of the target address.

From the elevated level of the roadway, Harry looked over the roofline of the houses and down the sloping land to the expanse of Sydney Harbour.

'Nice bloody view …'

Tanya interjected. 'How does a convicted ped afford this?'

'I did a title search last night,' said Trev. 'Place is owned by one Hilda Schwarz. Still lives there and is seventy-eight. Bernhard's dear old mother, me thinks.'

'Any other names linked to the address?' asked Harry.

'Not on the property registers, and we can't access the motor vehicle records, unfortunately. So, all we've got is what was in Tom's file. And that's got Bernhard periodically in and out of this address.'

Harry snorted. 'Still living at home with his mum? That'd be bloody right. No record of a Mr Schwarz senior? Or anyone else?'

'Not a trace, at least nothing connected to this address. It's all in Hilda's name.'

'So, from our chat last night I take it we're just watching today? Nothing else?' asked Tanya.

'Yep. Hopefully we'll get a good eyeball on Schwarz,' replied Harry. 'We need to confirm it's him before we can take the next step. And if he goes anywhere, we'll tail him and see what he does, who he meets.'

'So, if it is him are we going to grab him?' Tanya sounded a touch excited.

'Not today, Divine One, but we will. Soon.'

'And here was me hoping for some action on my first day.'

Trev laughed. 'As you're going to find out, Tanya, a lot of the work in this game is about as exciting as listening to a politician's press conference.'

'Ugh,' grunted Harry. 'I'd rather have a prostate exam from a gorilla.'

Trev turned back to Tanya. 'But you can do the camera-work today.' He pointed towards a rack next to her.

'Cool,' she said, sounding enthused again.

She picked up a Pentax K5 with a large zoom lens.

'This one?'

'Yep. You good with that from your lesson yesterday?'

'Sure am. I'll get a bit of practice on the seagulls while we wait.'

'Right,' said Trev to them both. 'I've got to get to work on rigging up the gear for Thursday night's fun, so Harry, you take the helm, mate, in case we have to roll. Tanya, you hop into Harry's seat.'

They played their musical chairs and settled in to wait. Harry pulled an iPod out of his backpack, plugged it into the van's audio, and turned around to the back.

'Bit of ELO, Trev?'

'Sweet, mate. Which albums you got on there?'

'Every single one, my friend.'

'Hours of bliss then.'

'Absolutely,' said Harry, as Jeff Lynne's voice started with 'Turn to Stone'.

Harry turned to Tanya. 'And if you even dare ask "who?" I will be docking your pay.'

Tanya pulled a face at him. 'Ha-ha, Mr PI. I've been through your CD collection. Electric Light Orchestra, and I actually quite like them. I remember our dad used to play them. On vinyl, too.'

Trev poured three coffees from a flask and passed two forward.

'Wish I still had all my vinyl albums,' said Trev. 'I had a great collection.'

'How come you got rid of them?' asked Harry.

'I didn't. An ex did. Burnt them in the backyard incinerator before throwing my bags out on the front kerb.'

Harry winced. 'Ouch. At least my ex-wife just walked and wanted fuck all to do with me, so I kept my vinyl.'

'I'll come over and have a look through sometime, mate,' said Trev. He sat at a mini workbench and spread electronic components out in front of him. He started whistling tunefully. He was thinking about the ex who had destroyed his record collection, along with his emotional balance at the time, many years previously.

Tanya sipped her coffee, silently singing along with ELO, thinking about her long-gone father.

Harry sang along as well, not exactly silently, thinking about his long-dead Orla. And he wasn't too tuneful either. He thought back to how Orla used to try to sing along when he put music on.

It was still only 7.15 a.m.

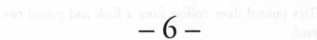

– 6 –

Dieter Schwarz had been lying low since the incident outside the school in Eastlakes last Friday, and he hadn't been out of the house since. It had been a close call and had unnerved him.

He'd chatted to the boy four days running and was on the verge of enticing him into his car. He worked his ploys meticulously, and this had been no exception: pick a poorer social area and scout for the poorer-looking kids walking to and from school, especially those taking a route down quiet streets alone. There was no point even trying anything around his area, he thought, despite the convenience factor. Firstly, it was too close to home for safety: he or the car might be recognized. Secondly, and more crucially, no kids around here even knew what a footpath looked like, except to view it from the elevated window of a luxury SUV as a designer-wear mummy dropped them off. And then, of course, arrogantly double-parked in the afternoon waiting for the little darlings. Plus all the silver-spooned brats had the latest mobile phones and were forever on them, another risk factor. No, the pickings were much healthier and safer around the housing estates with their violent welfare environments. Always a plethora of disadvantaged and needy kids desperate for attention and affection.

He'd been so close to getting real action on Friday that he was sitting in the driver's seat with an erection. The boy had just agreed to hop in for a ride home and a look at a new iPad when a large, unshaven bloke in a dirty singlet and shorts had emerged from the front door of a house and yelled, 'Oi, you!' He then started lumbering unsteadily but purposefully towards Dieter's car. The boy sprinted away down Florence Avenue. Dieter, instantly flaccid, wasn't interested in a close-up examination of the quality of the incoming gorilla's tattoos, so he gunned the engine and took off with a screech of tyres. He was still shaking when he got home to the lofty sanctuary of Vaucluse.

However, four days had now gone past without any police visits, so the singlet-clad gorilla had obviously not got his vehicle registration. Now he needed to get back out there and get some young satisfaction.

Dieter turned on the shower, let the hot water start flowing through, and stepped in. His thoughts, as usual before venturing out hunting, turned to his younger brother, Bernhard. They were only eleven months apart and looked so alike people had often asked as they were growing up if they were twins. Similar in looks, and similar in predilections, as it turned out. Hence why his thoughts always turned to his brother when he was mentally gearing up to go trawling for young flesh. The best way of telling them apart, but this required an intimate knowledge of them, was that Dieter loved little boys, whereas Bernhard passionately hankered for young girls. And a little too eagerly, in Dieter's view. Not that a raging lust for prepubescent female flesh was anything to criticize his brother for. Rather it was his lack of caution and circumspection about doing so in cahoots with others that was the problem. Dieter had always, bar once when much younger, hunted and feasted alone. No accomplices to prove a weak link or go off script. And if the selection and grooming were done properly and carefully, not too much risk of the child speaking out, at least not to anyone who'd listen. It was another beautiful feature of the kids in the gutter: they were naturally averse to speaking to anyone in authority, especially cops.

Dieter was immensely proud of himself for never having been caught. Unlike Bernhard, of course. Many years before, his brother had done two short jail stretches for molestation and a stint on probation for possession of child porn. Fortunately, each time he'd been arrested, Bernhard had been staying elsewhere. So, those were the houses the police raided. On the two occasions when the cops had arrived at Vaucluse, making their routine enquiries as they euphemistically called them, their wonderful mother, with fastidious preparation from Dieter, had assured the cops that Bernhard hadn't lived there for years. And so no search warrant had ever come close to violating the Vaucluse sanctuary. But it had got Dieter livid with Bernhard each time.

Still, despite Bernhard not being as careful as Dieter, many of his crimes, including the most serious one, were still unsolved by the law.

And it was the worst of Bernhard's crimes that Dieter always returned to thinking about, and it invariably unsettled him. These things always came back to haunt, eventually.

When Bernhard had come home at dawn that hot January morning eleven years ago now, hands dirty and shaking, it'd taken several minutes for Dieter to get him to talk.

When he had finished, Dieter yelled, 'You fucking idiot!' and shook him furiously in an extremely rare display of fraternal animosity.

The day before, Bernhard had been off cruising with his mates Herbert and Reggie. This was exactly why Dieter had such an issue with doing anything with an accomplice. Dieter wouldn't even go hunting with his brother these days. The limit of their cooperation was sharing their child porn finds and collections, as far as their differences in tastes allowed. In fact, the only joint foray had been as teenagers, when they'd lured an eight-year-old girl into a public toilet block one evening. That was the only time Dieter had ever been inside a female. Even then, as the leader of the adolescent predatory pair, he'd been canny in his methodology: the girl was a deaf-mute from the special-needs class at the local primary school, and Dieter had stalked her for three weeks first, before pouncing. Bernhard, as it transpired, so enjoyed the rape that he decided to stick with girls. So, their paedophilic pursuits had diverged. Even without that point of difference, Dieter still wouldn't have wanted the added risk of a co-offender. Bernhard, on the other hand, seemed to thrive on the mutual reinforcement and encouragement of the pack hunt. It also reduced his inclination to put much effort into careful grooming, hence his three arrests and convictions.

And so, according to Bernhard's account, on that summer day eleven years ago, the lusty trio motored past a young girl walking along the street in an average Sydney suburb. They'd grabbed the girl, and taken her back to Reggie's place where they'd raped her. Afterwards, they took her to the Royal National Park south of Sydney. Bernhard's version was that he had assumed they were going to just leave her in the bush, but Reggie said they couldn't let the girl live to tell what they'd done to her.

Bernhard told Dieter that he'd tried to persuade Reggie and Herbert that they didn't need to kill the girl. Dieter didn't openly express any disbelief, but inside he was quite certain his brother would have cut off his own scrotum if Reggie had told him to. Reggie killed the girl, so Bernhard and Herbert were accessories to murder.

And that was that, until a bushwalker stumbled on the grave, dug through by wild animals, a few weeks later. A police investigation kicked off and traipsed along very publicly for a while, then went silent. Nothing more was heard. Reggie had already by that stage taken the precaution of leaving Australia, never to return; Herbert had fled to Melbourne until the heat died down; and Bernhard laid low for months at the respectable Schwarz residence in Vaucluse.

Dieter remained amazed that the case had never been solved. But he should've known the calm was too good to be true. A couple of weeks previously, Bernhard received a call from an associate to say the cops, the Feds this time, were taking a fresh look at the case, some new task force, a cold case review. The associate, a discreetly like-minded man who worked in an administrative role in the office of the Commonwealth prosecutors, didn't know why the case was alive again, but had seen Bernhard's name, amongst others, on some affidavit material. Bernhard had not thought twice about the need to become scarce, and rapidly so. Without a valid passport, and a new application being out of the question, Perth was as far as he could run, and so he headed off to the west coast. Dieter kept in touch on the phone, advising his brother to stay away for as long as it took, and sending him cash. So far, so good: the Feds hadn't come banging on the door.

Now dressed, Dieter walked into the kitchen to have a cup of tea with his dear seventy-eight-year-old mother. The morning ritual, integral to the household, was a bit quieter now without Bernhard, but he'd be back, all in good time.

'Morning, *Mutti*,' chirped Dieter as he walked past her sitting at the table. Old Hilda Schwarz sat there taciturn and glassy-eyed, as was her Teutonic way.

Dieter made his tea and sat down opposite his mother, chatted to her about what he planned for the day, took her silent stare in his stride, and finished his cuppa. He stood up, rinsed his cup, and said, 'See you later, *Mutti*. Love you.' He walked out into the hallway.

He smiled at the thought of his wonderful mother, the one who kept on giving so generously with the house, her annuity and stock returns, and her fortnightly pension payments, both Australian and German. She had deteriorated rapidly as time went on. Neither Dieter nor Bernhard had the slightest intention of earning a living themselves. So, they nursed her by day and by night, with Dieter taking regular leave of absence to attend a night school course.

Dieter picked up the car keys and went out, carefully deadlocking the front door and the security screen behind him. He got into the blue Volvo, started the engine, and reversed out into the street. He headed off, this time to Malabar for the start of school.

He didn't notice a grey Volkswagen van pull out from the kerb about a hundred metres behind him.

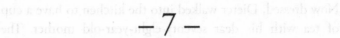

— 7 —

The heavy morning traffic in Sydney's eastern suburbs suited the PIs well, allowing them to stay comfortably hidden several cars behind the Volvo. Harry was at the wheel, having been sitting in the driver's seat when the car had pulled out of the Schwarz residence. Tanya had grabbed a few snaps as the car headed down Tivoli Avenue, getting the rego plate, but no clear shot of the driver.

Trev had put away his electronic components and was now perched behind Harry and Tanya, a digital video camera at the ready.

They'd crawled down Old South Head Road, all the way south on Carrington Street, and were now cruising through Randwick.

'So, I wonder where our friend Bernhard is off to, this fine winter morning?' said Harry.

'Clearly not shopping,' said Trev. 'We've gone past Bondi Junction, which would be his closest shopping centre.'

'At least it's easy to keep tabs on him in this traffic. Bloody Sydney.'

'And only getting worse.'

'Once we've confirmed it's him, Trev, let's get a tracker on the car at the first opportunity.'

'Yeah, easy. Got a nice little magnetic number I can stick up under the wheel arch. Battery's good for about seventy-two hours.'

'He's pulling into that service station,' interjected Tanya.

They were on Avoca Street in Randwick now, past the shops, and still heading south.

'Pull over here, Harry. This could be a chance. Let me know if it is him, and then pick me up the other side.'

'Roger that, mate.'

Tanya groaned. 'So cop, you two.'

'And roger that,' said Trev. They laughed.

Harry pulled the van to the kerb, into a bus zone. Trev grabbed a tracker from a drawer, slid the side door open, and hopped out.

Tanya was busy with the Pentax, focusing on the man climbing out of the Volvo now stopped at a bowser.

'Looks like him,' she said, squinting through the viewfinder and pressing the trigger.

Harry picked up the photo that Tanya and Sasha had copied from the AFP file.

'Yep, sure looks like our man.'

Harry stared at him as he filled the car. 'Schwarz, you fucker, I'm going to have you.'

Trev was standing at the bus stop pretending to scan the timetable, whilst Schwarz finished filling his tank. As soon as he headed for the cashier in the shop, Trev moved quickly, looking in at Harry as he passed the van. Harry gave him the thumbs up. Trev walked onto the service station forecourt. Passing the Volvo, he dropped a cigarette packet, and crouched down to pick it up. As he stood up again, his hand shot up inside the front wheel arch and then out again. He kept walking and came back out onto the footpath.

Harry slid the van past the petrol station and pulled up to allow Trev to climb back in.

'Nice work, mate.'

'Yeah, that was so smooth,' added Tanya.

'Now let's see if it works,' said Trev, opening up a MacBook Air, which he rested on the console between the two front seats. A map was on the screen, showing the streets around Randwick, and a blip was flashing in Avoca Street. 'That's our man,' said Trev, as the Volvo came back onto the street.

Harry let four cars go past and then pulled out to follow.

Tanya showed Trev the photos she had taken.

'Yes, our man all right. Good shots, too.'

With the GPS tracker working, Harry dropped the van back another half dozen cars behind the target, who was still heading south.

Fifteen minutes later they were in Malabar. It was a far cry from salubrious Vaucluse. The proximity to water was the only common denominator. But the median incomes couldn't have been more divergent. And that was considering those Malabar residents who had a job and an income that didn't come from the government. The stock of welfare housing, with its burnt-out car bodies and uncollected garbage bins, told the local story.

As the traffic thinned, Harry dropped right back from the Volvo, which was now out of sight, but still visible on the laptop in front of Trev.

'Hey, he's stopped. Pull over, Harry.'

The van slowed into the kerb. Trev pointed to the laptop and the map.

'He's there, on Franklin Street, and not moving.'

Harry looked closely at the map. 'And there,' he said, pointing at the screen, 'is Malabar Public School. The bastard's scoping out the kids on their way to school.'

'Prick. Let's move to where we can have a visual.'

Harry looked at the map again. 'Okay. We'll try over that side of Anzac Parade. Should be able to see across into Franklin and still have some distance from him.'

They had to detour around several side streets in order to get to their spot without going directly past the Volvo. Three minutes later they had pulled over in the northbound carriageway of Anzac Parade. The Volvo hadn't shifted and now they had a clear view of it about two hundred metres away. Tanya took a couple more snaps and Trev zoomed in with the video camera. Dribs and drabs of kids were wandering towards the school entrance.

'Do you think he'll try something?' asked Tanya.

'I doubt it,' replied Harry. 'If he grabbed a kid before school, then the balloon would probably go up as soon as the unlucky girl didn't show for class. More likely he's just checking out potential victims, so he can do more work on them.'

'I agree,' added Trev. 'Much more likely to try something after school. Wait for a kid on their own walking home.'

Half an hour later the trickle of kids had stopped and the Volvo started to move.

'Makes sense that he's hunting well away from home,' said Trev.

'Yeah. And this is a pretty poor area in parts, so he knows the easier types of victims to entice.' With that Harry punched the steering wheel. 'Cunt!'

Trev put his hand on Harry's shoulder. 'Easy, mate, we'll get him.'

'Yeah, I know.' Harry rubbed his face with both hands. How he wished he could turn back time, still have Orla to dote on. Now, however, his passion had to be vengeance.

'Let him run for a bit and then we'll follow out of sight. We can't lose him now unless he goes off on foot. Home to Vaucluse is my bet.'

Tanya made a noise, as if she was going to speak.

Harry looked over at her.

'Go on, ask. How do I think he enticed Orla into his car?'

'Well,' said Tanya softly, 'I thought with you being a copper at the time you would have taught her all about stranger danger and all that stuff.'

'You have no idea. Taught her that until she could recite what I was going to say before I opened my mouth.' Harry turned his head and stared through the windscreen. 'All I can assume is that Orla was grabbed. She'd never have got into a car herself. Not for anything.'

Trev spoke. 'His MO might be to watch for a few times before he grabs?'

'Yeah, or he might have evolved into more subtle and less hurried attacks. What is clear, however, is that he wasn't here this morning to recruit for the girl guides.'

'Agreed,' said Trev. 'Regardless of MO, he's planning something.'

Trev pointed at the laptop screen. 'Looks like he's going back the way he came. Homeward-bound, for a nice morning tea with dear old Mum.'

'So what are we going to do?' asked Tanya. 'Surely we're not going to sit and watch him grab a kid?'

'Not if we can help it,' replied Harry.

Tanya continued. 'Well, why not let the cops know that he's up to something? Let them stop him?'

Trev joined in. 'Because either they'll say there's not enough to go on at the moment, or if they do take an interest, then that buggers up our plans.'

'So do *we* have a plan?' asked Tanya.

Harry smiled at her. 'Don't get testy, Divine One. You are very much part of the team. We haven't done anything more than discuss a couple of ideas. Nothing settled yet. But now, I think we're going to have to bring it on, otherwise another kid's going to join Schwarz's trophy list.'

'Yuk,' said Tanya. 'Why don't you just knock him off today? You said you were going to kill him.'

'Oh, I am, nothing surer,' said Harry through gritted teeth. 'But we can't just rush in there and do it. We need to interrogate him first to find out what he did exactly, and everything he knows about the other two.'

'I thought the term was "interview", not "interrogate"?'

Harry and Trev laughed.

'That much is true in professional life,' replied Harry. 'But this one *will* be a good old-fashioned interrogation, with every brutally effective technique in the book.'

Trev chuckled. 'And some not in the book. Bernhard Schwarz won't know what's hit him.'

Harry continued. 'I think Friday has to be the day. Thursday evening we've got the harbour hoedown to deal with, so no chance before then.'

'And at least we'll know what times he'll likely be out and about. Granted it's only day one, but I know these pricks. I'd put money on his regular MO being prowling around school hours.'

'Yep. So, we cover his school run this arvo, and both runs tomorrow and Thursday. Then we grab him first thing Friday morning. Cool with that timing, Trev?'

'Going to have to be, mate. Just a few things to get organized beforehand, like a car, drugs, implements. Everything for a smooth and successful abduction, really.'

Harry turned to Tanya. 'You all good?'

'Of course.' Tanya sounded defensive. 'You're not leaving me out, Harry.'

'No intention of that. But it's going to be nasty, very nasty, so just checking, that's all.'

'Yeah, well, thanks. I'm no stranger to nasty. So, end of discussion, I'm in.'

'And Sasha?' asked Trev.

'No, she's off with Tessa for a fashion expo in Brisbane on the weekend. She's good for the job Thursday evening, but flies out Friday.'

'Tessa doesn't need you at the moment?' asked Harry.

'No. She said I could go if I wanted to, but what I wanted was to get some PI action.' She smiled at Harry. 'Plus, I think Sash's new male interest is going.'

'Ah, so last night's date was a success?'

'Yep. Sash texted me this morning, on her way home.'

'Oh, the dirty stop-out,' said Trev.

They all laughed.

Harry started the van. 'He still heading to Vaucluse?'

Trev looked at the laptop. 'Yep. Let's meander that way ourselves.'

Harry moved the van out into the traffic.

'But what if he grabs a kid on one of the outings before Friday?' asked Tanya.

'We'll have to intervene, of course,' said Harry, 'but that'll fuck our plan right up.'

'Not too much chance, though,' added Trev. 'He was just looking on this morning, so I think he's right at the start of his hunt. Probably several more days of watching before he singles out a target to work on.'

'These people really need to fucking die.' Tanya almost spat her words out.

'Well ...' started Harry.

'Not just him, Harry, all of the scum.'

Harry and Trev both nodded and the trio settled into a brooding silence as the van headed north back to Vaucluse.

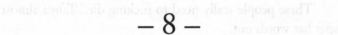

– 8 –

Wednesday slid by uneventfully, at least in as much as they shadowed Schwarz to the school in the morning and afternoon, and he didn't touch any kids. Only window-shopping, it seemed, although Harry and Trev knew damned well another victim was in the making. Only if Schwarz had his way, of course, and fate, Kenmare-style, was destined to intervene.

By contrast, Thursday was a flurried juggling act as Harry and Trev found themselves busier than a one-legged man in an arse-kicking contest. The pair of them had done the morning school run again, tailing Schwarz to Malabar and back. Tanya had been dispatched by Trev with a precise shopping list that had Harry gawking in curiosity: she was to get two sets of skimpy lingerie, decorated with as many sequins and beads as possible. Before Tanya was able to ask, 'What the fuck?', Trev had left the office with Harry. His parting words were, 'A vital part of the operation tonight, Tanya. And don't forget to keep the receipt. I want to hear Harry explain that business deduction to his accountant.'

Harry was still looking quizzically at Trev as they moved off in the van.

Trev grinned at him. 'Mate, this will be my finest piece of covert surveillance work yet: Operation Pussycam.'

Before Harry could ask, Trev continued. 'I'll explain it all when we get back to the office and the gear is finished. Need that underwear first.'

Back at the office by mid-morning, Trev took possession of two matching sets of purple lingerie, heavily sequined in magenta with black beading along the edges.

'Spot on, Tanya,' said Trev, and he disappeared back down to the workshop in his van.

Tanya looked at Harry with raised eyebrows. 'How is lingerie going to help with surveillance?'

'I don't know, babe. He said he'd explain when he was finished.'

Tanya rolled her eyes. 'Okay, what time do I need to be here by?'

'Four o'clock. We should be back from tailing Schwarz around then,' said Harry. 'You'll bring Sasha?'

'Yeah, of course. See you then, Mr PI.'

Tanya gave him a lingering kiss and left the office.

Harry got busy working the phones.

He returned a call from Miss Andromeda and found out that the hookers for the boat party that night had been arranged through Eternal Escorts, a new high-end outfit. They would be meeting with the boat of the moment mid-harbour.

Clever, thought Harry. No chance that way of anyone seeing the First State Transit bigwigs and union bosses having young, salacious women boarding their boat at whichever dock they left from.

Andromeda knew the owner of the escort service well and had assured Harry that he would get all the cooperation he needed. Harry smiled to himself. He, too, knew the owner of the new escort firm. The delectable Sandrine Gazeau, also known as Madame Méchante, had been a client of Harry's about six months earlier. It had been her case that led, eventually, to the demise of that piece of shit Commander Mervyn Lowe. Harry thought wistfully back to that day Sandrine, the French Tunisian goddess, had sat across his desk, looking like Cleopatra and getting Harry hard. Ever since, he'd wanted to get naked and filthy with her, but she had not succumbed to his charms. Not yet, anyway. Harry always lived in hope. Now Sandrine was expecting Harry's call.

First, however, he called another number from his recent exploits, and one that he had contacted on Monday in preparation. The phone was answered in a heavy Jamaican lilt, 'Hallo.'

'Mama Jocasta? It's Harry Kenmare again.'

'Ooh, Mr Harry, always be good hearing from you.'

'How are you today, Mama?'

'Very good, Mr Harry. You know I be a glass-half-full type of girl.' She chuckled lightly.

Harry tried to force the visions of milk out of his mind. He shivered as he remembered the intricacies of Club Mammary and that wretched breast-feeding councillor gorging himself in the fetish club.

'So, Mr Harry, you still need Zanza?'

'Yes, Mama, like I mentioned on Monday, and it involves good payment, of course.'

'Ooh, yes. Payment is always good. Zanza is looking forward to some more exciting work, I think.'

'And your security at the Club is still okay tonight?'

'Yes, Mr Harry, all good. A friend of Zanza come for the evening. Not big as Zanza, but plenty man enough to deal with the big babies who come here if they misbehave.'

'Cool, I really appreciate this, Mama.' So they settled the details and Harry hung up, promising to have a drink with Mama soon.

His third call was to Sandrine at the escort agency. That voice, simultaneously sultry and managerial, had Harry getting movement in his loins. He closed his eyes as the French accent dripped into his ear like warm treacle.

'Harry, always so good to hear from a real man, my favourite detective.'

'Sandrine, I'd be your favourite sex slave, too, given half a chance.'

She laughed. 'Yes, you'd like that, wouldn't you?'

'You have no idea.'

'Well, good detectives are supposed to be patient, yes?'

'Yeah, but I'm also a bloke and you are the most beautiful, sexy woman that Carthage ever produced.'

'Ah, yes, the expert art of flattery, Harry Kenmare-style. Show as much expertise with patience, and you'll be rewarded, *mon cher.*'

She blew him a loud kiss. Harry's erection completed itself and he groaned.

'Okay, the business Andromeda mentioned?' she asked.

'Yes, I need your assistance, Sandrine. Let me explain.'

Harry's proposition was a *fait accompli* and Sandrine happily agreed to have her girls accompanied by two lingerie waitresses, a bonus for the client, as well as Harry's chosen minder for the jaunt. Harry pictured the gigantic Zanza and thought that the term 'minder' was about as adequate as referring to Scarlett Johansson as 'a good sort'. However, Sandrine could see the magnificent African for herself this evening.

Lunch for Harry and Trev was pork rolls from the Vietnamese bakery up the street. It was one of Harry's go-to meal spots during the day. Apart from being only five bucks, the garlic mayo in place of butter, and the pork paté and meat slices, together with crisp vegetables and fresh coriander, made him salivate every time.

As much as the pair felt like indulging in a post-lunch Jameson or three, the afternoon surveillance remained to be done, so they fought back their thirst.

They were back in Harry's office just shy of 4 p.m., the afternoon surveillance having yielded nothing new.

The twins sauntered in ten minutes later.

The foursome sat around the office with a coffee and smoking as Harry detailed the plan for the evening on the boat.

Tanya and Sasha, who were to accompany the two escorts, would be wearing concealed cameras, rigged for sound as well as vision.

'So, you two will be in the main cabin where all the interesting action will happen, and then we'll see it all on film, in glorious technicolour. And Zanza will be a man-mountain guarantee of your safety.'

Sasha laughed. 'Pity we won't be able to film those girls at work in the other cabins. It'll be an Oriental shagfest.'

'Sasha,' said Harry, 'my idea of "interesting" is a suitcase full of dirty cash changing hands. I definitely do not want to watch some corrupt Beijing bureaucrat waving his cock around like a rampaging Nanjing noodle.'

The girls chuckled.

Trev had pulled the two sets of lingerie out of a box next to him. Everyone was now watching.

Tanya dived in and tackled the elephant in the room. 'I get wearing bugger all, being the general idea of a skimpy waitress, but how the hell are we supposed to hide cameras in those?'

Trev, smiling, picked up a pair of panties. 'So, the sequins and beads at the top hide a fibre-optic lens and mini-microphone.' He held up the sassy purple number, demonstrating the front to the twins and Harry. 'See, you can't notice anything from the outside. You'd need to get to within about thirty centimetres, and even then you'd have to suspect something and be looking for it.'

Harry interjected, 'But there has to be a device attached.'

'Patience, mate. The fibre and mike lead run down inside the fabric to this little connector.' He draped the micro leads across his index finger with a tiny copper connector stub joining them at their ends. He reached into his box with his free hand and produced a clear silicone tube about the size of a slim panatela cigar container. Tiny electronics were visible inside. 'The connector plugs into the end, here, and up it goes. The recording chips are inside with power supply. Should be good for four to six hours,' said Trev chuckling. 'Brings a whole new meaning to "lights, camera, action!" doesn't it?'

The twins laughed, wide-eyed.

'Talk about exploiting our femininity,' said Sasha.

Trev smiled at her. 'The high-tech version of using your beautiful bodies, but for a totally noble cause. My polite name, which I'll be using in the patent application, is "pussycam".'

'In-bloody-genious,' chipped in Harry.

Trev spoke to the twins. 'I'll leave you both to do the fitting.' He smiled somewhat sheepishly. 'I've already tested them.'

Sasha chuckled again. 'That was the dry run, I suppose?'

Trev deftly produced a tube of lubricant from his box of tricks. 'Because I'm a considerate type of guy, girls.'

Tanya had now taken hold of one the rubbery tubes and was examining it more closely. 'Actually, Trev, if you were really, truly considerate, this would have a vibrate setting on it.'

After the laughing subsided, Trev said, 'I'll bear that in mind for the two-point-zero version.'

'We can help with the design for that,' said Sasha, grinning.

'Yeah, could probably do with that help.'

Tanya winked at him.

Harry lightly banged his desk. 'Okay, let's focus on the job, please.'

'Yes, boss,' said Tanya.

'We'll go and try our equipment on,' added Sasha.

The twins headed out to the bathroom, carrying their high-tech lingerie.

They returned a couple of minutes later, smiling.

'All good?' asked Trev.

'Yep, and everything fits, so to speak,' said Sasha.

'A nice tight fit,' said Tanya, pouting at Harry.

With that, the twins dropped their jeans, revealing the sequined lingerie bottoms. They twirled in front of Harry's desk and then bent over theirs, gently waving their perfect buttocks. They both giggled.

Harry groaned and thought that it was an afternoon for getting a hard-on in the office. He noticed that Trev was entirely focused on his laptop screen. Oh, well, his loss if he didn't want to salivate over the rear view of the twins.

'All right, thank you for that magnificent display, ladies, but can we please get back to business?'

'Just letting you inspect your personnel, boss,' said Tanya.

'Reminding you that the money you pay us is very well-spent,' added Sasha.

'Yes, thanks for that. Now, let's go over the details again. The job's on and we need to get everything right.' He drew on the last of his cigarette and stubbed it out. 'And then we'll grab a bite to eat. We're due at the wharf at seven.'

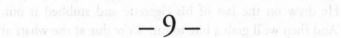

— 9 —

Julian Rhodes, Chief Controller of First State Transit,
stood on the rear deck of the large yacht, admiring the
incomparably beautiful Sydney Harbour whilst sipping a glass
of chilled rosé. He gazed appreciatively at the kaleidoscope
of colours from all the city lights reflected off the dark
water. From the boat, he could even see his harbourside
apartment building in Neutral Bay in the distance. Rather
more salubrious than an evening drink on the grimy river
Thames in his native London. In fact, it was all a bit of a gag
out here, teaching these colonials how to run a rail network.
Waterfront digs, over half a million a year, and since he'd
come out in 2009, he'd been able to surreptitiously clear out
the locals from the top echelons of First State Transit. This
paved the way for him to bring out several of his trusted old
colleagues from the regional rail network he'd run back home.

His deputy, Horace Briggs, who had joined him from
London, was currently in the luxurious main cabin. He was
attempting to be civil to the union thugs whilst ingratiating
himself with the Beijing executives, who were still hanging
on to the large briefcases and tote bag they'd come on board
with. Rhodes was disgusted at the thought of having to
share the deal with the TBFU idiots, those self-professed
working-class heroes, but it was the only way.

He took another sip of wine. Still, by the time this evening was over and done with, everyone would be happy: the Orientals would have the largest rail contract in the Asia-Pacific region since the days of the Raj; he and Briggs would be rather wealthier, and tax-free; and the oh-so-socialist unionists would be rolling in it, too. Hell, even the hookers, who were due any minute, would be taking home a bundle of cash. The ever-loyal and cunningly astute Briggs, who had worked in the Far East, had assured him that girls were needed to show good faith and seal the deal. Then he'd put together the five grand cash needed for the two high-class escorts. Oh, well, a drop in the ocean, or harbour, he sniggered to himself, compared to what was in those briefcases waiting for them.

The mid-harbour meeting had been Briggs's idea as well. It meant no chance of any prying eyes or ears. Rhodes had raised the obvious question of the hookers, but Briggs assured him that high-class prostitutes never repeated anything, their livelihoods depending on absolute discretion. Briggs did seem to have picked up a lot of varied experience during his Hong Kong and Korea years, thought Rhodes. Well, should all be a walk in the park, then. He took another sip of wine.

The foreshore park next to the wharf in Pyrmont was deserted as Harry and his team waited in Trev's van. A taxi pulled up and the twins gasped as Zanza extricated himself out the back door. The cab pulled away and the big man walked over to the van.

'Fuck, he's huge,' said Tanya.

'Yep, about two hundred and twenty centimetres and I reckon at least a hundred and sixty kilos of pure muscle,' said Harry, getting out of the van and shaking hands with Zanza.

'I'm liking him,' said Sasha under her breath. 'Bet he's built elsewhere, too.'

She caught Trev smiling. 'I'm sure he is.'

Just then a sleek, black Peugeot pulled up. Sandrine and two younger women, every bit as beautiful as the Tunisian temptress, got out of the car and came over.

Sandrine gave Harry a kiss on the cheek. 'Hey, my handsome detective. This is Carla and this is Lauren, for the evening engagement. If you could get them a cab afterwards that would be much appreciated.' Her hand lingered on Harry's buttock.

'Of course, no problem.' Harry caught Tanya looking over and grinning.

There was engine noise from the wharf as a water taxi pulled in and tooted.

'Okay, team, good luck and see you soon,' said Harry.

The four girls and Zanza headed towards the water. Harry watched the to-die-for young women wandering off with the big African man towering over them. He grinned and turned to Sandrine.

'I don't think they are at any risk at all.'

'No, he's just the man for the job,' said Sandrine. 'I won't ask anything else, despite my curiosity.' She ran her finger down Harry's nose, lingering on his lips. 'So, my detective, I'll be off, but do stay in touch.'

Trev was looking on smiling.

'I certainly will … '

Before Harry could continue, Sandrine's finger was replaced with her mouth and she gave Harry a kiss with plenty of tongue.

Harry moaned. 'I could do with a whole lot more of that, babe.'

'All in good time. *Au revoir*, gentlemen.'

She climbed back into the Peugeot and drove away.

'Bloody hell, mate,' said Trev. 'Where do you find them?'

'She was the one who started the whole Lowe thing, back in February.'

'Oh, she's that client. Now I can put a face to the name. Fine-looking lady.'

'Not wrong. I'd crawl over a mile of broken glass to get her naked.'

'Brother, I'm surprised you haven't already. Losing your touch?'

'Bugger off. She's just playing tough to get, Trev. She's yet to be won over by the Kenmare charm.'

'Maybe she wants commitment, Harry, before you get to hit a home run.'

Harry chuckled. 'I hope not, because my commitment days are well and truly behind me. Kissed them goodbye with the divorce. Vowed never again.'

'Wasn't just Orla, then?'

'No, mate. The marriage was fucked well before Orla was taken. The ex had been screwing around, including with another detective.'

'Ouch, not cool at all.'

'Then the bitch just used Orla's death as an excuse to call it quits.'

'Sounds like a class act.'

'Yep, so I promised myself I would never get into that sort of relationship again. And I'm liking it that way, believe me.'

Trev laughed. 'You're sure as hell not short on action, Harry.'

'Make hay whilst the sun shines, brother. Could drop dead tomorrow.' Harry lit a cigarette and passed the packet to Trev.

'A bit of music, I feel,' said Trev, lighting his smoke.

'Sounds good, all we've got to do is wait.'

'Bit of Pink Floyd okay, mate?'

'Cool,' said Harry.

Rhodes watched a water taxi approaching. He could see female heads inside, although there seemed to be four, not two as arranged. And there was a dark, decidedly non-female head looming above the girls. He stepped towards the door to the main cabin.

'Briggs, my man, on deck if you would.'

His deputy emerged, steadying his wine glass to allow for the movement of the swell, and looked towards the rapidly closing boat. 'Ah, the entertainment is arriving. Super.'

The pair chinked glasses.

The water taxi edged alongside and one of the hired deckhands came down from the control deck and roped the boats together.

Rhodes and Briggs nearly dropped their wine glasses as over two metres of the finest African masculinity stepped onto their deck, with a reserved nod in their direction. The Englishmen remained speechless as Tanya and Sasha were helped aboard by Zanza, followed by an equally stunning third blonde and a beautiful dark brunette.

Sasha broke the silence. 'So who's organizing this?'

Rhodes and Briggs looked agape, like two 1970s boarding schoolboys who had uncovered a tuckbox full of *Mayfair* and *Penthouse* magazines.

Briggs stammered, 'I, I am.'

'Okay,' said Tanya, 'these are the rules for the evening.'

She indicated the other two girls, the blonde and the brunette respectively. 'Carla and Lauren are your escorts, as ordered. It's full service for your two overseas guests, but it's the cash upfront now, to our minder here.'

She touched Zanza's arm, bare despite the cold air, and more muscled than most men's thighs.

'Full service means straight sex. Anything else, including anal, is extra. So are any additional clients. So, you negotiate directly with the girls and they set the prices for any extras. All good so far?'

Rhodes was speechless. He'd never heard a woman talk about anal sex. Being rogered in the Harrow changing rooms was his idea of it. Briggs, only marginally more composed, although equally reticent about sexual talk, and also a Harrow old boy, nodded at her.

'Yes,' he whimpered.

Tanya continued. 'Me and my sister here are a bonus the boss threw in for you. We'll go topless inside and serve drinks. You can enjoy looking all you like, but no touching. Understood?'

The two men nodded.

'And our minder here is Zanza. He's very, shall we say, protective.'

The two Englishmen recoiled as the giant African stepped forward, placing his hands on Tanya's and Sasha's shoulders.

Sasha took up the theme. 'Anybody breaks the rules, Zanza deals with them. Clear?'

'Yes, absolutely,' murmured Rhodes, whilst Briggs nodded again. Rhodes looked at his deputy, raising his eyebrows.

'It's fine,' whispered Briggs. 'They usually have a minder with them.'

He led the group inside the boat.

Tanya looked around the lounge area. It was a panoply of polished mahogany, red velvet, smoked glass, and gilt metal fittings. She thought it could easily double as the front room of an expensive brothel. Quite appropriate, really. She was happy, however, that the heating was working a treat, given she and Sasha would soon be topless.

It was left to Briggs to explain the rules to everyone else, the young Beijing interpreter rattling off the Mandarin version through a slightly embarrassed smile.

A few minutes later all four girls emerged from the bathroom. The two escorts, holding small clutch bags, wore translucent negligées providing a glorious view of expensive lavender-coloured lingerie beneath. They sashayed straight over to the two Chinese businessmen sitting on a couch. The interpreter introduced them as Mr Wu, the boss, and Mr Chen, and then himself as Mr Sung.

Carla and Lauren squeezed seductively into the available gaps, putting their arms around the two grinning men, to appreciative male noises.

Tanya and Sasha, wearing only heels and the spangled lingerie bottoms, did a strut around the room, giving every man in there a good close look at their pert, magnificent breasts, and smiling saucily.

Kevin Brogan, the TBFU state secretary, spoke, without raising his gaze from nipple level. 'Great fucking tits!'

'Well, enjoy the view, gentlemen,' replied Sasha.

'Now, let us refill your drinks,' added Tanya.

The twins completed their teasing circuit and went to the bar. Of course, their little parade was not really about showing off their bosoms. Rather, they had ensured close-up camera footage from their crotch cameras of every participant in the room.

Brogan turned to Rhodes and Briggs. He couldn't stand either of them, with their superior upper-class English attitudes. And they were doing their best to fuck over the workers and remove conditions that had taken the union decades to institutionalize into the railways. Still, this deal was $250k a piece for him and his mate, and that sort of cash spoke louder than comradeship. He swallowed his Aussie working-class pride, at least partly.

'For a pair of poncy poms, you've done bloody well with the sheilas here,' he said, waving his hand at the beautiful women.

'Fuckin' oath,' chimed in Jim Macadam, the TBFU assistant state secretary.

Rhodes took a rosé from Tanya and cleared his throat, looking over at the Chinese executives, who were grinning like Cheshire cats.

'Gentlemen, let's get the formal side of the evening done with. Then we can relax and enjoy the company.'

Rhodes couldn't see why any of this was funny to the damned Orientals. He didn't realize that 'poncy poms' had gone into Mandarin as well.

All seven men, the translator included, moved to the dining table. Mr Wu and Mr Chen extricated themselves from the escorts, now in only their lingerie, and brought the closely clutched briefcases with them.

Briggs distributed voluminous piles of contract documents around the table. Rhodes then took the lead, pausing every minute or so to allow the interpreter to catch up. However, given that copies in Mandarin had been given to the visitors, the discussions were over and done with in ten minutes.

Tanya and Sasha discreetly sidled around the table giving the covert lenses and microphones the full benefit of the proceedings. At one point Tanya moved in next to Rhodes at the head of the table, on the pretext of picking up his empty glass and moving her breasts to within a bee's dick of his face. She'd picked her mark well, with Rhodes being entirely and helplessly distracted by her, his hands dropping away from the documents. Meanwhile the fibre-optic lens above her crotch got a close-up of the papers in front of him. She picked up the empty wine glass, pouted a kiss at the wild-eyed Englishman, and moved to the bar, over-emphasizing her swagger.

'Great arse, too,' drawled Brogan, followed by a loud belch.

'Fuckin' oath,' added Macadam. 'That'd be a nice bit of tail. Could see myself chock-a-block up there.'

'And only for your viewing pleasure, gentlemen,' reminded Sasha, having to fight the urge to vomit at calling two such arseholes 'gentlemen'. She indicated Zanza, who stared implacably at the two unionists.

'Of course,' she continued, 'the ladies on the couch will be more than happy to entertain your custom after your guests have had their yum cha.'

A quick translation by Sung and then sniggering from Wu and Chen.

Brogan turned to Macadam. 'Jim, me mate, reckon we can treat ourselves then. We'll sure be able to afford it. Won't even need to use the work credit card this time.' He pointed to the now-open briefcases on the table, loaded with cash.

Macadam chuckled. 'Fuckin' oath, Kev. We'll give 'em one for the working man.'

Rhodes looked at Briggs and rolled his eyes. He loathed Brogan, Macadam, and all their cohort. Still, think of the dosh, just keep thinking of the dosh. Which is exactly what seemed to him to be in Briggs's eyes as he nodded, tipping his hand almost imperceptibly towards the briefcases.

All the signatures done, hands shaken all round, and briefcases slid along the table, one for the First State Transit pair, the other for the union duo, the head Chinese man, Mr Wu, pointed at Tanya and said something to his interpreter.

Tanya looked nervously to Zanza. The big man tensed up ready for action, and cracked his knuckles with a steely look in his eyes.

The interpreter addressed Tanya. 'Mr Wu ask you please get toast glasses, so they can do traditional salute to good business.'

With that, Wu produced a bottle from his tote bag. It was clear liquid with Chinese script on the bottle.

Tanya breathed a sigh of relief and Zanza noticeably relaxed. She got seven shot glasses and took them over to Wu, who nodded his head in appreciation, although looking at her breasts.

Wu handed the bottle to Tanya, and said something in Mandarin.

The interpreter spoke. 'Please, you fill glasses and pass around.'

Wu then said something else.

'Mr Wu says our tradition is to drink the bottle of baijiu,' said Sung.

'What the fuck is by-gee-ooh?' interrupted Brogan.

The interpreter smiled. 'Traditional spirit drink of People's Republic. Like vodka, but better. Stronger.'

He turned to Tanya and pointed to the glasses, then looked back at the group.

'Mr Wu says bottle to be finished, then play time with ladies.'

A sudden nervous look appeared on his face as he glimpsed Zanza and he hurriedly added, 'Those ladies over there,' pointing to the escorts lounging wantonly on the couch.

'No problem,' said Tanya, and she filled the shot glasses.

Sasha took two of them to the Englishmen up the table. Tanya slid two over to the unionists, wishing she could spit in them on the way, whilst the three Chinese guys picked up theirs.

Wu, Chen and Sung stood and held up their glasses, looking at the Westerners. Standing was clearly the go and the other four men hauled themselves onto their feet. As the other glasses were raised, the Chinese men said something in unison, then swallowed their drinks and banged their glasses down on the table.

The other men followed suit.

'That's fuckin' rocket fuel,' gasped Brogan.

'Fuckin' oath,' wheezed Macadam.

There was complete silence from the English end of the table.

Tanya refilled the glasses.

Brogan and Macadam looked pretty happy with the idea, Briggs less so, and Rhodes looked as if he was gagging on an English school dinner.

Tanya looked at him. What a fucking lightweight.

Sasha smiled at her, as if reading her sister's mind. Meanwhile, in the guise of being a horny temptress, she manoeuvred herself close to the table to look straight into the open cases of cash.

Back at the Pyrmont wharf, the partially lowered windows of the VW van were seeping a mixture of smoke and *Wish You Were Here* into the cold night air.

'I always hate this bit,' said Harry.

'Yeah, the waiting without being able to do anything. Definitely the worst part of the job.'

'And all the things that could go wrong just start marching around your brain like a nasty little Pac-Man.'

Trev laughed. 'I like that. Still, the safety of the girls is the number one priority, and we couldn't have that better covered. These white-collar crooks won't have any weapons. It's not a mafia meeting, or anything heavy like that.'

'True, and even then, unless it was a bloody machine gun, I'd still put my money on Zanza.'

'And with both the girls wired up, we can even survive one set of equipment failing.'

'Yeah, I know. All sounds fine when you pull it apart logically. Just those twitches in the gut, you know.'

'I know exactly what you mean, Harry.' Trev picked up the cigarette packet from the dashboard. 'Is this your last one?'

'Go for it, mate. I've got another packet.'

Ten minutes later on the boat, the baijiu bottle was empty. Rhodes had rushed to the toilet and Briggs was looking decidedly queasy. The unionists had ordered more drinks, going back to beer, and Sasha filled their order. Wu and Chen had disappeared into the bedroom with the escorts.

Unfortunately, the boat-builder hadn't included sound-proofing in the nautical specifications. So, whilst the crotch cameras weren't getting any orgiastic vision, the labial listening devices were another matter altogether.

The twins had no idea what the shouts and hollering in Mandarin were all about. The only hint was the fact that the young interpreter had turned a shade of beetroot and wore a sheepish grin. However, the enthusiastic verbal contributions from Carla and Lauren, whilst no doubt encouraging for the Chinese men, were probably wasted in their precise meaning inside that bedroom. Explicitly audible to the twins' microphones were clichéd gems such as, 'Oh, give it to me, big boy,' 'Fuck me harder, you stud,' and 'You're so big you must be the king of China,' all uttered several times at volume.

Tanya had to suppress a giggle, although she was glad she wasn't providing that part of the service. Even if the howls of paid-for desire were largely superfluous in the boat's bedroom, they'd go down a bloody treat at any ICAC hearings later on. Harry had explained this whole process to the twins, but stressed any public revelations would be weeks or even months away, and that was assuming they got all the evidence tonight.

The screams of mock rapture, however, were in this moment certainly not wasted on Brogan and Macadam, who were now visibly itching to tag-team the Chinese pair. Twenty minutes later, after a quick exchange with Carla, and a large wad of cash handed by Brogan to Zanza, that is exactly what they did.

Rhodes had come back from the bathroom, still looking green, and now drinking soda water.

Tanya couldn't help herself. 'Hey, sugar, you going for your turn next? Sloppy thirds?'

Rhodes glanced at her as she wiggled her breasts in front of him. His eyes then lost their focus on her chest. He suddenly upped and ran for the bathroom again.

'Guess that'd be a "no", Sis,' said Sasha, smirking.

Briggs, obviously made of slightly sterner stuff than his boss, was enjoying another drink with the Chinese men, the interpreter his normal shade again and translating a most voluble conversation.

Half an hour later the assignment was over and the twins, the escorts, and Zanza were sitting in a water taxi heading back to the wharf.

Zanza handed two wads of cash to the escorts. They both thanked him, and he nodded an acknowledgement with a smile.

Sasha spoke to them. 'Profitable evening, then? Hope you charged those union wankers well.'

Lauren, the brunette, replied, thumbing the wad like a deck of cards, 'You bet, sister, they were gagging for it. Could probably have gone even higher, but didn't want to waste time haggling, so two grand each is pretty all right for fifteen minutes' work.'

'And that included foreplay,' added Carla, laughing.

The other girls joined in the merriment.

'So, all tough-man bluster and no stamina,' said Tanya.

'Yep, and smaller peckers than the Chinese guys,' replied Lauren.

Carla resumed, 'And what the hell was with those cases of all that cash? Drug-dealers?'

'No idea,' said Tanya, completely poker-faced. 'Could be drugs, I suppose, although that English guy in charge wouldn't be able to tell the difference between a spliff and a dog turd, so I doubt it. But something dodgy, obviously.'

'Yeah, that's what we figured, too,' said Lauren. 'So, we thought there wouldn't exactly be any complaints to the cops about a little extra missing.'

She produced a chunky wad of notes from her make-up bag.

'Helped ourselves to a little tip while everyone was saying goodbye. You two still had those puppies on display and every set of male eyes in the room was getting a good last look. No one was watching the cash. Just a pity we didn't have a damned bigger bag.'

Tanya looked at the bundle, which she thought must have been at least ten grand. She smiled. 'Way to go, sisters.'

All the girls laughed. Zanza cracked a huge grin as well, and gave the thumbs up with both hands.

The water taxi slowed as it pulled into the wharf. They all alighted and walked up the pontoon to the waiting Harry and Trev.

'How did it go? We've been sweating here,' asked a visibly anxious Harry.

'Like clockwork, Mr PI,' said Tanya, grinning at him.

'Wouldn't have expected any less,' added Trev. 'Now fingers crossed everything worked.'

'And we can't wait to get changed, if you get my meaning,' said Sasha.

'Okay, less said the better,' Harry threw in quickly, before the escorts heard anything they didn't need to know.

He turned to Carla and Lauren. 'The cab over there is for you lovely ladies. Thank you for your work.'

Lauren smiled at him. 'Well, handsome, any other time you need staff we are definitely available. Seems you already know our boss.' She smiled at him.

The two of them walked off to the cab, as a second one pulled up.

Harry turned to Zanza and handed him an envelope. 'Many thanks, my friend. We could well have more work for you in the future, if that suits you?'

Zanza nodded his head, making a noise in his throat. He shook hands with Harry and then Trev.

'Thanks for looking after us, you hunk,' said Sasha. She touched his arm as he bent down and kissed her on the cheek.

Then he kissed Tanya, also on the cheek, and headed for the waiting taxi.

'You can change in the van,' said Trev to the twins. 'There's a blue tray on the workbench for the devices.'

'Cool, won't be long,' said Sasha. 'Then drinks, we've earned them.'

Tanya turned to Harry. 'Yeah, we sure have. I'm no expert, but I reckon there must have been several hundred thousand in the briefcases out there.'

Harry whistled. 'Can't wait to see and hear the recordings. Sydney's elite at their corrupt finest.'

— 10 —

H arry was awake before 5 a.m. on Friday, after a restless sleep, in anticipation of the hunt later in the day. The first slice of vengeance for Orla was nigh, and his adrenal glands were working harder than a dissident in a Soviet salt mine. He was in his office by seven, then texted Trev, who replied he would be on his way shortly, and began composing his anonymous letter to the ICAC to accompany the footage from the previous night's operation. He had yet to see it as Trev needed to download and copy it from the two crotch cameras.

Barry Stoddart had made it abundantly clear that his fingerprints were to be nowhere near whatever evidence was dropped into the ICAC. He just wanted the job done. Harry marvelled at the courage of the man's convictions. Still, business was business, and the end result would be the same. Mind you, over at the union head office, they'd probably just have one corrupt regime replaced by another one. The more things changed ...

Trev arrived half an hour later, carrying a bag of tricks, French pastries, and two coffees, an extra shot in each.

'You're a sight for sore eyes, mate,' said Harry, taking hold of a coffee.

'Can never have too much caffeine at this end of the day. Especially since I was up half the night working on our project.'

Harry frowned. 'I thought you were doing that this morning?'

'There's a bit left to finish, particularly some editing to hide the faces of the girls and Zanza. But I couldn't wait to have a look.' Trev had a wicked grin on his face. 'Harry, it's sheer bloody dynamite.'

Trev handed him a USB. 'Mate, that's a copy of the unedited feature film. You enjoy that and your brekkie while I finish the version for ICAC.'

'Sweet,' said Harry, inserting the stick into his MacBook, and taking a bite of a *pain au chocolat*.

Through the pastry chewing he said, 'I've done the anonymous tell-all letter for ICAC, and Sasha will drop the parcel at their front counter this arvo, on her way to the airport. Tanya's going to come with us.'

Trev stopped his computer work and looked over at Harry. 'Mate, I know she said she's not going to be left out, but you sure she should come along? And I don't mean anything against her, I love the girls, but it's going to be a real brutal evening.'

'Yeah, don't I know it. And that is, of course, the general idea.' Harry paused. 'Anyway, after our initial chat about it on Tuesday, I did suggest to her that she might be better off not coming. Let's just say I can still feel the slap, and I won't be making a similar suggestion again.'

Trev chuckled. 'Wish I'd been a fly on the wall for that.'

'Bugger off, Trev.' Harry smiled at him and started the video.

Over an hour and numerous comedic comments later, Harry was done.

Trev looked up from his screen. 'Pretty damned good, isn't it?'

Harry lit a smoke and passed the packet to Trev. 'Mate, by the time ICAC has finished with that lot, they're going to be more screwed than a cheerleader at a grand final after-party.'

'And then some. Smug bastards won't be grinning so much then.'

Harry mimicked Macadam from the recording. 'Fuckin' oath, mate.'

They laughed.

'If only we could have a celebratory drink,' sighed Trev.

'It's going to be a long wait for that first one later tonight,' lamented Harry.

The icy southerly August wind howling down the streets was perfect for the purpose at hand, keeping all the Vaucluse residents comfortably tucked up in their heated luxury dwellings in the middle of Friday afternoon.

In Towns Road, around the corner from Tivoli Avenue, nobody took any notice of the grey VW van and a white Holden Commodore sedan parked in front of it.

Harry got out of the van and turned back to Tanya in the cab. 'So, Divine One, all clear?'

'Yep. Wait for your message, go to the house and back into the driveway as close to the front door as possible.'

'Sweet. See you very soon. And welcome to your first serious crime.' He winked at her, and got blown a kiss in return. He then walked towards the Commodore as Tanya slid behind the steering wheel of the van.

Harry, unusually in a tie and jacket, got into the passenger's side of the car, enjoying the blast of the heater that Trev, also in a jacket and tie, had on full bore.

'The old suit is a bit snug these days,' said Harry.

Trev laughed. 'Yeah, I hate wearing them, too.'

'At least yours still looks like it fits you.'

'We need to get you down to the gym, mate.'

'Whatever, smart-arse.'

'So, all set, Harry?' asked Trev.

'Yeah, mate.' Harry slipped his seat belt on. 'Let's do this, Detective Sergeant Matson.'

'Roger that, Detective Sergeant Kenmare.' He grinned.

Harry stared ahead, anticipating finally meeting one of the scum who'd taken his Orla. He was looking forward to this: the first act of vengeance in his three-act quest.

Trev pulled away from the kerb and headed into Tivoli Avenue. The Commodore's number plates, registered to Hertz, were lying face down at Harry's feet. Trev had put dodgy ones on the car for the trip to Vaucluse, to be switched back in an hour or so, before he dropped the car back to the rental depot in Darlinghurst. And his VW van would have its real plates restored as well, before their felonious trip west over the Blue Mountains that evening. False plates were great in case of nosey neighbours jotting them down whilst they were at Schwarz's house. But they certainly wanted the real article back in place before hitting the highway: a routine police stop revealing false plates would suddenly become anything but routine.

Dieter Schwarz was sitting at his kitchen table reading the *Daily Telegraph* and sipping a cup of tea, his mother as serene and laconic as always. He jumped as the doorbell sounded.

Strange, he thought. He certainly wasn't expecting anyone. One of the benefits of living in such a swanky enclave was the scarcity of door-to-door pests. He thought he'd lie low and ignore it; they'd move on soon enough. By the third time the ring was rather more insistent, and accompanied by a solid knock on the door. He snuck into the front room where he could get a view of the porch and driveway without being visible himself. He saw a newish white Commodore sedan parked behind his Volvo. Then he saw two largish men at the front door, both dressed in suits, short hair, one with a slight beer gut, and the thinner one holding a clipboard.

Shit. Cops. Detectives. Maybe the Feds were finally looking for Bernhard. Dieter definitely didn't want them sniffing around looking in windows, so best to talk to them at the door, appear eager to help, and tell them that Bernhard had gone away. Or, better still, had moved out. He walked into the hall and opened the front door.

The one with the clipboard spoke as they raised leather wallets with metal badges.

'Mr Schwarz?'

He looked at their badges. Shit, not Feds. They were state police. 'Yes?'

'Detective Sergeant Black and my offsider, Detective Sergeant Hand. We're from Eastern Beaches Detectives Office.'

'Is there a problem, detectives?'

'We just need to ask you a few questions, Mr Schwarz. Maybe we could come in. Shouldn't take more than a few minutes.'

He sure as hell didn't want them in the house, and his mother wasn't exactly up for any guests. 'Why can't we just talk like this, here?'

'It's a bit of a sensitive matter, Mr Schwarz. More discreet to chat inside.'

Dieter's mind was racing. They clearly didn't have a warrant of any sort, or they would have said so and demanded entry. So, he stood his ground. 'If it's all the same to you, Detective, we'll talk here.'

The second and chunkier one, who was staring filthily hard at him, spoke in a low, menacing voice, almost a growl.

'Listen, pal, we can do this the easy way, or the very fucking hard way.' There was a malevolent smile on the cop's face. 'If you want us to start having a loud conversation out here about your car there being seen trying to pick up kids down at Malabar, then we'll play it that way. Should definitely make an impression on your neighbours.'

Dieter swallowed hard.

The first one smiled at him. He must be the good cop of the routine. Then the bad one continued. 'And then we'll do a bloody door-knock up and down the street, asking if any of the oh-so-respectable locals have ever seen kids being brought into this house.'

Dieter's hesitation ended abruptly. 'Okay, okay, you don't need to do anything like that,' he said quickly. He unlocked the security door and opened it. 'Come in, detectives. We can chat in the front room just here.'

He needed to stop them getting any further in towards the kitchen, not to mention the special private room that he and Bernhard shared. He led the pair into the front sitting-room.

'Now, how can I help you today, detectives?' he asked through a nervous, forced smile.

The slimmer of the two, now facing him, spoke. 'This is your mother's house, isn't it?' he asked.

'Yes, Detective. But she is away visiting relatives in Germany.'

The same cop continued. 'That your car out there? The blue Volvo?'

'Yes, Detective.' His mind was racing, trying in the typical suspect's way to guess what the cops already knew, and how unhelpful he could be without appearing to be so. Dieter decided not to volunteer Bernhard's name at this stage.

'You been down at Malabar this week, outside the school?'

'Uh …' Dieter was panicking now. 'Let me think …'

As he stared at the nicer cop's out-of-fashion red and gold striped tie, wondering how to answer, he didn't notice the heavier, nastier cop disappearing behind him.

And then it was too late.

Harry grabbed Schwarz, wrapping his right arm around him and pinning his upper limbs. His left hand clamped like a limpet over the molester's mouth and pulled his head back. Harry wanted to snap the bastard's neck right there and then, but he needed a confession, and to find out exactly what poor Orla had gone through. It took all his restraint not to kill Schwarz on the spot.

In one fluid movement, Trev dropped his clipboard and pulled a syringe from his inside pocket, flicking the cap off as he stepped up to Schwarz, who was struggling against Harry's clam-like grip, his muffled shrieks of fear failing to make it past Harry's hand. Trev stuck the needle straight into Schwarz's neck, easing the plunger down all the way. A hefty dose of Midazolam coursed into Schwarz's bloodstream and within seconds he went limp and his knees gave way. Harry lowered him to the floor.

'You sure know your drugs, brother. I've never heard of Midaz,' said Harry.

Trev chuckled. 'Mate, one of the benefits of having a doctor as a regular fuck buddy.'

'I guess abduction methods must make for a different sort of pillow talk.'

'I like to keep it spicy.'

It was Harry's turn to laugh. 'So does your doctor friend supply the shit as well?'

'Hell, no. I've got other, less respectable, contacts in that scene. And for a price, you can literally get anything.'

'Ah, Economics one-o-one. Gotta love capitalism.'

'Exactly, brother.'

Harry checked Schwarz's pockets and found a Samsung phone, but nothing else.

'He put his keys down on the hall-stand,' said Trev. 'And it looked like a wallet next to them.'

'Cool,' said Harry. 'We'll take them and then we can come back and inspect at our leisure after the dirty deed of justice.'

Harry texted Tanya.

Trev went out and came back with two sets of keys and a man's leather wallet. He shoved them into his inside jacket pockets. Then there was the noise of an engine slowly approaching up the driveway.

Harry opened the front door. Trev was behind him and tried a couple of keys in the door to make sure they had the right ones.

The back of the dark van came to a stop about two metres from the front door, far enough out to allow the van's rear door to open, but close enough to render the entry to the house invisible to anyone else. Harry stepped out onto the porch and opened the van door.

Tanya turned around and smiled at him. 'As requested, boss.'

'Excellent work, babe. You stay right there and we'll be ready in no time.'

'Cool.'

Harry and Trev returned to the sitting-room and went over to the unconscious Schwarz. Harry grabbed him under the arms and Trev took his legs. They hauled him out of the room, through the front door, and into the back of the van.

The pair stepped back from the vehicle. Trev locked the house up, pocketing the keys. Harry closed the back of the van, and climbed into the passenger seat. He lowered the window. Tanya was still behind the wheel.

Trev came up to the window. 'See you at that car park and we'll sort out the plates, and then drop the car back.'

'Sweet,' said Harry. 'And then it's, "Go west, young man," as the song goes.'

Trev grinned and gave him the thumbs up. He walked over to the Commodore, hopped in and backed it out into the street. He drove off.

Tanya started the van, and then headed off after Trev.

– 11 –

The grey van, with its eclectic human cargo, cruised westwards through the Blue Mountains: two rugged ex-detectives accelerating into the criminal life, one beautiful young woman joining them as she sought to escape her damaged past, and one sedated paedophile who, had he been conscious, would have been pleading for his own monstrous existence.

Trev was driving at a sedate pace, attention from the highway patrol cars being the last thing they needed. Harry was staring pensively through the windscreen, drawing slowly on a cigarette. Tanya was in a jump-seat in the back, ready to squirt a dose of Midaz up Schwarz's nostrils if he stirred. Not that he'd be able to do anything if he did come out of the chemical cloud. If he'd been bound up with any more cable ties, he would have qualified for first place in the Electricians' Guild annual bondage challenge. Trev had also ensured that all their phones were turned off to make them untraceable. The only device still active, in case anything online was needed urgently, was a spare iPad Trev used with a falsely registered, prepaid SIM card.

As the van descended onto the Western Plains, the sun was sinking slowly towards the hazy horizon. Its waning rays bathed the roadside sandstone outcrops in a warm, deep golden hue, highlighting their natural layers of yellow, orange, and pink, making them appear to glow. In the same fading amber light, the gnarled, brown gum tree trunks with their sappy excretions resembled well-oiled pork crackling. The van windows were down, letting out the tobacco smoke and welcoming in the pervading waft of eucalyptus oils, carried in on the cool air. It was an Australian country road at the end of another sunburnt day.

With the enormity of the afternoon so far, the trio were predominantly silent, all grappling with their own thoughts in their own private ways.

Harry was relishing the prospect of getting Schwarz's confession and then killing him.

Trev, more practically minded, was speculating as to exactly how much pain Schwarz would take before he confessed.

Tanya was flying high on the day's adrenalin rushes, which beat the hell out of the fashion industry.

With the now dying winter sunrays coming horizontally into the van, the resolute faces of the three sleuths took on a radiant, sun-tanned look: three classical, bronzed avengers gazing westwards to destiny.

It was twilight when they turned off the Great Western Highway and headed north. Darkness had descended as they finally arrived at their destination about an hour later. The van's headlights picked out an old miner's cottage at the end of a disused track through a patch of dense forest. Trev put the handbrake on and turned off the engine. Before the headlights went out, Harry saw the remnants of a mineshaft derrick about twenty metres to the side of the shack.

'Well, team, welcome to the arse-end of Sofala,' said Trev. 'Hard to believe this whole area was teeming with miners a hundred and fifty years ago. Now it's just another ghost town.'

'Suits us perfectly then,' said Harry.

'Exactly.'

'How close to town are we, brother?'

'About eight kilometres, and there's bugger all within at least three. I checked carefully when I was making the selection.'

'Cool.' Harry turned around to Tanya. 'And how's our sleeping beauty back there?'

'Not a peep,' replied Tanya, 'and he's still breathing.'

'Just as well,' said Trev. 'Dead men don't talk, which would rather defeat the purpose. I'll bring him around with a shot of Flumazenil as soon as we're set up.'

'Trev, how do you know all this shit?' asked Tanya. 'You used to be a copper, not a doctor.'

'He just sleeps with a doctor,' chipped in Harry.

'Not for a while,' said Trev quietly.

'Well, that would certainly make for a different game of doctors and nurses,' said Tanya, poking Trev in the ribs.

'Sure does,' he replied.

All three of them climbed out of the van.

'Fuck me, it's cold,' said Harry.

'Yep, heading for three degrees up here tonight,' said Trev.

'A cold night in hell, then.'

Tanya gasped as she looked up at the night sky, still indigo towards the western horizon. 'The stars are so bright out here, you just don't realize in the city.'

'Yes, beauty up there and ugliness down here,' sighed Harry. He caught Tanya's eyes as she lit a smoke. 'And some real beauty down here, too.' He smiled at her.

'Smooth.' She blew smoke in his direction.

Trev slapped him on the shoulder. 'When you've finished with your attempt at poetic philosophy, big boy, we've got work to do.'

'Smart-arse.'

Trev opened the large back door of the van. He stepped in and knelt next to Schwarz, checking his pulse. 'Still out to it, but alive.'

He stepped away and passed two electric hurricane lamps to Harry along with a Maglite torch. 'See where you can set them up inside, Harry.'

'No worries.'

Harry wandered off to the shack, turning the torch on and walking in through the gap that once held a door. Trev came in behind him with a metal garden chair. He walked over to an upright timber joist in the middle of the one-roomed cabin. The joist was still doing a solid job at holding up the main roof beam, although the corrugated iron sheets above looked more like Swiss cheese than a roof covering. Harry had put the lamps, now providing a sombre but adequate illumination of the room, on wooden shelves. Trev went out and returned with a rope. He used it to lash the chair to the joist. He tried to shake the chair with his hands.

'Solid as a rock and our little stage is set.'

Harry spat onto the dirt floor. 'Act one, scene one. Enter stage left one paedophile.'

The pair walked back out to the van. Tanya was still smoking and was holding a camera.

'Hey, Tan, don't forget, all ciggie butts in the ashtray.'

'Yes, Trev.' He couldn't see her rolling her eyes in the dark.

'What's with the camera?'

'Just going to take some pictures of the stars. I've never seen them like this before.'

Harry pointed over towards the south. 'You see those two really bright ones, look like they're in a line?'

'Yep,' she replied.

'The pointer stars: Alpha and Beta Centauri. Follow them upwards, and there's the Southern Cross.'

She looked in the direction he was indicating. 'Oh, awesome.' She took a couple of photos.

The two men went to the back of the van and grabbed Schwarz by his feet, dragging him out.

A pair of bush stone curlews let out their chilling shrieks from nearby, loudly interrupting the cacophony of nocturnal outback creatures, dominated by croaking frogs and yapping sugar gliders.

Dieter Schwarz gradually became aware of his surroundings as his eyes began to refocus. His head felt groggy, his mouth was parched, and his wrists and his ankles screamed in pain. He tried to move his limbs, but he couldn't. He knew he was in a sitting position, and he seemed to be fastened to the chair he was on. Initially, a couple of bright lights filled his vision, but then he started to make out two human shapes in front of him. He saw a blur of movement and then he felt a huge pain searing through his left cheek. His awakening accelerated rapidly.

'Wakey, wakey, you piece of shit,' growled a slightly familiar voice in front of his face.

His near-vision focus returned and he recognized one of the cops from his house. The man stood back. This wasn't his lounge room, though. Then he saw the other cop. But they were no longer in suits. He seemed to be in an old shed. Then he saw a young woman leaning against the wall. Despite the cigarette between her lips, Dieter thought she was pretty, if you were into that sort of thing: adults. There was a card table a couple of metres to his left with a variety of implements on it. Then it suddenly registered that he was completely naked. This wasn't good, not good at all.

There was a loud bang on the roof, followed by a throaty growl. Tanya jumped.

'Just a possum, babe,' said Harry.

'And judging by the bang, a fricking well-fed possum,' added Trev, as he stood next to Schwarz and gave him another injection. He spoke into the captive's ear. 'Bit of sodium pentothal, my friend, the old truth juice.' Trev stood back.

Harry stepped in towards Schwarz, who closed his eyes, flinching, but then opened them again when no blow arrived.

Harry was holding a photo about thirty centimetres in front of him. 'Recognize her? Eleven years ago?'

'No,' he gasped.

'Really?' growled Harry. 'You and your scum mates raped and killed her.'

'I ... I ... I don't know what you're talking about,' stammered Dieter.

'She was my daughter,' roared Harry. 'You cunt!'

This time he didn't have time to flinch before Harry's fist torpedoed into his face, nearly taking his head off. Blood started running from his nose and then from his mouth.

'You're going to tell us everything before we're finished, Schwarz.'

'Honestly,' he stammered, 'I don't know that girl.'

'You're a fucking child molester, Schwarz. We know that. We're both ex-detectives, and we've still got plenty of contacts. How do you think we found you?'

Dieter looked at them. It seemed as if he was considering his next response carefully, as blood ran down his chin. 'But ... but I like little boys, not girls. Never touched a girl in my life. I swear to God.' Dieter wasn't about to add to his problems by disclosing his teenage rape of the deaf-mute girl.

Tanya couldn't help herself. 'Oh, and that makes it so fucking all right, I suppose?' She strode over and spat in his face. 'You fucking monster. I really hope these two make you suffer.'

Her globule of saliva meandered its way down his cheek to mingle with the blood. Harry held up his hand towards her and she moved back.

Harry gave Dieter three rapid fists into his stomach. 'You're fucking lying, Schwarz!'

Harry sunk his fist in again. 'Tell me the fucking truth!'

Dieter was sobbing and struggling for air. 'I ... I don't know that girl, honestly.'

'Time to get serious then,' said Trev. He picked up a handheld blowtorch from the little table, ignited it, and turned up the gas supply to produce a roaring blue flame as he stepped towards the captive.

Dieter gasped and begged, 'Please, no, I don't know anything.'

Harry pulled out a black leather gag ball from his pocket and rammed it into Dieter's mouth, securing the strap behind his head. Then he lowered his mouth to his ear. 'And when my mate here has finished his little tricks, you, Bernhard, are going to tell us everything.'

Dieter made all sorts of muffled noises, looking pleadingly at Harry, who took several paces back.

Trev moved the flame towards Dieter's chest and proceeded to barbecue both his nipples into masses of blackened deformed flesh.

Dieter convulsed in pain, at least as much as his lashings would permit, and his stifled screams shook his whole face. His bladder and bowels gave way at the same time. The smell of excrement fused with the pork-like stench of burnt human meat.

'Ready to talk now, fuckwit?' hissed Harry, removing the gag.

It sounded as if Dieter was going to choke, but then some noises started. 'I'm ... I'm not Bernhard. I'm Dieter. Bernhard is my brother.'

Harry snorted. 'Yeah, righto. And you just happen to look a dead ringer for Bernhard, and drive Bernhard's car. Let's try again.' Harry shoved the gag back in his mouth.

Dieter was wide-eyed with terror and struggling to scream as Trev moved in again. 'You should have been castrated years ago, Bernhard. Would have saved countless kids. I think I'll do it now. Better late than never. And you certainly won't be needing your balls again after tonight.'

With that, Trev lowered the roaring blowtorch and there was a slight blaze as Dieter's pubes caught alight briefly, and then his scrotum blackened and melted. Harry winced as he watched. Dieter simply passed out.

Trev turned the blowtorch off. Then he picked up a syringe and stuck it in Dieter's arm. 'Ritalin, a stimulant,' he said to Harry.

Dieter came to, and Harry removed the gag. He put the photo back in front of his face. 'This was my daughter, Orla. Now, we know that you and your ped mates, Reggie and Herbert, abducted and raped her. Then you killed her and buried her in the Royal National Park. We know all that, Bernhard. What we want to hear from you is exactly what each of you did to her, whose idea it was, who else was involved, then or later, and where fucking Reggie is now. And I mean precisely where he is.'

Dieter dribbled a mixture of blood and vomit.

'But ...' he whispered.

'No, no "buts", Bernhard. There's plenty more pain available if you choose that path.'

Dieter started crying.

Tanya's voice came in from the background. 'Oh, fucking spare me, please.'

Harry leaned close to Dieter. 'Come on, out with it.'

Dieter looked up at him, his face screwed up in pain. 'I, I do know about your girl. But I wasn't there, I swear. Bernhard told me about it. But I am Dieter. You must believe me, please.' His crying increased.

'Not this shit again,' said Trev, picking up a pair of bolt cutters. 'Which finger shall I start with?'

'Please!' wailed Dieter. 'You must have my wallet, my phone maybe. I can show you. I'm Dieter.'

Harry and Trev looked at one another. Trev put down the tool and went out to the van. He came back with the bag containing the items they'd taken for later examination from the Vaucluse house and from Dieter's pockets. He took out the wallet, opened it and pulled out a driver's licence.

'Fuck.'

He passed it to Harry.

'Dieter Jürgen Schwarz. Date of birth twenty-nine twelve seventy-one,' read Harry.

'Could be a fake,' said Trev, 'though it's a pretty good-quality one if it is.'

He went through everything else in the wallet.

'Everything's in the name of Dieter.'

'And, and on my phone you'll find Bernhard's number,' added Dieter desperately. 'I can give you the code.'

Trev chuckled. 'Don't bother, I worked it out already. Got a nifty little machine for that. Two nine one two.'

He paused, and then laughed.

'Your birthday, fuckstain. Not very original for a PIN, but you're not alone on that score.'

Dieter continued to sob and whine.

Harry picked up the phone and looked over at Trev. 'Okay to play?'

'Yeah. That's why I cracked it before we left Sydney, to disable the position settings and put it on airplane mode. Didn't want to turn it off like ours in case we needed to look at it during our little chat. But airplane mode makes sure there's no signal from it.'

'Cool, didn't know that,' said Harry. He went to the contact list and scrolled. 'Can't see any Bernhard here, Bernhard.'

'No, no, it's under *Bruder*, my brother.'

'That could be convenient bullshit.'

'But look at the photos, too. You'll see some of both of us together.'

Harry and Trev peered at the screen, trawling until they found a close-up of what appeared to be two Schwarz men together.

'Bugger me, they could be twins,' said Trev.

Harry turned back to Dieter. 'Okay, so where the hell is Bernhard then?'

'In Western Australia. He left a few weeks ago when he found out the police were looking at him again.'

'How did he find out?' asked Harry.

'I don't know.'

'Fuck you,' said Trev, picking up the bolt cutters again.

'Okay, okay! He's got a friend in the office of the DPP.'

Trev whistled. 'Is that right? What's the friend's name then?'

'I'm not sure, Simon something. Really I don't know anything more about him.'

'So where is Bernhard in WA exactly?' asked Harry.

'I've got it written down at home. Please, take me back there and I'll help you all you want.'

Trev climbed out of the back of the van and walked over to where Harry was standing having a quiet chat with Tanya in the darkness. The choir of night creatures, with their chorus of shrieks, growls, clucks and chirps, had stopped. It was almost as if they knew a pregnant pause was necessary at this point in the script.

'Well, we've got the wrong Schwarz brother. I just did some more checks looking for a Dieter, and, sure enough, there is a Dieter born a year before Bernhard.'

'So nothing came up before?' asked Tanya.

'No, but we weren't looking for any name other than Bernhard,' said Trev.

'Fuck,' said Harry. 'And double fuck. I was quite prepared to kill the scum who took Orla, but this ...'

'Yeah, but we can't really let him go, he's seen our faces.'

'I know, but ethically this is a mammoth problem, brother,' said Harry. He lit a smoke and passed the packet to Trev. 'I can deal with avenging Orla,' he continued. 'This, on the other hand, would be more like vigilante execution. And where does that stop?'

'Fucking hell, mate, we don't have the luxury of getting too philosophical here.'

'All right, let's think this through.'

Tanya started to walk off. 'I'll leave you two to your moral dilemma.'

Harry looked over at her again a minute later. She was leaning against the van next to the open door, having a smoke and pulling her earphones out of the door pocket.

Harry looked back into the cold, dark bush.

'Harry, I get your issue, but he can't live, can he? Not now, not after he's seen us?'

'No, that can't happen, obviously.'

'So, we have to kill him, mate. We've no choice.'

'Yeah, but as I said, he's not one of Orla's killers.'

'Still a fucking paedophile. Plenty of other victims who we'd be doing some justice for.'

'There is that.' Harry paused. 'Hey, maybe we can convince him to kill himself, or face hours of more torture?'

Trev snorted. 'Good luck with that idea, mate. Sounds good in theory, but most of these cunts are so egotistical that suicide would be the last option for them.'

'Fuck!' said Harry.

In the background, the night creatures continued their chatter.

Tanya waited for the guys to fall into deep deliberation again. She reached back into the van door pocket, and then walked quietly into the cabin.

Dieter looked up at her as she stood in front of him.

Tanya sneered down at the trussed and bloodied man. She tried to breathe through her mouth to avoid the foul stench of burnt flesh and shit. She stared at him. No amount of suffering was too much for these monsters in her view. Just like the stepfather who had ruined her and Sasha's childhoods, this vermin was a complete waste of oxygen.

'Please, please,' he begged. 'Get them to take me home and I can help them.'

Tanya smiled contemptuously and again spat in his face, imagining it was her stepfather.

Dieter's expression changed. 'Fuck you, you little slut.'

'Oh, is that right?'

Tanya reached into her cargo pants pocket, coming out with a .38 Special that she'd retrieved from the van door. She levelled it at Dieter's forehead.

He tried to laugh, with a mixture of blood and mucus bursting from his nostrils. 'You wouldn't have it in you. Besides, if that were the plan here, they would have done it already. I didn't touch his daughter, and he knows it.'

'Maybe they hate all paedophiles. Think they should all die.'

'Huh. As I said, they would have killed me already. Now they don't know what to do. I can hear them arguing out there.'

'Well, fucker, you don't see me joining in the argument, do you?'

'You're not a killer. You're nothing without those men out there.'

A slight smile tweaked the corners of Tanya's mouth. She brought her left hand onto the butt of the revolver to join her right, and then she pulled back the hammer. The stubby barrel remained rock steady about fifteen centimetres in front of Dieter's face.

'His daughter, Orla, or not, you're still a fucking child molester.'

'I love children. I don't hurt them.'

'Oh, spare me that perverted self-justification. No doubt my cunt of a stepfather used the same lines with his mates.'

Dieter sneered at her. 'Bit of sweet meat, were you? And now you feel sorry for yourself, and angry because really you enjoyed it.'

'No, I'm getting on with my life. But you're not. All molesters deserve to die in my books. And, you piece of shit, I am plenty, with or without those guys out there. Take that as your last lesson, arsehole.'

Dieter's expression changed again, revealing his realization that she did have it in her.

Tanya's index finger squeezed down on the trigger.

A blast shattered the night and nature went suddenly silent again.

Harry and Trev ran towards the shack.

Tanya was standing back from Dieter, now lifeless with a neat .38 calibre hole between his eyes, a slow dribble of blood running down the bridge of his nose. Harry looked at Tanya. He was speechless. She passed him the Smith & Wesson, and lit a cigarette. She smiled at Harry. 'I didn't share your ethical dilemma. I lost my childhood to these filthy scum. They all need to die.'

'Okay,' was all Harry could come up with.

Trev regained his composure first. 'Well, it was really the only solution. So, let's finish it off. Come on, Harry.'

Tanya watched, holding the torch, as they threw Dieter's body down the mineshaft near the cabin. There was a thud as it hit the bottom about ten metres down.

'Hold your noses,' said Trev, opening a sealed bucket he'd got from the van. He tipped its dark, sloppy contents down after the body.

'That stinks!' said Tanya.

'Blood and offal,' said Trev. 'It'll attract all the meat eaters out here. Schwarz will be an unidentifiable skeleton before the week is out.'

'Meat eaters?' asked Tanya.

'Plenty of them,' said Harry. 'Feral cats by the hundreds, then goannas, and the bush rats. They'll all do the job.'

'The cycle of life,' added Trev.

'Oh, so now it's your turn for philosophy, is it, smart-arse?'

'Yeah, that's right. Now let's get out of here.'

They packed up their accessories, jumped in the van, and began the trip back to Sydney.

– 12 –

It was dark the following evening as the grey van, again with number plates of convenience attached, reversed quietly into the driveway of the Schwarz residence, blocking the front door from view.

As Trev exited the van's back door, Harry turned to Tanya. 'We'll be as quick as we can. Any sign of movement out here, you text us. And keep the van locked.'

'Cool.' She smiled at him. 'Not leaving me a gun then?'

'Funny, ha-ha, Miss Trigger.'

With that, Harry stepped out of the van, closed the door gently behind him, and joined Trev who was opening the front door of the house with Dieter's keys. The pair stepped into the dark hallway and closed the door silently. They were both wearing cotton forensic gloves.

They stood listening in the darkness. After a couple of minutes Harry whispered to Trev. 'Not a sound, think we're good.'

'Yeah. We'll just use the lights. Being a ped, I'll bet all the windows are well and truly covered for total privacy.'

Harry flicked on the light switch for the hallway and the pair squinted as their eyes adjusted. Harry turned to Trev. 'I reckon we'll find what we want in his bedroom or there'll be a study or den-type room.'

'Bloody den of iniquity more like.'

'Right, we know that's the lounge,' said Harry, pointing at the first doorway on the left.

Trev looked into the doorway opposite. 'Dining room.'

They walked cautiously along the hallway. Harry was about to step into the next door on the left when he threw himself back against the wall and pulled his .38 out of a shoulder holster. Trev took the cue and drew his piece as well. Harry motioned to the room and mouthed to Trev.

'There's someone sitting in the kitchen.'

Trev leaned against the door-frame and peeked around the edge. He stood completely still and waited for a minute. Then he whispered in Harry's ear.

'A woman. Not moving at all.'

'Asleep, you reckon?' Harry breathed.

'We're about to find out, 'cos we can't back out now.'

'And when she sees our faces?'

'We'll use the fake IDs. Give her some story about finding the door open on a routine visit.'

Trev put his hand around the door-frame, feeling for the light switch. Harry moved into the doorway and levelled his revolver.

The bulb blew as the light went on. The figure in the chair, her back to them, didn't move a millimetre in the gloom.

They paused, but then Harry slowly moved forward, circling around behind the motionless woman. Trev approached from the near side.

'Hello, madam,' said Harry, in a typically gruff, copper way.

Nothing.

Harry was now on her far side and looking at her face. 'Mate, her eyes are wide open.'

Trev moved in and put his fingertip on the side of the woman's neck.

'She cold?' asked Harry.

'More like room temperature. Weird. No pulse, that's for sure. She's definitely dead. Or else a very realistic mannequin.'

Harry leaned in close to old Mrs Schwarz's face. He blew gently and a light sprinkle of dust came off her cheeks. Harry stared closely at the open eyes. He flicked on his torch. 'Jesus wept!'

'What?' asked Trev.

'Mate, she's fucking stuffed.'

'Yes, mate, exactly. I said she's dead.'

Harry was grimacing. 'No, she is literally fucking stuffed.'

'What?'

'Glass eyes, mate, have a look.'

Trev leant in from the other side. He scrunched up his face in horror. 'Bloody hell!'

'Looks like Dieter and Bernhard really are mummy's boys. Typical fucking peds,' said Harry.

'Just couldn't bear to part with her, I guess.'

Harry picked up a sheet of paper from the top of a neat stack on the kitchen table opposite the late Mrs Schwarz and put his torch light on it. He laughed. 'Crafty little bastards.'

'What is it?' asked Trev, as he walked around the table.

'A bank statement for one Hilda Anna Schwarz. And there are fortnightly deposits from Centrelink, as well as something German on a regular basis. Last deposit was a week ago.'

Trev laughed this time. 'Mate, I've seen the dead-man welfare scam done before, but never actually in the presence of the deceased party.'

Harry pulled out his iPhone and photographed the bank statement, then Mrs Schwarz's serene face. It was anaemic and completely without lustre. She had a somewhat musty smell to her, with a hint of naphthalene.

'Trev, just hold the statement next to her face, will you?' He took another shot.

'Let's find Dieter's stuff,' said Trev.

Within two minutes Harry had found the room they were looking for and turned on the light. 'In here, Trev.'

Trev joined him and they stood there contemplating the depraved scene in the room, the size of a tiny bedroom. There were a number of child porn photos, some clearly home-made and others cut out of magazines, on the wall behind a bench-desk running along the length of it. The desk was disgustingly demarcated into two halves, one with naked boys and one with naked girls. The male side had two laptops open on the benchtop, the female side had a clean rectangle shape on the slightly dusty surface.

'Think that's where Bernhard's machine would've been,' said Harry. 'Plus that's the girl side of the room. Dieter said he was into boys. And they do usually stick to one or the other.'

'Sick fuckers,' said Trev, looking around the pictures. 'You know what always strikes me when I've seen these sort of pictures before?'

'That a picture doesn't even begin to depict the tragedy for these kids?'

'Okay, there is that. But it's always this similar look the kids have, almost as if they simply don't understand.'

'And it's that naïvety that these bastards prey on. But you're spot on, the kids in the pictures do usually look a bit blank.'

Trev picked up one of the laptops. 'I'll take Dieter's computers, however. And those hard drives over there.'

Harry got busy going through a drawer unit.

Trev leant towards a frame on the wall next to Dieter's half of the desk. He laughed. 'Bugger me, a City Night College certificate in taxidermy awarded to one Dieter Schwarz.'

'Can't ask for any more devotion to a mother, can you?'

They continued their search of the room.

Fifteen minutes later they emerged from the house, waving goodbye to the old woman, with Trev adding, '*Auf Wiedersehen, Frau Schwarz.*'

Harry was carrying a bag with two laptops in it, as well as a stack of documents and two external hard drives.

As Trev closed the front door, Tanya opened the rear door of the van from the inside. Harry looked at her face, still entirely stunning in the gloomy light.

'Babe, your beauty is all the more appreciated after what we've seen in there.'

'You expected bad, though, didn't you?'

'Yeah, but bloody hell, that was fucking dreadful. Kiddie porn all over his room and a stuffed, literally stuffed, like taxidermy, old mother in the kitchen.'

Tanya raised her eyebrows. 'What?! I don't suppose I can have a quick look?'

'Why would you want to, babe?'

'I'm learning the trade, remember? Plus I'm not exactly innocent in this field.'

Trev pulled a digital camcorder out of his inside jacket pocket. 'It's all filmed, Tanya, if you really want to. Right now, we need to get going.'

Tanya nodded.

Harry chuckled. 'You mean "decamp", Detective Sergeant Matson.'

'Indeed I do, Detective Sergeant Kenmare.'

They both laughed as they climbed into the van.

Tanya rolled her eyes and sighed. 'Don't give up your day jobs, boys. You'd starve doing stand-up.'

Harry clambered into the driver's seat and started the van. They slowly eased into the road and discreetly headed off towards the city.

An hour later, they were sitting in Harry's office.

Trev had both the laptops from Schwarz's house up and running. 'Dieter obviously felt completely secure in his place, all the passwords are saved in the browser on this one.' He pointed to the HP machine he was playing with.

'What about the Samsung?' asked Harry.

'That's all kiddie porn, mate. Seems he uses one for that, and then this one for everything else.'

Tanya lit a cigarette and poured herself a second vodka. 'So, this welfare scam, how much would he have got?' she asked.

'Depends when the old lady died,' said Harry, leafing through a stack of papers in front of him. 'But it looks as if there's the Centrelink payments here, then the German payments, presumably pension as well, and some other regular deposits. Quick estimate, I'd say about seventy grand a year.'

'And then every month, Mrs Schwarz generously transfers several thousand dollars into Dieter's account. The amounts vary, too, so less suspicious if anyone cared to look,' added Trev. 'Presumably Dieter then gives cash to Bernhard.'

'And so you can access Dieter's account then?' asked Tanya.

'Yep, here it is.' Trev made a few keystrokes. 'We could clear it out if we wanted. Current balance is over two hundred grand.'

'We don't want any of his filthy ped money, unless it's to finance more hunting,' said Harry firmly, refilling his and Trev's whiskey glasses.

Tanya smiled back at both of them.

Harry frowned. 'What's going on in there, Divine One?'

She grinned broadly. 'A devious idea coming together.'

'Go on,' said Trev.

'Well, he won't be using his money, but lots of kids could. A bit of ironic justice.'

Harry was still frowning. 'Please explain, babe.'

Tanya was still smiling. 'Set up some regular direct deposits to various charities that help kids. And Dieter, the filthy piece of shit, will be giving until the money runs out.'

'Actually,' said Trev, 'the money will keep flowing into both their accounts until someone finds out they're dead. So, could be a while.'

Harry roared laughing. 'This is priceless, Tanya, absolutely bloody priceless.'

'I love it, too,' said Trev, 'but no religious charities.'

'Totally agree,' said Tanya. 'They're all self-serving rorts. So, I reckon Médecins Sans Frontières for a start. All those hospitals they run in shit-fights around the world. A great cause.'

'Very nice,' said Harry. 'And our friend Zanza would no doubt approve of that.'

Tanya continued. 'Then maybe UNICEF, and the children's hospitals here, and the Clown Doctors program.'

'What's that one?' asked Trev.

'They go around providing entertainment for kids who are in hospital, especially ones with cancer.'

'All sounds bloody good to me,' said Harry. 'Who would have thought Dieter would have developed such a social conscience? Funny how life goes.'

Trev chuckled. 'There's a surprise at every corner, that's for sure. I'll get the deposits for the charities set up in the morning. Now for his emails. Let's see if we can find Bernhard.'

Trev started scrolling through Dieter's email account, whilst Harry leant back, put his feet on his desk, and lit a Marlboro, sipping on his Jameson. Tanya absorbed herself with her iMac.

About twenty minutes later, Trev turned to Harry. 'Oi, wake up, brother. Come and have a look at this.'

Harry swung his feet off the desk and walked over to the meeting table where Trev was working.

Trev pointed at the screen, as Harry leant in. 'This email was from Bernhard last Monday, letting Dieter know he's got a PO box now, and asking for more money to be sent.'

'Where's the PO box?'

'Some place called Chidlow, postcode six-five-five-six.'

'So, Western Australia then.'

Harry turned to Tanya. 'Hey, Tan, can you please look up Chidlow, C-H-I-D-L-O-W, on Google maps?'

A minute later, Tanya said, 'Got it. Inland from Perth. Looks about forty or fifty kilometres.'

'Right,' said Harry. 'Looks as though we're going to the west coast for a spot of ped hunting.'

Trev closed up the two stolen laptops. 'All done here for the moment. Let's get out of here for a more relaxed drink.'

'Sadly a bit late for the Emerald Bar,' said Harry. 'Why don't we have a few *chez moi*, and you can crash on the couch, Trev.'

'Suits me, mate.'

Several drinks at Harry's bachelor pad in Ultimo saw them call it a night, saluting each other all round for a job well done. Harry gave Trev a couple of pillows and a doona. Tanya gave Trev a kiss goodnight.

In Harry's bedroom, Tanya stripped faster than Harry. She lay back naked on the bed, looking seductively at Harry, who was trying to get out of his trousers without falling over. Tanya giggled. He finally joined her, unclothed, on the bed and placed a hand over one of her breasts as their tongues met in a wetly urgent kiss.

Harry came up for air. 'You are utterly wonderful.'

'Bet you say that to all the bad-arsed chicks,' she teased.

Harry chuckled. 'Well, maybe some of them, but none as gorgeous as you, ever.'

'Smooth. But I like that.'

'Forgetting possessiveness or any of that shit, you mean the world to me, Tanya.'

'Mmm. Is that PI speak for "I love you"?' She poked him in the ribs, but at the same time ran her tongue over his lips and kissed him.

'Yes, babe, I do love you in my own way. I'm not a conventional, homely, one-woman type, but you know that.' He held her tight in his arms.

'And nor am I,' she replied. 'I'll always be myself but, Harry, I do love you. You are a good, good man, and I want you in my life always.'

They kissed.

'So, you and Sasha going to come on the Perth trip?'

'I am, hell yes. Sash won't be able to, though.'

'Why not?'

'Couple of appointments.'

'What sort of appointments?'

'Some medical check-ups. Don't really know much else at the moment.'

'You mean lady stuff?'

'Yeah, Mr PI, that's right. Lady stuff. Want more detail?'

'Ah, no, thanks anyway.'

She ran her tongue over his lips again.

'Now, Mr PI, shut the fuck up, forget about going west, and head south, big boy. And do not surface until I say.'

Harry grinned. 'Yes, boss.'

Harry's face started sliding down Tanya's chest, licking her breasts on the way. He was lingering there, his tongue working her nipples into hard points. She hurried his journey, shoving his cranium downwards along her flat, toned belly and opening her thighs. When his face was buried in her moistening crotch, resplendent with her full Brazilian, she wrapped her legs around his head, using her hands to hold it between her legs. It was hardly necessary: Harry's eagerness in this pursuit made the most zealous of missionaries look like reluctant novices. Harry's tongue eagerly started its magic, writhing like an eel in the wetness of her vagina, working on her clit.

Out on the couch, as Tanya's moaning increased in volume, Trev groaned and grabbed one of his pillows, shoving it over his head. He closed out the noise of Tanya's delight. In the self-imposed total darkness, and behind his closed eyes, the image of Jean-Louis came to him, as it did most nights. And despite the years, the power of his love never diminished. In his reverie Trev reached out, pretending he could stroke Jean-Louis's face. Then a tear fell from the corner of Trev's eye, immediately soaked up by the pillow. A few minutes later he fell asleep.

* * * * *

PART 2

HARRY'S WESTERN

But the scent of her lingered on in the small room and even as he strolled to the shower the memories were falling into line. Lissa was some girl.

- William Ard

A man has missed something if he has never woken up in an anonymous bed beside a face he'll never see again, and if he has never left a brothel at dawn feeling like jumping off a bridge into the river out of sheer physical disgust with life.

- Gustave Flaubert

– 1 –

Harry sighed with pleasure as he sunk the ultra-sharp boning knife into Bernhard Schwarz's pelvic area, pushing hard with a circular motion to excise his genitals. Bernhard's screaming was stifled by the bloody penis and scrotum being rammed into his mouth until he choked on his own testicles.

Harry opened his eyes, returning from his fantasies, as the train entered a curve and the sunlight hit his face. It was an unseasonably warm September afternoon and the long, silver Indian Pacific meandered its serpentine path through the Blue Mountains, heading west out of Sydney. It had been a couple of weeks since Dieter Schwarz's demise and a long way further to the west lay Bernhard's date with destiny.

'You daydreaming, mate?' asked Trev from across the table in the bar carriage.

'Sorry, didn't mean to zone out. Where's Tanya?'

'Went back to her cabin to make a call to Sasha. She got a text from her.'

'She probably got the appointment through for the tests. Let's hope it's nothing.'

'Well, she's young and fit. Doctor's probably just being extra cautious.'

The waiter came past and Trev held up his fingers. 'Three more please, mate.'

'Certainly, sir.'

As he walked away towards the bar, Tanya returned and sat down next to Harry.

'All okay, babe?' he asked.

'The tests are set for Friday, but we won't know anything until next week.'

Trev took her hand across the table. 'She'll be okay, Tan. I'm sure the doctors are just being careful.'

Harry put his arm around her. 'Yep, it'll all be fine.' He kissed her on the temple.

Tanya looked out the window. 'Shit, I could kill for a smoke right now.'

Harry laughed. 'The one downside of this otherwise magnificent method of transport: no smoking until the first stop. And that's Broken Hill in the morning.'

'But we are well stocked on Nicorettes, and the bar is limitless. We'll survive,' grinned Trev.

Tanya took a large swallow of her vodka lime. 'I can't believe I agreed to this. Three days until Perth. Three fucking days! They have invented aeroplanes, you know!'

'And we need the van with all its gear, as well as the weapons.' Trev waved in the direction of the back of the train, where the van was nestled on the car-transporter wagon hitched to the end of the silver snake.

'Plus,' added Harry, 'our fake IDs were a breeze getting on this. It's nowhere near the scrutiny we might have had at the airport.'

'And hence the unidentified phones we gave you and Sasha, so you could still talk to each other and there's no trace back to either of your names,' said Trev.

Tanya groaned. 'I know. But still, three days.'

Harry put his arm back around her shoulders. 'Babe, three days of relaxation, great food, endless drinks, and over four thousand kilometres of Australian scenery.'

'Stuff the scenery.'

'Well, what about the company of two of the finest fellas you'll ever meet?' said Trev chuckling.

Tanya closed her eyes. 'And it's going to be three very, very long days,' she moaned.

Both the blokes laughed.

Later that evening as the train ambled westward, the trio were sitting in the restaurant car, having gorged themselves on a three-course dinner including kangaroo, barramundi, and a delicious Margaret River cheese platter to conclude. Three bottles of Barossa cabernet sauvignon had assisted, and were now reinforced by cognac for the guys and a Cointreau on ice for Tanya. Harry swallowed the last of his drink and put the brandy balloon down gently.

'Well, team, in the absence of being able to enjoy a cigar, I'm going to pass on a second cognac and hit the sack.'

Tanya looked at Trev's glass, which was still in business. 'I'm going to have another, so Trev doesn't have to drink alone.'

Trev laughed. 'Never worried me before, but very happy for the company. Otherwise I might be left to talk to those sisters over there.' He subtly indicated in the direction of two Franciscan nuns having a cup of tea. 'And then I'd simply end up telling them what I thought of the bloody Catholic Church and it'd get untidy.'

Tanya glanced in their direction. 'Yeah, they've been giving me filthy looks for the last hour they've been here.'

'See you pair of drunks in the morning then,' said Harry, as he belched audibly. '*Excusez-moi*! Better out than in.'

There was an audible 'tsk tsk' from the holy table.

Harry exhaled in the opposite direction before leaning in to give Tanya a kiss goodnight. He'd been aiming for her cheek, but she turned quickly, planted her lips fully on his and rammed her tongue into his mouth, making loud groaning noises with it.

The gasps of opprobrium from the nuns were more stridently judgemental than a Sunday sermon.

Tanya turned to face them. She smiled and stared at them until they looked away.

'Pure style, Tan,' said Trev, clinking his glass against hers.

Harry laughed. 'Is it safe for me to leave you two here? We don't need a religious fight in the dining car. And I don't mind the fight, but the publicity wouldn't help.'

'Depends,' replied Tanya.

Harry raised his eyebrows.

She continued. 'If the sanctimonious old crones say anything, then I won't be sitting here quietly. It'll be on.'

Harry didn't need to worry. At that moment the righteous sisters got up and scurried away in the other direction. They didn't even get to see Tanya's raised middle finger.

'I'm out of here,' said Harry. 'Good night and sleep well. And we can sleep in as long as we like.'

Tanya and Trev both said, 'Good night', as Harry upped and walked off towards his cabin two carriages away.

Trev signalled the waiter for two more drinks. Tanya was looking pensive and swirling the ice cubes around in her glass.

'Sasha?' asked Trev.

'Yeah. I can't help being worried.'

'Of course, Tan. But at her age I'm sure it'll be okay. It's really rare for young ones like you two to have any really serious issues.'

'I keep trying to remind myself of that, but …'

She went silent.

'Want to talk about it?'

'It's just that, finally, for the first time in our lives, things are going well for us. And now this. It would be so unfair.'

The new drinks arrived. Tanya paused and stared into the dregs of her old one. 'Ironic, really. First lucky break we ever got, as it turned out, was being naked on all fours with Harry going hard from behind.'

'An image I so do not need,' said Trev.

Tanya chuckled, then looked at him. 'Trev, does he know you're gay?'

Trev smiled. 'We'll come back to that. You go on.'

She looked down again. 'Here we are, less than a year later. Out of the parlour, making good money and having exciting work with you and Harry. Got the part-time fashion design apprenticeships with Tessa. Thanks to her contacts, we've made some serious money modelling lingerie for magazines. It almost seems too good to be true, and so I'm scared of losing something.'

Trev touched the back of her hand. 'You two are inspirational, Tan. Don't bloody forget that. You were dealt a real shit hand and you've turned it around. Be proud of yourselves. And our thoughts for Sasha.'

He raised his glass, as did Tanya. 'For Sash,' she said.

They drank.

'All right, enough about me. You're not escaping the question, Mr Trev.' Her radiant smile lit up her beautiful face.

'Honestly, we've never actually discussed it. But I'm guessing he's worked it out, given we don't exactly banter together about all the gorgeous women in our world, you two at the top of the list ...'

'Smoothy,' interrupted Tanya.

'And that's what you'd expect if we were both straight.'

Tanya nodded. 'Yeah, I suppose. Just seems strange that you're such good mates and yet haven't talked about it.'

Trev laughed. 'That's because you're approaching it from a female perspective where you talk about everything. Us blokes, a lot of stuff remains unspoken. I'm not saying that's always a good thing, but it's reality.' He took a sip of cognac. 'Anyway, it's not likely to bother Harry. He's nothing if not progressive in his views, plus he'd probably appreciate the reduced competition.'

Tanya laughed this time. 'He doesn't have to worry there. He punches well above his weight in the lady department. I think it's his huge, rough-edged charm. And the evident decency and honesty.'

'He's certainly not lacking on that score, our Harry.'

'So, Trev, what's your story here?' She looked him in the eye again.

'What do you mean?'

'Don't be coy. I know that we're both here helping Harry with hunting down his peds. But he mentioned before we left that after we've done Schwarz, then you had something to do before we could go home to Sydney.'

'Yep. Let's just say some unfinished business with the wonderful Catholic Church. Hence my earlier comment.' Trev paused and swallowed more cognac.

'You can't stop there.'

Trev took a deep breath. 'I went to a Catholic boarding school in Queensland. Awful bloody place. I was fourteen when it happened. I already knew I was gay, but obviously kept my mouth shut and tried to blend in. But one day, four of the older boys dragged me into the changing rooms, told me that faggots needed to be punished, and then beat me up.'

'I'm sorry, Trev. Gay kids got bullied at our school, too. I can only imagine how much worse it was back in your day.'

'Yeah. I had quite a few cuts and bruises after that beating,' he continued. 'So the nursing sister had to patch me up, and the headmaster, Father Barwick, was informed. After the nursing station, I got called into Barwick's rooms. He demanded to know what had happened, so I told him. He asked me if I was gay, and I said yes. I thought I was safe in there. He then made some comments about "all God's children" and the like, poured me a sherry, and we talked about study. Several sherries later I was pretty tipsy. Then he raped me.'

'Oh, God, no. I'm so sorry, Trev.' Tanya took his free hand in both of hers.

Trev took a swig of cognac and looked out into the dark landscape. He turned back to Tanya. 'It happened again several times before term ended. When I went home, I eventually told my good Christian mother about it. She told me I was an evil, ungrateful little liar and called my good Christian father, who proceeded to beat me so badly I spent a week in hospital.'

'You're kidding?'

'Sadly, no. My father was a prick. Then the police and social services became involved. I never went home again, and instead went to live with an aunt and her family in Brisbane.'

'Was anything ever done about the priest?' asked Tanya.

'I did try to talk to people about it, and my aunt supported me every time, but anyone in authority just told me to be quiet and that that part of my life was behind me. To this day I've never been able to swallow injustice.'

'I'm with you on that.'

'Later I joined the cops, thinking I might get to right some of the wrongs out there. Turned out I was wrong. And then you already know all about my leaving the Force.'

'That's so awful, Trev. Does Harry know all this?'

'Not all the gory details. But he does know that I was raped by a priest.'

'So, what's the link in WA?'

'After I'd started in the cops, I lodged an official complaint of sexual assault so I could have the priest investigated. I made my statement, but before the detectives could interview him, the wonderful Archbishop had transferred him to WA, out of reach of the Queensland Police. They ended up dropping the case as they told me there wasn't enough evidence to warrant seeking extradition. One of the detectives did tell me on the quiet that the diocese had been tipped off that the investigation was underway.'

'Who the hell would tip them off?'

'Tan, you have to understand the Catholic brotherhood infiltrates across our institutions. There are plenty of senior police whose loyalties are elsewhere, well away from serving their communities.'

'Wankers.'

'Anyway, that was twenty years ago now. Then last year, out of the blue, a former colleague in Brisbane called me to say that there had been an enquiry from the WA Police about Father Barwick. So, it seems he's still alive. I thought I needed to have some therapeutic words with him while I still could.'

'Are you going to kill him?'

'I'd rather see a full public confession, and maximum public damage to the Church, but we'll have to wait and see. Got to find him first.'

Tanya took Trev's hand again. 'Thank you for sharing.'

'I knew you of all people would understand. Seems as though we're all hunting demons.'

'You bet. Sasha and I've got our paedophile stepfather to deal with yet.'

Trev raised his glass. Tanya followed suit.

'To justice,' said Trev.

'To vengeance,' replied Tanya.

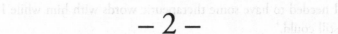

– 2 –

The next three days were a blur of eating, drinking, chatting and sleeping for the trio as the train rolled sedately across the vast Australian outback. The three scheduled stops – Broken Hill, Adelaide, and Rawlinna – became nicotine marathons. For the six-hour stop in the South Australian capital, they headed into the city itself, getting well-fed and watered in an inner-city beer garden. Then it was back on board the metal snake to cross the endless Nullarbor Plain, which bored Tanya senseless.

Saturday morning saw the train pass through Kalgoorlie and across the Wheatbelt. Springtime in Western Australia meant the renowned and unique wildflower season. As they rolled through the undulating countryside east of Perth, the cleared hillsides were carpeted with a floral shagpile of colour. Vibrant expanses of pink, yellow and white everlastings, patches of electric-blue leschenaultias, and the scarlet and jade green kangaroo paws captivated the eye. It was like rambling across vast slices of fairy bread, something out of the imagination of Roald Dahl. Even Tanya noticed, from the depths of her ennui, the prettiness of the landscape.

The train crawled into the city mid-afternoon and the van was offloaded at East Perth Station, watched by the three chain-smoking sleuths, all feeling that slight trepidation that accompanies the arrival in a new city.

Trev looked over at the skyscrapers of the CBD. 'Be good if we have a chance to look around, mate.'

'As long as we've got some time left after both jobs are done,' replied Harry. 'We should do, I reckon, as the return train isn't until tomorrow week.'

Tanya groaned. 'Another three days of that fricking train. Aaagh!'

They climbed into the van and Trev started it up. He turned to Harry. 'Mundaring, wasn't it, mate?'

'Yeah,' said Harry. 'There's a motel on the highway and that puts us only about fifteen minutes from Chidlow, so we can operate from there.'

Trev opened up a street directory.

'That's a bit retro, Trev. What's wrong with the satnav?' asked Tanya from the jump-seat behind the blokes.

'Tan, just like the phones, we don't need any unnecessary traces that we're here.' Trev passed the map book to Harry and they moved off.

'So, what's the next part of the plan?' asked Tanya. 'You didn't go into any detail on the train.'

'No, and that was deliberate,' said Trev. 'Too many people in close proximity and thin walls.'

'So, tell me now.'

'We're going to lure Schwarz to the post office and then follow him using a tracker to find out where he's living,' said Harry. 'And then we'll pay him a late-night visit.'

'And you know what happens then,' added Trev.

'Yeah,' said Tanya. 'Guess I don't have to pull the trigger this time, though.'

'Damned right,' said Harry. 'Bernhard is all mine.'

'So, how are we going to get him to the post office?'

'A cunning plan,' said Trev, doing his best impersonation of Baldrick from *Blackadder*.

Harry chuckled. 'Love it.'

'Going to message him from Dieter's phone to say a registered letter with money has been sent to his PO box and will be there Monday,' continued Trev. 'And we'll be watching.'

'And that, Divine One, is where you take centre stage,' said Harry.

'What do you mean?'

'He'll be pretty cagey, being basically on the run, so if he gets any sniff of either of us likely lads, he'll be off. A young lady, however, not the same problem. So, you're going to be near the post office to stick the tracker on whatever vehicle he's driving as soon as he goes in to pick up his mail on Monday morning,' explained Harry.

'Why can't we just follow him?'

Trev joined in. 'It's semi-rural up there from what I've seen on Google. So, very little traffic. Our van tailing him would stick out like a whiskey in Mecca.'

'Cool,' said Tanya. 'So what are we doing tomorrow then?' She yawned emphatically.

'Keeping a low profile,' said Harry. 'Hopefully the motel has got cable TV, and we'll get in plenty of grog for this evening.'

'I'm choosing the TV channels then, since I have to sit around even more,' said Tanya defiantly.

'Deal,' said Harry, lighting a cigarette.

They drove east on Guildford Road, coming into Midland about twenty minutes later. Trev pulled into a car park in front of a shopping centre.

'CommBank cash machine over there, I spy,' said Trev. 'We need to top up so we don't use our credit cards.'

'And your ATM card?' asked Tanya.

Trev and Harry both laughed.

'Not his card, babe,' said Harry. 'Good old Dieter is once again contributing to the operation. Can't believe the bastard's generosity.'

'And the dumb fuck had the same PIN for his cards as his phone,' added Trev, 'which ...'

'Which was his birthday,' completed Tanya. 'Some people are seriously stupid.'

Trev got out of the van and walked across the car park to the ATM. He came back a couple of minutes later and pulled out a wad of yellow $50 notes.

'Two grand in lovely pineapples. Should keep us going for a day or so.'

'Excellent,' said Harry. 'First things first, bottle shop.'

They pulled back onto the Great Eastern Highway, heading towards the hills of the Darling Scarp. A slight detour through a drive-in bottle shop netted them enough Jameson, vodka, and red wine to fuel a week-long cabinet meeting. A couple of cartons of cigarettes topped it off. They resumed their journey east, climbing Greenmount Hill.

Outside Mundaring, Trev pulled the van over short of the entrance to the Paradise Motel. The website had advertised it as, 'Your Oasis in the Hills – Heaven for the Weary Traveller'. The three of them peered at the joint, its pot-holed driveway bordered by dead grass, liberally adorned with faded soft drink cans. A long-dead rosebush had captured yellowed sheets of newspaper on its thorns.

'More like paradise fucking lost,' said Harry.

'In my experience, the shabbier, the more discreet,' said Trev, handing Dieter's wallet to Harry and stuffing a load of the recently acquired pineapples into it.

'Indeed,' said Harry. He turned to Tanya. 'Tan, pass me my travel bag, will you? I'll go and check in, so to speak.'

Trev laughed.

'So why aren't we driving in like normal people?' asked the stubbornly logical Tanya.

'Aside from arguing about us being normal, the point is that we don't want any vehicle details noted. Just a single wandering bloke walks in off the street, that's it,' said Harry.

And with that Harry took his bag and got out of the van, walked along the kerb and into the driveway of the decrepit establishment.

The paint job, formerly white presumably, was now diesel-exhaust grey. The guttering around the front of the roof had rusted through in places, leaving brown trails down the walls, like giant skid marks. A large concrete planter box next to the front door held a miserable palm tree, fighting for its life, and losing, only having the cold comfort of outlasting the rosebush. To top off the *Vogue Living*-worthy appearance, the sign above the door had lost a few of its plastic letters, or maybe they'd escaped. Harry noted with satisfaction several vehicles, including two vans, dotted in front of rooms, so new arrivals wouldn't raise any particular interest. He stepped into the front of the P RAD S MO L.

After his vision adjusted to the fog of cigarette smoke with a bouquet of BO, he saw a middle-aged bloke behind the counter, newspaper spread out in front of him, smoke in one hand and a stubby of Emu Bitter in the other. He belched as he looked up at Harry.

'G'day, mate. Welcome to the Paradise Motel,' he said in a broad, raspy Australian accent.

132

Harry took in the deeply tanned and lined face, silver crew cut, and fading tattoos on both forearms. Ex-military surmised Harry, and exactly the sort of laid-back Aussie bloke he found so easy to get on with at first encounter. Years as a cop had left him an expert at talking to the common man.

He walked up to the reception desk. There was a tatty sign that read, 'Bob Gauntlett – Proprietor'.

'G'day, mate. Passing through, bit of business to do, you know. Need a room for a couple of nights. Maybe a bit longer.'

'Well, this being a motel, mate, rooms is what I do. Eighty for a single. They've all got an en suite and cable.'

He pushed a guest register in front of Harry with a half-chewed biro.

'Just need some details, mate, and a credit-card imprint. You can settle the bill however you like. Cash is fine, of course.' He smiled at Harry, who had Dieter's wallet out, making the cash conspicuous.

Harry was ready to assume the Germanic identity and use the credit card if he had no choice, but he was angling for a cash transaction. 'I actually need a twin. How much?'

The man raised his eyebrows.

Harry jumped in. 'Got an old mate meeting up with me tomorrow. We're going to get on the piss, so he'll need a bed, too. And we don't share.'

The man grinned. 'Yeah, you don't strike me as one of them.' He looked down at the open wallet and stared at the thick wad of yellow banknotes.

Harry sniffed opportunity. 'Mate, is there a rate for a twin room, with a fridge, and without the paperwork?'

The man looked him in the eye. 'For a true-blue fella like you, there's always a rate. Try me.'

Harry was confident a deal could be had, but the motelier clearly looked as if he played poker. Harry needed to show a hand: bluffing could turn things sour quickly. And a bit of theatre was called for, some dramatic embellishment. Harry looked around in both directions, then back at the man. He slowly pulled out a wad of fifties and deliberately counted them one at a time onto the counter. He reached a grand.

'Bob, isn't it?'

'Yeah, mate.' Bob was ogling the pile of cash hungrily. He wore the face of a guy in a strip joint as a naked lap dancer approached.

'If I may,' oozed Harry, 'what say you to a nice round grand for three nights? If I need to extend I'll drop you another bundle.'

Bob was nodding.

Harry really wanted to seal the deal. 'Oh, and one more thing.' Harry lowered his voice. 'Can you point me in the direction of where a bloke can get a root around here?'

Bob roared laughing. 'Fella, you really are dinkum, aren't you? Deal!'

The speed with which he swept up the arrayed banknotes betrayed a card-playing dexterity. The grand disappeared into Bob's back pocket. He took the guest register and put it on the counter to his side. He opened a drawer and handed Harry a maroon business card with gold lettering, 'Heidi's Harem', and a mobile phone number.

'The girls there will come up here no problems, they're used to the place. And they're all pretty okay, from what I've seen anyway.' Bob winked at him.

'Cheers,' said Harry, pocketing the card.

134

'Or,' continued Bob, 'if you want to save some cash, you can go over to the pub any evening and ask the barman to point out Shazza, the town bike. Buy her drinks for the evening and done deal, mate. And she's filthy.' He winked at Harry again. 'She'd look after you and your mate at the same time.'

'Sounds like a lady of the world,' said Harry.

Bob laughed. 'Mate, Shazza couldn't spell lady, but she bangs more than a dunny door in a storm. And take it from me, fella, she likes it in every hole she's got.'

'Always good to have options,' replied Harry, grinning.

'No worries, mate.' Bob handed Harry a key and a card. 'Welcome to my humble resort,' he said. 'Room two eleven. Nice and quiet, around the back.'

'Perfect, thanks.' Harry picked up his bag.

'Enjoy your stay, mate, and my mobile is on the card if you need it.'

'Cheers.'

Harry turned and walked out onto the porch, and then down a side passage that cut through the single-level building to the rear.

Harry opened the door of two eleven and went inside. The room was as shabby as the exterior of the place. Harry dropped his bag on a tired-looking armchair, which was doing its best to manage a compatible relationship with the threadbare carpet – it was a competition of the worn and weary.

He checked the sheets on the two beds, the towels in the bathroom, and the toilet bowl and vanity.

Okay, it was scruffier than a Bali street dog, but it was at least clean. Decrepit he could do, stained sheets and pubes on the toilet seat he could not.

He pulled out his backup phone and texted Trev. A minute later the grey Transporter pulled up outside the room.

Tanya walked in, Trev following, and looked around her.

'Fucking hell, Harry, I'd hate to see what sort of place you'd get for a girl who wasn't great in bed.'

'Babe …' started Harry.

Trev interrupted, 'One without a bed!'

They all laughed.

'We'll unpack and then go find some takeaway dinner, and breakfast supplies for here,' said Harry.

'I'll go get the grog,' said Tanya. 'I really need a drink now.'

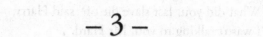

– 3 –

It was mid-morning on Sunday before anyone stirred, thanks to the amount of red wine used to wash down the takeaway Chinese banquet the previous evening, not to mention the spirits that followed dinner. The chipped melamine table was littered with empty bottles and smeared plates. Odorous plastic food containers competed with the taint of cigarette smoke. The trio had decided to go hard as nothing was happening until Monday.

Trev got up first, and headed for the bathroom. The toilet flushed and then the shower started.

Although Harry and Tanya had shared one of the two double beds, it had been a celibate night, partly due to the volume of alcohol and partly due to Trev's presence.

So, Harry, despite his fuzzy head, woke with an erection like an obelisk. Tanya was lying looking at him and the prominent bulge under the bedclothes.

'Morning, Mr PI. I'm happy to see you, too.'

She ran her tongue around her lips and caressed the blanket on top of his cock. 'Ooh, so near and yet so far!'

Harry groaned. 'Piss off, you tease.' He poked her in the ribs and she squealed, then giggled.

Trev came out of the bathroom whistling, in only his boxer shorts. Harry quickly turned on his side to hide his stiff member.

'Morning, team,' said Trev, rather too chirpily for Harry's liking.

'What's the chance of a girl getting a coffee from a sensitive, attentive guy?' asked Tanya.

'What did your last slave die of?' said Harry.

'I wasn't talking to you, Mr Hard.'

Trev laughed. 'Tan, for you, anytime. Milk? Sugar?' He winked at her.

'That's the way it's done, Harry, you see?'

'Bugger the pair of you,' said Harry. 'But I'll have one while you're at it, Trev.'

'Yeah, yeah.' Trev went over to the small counter above the fridge and put the kettle on. He turned back to them. 'After I've had a cuppa, I'm going to slide over to Chidlow and do a bit of a recce.'

Harry thought about going along as well, but then he considered his erection and the gorgeous woman next to him. Despite being a team player, there was no contest. 'Good idea, mate. Look less suss with one guy on his own.'

Trev grinned and made the coffees. Ten minutes later he was gone. The VW's engine started outside the room.

In one movement, Tanya had her knickers off and was astride Harry's face, reaching back, grabbing his cock. 'Right, no time for foreplay,' she grinned at him.

'Probably not,' mumbled Harry, making it sound like her crotch was talking, some feat of vaginal ventriloquy.

'You mentioned a slave before. Now I've got one. Work, slave!'

Muffled sound emanated from Harry as Tanya's crotch smothered his mouth. She rode his face rhythmically, every now and then sliding forward a little bit extra so his tongue lightly flicked her anus. As she got close to climaxing, she let go of his cock to grab his hair with both hands and her thighs tightened in a spasm against the sides of his head as she orgasmed. She threw her head back and shouted towards the ceiling, 'Damn, you're a good slave!'

Her thighs released and Harry gasped in air. She slid down his body until their faces were together. She kissed him, licking some of her wetness off his face. 'Thank you, Mr PI. Much needed.'

'My pleasure, Mistress Tanya. And no blood nose this time. Bonus.'

She chuckled as she slid her dripping pussy onto his cock.

Harry groaned. 'Oh, yeah. Much needed, too.' He gripped her hips as she rode up and down, his eyes closed in rapture.

Tanya leant to the side and grabbed a tube of lube from her bag on the bedside table. Harry looked over, then followed the tube back with Tanya's hand. Grinning, she squeezed some gel onto her fingers and kept riding him. She reached around behind herself with the dollop of lube. Then she came off Harry's cock, grabbed it in her hand, and pushed it back a fraction in her crotch. She slowly lowered her arse, closing her eyes and groaning as Harry's member gradually slipped into her anus.

'Jesus wept, that's tight!' gasped Harry.

'Don't you cum too quickly, boy, I want to savour this.'

'You and me both, girl. I'll try to picture something awful.'

Harry struggled against the prevailing pleasure. He had to stave off his orgasm as long as humanly possible, which was a hell of a tall order. He was all the way in her now. She slowly lifted herself back up. And then slowly down again.

'Oh, fuck!' Harry closed his eyes again: looking at the naked Tanya riding him was hardly conducive to delaying his climax.

'Think of Club Mammary!' exhorted Tanya.

'Oh, yeah, that works. Nappies, baby powder, breast milk!'

'And fat, corrupt councillors!' added Tanya.

'That'll make me last a while. Just don't you tickle my balls.'

Tanya's sliding her arse up and down Harry's cock gradually gathered speed as she loosened up. Now she was playing with her clitoris, eyes shut, finger circling intently. 'My nipples, slave!'

Harry grabbed some gel and started massaging her breasts.

She rode faster.

'Far out, I can't last much longer,' cried Harry.

'Hold it! Hold it!' Tanya's finger was going hell for leather on her clit, and three fingers from her other hand were now in her pussy. She screamed as she came.

Harry promptly exploded deep inside her arse, with a yell almost as loud as Tanya's.

She flopped down on his chest, leaving him inside her.

'Babe, that was fucking fantastic,' said Harry, kissing her neck.

'Yep. I even forgive you now for this shitty motel.'

They kissed tenderly, Harry stroking her face as she lay against his chest.

Trev, erring on the side of extra consideration, didn't return for two hours. Tanya and Harry were showered and dressed when he walked back into the room. He grinned as he took in the musky overtone hanging in the air, despite the stubborn challenge from last night's Chinese leftovers and this morning's cigarette smoke. He winked at Tanya, who stuck her tongue out at him.

'Well, Chidlow's not exactly a thriving metropolis, that's for sure,' he said to them both.

'How's the post office look?' asked Harry.

'It's combined with the newsagent. PO boxes are out on the front wall.' He looked at Tanya. 'There's a real estate agency right next door, so perfect cover for you to be looking in the window while you wait.'

'What's the area like for surveillance?' asked Harry.

'The whole street set-up is pretty open, so we can get a good line of vision from a fair distance away. Downside is we can't get too close, so you'll need to be careful, Tan.'

'Always. But how'll I get a chance to get to his car if the boxes are out the front?'

'The message we sent to him said it was a registered letter. So, when he finds it's not in the box, which it wouldn't be anyway, he'll have to go inside to the counter to ask.'

'Sounds reasonable,' said Harry. 'As soon as you've stuck the tracker on his car, babe, you start walking down the street towards us. Once he's out of sight, we'll come and scoop you up.'

'Cool. But how do we know what time he'll be there? Look a bit fricking weird if I'm hanging around outside for too long.'

'Shouldn't be an issue,' replied Trev. 'I checked with the shop on the phone. The PO boxes get sorted between nine and nine-thirty every weekday. My bet is Schwarz will be bang on time by nine-thirty to get his filthy hands on the cash he's expecting.'

'I agree,' said Harry. 'So we'll get you in position before nine, babe, and it shouldn't be more than half an hour tops for you to wait around. You could even be in the newsagent browsing, buy a magazine or two, and then as

141

soon as he walks in, you walk out, do his car, and then be looking in the real estate window when he goes.'

'Okay,' said Tanya, nodding. 'I'm cool with all that. Now let's get some food, I'm famished.'

Lunch was pizza, with beer. The afternoon was movies on cable, Tanya's choices including both *Sex and the City* films, with more beer. Dinner was Chinese again, with wine. Given the operation the next morning, they all took it a bit easier than the previous evening.

After dinner, Harry and Trev were sitting outside on the little verandah at the front of the room, drinking Jameson and smoking. For September, it was remarkably warm, and completely still. Their combined cigarette smoke loitered around them like a fog. Tanya was sitting on a bench about fifty metres away in the botanical graveyard that held itself out as a garden. She was talking to Sasha on the phone.

Harry refilled his and Trev's glasses. 'Mate, I meant to say thanks for our little privacy this morning. Made the most of it, and much appreciated.'

Trev turned and grinned at Harry. 'Yes, mate, I know. Room smelt like a bonobo's boudoir when I got back.'

Harry laughed. 'Bugger off.'

'Harry, you are the poster boy for the punching-above-your-weight club. Your charm is something to behold.'

'Sometimes I can't quite believe it myself. The epitome of friends with benefits.'

'Good job Kenmare and Associates doesn't have a code of conduct. Shagging the staff might be a problem.'

'Code of what?'

They both laughed.

'And how about you, Trev?'

'Meaning?'

142

'Any horizontal action, mate?'

Trev took a sip of his whiskey. He was hesitant.

'Don't go shy on me, mate.'

'Well …'

'Come on, Trev.'

'Harry, I don't mean to drop this on you, but you do realize I'm gay?'

'I'd figured, mate.'

'How so? Tanya give you a hint?'

'No, not at all.' Harry took a mouthful of drink. 'No, I had wondered for a while, since you never, ever talk about women, or rooting, and we have spent a lot of time sitting around together, chewing the fat.'

'That we have.'

'But the clincher was that day in the office when the girls were messing around and trying on their pussycam lingerie bottoms.'

Trev laughed. 'Yeah, I remember.'

'Well, remember when the two teases bent over their desk, their delicious derrières in full view and leaving nothing to the imagination?'

'Yep.'

'Mate, I got a boner like a karri tree, nearly blew my load, and couldn't take my eyes off them. You didn't even seem to take any notice. And I figured for a guy not to be helplessly fixated on those gorgeous arses, he had to be either dead or gay. And you're still very much breathing, my friend.'

Trev chuckled. 'Yeah, the display was for your benefit, mate. The girls already knew I was gay.'

'Well, good on them. I still have dreams about that image,' said Harry, gazing over in Tanya's direction.

'Mate, about what I was saying?' said Trev.

Harry looked back at him.

'So we're all cool, yeah?' asked Trev.

Harry frowned momentarily, then grasped the question. 'Shit, of course we are, Trev. You're my mate, and that's all that matters. Cheers.'

They chinked glasses.

'So my question remains, however. Any romantic interests?' asked Harry.

Trev laughed. 'I'm not getting off the hook, then?'

'Nope. You know me far better than that.'

'Yeah.' Trev looked into his glass. 'A bit of casual action. Nothing romantic, Harry.'

'You looking?'

'No. I had a partner for years, Jean-Louis. But he died. Killed.'

'Shit. I'm sorry, mate.' He reached over and laid his hand on Trev's shoulder.

'Story for another time, Harry. For now, I don't want anything emotional. A casual root now and then will do me fine.'

He looked back into his glass, and then over at Harry. There was a slight smile again. 'Rather like you really, big boy.'

Harry grinned. 'Let's have another drink, mate.'

144

— 4 —

No one took any notice of the grey VW van sitting on the grass and dirt verge of Thomas Street in Chidlow. Fortunately for the team, there was scant human movement anywhere, no one to take any notice, despite it being Monday morning. Before Mr Henry Ford, it would have been called a one-horse town, and that would have been with artistic licence.

Trev and Harry were sitting in the front seats, discreetly peering through binoculars at Tanya, who was studying the display window of the real estate agency about a hundred metres away. It was hard not to look out of place in this dead centre of nowhere. Harry had made a couple of quips as they arrived about the realities of these close, in-bred communities. Tanya was dressed down in old jeans and a hoodie. Trev had at least tried to make the van a bit more innocuous by slapping two of his collection of magnetic business signs on the sides of the vehicle.

Today they were a truck from Telstra, ubiquitous enough to not raise an eyebrow anywhere in Australia. Given the nature of this little backwater, it was a much more prudent choice than most of Trev's more interesting signage possibilities: 'Bright Light Electricians', 'Kev's Karpet Kleaning', 'Pierre the Parisian Plumber', or 'Dennis the Dirty Dog Washer'. Trev had found them all mighty useful in his surveillance work. But today the signage was boring old 'Telstra', the roof racks back on the van with the obligatory ladder tied on, an accessory Trev had bought the day before for the sake of authenticity.

Harry lowered his window and lit a smoke. He offered one to Trev, who took it, lowering his window halfway.

'This place just pumps, doesn't it? I've seen livelier morgues,' said Trev, blowing smoke out the window.

'Not wrong, mate. I reckon if you farted in public here it'd be front page news.'

Trev chuckled. 'We'll soon fix that for them.'

'Oh, yes we will. Let's just hope the bastard turns up.'

'He's on the run and probably desperate for cash. He'll be here.'

They saw Tanya saunter into the newsagency-cum-post office a minute after nine. By ten past nine, there had been three false alarms with cars pulling up, but no sign of Bernhard Schwarz.

At nine twenty, Trev quickly raised his binos again.

Then suddenly, 'You've got to be joking!'

'What?' said Harry.

'That sure looks like him and he's on a bloody bicycle!'

'What the fuck?' Harry refocused his lenses. 'That's Schwarz all right. But Tanya's not going to be able to stick the tracker on the bastard bike!'

'Fuck, fuck and triple fuck!' Trev pounded the steering wheel.

They watched in stunned disbelief as Schwarz propped his bicycle up against the fence, and walked up to the PO boxes. He opened one, peered inside, and then closed it. He walked briskly into the shop.

Exactly on cue, having seen Schwarz come in, Tanya came out of the newsagency, a magazine in her hand. She looked around her, but there wasn't a car in sight. Then she noticed the bicycle. Oh, shit, she thought. What the fuck am I going to do with that?

She looked in the direction of the van, as if hoping for a telepathic solution. Well, you guys didn't think of this, did you? She had to think fast. The plan had certainly not factored in a paedophile on a pushbike.

Her phone vibrated with a message.

It's a no go. Start walking. Hx

She moved back to the real estate window.

Then Schwarz came out of the shop, empty-handed, and went over to his bicycle.

Tanya moved.

Back in the van, Harry and Trev had the tension sweating from their pores. Harry was staring through the windscreen whispering expletives under his breath. Trev was squeezing the steering wheel with both hands, having put the binoculars down.

'What the hell is she doing?' gnashed Harry.

'Fuck knows,' said Trev, his voice apprehensive.

They lit two more cigarettes. The muttered expletives kept rolling.

Tanya wandered over to Schwarz. 'Excuse me?' she said, putting a timid, unconfident tone into her voice.

Schwarz turned and looked at her. 'Yes? Can I help you?'

Tanya moved closer to him. She glanced at his grubby jeans and stained fleecy sweatshirt. He had a distinct odour wafting off him, like a freshly fertilized garden bed. Part of Tanya wanted to gag, both from the smell and her opinion of paedophiles. The other part wanted to spit in his face.

She fought down all her emotions before responding. 'I hope so. Been looking at houses for rent in the window there. You live around here?'

'Why?'

'I just want to know what it's like. The locals, the town, you know. I need somewhere quiet with nice people.'

He stared at her.

She threw out the bait. 'It's for me and my two little girls.' She forced a tear down her cheek and looked at her shoes.

Schwarz's stony expression suddenly melted, and was replaced with apparent concern. 'Oh, I see. Are you okay?'

She looked up again. 'Sorry, I hate crying. It's all just too much at the moment.' She made an effort to sniffle. 'Got beaten up, again, by the boyfriend. Been at a refuge in Midland with the twins. Just need somewhere away from it all where we can be safe.'

She started crying harder.

'I'm so sorry to hear that.' Schwarz put a hand gently on her shoulder.

Back in the van there was an explosion of nuclear proportions.

'Move it, Trev,' shouted Harry. 'I'll take the cunt now!'

'Harry, settle! He's hardly likely to do anything out front of the shop. In fact, he's hardly likely to do anything at all. She's ten years too old for him.'

Harry took a deep breath, put his binos down, and lit another smoke from the remains of the previous one. He nodded at Trev, his jaw clenched and his teeth gritted.

'I don't know what she's up to,' said Trev, 'but she's a super-smart girl and she can handle herself. If he did try anything, she'd kick the living shit out of him. I'd put money on it.'

Harry relaxed slightly. 'Actually, that would be entertaining to watch.' He drew hard on his cigarette.

They resumed observing through their binoculars.

'So, twins, eh?' said Schwarz, smiling at Tanya.

She caught the gleam in his eyes. You fucking scum, she thought. But he had taken the bait. She could see that in his odious eyes.

She pulled a tissue out of her handbag and wiped her tears, putting on a nervous smile. 'I've got a photo here,' she said, rummaging in her bag and pulling out her purse.

Schwarz was silent, and leaning his head in towards her eagerly.

She opened her purse and showed him a photo of her and Sasha as kids. It was the last photo they had before their father had gone away with the army, forever. She and Sasha both kept a copy in their purses.

'That's Angel,' she said, pointing to her younger self, 'and that's Sunray.'

'Ooh, beautiful names for two adorable little girls,' gushed Schwarz.

'They're nine next month.'

'What a wonderful age,' said Schwarz, smiling. 'Please excuse me, but you don't look old enough to have nine-year-olds.'

Tanya put on an embarrassed look and cleared her throat, audibly. 'I got pregnant when I was fifteen. I'm twenty-four now.'

'Oh, I see.' Schwarz paused, and looked at the photo of the twins again. 'If you don't mind me asking, is their father the same guy who beats you up?'

'No, that's another great choice I made.'

She pointed at the photo. 'Their father went away. Never came back.' The tears this time were real.

'Gee, that must be awful tough on you now. If I could help in some way.' He looked enquiringly at her.

She wiped her eyes, smelling the swallowing of the hook. 'Oh, mister, I only just met you. I couldn't possibly impose.'

'Nonsense, I'd love to help out. And I'm not the sort of guy who'd ever lay a finger on a lady like you.'

No shit, Sherlock, thought Tanya. Too much tits and pubic hair for your liking, you fucking rock spider.

She found the nervous look again. 'Well ...'

Schwarz held out his hand. 'I'm Bernhard. My friends call me Bernie.'

She hesitantly took his hand. 'Lorelei.'

Had Schwarz known a bit more about his German ancestry and Germanic folklore, the name would have struck a chord perhaps. But he didn't, and it went over his head.

Tanya, on the other hand, had remembered it from idly browsing through a coffee-table book on mythology at Harry's apartment whilst he was making her dinner one night: Lorelei was the siren on the Rhine who lured men. She enjoyed the image, and she was enjoying the role. It sure beat standing in lingerie in front of a camera showing off her curves.

150

'That's a lovely name, too,' said Schwarz. 'So, did you see any rentals you like in the window?'

'Not in my price range, everything is so expensive. And I need to get right away from the refuge. Arsehole knows I'm there and if he gets pissed one night, he'll come looking for me.'

Schwarz positively beamed at her. 'Hey, tell you what. I've got heaps of room at my place. It's a little bit out of town, but nice and secluded. Bit pongy I'm afraid, that's the only downside.'

Tanya frowned.

'I'm filling in as caretaker at a piggery,' said Schwarz.

'Oh,' said Tanya. 'But I really don't want to impose.'

'Not at all, not at all,' replied the increasingly enthusiastic Schwarz. 'Look, why don't you come and have a look, then you can decide. I presume you've got a car?'

Schwarz looked around. There was nothing within fifty metres of the shop.

'Yeah, yeah,' said Tanya hurriedly. 'But it's outside the hotel down there. I wanted to walk around a bit, get the feel of the place.' She indicated back up the road to where there were now three or four cars parked on the gravel strip out front of the pub and bottle shop.

'But I'm going to be overdue to get back to my girls.'

'Oh, I see,' said Schwarz, looking crestfallen.

'But I really would like to have a look, really I would. Can I come tomorrow evening? I should be able to organize a carer again at the refuge.'

Schwarz's face lit up instantly. 'Of course, Lorelei. Have you got a pen and paper?'

She pulled a biro out of her bag. 'Here you go. Just write on the back of this,' she said, passing him a copy of *New Idea*.

He scribbled and handed the magazine back to her. 'There's my number and the address. It's about three kilometres out of town on Rosedale Road. You can't see the house or piggery from the road, but there's a sign at the start of the driveway. Come by tomorrow evening. Just call or text me first.'

'Oh, thank you so much, Bernie. This is so kind of you. I'll call you tomorrow as soon as I know what time I can get away.'

'Great. See you tomorrow, Lorelei. Bye.'

She gave a little wave as he hopped on his bike and pedalled off down the street, whistling loudly.

Back in the VW van, there were two thunderous sighs of relief.

Tanya loitered outside the real estate window again, keeping the corner of her eye on the pedalling paedophile until he turned a corner and disappeared. She gave it a couple of extra minutes, then sauntered back along the street towards the VW van. She stopped outside the pub and texted Harry.

All clear behind me? Tx

Straightaway her phone buzzed in response.

Yes babe come in Hx

She crossed over the road without turning back and climbed in the side door of the van.

'What the fuck?' Harry couldn't help himself.

'Relax, Mr PI.'

'Do we need to do the lesson on sticking to plans again?'

'Oh, what? Sticking a tracker on a bicycle? Bloody great plan!'

'She does have a point,' said Trev, a slight smirk on his face.

Tanya kept going. 'Yeah, remember the lesson about adapt and improvise? Well, that's what I did.'

Harry took a deep drag on a cigarette, and exhaled slowly, calming himself.

'Okay, point taken. So, what did this impro consist of?'

'I used my feminine charms and wiles, Harry.'

Trev chuckled loudly.

Harry frowned. 'You're not going to tell me you got a rampant paedophile to get a boner over you?'

'No, of course not. But I had him just about blowing his load over a single mother with nine-year-old twin girls, at a women's refuge, who needs alternative accommodation in a hurry.'

She pulled out her purse and showed them the photo.

'See? My twin girls. Right up his alley. He couldn't offer hospitality fast enough.'

Trev roared laughing. 'Tan, pure style, brilliant!'

Harry grinned and shook his head. He, too, laughed. 'Yeah, okay. I'll concede that. So, what's next?'

She passed over the *New Idea*.

'There's his phone number and address. He introduced himself as Bernhard, too. He's a caretaker on a pig farm out of town. And I'm going around tomorrow evening to check it out before I move in with my girls.'

Tanya sat back in the jump-seat looking smug, and lit a smoke.

Harry and Trev both looked at her in admiration.

'An isolated piggery. Sounds perfect,' said Trev.

'Bloody oath,' replied Harry. 'But glad I won't be buying my bacon around here in the future.'

Trev grinned. 'Ooh, no!'

He looked at Tanya. 'We'd better get you an old car, single-mother style, to turn up in.'

'Definitely,' said Harry. 'Bound to be a rent-a-wreck place in Midland. We'll sniff around online back at the room.'

Trev started the van, did a U-turn, and they headed west out of Chidlow, back to their salubrious accommodation at the Paradise Motel.

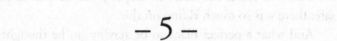

— 5 —

Bernhard Schwarz was walking on air as he cleaned up his spartan, secluded lodgings on Tuesday afternoon. It'd been months since he'd had any real sex action. He did have a pretty hefty collection of videos on his laptop to masturbate over, but watching the same kids again and again was getting a little routine. Plus you simply couldn't go past real flesh, he thought dreamily. One film he never tired of beating his meat to, however, was the one of him, Reggie and Herbie gang-banging that cop's daughter in Sydney all those years ago.

Seemed like another life: big, bustling Sydney; his mates that he could hunt and play with; never any shortage of young things.

Yes, that video was an oldie but a real goodie. Perhaps it was because he starred in it that it really got him aroused. He'd even managed to synchronize his masturbating to climax in time with his orgasm in the film footage. Such an artiste, he thought to himself, gazing wistfully at his computer desk in his bedroom.

Oh, well, back to tidying up. Need to impress Lorelei and get her daughters here, under his roof. They obviously needed a daddy figure to protect them. He was the man. Hell, he had scored luckily there: nine-year-old twins and a desperate single mother. It was like winning the Powerball for paedophiles. He bent down beneath the desk and scooped up the collection of tissues in varying states of dampness. Not that he intended letting Lorelei look into his bedroom when she came to inspect, but he had to be safe: there was so much riding on this.

And what a perfect place to be staying in, he thought. So secluded no one could hear the screams. Or if they did, they'd assume it was the pigs. There were hundreds of noisy porkers in the sheds.

The piggery was owned, via a corporate entity, by a prominent Perth businessman, Xavier Slade. Not so prominent were this businessman's interests outside his family, his church, his Rotary Club, the disadvantaged-children charities he publicly supported, and the state Liberal Party.

His alter ego lived on the dark web and his real passions were his activities that were fed lasciviously from that cesspit. Bernhard had been supplying Mr Slade with good juvenile imagery for years and was friends with him, as much as that concept was relevant in that world. When Bernhard had had to run from Sydney, he'd put out word in his dark community for help.

And so he'd ended up with this caretaker's house at the piggery in WA. He didn't have any caretaker's duties to perform. The place was semi-automated for food, water and waste disposal for the beasts, with an overseer visiting once a week on a Sunday. And he never came near the house. It was perfect, really. Now Bernhard just needed real live captive flesh.

During the drive from the airport to the piggery, Mr Slade had explained that he did occasionally visit the house for the purposes of indulging in private, when prepubescent carnal opportunities presented. But he added that if that all-too-rare chance did arise, then he was sure Bernhard would be more than happy to join in. Other than that, Mr Slade instructed Bernhard to lie low, only visit the local shops when he absolutely needed to, not to get friendly with anyone, or to have any visitors to the property.

Now, several weeks later, Mr Slade's advice was being washed into oblivion by a tidal wave of testosterone and Bernhard's desperate libido. Had he been thinking anywhere near clearly, Bernhard may have slowed enough to reflect that the whole encounter with Lorelei was a little too good to be true. However, his synapses were swimming in predatory hormones and his mind was in wild fantasy mode. Damn, nine-year-old twins! He started the vacuuming with a smile, and an erection.

Back down the highway towards the city, the three tourists from Sydney, who *were* thinking clearly, were readying themselves for Schwarz's date with destiny. Earlier that morning, Trev had walked into a joint called Rent-a-Heap in the industrial backblocks of Midland, having surveilled it, done a few online checks, and decided it was dodgy. His opinion was confirmed by the appearance of the owner: dirty black leather, tattoos on every visible skin surface, including tear drops on his left cheek, and his outlaw motorcycle gang colours proudly displayed on his leather jacket. The bloke was simply Mr Bad-Arsed Bikie, and the car-hire business was clearly a money-laundering front.

Perfect, thought Trev, as the bikie showed no interest in formal paperwork and a lot of interest in a fistful of fifties. Trev left five minutes later in a clapped-out Toyota Corolla. Its engine coughed as if it had terminal bronchitis and it ran as roughly as a mouthful of gravel. It was the perfect car for a down-on-her-luck single mother. Going back past the shops, Trev stopped at a Vinnie's store, bought some old kids clothes and a couple of stuffed toys and a pair of Barbie dolls. He casually threw them around the back seat and back shelf of the car. Then he headed back to the motel at Mundaring.

He found Harry making a coffee. 'Yes, please. White and one.'

The bathroom door was open and Tanya, dressed, was drying her hair. The confined air in the room was again redolent of sex.

Trev made a show of sniffing, then grinned at Harry. 'Ah, standard variety today, mate?'

Harry sipped his coffee and gave him the bird. 'Make your own, smart-arse.'

Tanya emerged from the bathroom, smiling at Trev. 'Yeah, like you'd know, not,' she said.

'Oh, touché, babe.' Trev laughed and made his own coffee, and one for Tanya.

The three sat down to discuss the plan of attack.

Tanya, proud of her achievement the previous day, was naïvely confident in the outcome. Harry, having seen so many meticulously planned and utterly foolproof fuck-ups in his police career, had misgivings about the way things had gone down so far. However, he was brought around to optimism by Trev, who had a more positive outlook. He'd concluded that once in a blue moon, the good guys got a pure lucky break.

And were it not for that fickle wench, Lady Fate, a pure lucky break is exactly what it would have been.

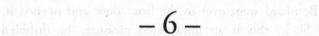

– 6 –

Bernhard looked around at his tidied living quarters. Given the usual shambolic mess he was happy to wallow in, the place almost felt like a stranger's house.

Lorelei had texted him during the afternoon to confirm it was still okay to visit. He'd eagerly responded, telling her to come up about 6 p.m. He figured a quick inspection by her, lots of supportive and sympathetic charm oozed by him, and hopefully she'd move in straightaway, with her nine-year-old twins, his two new playthings.

He was sitting on the old vinyl couch, watching the start of the five o'clock news bulletin, when he heard a car approaching, over the never-ending cacophony of pigs grunting and squealing. He checked his watch and frowned. Maybe Lorelei was really keen, or maybe she was hopeless at telling the time. Whatever, either way it worked for him.

He walked over to the lounge room window and saw a deep blue Jaguar sedan pulling up in the front yard.

Shit! Mr Slade. What was he doing here? And there was another man, younger and rotund, in the Jag's ample front passenger seat. Bernhard didn't recognize him, but he looked like Billy Bunter.

Mr Slade got out of the car, saw Bernhard through the window, and waved. Bernhard waved back. Billy Bunter also got out and went round to the boot of the car. He disappeared behind the boot flap as it swung upwards. Then he reappeared hefting a large canvas sack over his shoulder. They both walked towards the house.

Bernhard went over to the front door and opened it. 'Mr Slade, this is an unexpected pleasure,' he dribbled obsequiously.

'It's going to be a lot more pleasure than that, Bernie,' replied Slade in his deep, mellifluous voice, sounding like an operatic tenor.

Bernhard raised his eyebrows, looking at the younger man with the sack on his shoulder.

'Bernie, meet my nephew, Grant. Grant, meet Bernie.'

The nephew grunted, followed by a faint, 'G'day.'

Bernhard stood aside to let them through the front door.

'Drop her on the couch,' Slade directed his nephew. 'Close the door, Bernie, and then come and see what we have in store for the evening.'

Bernhard obeyed and then walked behind Slade into the middle of the room. Grant was in the process of tipping a bound and gagged young girl out of her canvas confinement.

Bernhard looked at the girl's terrified eyes. He'd seen that exact expression before, many times, but especially memorable was that cop's little girl. This girl was a similar age, about ten. She was skinny and pale, with matted long brown hair. Her grimy, tear-stained face matched her grubby shorts and T-shirt. And she had soiled herself.

Slade put his hand to his nose. 'Take her to the bathroom and wash her,' he said, looking at Grant.

'Yes, Uncle.'

Slade turned to Bernhard. 'You, too, Bernie.'

160

'Yes, Mr Slade.'

'And no fucking her yet, you two. I get first go. Understand?'

'Yes,' they replied, heading for the bathroom out the back with Grant carrying the girl awkwardly, as if trying not to get excrement on himself.

Five minutes later, a clean, naked, and trembling girl was dragged into the main bedroom where an equally naked Slade was slouched on the double bed like an omnipotent Roman emperor waiting for the female captives from his latest campaign.

Grant hurled the girl onto the bed where Slade grabbed her hungrily.

Grant and Bernhard both rushed to get their clothes off.

An hour later, their depravity sated, at least for the time being, the three paedophiles sat in the lounge room in their underwear drinking beer and comparing obscene anecdotes about their most recent rape.

The now catatonic child lay on Bernhard's bed.

They were exploring ideas for using Bernhard's video camera with the girl when there was the sound of a vehicle coming up the driveway.

'Who the hell could that be?' said Slade, clearly alarmed.

They all dived for the bedroom, grabbed pieces of clothing, and closed the door behind them as they went back into the lounge room. Slade and Grant were rapidly throwing their shirts and trousers on, whilst Bernhard made do with shorts and singlet.

The car engine sounded as if it was now idling out the front near the Jaguar.

'Bernie! Any ideas?' inquired Slade.

'Um, well ...'

'I fucking told you no visitors! None!' shouted Slade.

'Mr Slade, I can explain,' pleaded Bernhard.

'Try me, and it'd better be really bloody good!'

'She's … she's a single mother, got nine-year-old twin girls, and she needs urgent accommodation. I couldn't turn that down.'

'Twins?' said Slade, calming down a touch, but frowning at Bernhard.

'Yum yum,' murmured Grant.

'And where did you meet this single mother, Bernie?'

'She was at the shops when I went to pick up my mail yesterday. She was looking in the real estate window. We got talking.'

Slade frowned. 'Who started the conversation?'

Bernhard paused to think. 'Um … she did.'

'And it didn't strike you as just a little convenient that a single mother with young female kids chose to approach you?'

'Well … no, not really.'

Slade shook his head in exasperation. Grant was surreptitiously peering around the edge of the front window. The car engine had now stopped.

'Just a young woman, Uncle. Looks like she's fiddling with something on the front seat. Car's a total shit-box. Oh, and I can see a couple of toys on the back shelf, teddy bears or something.'

'No kids with her?'

'Can't see any.'

'No,' said Bernhard. 'She was coming up to check out the spare rooms before bringing the kids up.'

'Right,' snapped Slade, looking tense. 'You answer the door and invite her in. No point in us hiding since she's seen my car. Introduce us very briefly as the farm owners making one of our regular visits. Then show her the spare rooms and get her out of here pronto. Got that?'

'Yes, Mr Slade. No problems.'

'Are you sure? We don't need any bloody problems.'

'I'm sure, Mr Slade,' said Bernhard.

'Twins, Uncle, that could be sensational. Think of the videos.' Grant was licking his lips.

'Yes, mate, I'm well aware of the wonderful possibilities. But all in good time.'

He turned to Bernhard. 'And we're going to be having a serious chat about why you should do as I tell you, Bernie.'

'Yes, Mr Slade. I'm sorry. It's just, twins …'

'Yes, yes, all right. If you can pull this off, Bernie, I'll consider forgiving you for not doing as you were told. In fact, I'll even let you have first bite of the cherry, one of them, anyway.'

Bernhard smirked. 'Thank you, Mr Slade. I won't let you down.'

Slade turned back to his nephew, who was still grinning wetly. 'Grant, lock the main bedroom door. Tie her up and gag her if she's conscious. Now!'

'Yes, Uncle.'

Grant moved quickly into the hallway. He opened the bedroom door, looked at the silent body on the bed, and retrieved the key from the inside of the door lock. He closed the door, locked it, and pocketed the key. He walked back into the lounge and joined the others, sitting down.

'She all quiet?' asked Slade.

'Yes, Uncle, out like a light.'

They waited for the knock at the door.

— 7 —

The delicate glow of the day's final sunrays reached out from the western horizon as Tanya pulled the sputtering Toyota rust bucket into the driveway of the piggery. She hoped the engine would last the distance, although it sounded like a feeble asthmatic gasping for air. The VW van was about a hundred metres behind her.

The plan was simple enough: have a look at the place, engage in an enthusiastic chat with Schwarz, and suggest a cup of tea. Then ask to use the bathroom and text Harry and Trev, who, having stopped short of the driveway to wait, would slip in like a malignant evening fog and take care of Schwarz. Easy. What could go wrong?

The gravel driveway ran uphill for a distance, curving through jarrah trees and wattle bushes. A scattering of grass-trees added a Doctor Seuss-like ambience to the woodland. A kookaburra cackled loudly as the Corolla rolled over the crest and almost straightaway into the large clearing in front of the house, with the piggery sheds off to the right.

'Oh, fuck!' said Tanya, as she took in the blue Jaguar. She thought quickly. It was too late to back out: that would blow it all. Who the hell could this be? And a new, extravagant model by the looks of it. It didn't feel right. She started to feel a bit nauseous. No, hang in there, girl, you can pull this off, she told herself. But she needed to let the guys know.

She pulled up and left the engine running. She saw the edge of a curtain move in the main front window. She leant over the front passenger seat as if rummaging in her handbag. Her thumbs moved swiftly on her iPhone.

> Flash car here. May have company. Will suss out. Msge within 10 mins. If not, help me. Tx

She switched the phone to silent and put it back in her bag. She turned off the engine, and got out of the car. She never saw Harry's response.

She walked up to the front door, working on her desperate-single-mother demeanour. She knocked.

Schwarz answered it straightaway. 'Hi, Lorelei. Great to see you.' He grinned insipidly at her.

'Hi, Bernie. You too. I hope this isn't inconvenient,' she said, indicating the Jaguar.

'Oh, no, not at all. That's just the owners popped in for a visit. You can still have a look and then be on your way, back to your girls. The owners won't mind.'

'Great,' gushed Tanya. 'I'm so hoping this will be an answer to all my prayers.'

'I'm sure it will be, Lorelei.'

She followed Schwarz into the living-room saying 'Hello' to the two men sitting there.

'Don't mind us, love,' said the older one, looking her up and down.

The pair resumed talking, about pork prices from what she could hear. They seemed to pay no further attention to her.

Tanya noticed that all three men were barefoot. She looked over to the inside of the door, but saw no shoes. Something wasn't right.

'I'll show you the two spare bedrooms,' said Schwarz.

She smiled at him, glancing at the two men on the couch. They were definitely taking no notice of her. Okay, maybe it was nothing.

'This way,' said Schwarz, touching her shoulder.

'Okay,' she smiled at him again. 'Let's have a look, Bernie.'

He led Tanya down the corridor towards the back of the house, past the closed door of the main bedroom, which he indicated to her was his room.

– 8 –

Out on the road in the van, Harry was staring at his phone screen with his last text message.

Get out NOW! Hx

There'd been no reply.

Either Tanya hadn't seen Harry's instruction or she was ignoring it.

Harry, swearing like a trooper with the clap, texted again. Nothing.

Then he called.

No ring. Voicemail.

'Trev, I don't like it at all.'

'Me neither. But if we charge in there and it's all okay, then we're stuffed. We need the visitor to clear off so we can grab Schwarz alone.'

'Yeah, but if she's in trouble, every second counts.'

'I know, so do we risk it now, or wait until the ten minutes is up, as she said?' asked Trev, looking at the dash clock. 'It's only been six minutes.'

Harry banged the dash with the edge of his fist. 'Hell, Tanya, why couldn't you do as I said?' he yelled.

'Mate, she might not have even seen the message. She's obviously using initiative, a good quality.'

'Not if it gets you hurt.'

'Harry, Tanya understands how important this is and that there'll only be one chance. She said ten minutes. So, we give her a call at nine and a half. If she's okay, she'll answer. If not, in we go, guns blazing!'

'Fuck!' yelled an exasperated Harry. 'Yeah, okay. But if we do that we're going to have to drag Schwarz out in full view of his visitor.'

— 9 —

In the lounge, Slade interrupted his nephew's small-talk about the piggery. In a lowered tone he said, 'There's something not quite right about that Lorelei.'

'What do you mean, Uncle?'

'Every vulnerable, battered single mother I've ever met has had an overwhelming exhaustion and fear in their eyes. And I've met quite a few, believe me. It's a great way to access kids.'

'I didn't get a good look at her eyes. She's not my cup of tea,' replied Grant.

'Obviously, mate, nor mine. But I always look at the eyes. They are the windows to the soul. And Lorelei, she is way too alert and observant. Plus she looks pretty young to have nine-year-old kids.'

'Yeah, but it's possible. She could have had them real young, or she looks real young for her age.'

'Mate, switch on, or one day you'll come unstuck. Yes, it is possible. But a young mum with twin girls walking in here looking for a place to stay is about as likely as you winning the lottery.'

He stopped talking as Schwarz came out of the corridor with Tanya behind him.

As they came back into the lounge room, Schwarz turned to Tanya. 'So?' he said, hopefully.

'Bernie, it's perfect.' Tanya did her best forlorn look. 'When can we move in?'

'As soon as ...'

Before Schwarz could finish, a muffled groan came from behind the closed door of the main bedroom.

Tanya turned towards the noise, but there was no further sound. She turned back as Slade and his nephew got to their feet. She'd lost the pretend dejected manner. She was looking for an easy exit. Slade, seeping rat-cunning, picked her look.

'Bernie, block the hallway,' he yelled. 'Grant, grab her!'

As Schwarz moved to the hall entrance, Tanya decided he was the weakest link. She went to rush him and get past to the back door, ready to belt him as hard as she needed to.

However, for a seriously obese man, Grant moved surprisingly quickly. As Tanya lunged at Schwarz, Grant closed in behind her, grabbing a handful of her hair and pulling her backwards. Tanya yelped in pain, then swung her fist at Grant instead. But she was off balance and her punch missed its target, his nose, and glanced off the side of his flabby face into his ear.

'Bitch!' he growled, as Schwarz came in behind Tanya, grabbing both her arms. Grant seized the moment and drove his fist hard into her stomach.

Tanya doubled over, winded and retching.

'Get me a kitchen knife,' Grant commanded Schwarz. 'And make it large and sharp.'

Slade stepped over and picked up Tanya's handbag from the floor next to her.

Schwarz came back from the kitchen with a carving knife, handing it to Grant, who hauled Tanya up by her hair. She mustered some energy and plenty of courage, and swung at Grant again, but he twisted her around and she missed. He then pulled her into him so he was holding her from behind and put the knife blade up to her throat. 'If you move again, bitch, I'll slash you,' he growled in her ear.

Tanya gagged as Grant's fetid breath breezed past her ear and around her face like a noxious cloud of tooth decay, blending wickedly with the waves of body odour oozing out of him. Didn't take too much exertion for him to be running in sweat, she thought, desperately willing her anger to prevail over her fear. She knew that fear would leave her a victim, as she had been as a child, whereas anger might, just might, give her the edge she needed to survive.

She quietly prided herself on her toughness and self-reliance, attributes learned the hard way from a young age. And she was always rebuffing Harry when he was overprotective, despite his protestations to the contrary. However, right now, she was hoping Harry would default to being protective. And fast!

Slade was going through Tanya's purse. He pulled out her driver's licence. 'So, Lorelei, wasn't it?' He smiled fiendishly at her.

She glared daggers in return.

'Or maybe Tanya? Tanya Roberts of Surry Hills, New South Wales?'

She continued glaring at him.

'So, Tanya, what the fuck is Tanya Roberts of New South Wales doing here in my piggery in WA?' He came around the edge of the couch and leant in close to her face. 'Speak up, you little bitch,' he hissed, spittle landing on her nose and cheeks.

She said nothing.

He stepped back slightly, and slapped her across her face. It was so sharp and hard that Tanya's vision blurred.

'Fuck you,' she gasped.

Slade gave a thin laugh. 'Oh, my, such bravado.'

He slapped her face again. This time he split her bottom lip and a little fleck of blood appeared.

'Fuck you again!' This time she spat at him, getting him on his face.

He took out a white silk handkerchief and wiped the saliva off. Then the thin laugh again. 'Actually, Tanya Roberts of New South Wales, we're going to fuck *you*. Not literally, of course. Not us. You would have been pretty tasty ten years ago, but not now. However, once we've got your information out of you, there's going to be a bit of a show over in the pig shed.'

Tanya stared at him, her vision still a little affected from the slapping.

'Not even curious?' Slade was smiling, and an evil laugh erupted, like pus from a sore. 'I'll let you know what you've got to look forward to.' He licked his lips and smiled at the other two men. 'So, Tanya from Sydney, we're going to take you to one of the pig sheds out there. We're going to tie you down, naked, with your legs wide apart. You probably like having your legs spread, but this will be like you've never known it before.'

'Fuck off!'

Slade glared into her eyes and viciously grabbed her crotch. He wasn't smiling any more. 'Next, we'll get a cloth good and dripping wet from wiping a few sows' vaginas, and wipe it over you. Then we'll bring in a prized mating boar who's hot to trot this week.'

Tanya swallowed and bit the inside of her cheek to try to keep her focus.

Slade smiled again. 'Then, Tanya Roberts, you little slut, we'll video the pig fucking you. Great money in these films, especially the snuff movie variety.'

The other two paedophiles laughed and made grunting noises.

Slade continued. 'You ever seen a large boar's dick, Tanya Roberts?'

Tanya tried to keep any look of horror off her face. She couldn't reply this time. She knew what 'snuff movie' meant.

'No, you haven't? Well, let me tell you, they're pretty meaty and shaped like a corkscrew. You'll know all about it when that goes up your sweet little vag with two hundred kilos of horny hog behind it.'

He let go of her crotch and reached towards her face. Instead of touching her, he took the carving knife from his nephew's hand. He put the point of the blade against the top of her left cheekbone.

'Hold her tight, Grant.'

'Yes, Uncle.'

'Now, Ms Roberts is going to tell us all about herself, isn't she?' Slade pushed the tip of the blade into her skin.

Tanya whimpered as the blade travelled south on her face, opening up the skin on her cheek. Blood started to trickle.

She tried to struggle, to get away from the steel blade, but Grant had her pinned tight to his body. There was a line of blood now down to her chin and a few small red droplets fell into her cleavage.

Slade gave the knife back to Grant. He pushed Tanya's hair back behind her right ear.

'Now, Grant, if she doesn't give me some answers to the next few questions, slice her fucking ear off.'

– 10 –

In the van, the atmosphere was tenser than a late-night front hallway with a wife awaiting the return of a philandering husband. Seven minutes had ticked over on the clock.

'So, it's disguise time,' said Trev, pulling two black balaclavas out of a pouch under his seat.

They put them on, and Trev started the van. He moved slowly along the road, lights off, until they were at the entrance to the driveway. They stopped, engine running.

Trev pulled his .38 Smith & Wesson out of his belt holster and checked the load. Harry did the same.

Trev then reached behind the seats to a metal trunk on the floor and pulled out a chrome-plated .357 Ruger Magnum and put it in his lap.

'Nice,' said Harry. 'Bit more punch than the old thirty-eight.'

'Exactly,' said Trev, reaching down again. 'And this, big boy, is for you, since we're talking more punch.'

Harry smiled as Trev handed him a cut-down 12-gauge Remington pump-action shotgun and a bag of shells. 'This brings back memories of dawn raids,' said Harry, quickly loading the magazine. He pumped a round into the breech.

Eight minutes.

Harry had his phone in his hand as he wished away the seconds.

The pair were silent.

Harry was looking at his phone and holding the shotgun.

Trev was staring straight ahead into the semi-darkness, patting the .357.

Nine minutes.

'Fuck it, that'll do.' Harry pressed the number.

Trev slipped the transmission into drive and gripped the steering wheel.

Straight to voicemail again.

'Let's go!'

'Roger that.'

Trev gunned the engine and the van, headlights now illuminating the scene, plunged into the gravel driveway and roared up the slope. They flew over the crest of the hill and almost drove into the front door of the house.

As they jumped out of the van, guns in hand, raised voices were coming from inside the house. One of them was Tanya's, emitting the words 'fucking' and 'cunts' in the same short, loud sentence.

The lock on the front door was hardly a match for Harry's violent and practised size-eleven boot, and the door-frame splintered as Harry's body followed his foot. The 12-gauge was in front of him, and Trev with the .357 Magnum at eye level was right behind.

Grant was still holding Tanya, knife at her throat, standing behind the couch. Slade and Schwarz were off to the left, staring in disbelief at the masked intruders.

Harry held the shotgun steady about two metres in front of Tanya and Grant. Trev covered the other two, who were close enough together to allow him to easily flick the barrel from one to the other.

The momentary silent pause was like a scene from the Phoney War, whilst the combatants took stock.

Harry, looking at the blood dripping down Tanya's face, broke the silence, looking over her head at Grant. 'Okay, fat boy, let the girl go or I'm going to fucking kill you.' His index finger was on the trigger of the Remington, ready to squeeze.

Grant looked stupefied by the new experience of facing a black mask, a gun barrel, and a large man threatening to kill him. The only familiarity here was being called 'fat boy'.

'Don't do anything, Grant!' shouted Slade.

'Shut the fuck up, arsehole!' yelled Trev, moving his gun barrel closer to Slade's face.

'I'll … I'll fucking cut … cut her throat,' stammered Grant, shaking now.

The knuckles on Harry's left hand were white from the pressure of grasping the shotgun slide.

'Let's calm down, everyone,' Slade said, in a lower, somewhat conciliatory tone and looking at Trev. 'Maybe if you guys can tell us what you want, we can sort that out, and then we can all get on with our days.'

Trev walked the two remaining metres over to Slade. He put the .357 muzzle almost up Slade's left nostril. He grabbed the back of Slade's hair. 'So, who are you? And who is Grant over there?'

Slade went pale.

Schwarz started edging towards the hallway. Trev, still holding Slade, swung the Magnum. Schwarz froze. 'Get back here, scumbucket. Kneel by the table there, hands on your head.'

Schwarz hesitated.

Trev cocked the hammer on the revolver.

Schwarz complied.

From somewhere, Slade dug up some ill-advised defiance. 'I'm … I'm not saying anything.'

'Really?' asked Trev. He quickly dropped the .357 barrel towards Slade's right leg, and pulled the trigger.

Slade howled in agony as his kneecap was obliterated and he collapsed instantly.

'Uncle!' screamed Grant, momentarily loosening his grip on Tanya.

She seized the chance and dropped out of his grip, straight down behind the couch onto the floor. She'd seen Harry using a shotgun on a firing range; knew he needed a wide-open target.

Harry was beyond talking any more. He, too, grabbed the moment.

His first shot blasted Grant directly in the chest. Harry immediately cranked the action and let a second round go. This one went a bit higher due to the recoiling of the gun. The first blast had driven Grant backwards and slightly lifted him. The second hit him square in the face, stripping his features off like a meat saw.

Over at the dining table, Schwarz pissed himself.

A few metres away, Slade was still groaning loudly on the floor, clutching at his shattered knee.

The aroma of blood, flesh, and cordite began to pervade the air.

— 11 —

The impasse was over and the PIs were in charge. Tanya got to her feet from behind the couch, touching her bloodied face.

'Let me have a look at that, babe,' said Harry. 'We need to patch it up.'

'We'll get to that,' replied Tanya. 'But there's someone in that bedroom there.' She pointed at the closed door at the start of the hallway.

Trev, who was closer than Harry, moved first. 'I'll check it, you keep these two fuckwits covered.'

'My pleasure,' said Harry. He moved to his left and raised the shotgun again.

Schwarz looked at the menacing barrel, but then copped a backhander from Trev as he walked past, which sent him sprawling.

Trev slowly moved into the hallway, the .357 raised and ready.

Tanya came around the couch and over to Harry. He chanced taking his eyes off the two peds, as they were both lying uselessly on the floor. His right hand remained holding the shotgun, but with his other hand he gently put his fingers under Tanya's jaw and lifted her face slightly. He inspected her wound.

'I know there seems to be a fair bit of blood, but believe me, a little bit of claret goes a very long way. The cut's quite shallow, which is lucky.'

'Yeah? Lucky? It fucks up doing any more modelling, doesn't it? And it fucking hurts.'

'Babe, when we get home, we'll get you a great plastic surgeon and get you fixed up beautifully, okay?'

'Thanks, Harry. Hell, I'm glad to see you two.'

'Yes, we'll discuss that later, the little question of following instructions. Now, here, take this and keep these two covered. You already know how it works.' He winked at her and gave her the .38 revolver from his belt holster. He moved over to check that Grant was dead.

At that moment a juvenile shriek sounded through the house.

Trev had entered the bedroom, smashing open the locked door.

'It's okay, little one, we're not going to hurt you,' he said in a soothing tone, although no doubt, given his black mask and gun, the captive child was thinking exactly the opposite.

He came back out and closed the door behind him. This time as he walked past Schwarz, he drove his toecap into the prostrate paedophile's groin, eliciting a high-pitched scream. He took another couple of strides and did the same to Slade, although his groaning hardly changed: the new pain in his groin wasn't enough to cut through the agony of his blasted kneecap.

Trev turned to Harry. 'Young girl in there. Naked and terrified. And at a quick glance, I'd say they've already raped her.'

'Fuck me!' said Harry. 'Any life-threatening injuries?'

'Not that I could see. I think she should be okay in there whilst we deal with this lot.'

'Talk about a great plan instantly turning to poo.'

'Not wrong, brother. Well, adapt and survive.'

'Yep. Mate, first up, can you grab the first aid kit from the van? We'll keep these two covered. Fat boy over there's dead.'

Slade groaned.

'Roger that.' Trev went out to the van and was back in a flash with the kit and an iPad. He stood next to Tanya and opened up the small red box. 'Gonna sting, Tan.'

Tanya braced herself and then gritted her teeth, swearing as Trev smeared antiseptic along her cut cheek. Then he applied overlapping plasters to cover the wound.

'That'll do for now.' He gave her a kiss the side of her head and put the first aid box on the table.

With that, Trev grabbed Slade by the hair. He screamed in pain. Trev dragged him semi-upright and hurled him onto the couch. He pushed his head back and shoved the .357 barrel in his face.

'Right, cunty, who's the little girl in there?'

Slade was struggling to form any words.

Trev put the gun barrel down to his undamaged knee. 'Want me to do the other one?'

'No ... no ... please!'

'So, who is she?'

'We picked her up at a youth centre.'

'Your wallet!' demanded Harry.

Slade clumsily dug into his trouser pocket and pulled out a stylish, black leather Oroton wallet. 'Here ... take anything you want ... please ...'

'Oh, we will,' said Trev.

Harry pulled out a driver's licence. 'Xavier Ernest Slade, born nineteen-fifty-nine, and you live in Dalkeith.'

'Flash area, from memory,' said Trev, taking the wallet from Harry. He pulled out the bank cards. 'Judging by that magnificent specimen of a car out there, you've got a bit of cash, Xavier?'

'Yes, yes. Look, I'll pay you whatever you want. Just please let me live. Please …'

'What's the set up here? Who owns the joint and are there any staff for the pigs?' asked Harry.

Slade explained his ownership and the overseer arrangements for the animals.

'Right, I want PINs and all your online banking details.' Trev waved the .357 encouragingly towards Slade's knee again.

'My PIN is six-zero-zero-nine, same for all my accounts.'

Harry looked back at the drivers licence. 'It's his bloody postcode.'

'It's true, really. I use that because I'm awful at numbers,' pleaded Slade.

Trev picked up the iPad and checked for a signal.

Harry looked over and frowned.

'Don't worry, I put a throwaway SIM in this as well.' He turned to Slade. 'Let's see about your bank then. Give me all your details.'

Slade rattled off his bank, branch, and numbers.

Trev entered them into the website, one at a time, getting the device to memorize them. 'Bingo! Good boy, Xavier, you did tell the truth.'

'Now. Let's give the fucking dog a biscuit, and then we'll talk to Bernhard,' growled Harry, taking off his mask. Trev did likewise.

Terror gripped Slade's eyes as he realized that, with his assailants unmasking themselves, he was a dead man. But before either the .357 or shotgun barrel moved on to him, Tanya stepped in.

'No, guys.'

'What?' said Trev.

'Look at this,' she said indicating her face. She turned to Slade. 'And he was going to film me being fucked by a pig. This scum is mine.'

Trev stepped back a pace. Harry moved slightly to cover Schwarz, although he wasn't going anywhere.

Tanya stood in front of Slade and pointed the .38 muzzle right in front of his face.

'Goodbye, fuckstain. The pleasure's all mine.'

There was a single blast as Tanya put a .38 hollow-point square between Slade's wide, staring eyes.

He slumped backwards, convulsed a couple of times, and died.

The trio of sleuths turned as one towards Schwarz.

Bernhard was lying on the worn carpet, one hand clutching his lower abdomen, the other wiping the tears and mucus off his face. He was having trouble focusing his eyes and his ears. He could hear the men shouting at Mr Slade. He heard his name. How did they know his name? Who were they? What was happening? Oh, Dieter, I need you now. '*Mein bruder* ...' he whispered.

Then the yelling stopped. The young woman said something. She must be with them, he thought. He quietly chided himself for being a little late figuring out Lorelei was a fraud.

He wanted to escape, but he felt too weak and in pain from the kicking. The front of his shorts was still warm and wet from where he had pissed himself. His eyes focused properly in time for him to look on in horror as the girl stepped forward and shot Mr Slade in the face. Bernhard watched as Slade died. He realized he was the only one left. He tried to move, but his body wasn't up for it.

The three killers then turned to look at him.

'No, please …' he wailed.

'Righto,' said the stockier of the two intruding men. 'Time for the real business.'

Then he heard a loud, wet, flatulent sound. As he watched watery muck the colour of the Ganges River run down his thighs, Bernhard realized he had shat himself.

– 12 –

Schwarz was naked and tied to a dining chair, which was in turn pushed against a wall. He was gagged. The room stank like a septic tank, with a lingering whiff of cordite from the gunshots.

'Tan, can you please go and see if you can settle that girl down. She'll probably appreciate a female face,' said Harry.

'No worries. What are we going to do with her?'

'We'll take her with us and drop her off outside a hospital or medical centre.'

'Just need to be a bit of a distance away, so we don't get caught on any CCTV cameras,' said Trev.

'For sure. But don't worry, babe, we'll get her close enough so we know she'll be okay,' replied Harry.

'And what about the gunshots?' asked Tanya. 'Do we need to hurry?'

'Won't be an issue out here. All farms and bush, plenty of people could be using guns,' said Trev.

'Yeah, I heard a couple of rifle shots when we were waiting out on the road,' added Harry.

Tanya nodded. 'Cool, I'll go and check on our girl.' She walked off to the bedroom, handing Harry the .38 on her way.

Without any preamble, Harry drove his latex-covered fist into Schwarz's guts. The captive wheezed through his gag and made a whimpering noise.

'Now, Bernhard, you maggot, you're wondering who the hell we are, aren't you?' Harry hissed in his face.

There was a zapping sound as Trev, wearing thick rubber gloves, smacked two electrical contacts together. It sounded like a blood-laden mosquito suiciding in a porch insect lamp.

'Men on a mission, Bernhard, that's who we are, plus a lady,' said Trev, zapping his metal prods again.

Harry lent into Schwarz and lifted the gag off his mouth. 'Remember a little girl you and your mates buried in the Royal National Park in two thousand and two?'

Schwarz looked at him. Even more terror invaded his eyes, if that was emotionally possible for him at this point.

Harry slapped him hard across the face. 'Remember?!' he yelled.

Schwarz looked at his assailant dumbly. That earned him a punch to the guts.

When he lifted his head back up from retching, Harry slapped his face twice. 'Remember yet?'

Schwarz nodded hesitantly.

'Her name was Orla. She was my daughter.'

Schwarz stared at the big man in front of him. He said nothing.

Harry slapped him again. 'Nothing to say, arsehole?'

'Sss … sss … sorry,' whispered Schwarz.

'Oh, you're going to be. You remember what her dad did for a living?'

Schwarz nodded again.

'I can't hear you!'

'Po … police officer.'

'Well done, Bernie.' Harry gripped Schwarz's chin, squeezing his face into a grotesque grimace. 'Bernie, you know what's worse than an angry cop who's after you?'

Schwarz shook his head. 'Uh … nuh … nothing?'

'Wrong! An angry *ex*-cop who's after you. I don't have to worry about the rules or procedures, or about my sodding career any more.'

Schwarz looked nervously at Trev as the contacts zapped viciously again. He felt movement in his lower body, but neither his bladder nor bowels had anything left to expel. He could taste blood in his mouth. He thought back to Dieter and their home in Sydney. His beloved brother had told him frequently that the cop's daughter episode would come back to haunt him. Oh, Dieter, why didn't I listen more to you? Why did I always follow Reggie? His wandering train of thought was interrupted by the young woman reappearing.

Tanya came out of the bedroom with a laptop and mobile phone. 'I've tried to calm her down. Won't say anything to me, not even her name.'

'Good effort, babe,' said Harry. 'We're getting to know Bernie here.'

'Just another fucking oxygen thief,' said Tanya. She put the devices down on the table near Trev's paraphernalia. 'Thought we could get the passwords from him.' She pulled a pen and notebook from her bag.

'Excellent idea,' said Trev, zapping again. 'I do love the noise these make. Don't you, Bernie?'

Schwarz shook his head. 'No … please …'

Trev stepped forward.

'Bernie, your PINs, now!'

Schwarz didn't need any further encouragement, let alone electricity, and he spewed out his codes and passwords, almost as if reading from a script. Tanya jotted them down. She tried the phone first.

'I'm in.' She put it down, and moved to the laptop and made a few keystrokes.

'Yep, in here, too.' A bit more tapping. 'And there's a whole lot of passwords stored in the browser.'

Trev looked over. 'Sweet, seems like what we need.'

Harry turned his attention back to Schwarz. 'So, how about some serious pain, Bernie, my mate?' he snarled. 'Bet my little Orla was in a whole lot of pain before you fuckers killed her.'

'It … it was Reggie. He killed her,' spluttered Schwarz.

'And you only raped her. That makes it all okay, does it?'

Schwarz looked inanely at him and said nothing.

Harry drove his fist into his stomach again.

'Give him a little taster, Trev.'

'Absolutely.' Trev shoved the electrified prods onto Schwarz's scrotum. The scream that came out was so high-pitched it was almost inaudible.

They gave him a few seconds, then Harry resumed his interrogation. 'Now, Bernie, you're going to tell us everything that happened with my Orla, and everything you know about Reggie Wheeler and Herbert Farr. And we've read the police file, so any bullshit and my electrical friend here will barbecue your genitals. Slowly. Understand?'

Schwarz nodded vigorously.

'Start talking!'

And Bernhard Schwarz sang like a bird, as if some desperate morsel within him thought it might save his life.

It was one afternoon in January eleven years ago. Bernhard was out cruising with his mates, Reggie and Herbie. They were in Herbie's car on the prowl for kids. Reggie, commanding the venture from the back seat, said he was desperate for a screw. They passed a young girl walking alone down a quiet street in Bexley. She was about ten, slim with brown hair, and wearing shorts and a T-shirt.

Reggie said she was pretty enough and the right age. She would do just fine. Bernhard said that it was Reggie's idea, but him and Herbie agreed. Reggie always made the decisions when they were together.

There was no one around, so Herbie swung the car around and slowed to a crawl at the kerb. Bernhard called out to the girl, who started walking more quickly. Herbie pulled the car into the next driveway, blocking the footpath. Reggie leapt out of the car, and grabbed the girl by her arm before she had time to run. He dragged her into the back with him and they drove off, heading for Reggie's place in Kogarah. They pulled in around the back of the house, completely unobservable to neighbours. Reggie dragged the girl, who was struggling and trying to scream through his hand, inside. They took her straight to Reggie's 'playroom' beneath the house. Reggie's late uncle built the underground space as a fallout shelter back in the early sixties when they were all the fashion. When Reggie inherited the house, he wasted no time at all in 'renovating' the basement chamber for future depravity.

Reggie threw the girl on the bed in the corner. She put up a ferocious fight as they stripped her, but she lost her vim after Herbie slapped her twice across the face so hard that she was stunned into semi-consciousness. Bernhard started the video camera that was mounted on a tripod, and then they got naked. They gang raped the girl on the bed, clothed in its never-washed sheets, as Reggie liked to enjoy the lingering odour of past conquests.

After the initial assault, whilst Reggie was helping himself to seconds, the girl mustered her voice. She screamed her dad was a cop and that he'd get them all and put them in prison. Reggie punched her several times in the face and she passed out altogether.

Harry thought back to the video snippet Tom had shown him of little Orla, crying and cowering on that bed. He remembered how stained, in a variety of colours, the sheets looked. He also recalled the chains and shackles attached to wall behind the bed.

He closed his eyes, took a deep breath, and looked down at Schwarz. 'You bunch of cunts!' he roared, raising his fist.

Trev took hold of his shoulder. 'Mate, let him finish since he's on a roll. Plenty of time for punishment.'

Harry lowered his fist.

As Trev zapped the electrics again, by way of gentle motivation, Bernhard returned to his appalling confession.

As they sat around after sating their lust, Reggie said they'd need to rethink this one. Herbie said he didn't think even his cop friend, who had been so useful in the past, would be able to help out. Reggie said they should take her for a little drive. They gagged her tightly with a tea towel and tied her wrists and ankles. Reggie took her out to the car, where Herbie opened the boot and Reggie dropped her in. Reggie told Herbie to drive south to the Royal National Park.

It was dark when they found the narrow bush track that led to a secluded clearing. Herbie stopped the car and Reggie pulled the girl out of the boot. He untied her and removed the gag. She spat at him. He belted her again and pushed her into the back of the car. Then they each took their turn with her on the back seat.

Harry growled like a predatory wild animal.

Trev again put his hand on his friend's shoulder. 'We're getting there, Harry. Hold on a bit longer, mate.'

'Keep going, fuckwit,' Trev said to Schwarz.

Bernhard spluttered, but found his voice again. 'I assumed we were going to just leave her in the bush, but Reggie said we couldn't let her live to tell. He got a shovel out of the boot and told me to dig a grave in the bush away from the clearing.'

He coughed. 'I did try to talk Reggie out of killing her, honestly I did, but Reggie said he wasn't going to prison for anything, and if we didn't get rid of the girl, we'd all end up getting caught.'

So, Bernhard did as he was told. When he was done, Herbie and Reggie dragged the naked, semi-conscious girl through the bushes and threw her into the newly dug shallow trench.

Schwarz stopped.

'Is that all?' yelled Harry.

'What do you mean?' asked Schwarz, dribbling.

'Who took her shamrock pendant? It wasn't on her body when she was found.'

Schwarz looked at Harry. 'Oh, yeah. I was forgetting that bit.'

'Well, fucking remember now!'

'Okay, okay. She was lying in the hole, murmuring and twitching slightly. Reggie bent down and grabbed a gold pendant around the her neck and ripped it off her.'

190

Schwarz paused and swallowed audibly.

Trev's electrodes zapped. 'Keep going, Bernie.'

'Okay. Reggie pulled down his zipper and said, "So, the daughter of a pig", and pissed on her. He took the shovel off me and drove the blade through her throat. She stopped moving or making any noises. Blood started flowing into the sandy soil. Reggie gave the me back the shovel and told me to refill the hole.'

Schwarz added that when the girl's body was found the following month, they all knew they had to lie low for a while. Reggie took off overseas. Herbie went to Melbourne to a friend's place. And he stayed quietly at his mother's house in Vaucluse.

Schwarz's voice petered out and his head dropped.

Harry stepped in and grabbed Schwarz by the throat. 'You fucking maggot!' He punched him in the guts.

'It was Reggie's idea to kill her,' spluttered Schwarz. 'Honestly, it was. I would have just left her there. But Reggie insisted. And Reggie always got his way. He could get violent when he didn't. Wouldn't have been the first time he hit me or Herbie.'

'So let's have everything you know about your two little maggot mates,' hissed Harry, releasing the pressure on Schwarz's throat.

Apparently Reggie Wheeler was now working at an orphanage in Laos, outside Luang Prabang. Schwarz gave them the details and mentioned all the emails he'd had from Reggie, who was always bragging about the attentive parenting he was providing to the poor Laotian orphans.

And Herbie Farr was banged up in a Victorian prison, Hopkins Correctional Centre in Ararat, to be precise. He wasn't due for parole for another eighteen months. However, he was, through his lawyer, trying to get an interstate prison transfer back to Sydney so his old mother, in increasingly and terminally bad health, could at least visit him before she croaked. Obviously with Herbie inside, there were no emails to Schwarz. But there had been the old-fashioned letters, and Schwarz had spoken to him on the phone recently. The Victorian prison authorities were dragging their feet on the transfer application and Herbie was worried his mum might die without seeing him again.

'Stiff fucking shit,' had been Tanya's contribution at this point, getting up from the table to spit in Schwarz's face.

'Yeah, I tend to agree,' said Harry. 'But an opportunity starts to present itself, me thinks.'

Trev smiled. 'I'm with you, brother. We definitely don't want to be waiting eighteen months, but if he has to be moved we may have options.'

'Yep, we'll work on that later.' Harry turned back to Schwarz and punched him again. 'One more subject to discuss, Bernhard, and that's the cops. You mentioned a cop friend.'

'It was Herbie's friend. He was the cop who died in prison recently.'

'Name?' Harry wanted to hear it from Schwarz.

'Mr Lowe. I think he was a superintendent. Something senior, anyway.'

'You ever meet Lowe?'

'No, never. Herbie knew a couple of cops who liked kids, but Reggie and me always steered clear of them.'

'You know any other names?'

'No, honestly I don't. I only remembered Mr Lowe's name when I saw the news about his death.'

Trev signalled Harry to step away from Schwarz. He whispered in Harry's ear. 'We need to ask about his DPP friend, the one who tipped him off.'

'Yeah, good point. I was forgetting about him. Bit too much going on in my head at the moment.'

'But we don't want to mention his brother yet, he might clam up on us. The stupid bastard thinks he can still get out of here alive.'

'I like your thinking. I will break the news to him before he goes, though.'

Trev smiled. 'Of course.' He moved back to Schwarz. 'And how come you're over here, Bernhard?'

'What do you mean?'

'Don't be tiresome, fuckwit. Why did you leave Sydney?' Trev picked up the electrical contacts.

'No, no, not that. I'll tell you. I got a call from a friend who works at the public prosecutor's office. He'd seen my name on some police paperwork.'

'His name?' asked Trev.

'Simon.'

'Simon what?' said Harry.

'Simon Abrahams.'

'Let's have a look, shall we?' said Tanya, picking up Schwarz's phone. 'Aha! Simon Abrahams is in there, and there are call records recently.'

'Good stuff,' said Harry. 'Okay, Bernie, my little mate. Now, we're going to go over it all again, for the video camera here. Plus, you're going to confess to any other child sex crimes you haven't been caught for. We might be able to give some other families at least an iota of closure.'

The shattered Schwarz looked up at him, tears dribbling down his cheeks. He opened his mouth soundlessly.

'Going to cooperate, Bernie, or would you like a recharge, so to speak?'

There was a sharp crackle as Trev touched the electrodes together again.

'I'll tell you everything,' pleaded Schwarz.

'Good,' said Trev. 'Then, in due course, we'll anonymously send an edited version to the cops to close off a few outstanding cases.'

Harry nodded. 'At the conclusion of our three-act play, that is.'

'Precisely,' replied Trev.

And so they recorded him for about forty minutes, retelling the killing of Orla, and then detailing one other abduction-murder, and three abduction-rapes.

Halfway through, Tanya took herself outside, to avoid using the .38 again.

When Harry and Trev were satisfied Schwarz had nothing left to give up, Trev turned the camera off.

'Anything else, mate?' Harry asked Trev.

'All good, mate. All yours. Want any tools?'

'No, just this knife.'

Harry turned to Schwarz and continued. 'This is just like when we interrogated Dieter the other week. Forgot to mention we had a little chat with your brother.'

'A rather final chat, as it turned out,' added Trev.

'What … what do you mean?'

'Dieter told us where to find you. Before he died.'

'Dieter's dead?' gasped Schwarz.

Harry nodded, smiling, letting the news sink in briefly. 'And here's where we say our goodbyes, Bernie.'

'No, please! Let me live! I told you everything, I promise.' There was a torrent of desperate tears cascading down Schwarz's face now, turning pink as they mingled with the blood.

'Yes, you probably did. But now, just as you took my Orla's life, I'm going to take yours.'

Harry leant into Schwarz's face. 'Look me in the eye, Bernie. I want to see the lights fading out.'

Harry's left hand gripped Schwarz by his throat and forced his terrified face to keep looking up into Harry's. 'This is for Orla.'

Harry's other arm moved suddenly and he thrust the carving knife deep into Schwarz's guts. Harry twisted the blade and dragged it up through the intestines and liver. Blood started running down Schwarz's naked abdomen and pelvis, streaming onto the floor and puddling under the chair on the rough carpet that was about twenty years past being absorbent.

Harry kept looking at Schwarz, his hand on his throat, like a human dimmer switch as the spark slowly extinguished in Schwarz's eyes. He was lingering, only those last reminiscences crawling around his monstrous mind.

Harry smiled bleakly at him. He withdrew the long knife blade. 'Bye bye, Schwarz, you cunt.'

Harry rammed the knife through Schwarz's sternum and deep into his heart. Schwarz's eyes momentarily widened, then closed as his head lolled back, Harry releasing his grip.

Harry stood back from his handiwork. He wasn't smiling any more. He pulled the latex off his hands. 'One down, two to go.'

Trev walked over, removing his rubber gloves, and gave Harry a hug, taking him by surprise. 'Well done, mate. I know it's bloody awful doing this, but Orla deserves to be avenged.'

'Thanks, mate. I fucking hate this business, but I'm not going to be able to get on with my life until the demons are slain.'

'Literally. And I know the feeling, mate. Thought you might have made him suffer a bit more.'

'No point prolonging things once we'd got the info we needed. Then it was just my revenge left, and I wasn't going to torture him for that. He's dead. That's my revenge. Justice is one third done.'

Harry checked up and down his front. 'And somehow I managed to avoid any blood spatter.'

Trev looked him over front and back. 'Yep, all good. Just running a nice sweat, that's all.'

'Hot work, Mr Matson.'

'And positively shocking, Mr Kenmare.'

– 13 –

Tanya walked back in at the precise moment Harry and Trev were hugging for the second time.

'How sweet. A butchers' bromance.' She looked at the just-departed Schwarz, gagging slightly as she took in his open abdomen. 'And good riddance to that piece of shit.'

'Yep, now we need to clean up and get out of here,' said Trev.

'Pigs?' asked Harry.

'Pigs,' replied Trev.

Tanya, missing the reference, looked around at the charnel house that was once a living-room. 'So, we just going to burn the place down to get rid of everything?' she asked.

'No,' said Harry. 'That would be great for clearing up the evidence, sure, but it'd probably start a bushfire. And we sure as hell don't want any innocent people suffering.'

'So, it's feeding time for the piggies,' said Trev.

Tanya looked aghast. 'You're not serious?'

'Absolutely,' said Harry. 'Pigs eat meat, no problems. We'll turn off their automatic feeding machines and chuck the bodies in. As soon as they're hungry, which being pigs they usually are, they'll devour the lot.'

'And we know from Slade that the supervisor will be back on Sunday, so he'll find the machine turned off, assume there was a technical failure, and turn it back on. The piggies will be a tad hungry by then, but they'll be fine. And the bodies of three peds will be no more.'

'Gross!' Tanya's face was scrunched up in horror. She looked around the room. 'And what about the blood in here, and all our fingerprints?'

'Oxygen bleach,' said Trev. 'By the bucket-load. There are drums of it out by the first shed. Saw them when I grabbed the first aid kit. They'd use it for cleaning out the pigpens.'

'Will that get rid of blood?' asked Tanya.

'Not fully,' replied Harry. 'But it'll degrade it enough to make it useless for analysis, destroy the DNA. At some stage someone might find it, but it won't be much use to identify these three.'

'And using it to wipe all the surfaces we've touched will definitely get rid of prints,' added Trev.

'It won't go down as the perfect method in the annals of cleaning up crime scenes, but it'll do. We'll take all Bernhard's identifying stuff, and these other two. And we'll ditch the Jag,' said Harry.

Trev shook his head. 'Crying shame that. I've always fancied a Jaguar Sports.'

'And the girl?' asked Tanya.

'We need to drop her off where she'll get looked after, and so that's a hospital. That's all we can do, Tan. We can't get any more involved than that,' said Harry.

Tanya nodded reluctantly. 'Okay. What do you want me to do? I'm so not volunteering for chopping up bodies.'

'Oh, where's your sense of adventure?' Harry gave a half-hearted laugh.

Tanya stuck her tongue out at him.

'Don't worry, Tan, we'll do that bit,' said Trev.

'Phew.'

Harry looked at her. 'How about you grab a couple of bags from the van and go around the place cleaning up anything at all that can identify any of these three. And collect all Schwarz's belongings from his room. We'll put them in the dumpster at the motel when we leave.'

'No worries,' said Tanya. 'But I'm not touching any of the bodies.'

'Don't worry, we'll check the pockets of these two dressed ones before we cast them over to the hogs.'

'Then put it all in the van,' said Trev. 'The girl goes with you in the Corolla. Harry'll drive the van, and I'll take the Jag.'

'Oh, and why do you get to drive the Jag?' challenged Harry.

Trev grinned at him. 'Just the way it is, big boy.'

Tanya went out the front door. Trev pulled sets of rubber dishwashing gloves out of his kit bag. He passed a set to Harry and put a pair on himself. He passed Tanya a pair of latex gloves when she walked back in a moment later.

Harry and Trev stripped Slade and his nephew, removing their pocket contents, watches and a large gold signet-ring from Slade. They then piled all their clothes along with Schwarz's in a heap.

Trev turned to Tanya. 'Tan, is there a washing machine out back?'

'Sure. There's a laundry next to the bathroom.'

'Cool. When you've done with bagging stuff, could you please stick this pile in the machine and set it on the longest wash cycle going?'

'No worries.'

Harry pulled a rug over to Schwarz's body, and untied the dead ped from the chair. They rolled him up in the rug, being careful not to let his intestines tumble out, and headed for the nearest pig shed.

Schwarz's body made a loud squelching sound as it landed in the wet slop on the floor of the first pigpen. The swine had backed off as the foreign pink object tumbled into their domain, but now they came forward for a sniff, with intestines and organs spilling out from the lengthy opening Harry had carved in the abdomen. Trev found the auto-feeder chute and controls. He turned the power supply off and, to be certain, moved the chute sideways away from the pen.

They were back a few minutes later with Slade's corpse. Most of the grunters moved back again as Slade was tipped into the pen beside Schwarz. Two huge porcine specimens, however, didn't budge an inch. They were too busy competing to rip out parts of Schwarz's innards.

Trev nodded in their direction. 'Bloody porkers are getting in even quicker than I thought they would.'

'Yeah, must make a welcome change from those dried food pellets they get,' said Harry, pointing at the hopper above the feeding chute.

'Looks as though these two big bastards are having liver for dinner,' said Trev.

'Ah, pâté de paedophile,' said Harry. 'They'll be demanding toasted baguette in a moment.'

Trev laughed. 'Bugger, forgot to bring it.'

Ten minutes later, the nephew's corpulent carcass was heaved into the pen, with Harry and Trev grunting more than the pigs.

'Bloody hell, he'll keep them going for a while,' wheezed Trev.

Harry looked at the horde in the pen. 'Now, little piggies, make sure you share, and eat up. That's all you're going to get until Sunday.'

Trev picked up the carving knife from the rug, lent over the railing, and opened up Slade's guts, followed by his nephew's.

'Just to encourage them, now they're getting a taste for it.'

'Yeah, good idea. Just remind me never to buy any bacon that says "produced in Western Australia".'

On the way out of the shed, the pair picked up a drum of bleach between them and carted it back to the house.

Tanya was standing in the lounge, gloves off.

'Guys, I've wiped all the surfaces we could have touched. I found cleaner under the sink, so I used that. Bags of stuff are in the van, and the girl is dressed.'

'No name?' asked Harry.

'She's still not saying anything. I did manage to get a nod from her, though, when I told her we were taking her to a safe place. And got another nod when I said it was really important not to mention us, because we'd sorted out the guys who hurt her.'

'Good thinking, babe,' said Harry. 'Okay, take her out to your car, and stay with her. We'll wrap up in here.'

Trev, meanwhile, had grabbed the bucket Tanya had finished with and put it next to the drum of bleach. He'd already taken the cap off.

'Give us a hand, Harry.'

The pair tipped the drum and filled the bucket. They waited discreetly as Tanya took the young girl out of the back door of the house.

Trev went into the main bedroom, looked at the wet stains on the sheets, and spread bleach all over the bed. Then he went back into the lounge.

They refilled the bucket six times, drenching the bloodied areas of the floor and the chair where Schwarz had died. Then two bucketfuls were heaved onto the wall where the shotgun blasts had sprayed morsels of Grant's fleshy face.

'Best we can do,' said Harry.

'Yeah. Can't do much about all the hairs that'll be around, but at least this will make it a prick of a job to identify anyone.'

'And we'll be long gone,' said Harry. 'I seriously doubt there'll be any records at all linking Schwarz to this place.'

'Or linking him to Slade and his nephew.'

'And no bodies anywhere, either,' said Harry.

'Exactly. So, worst case scenario, there could be three missing person reports, but one back home in Sydney with the other two here. And then perhaps someone finds indeterminate traces of blood in here at some stage. Sounds like a bitch of an investigation to me.'

Harry chuckled. 'Yeah, one most detectives wouldn't break a sweat over. I don't think we need lose any sleep.'

'Exactly. So, as the Russians say, mate.'

'Yeah, let's fuckenoffski,' said Harry.

The pair walked out, Harry closing the front door behind them. Tanya was leaning on the bonnet of the Corolla having a smoke. The young girl was huddled in the front passenger seat.

Trev put the empty bleach drum down next to the stack of full ones. As he walked back to the others, he peeled off his gloves, dropping them in the bag Harry proffered, with the other pairs. He rummaged in the plastic bags of items Tanya had collected and emerged with the keys to the Jaguar. He grinned at Harry.

'Right, let's hit the road. You good to go, Tan?'

'Yep.' She ground out the cigarette in the red dirt, picked up the butt, and got into the driver's seat of the shit-box Toyota.

Harry walked over to her. 'Follow us. We'll head for the hospital at Midland, best option. You drop her off down from the entrance, so no surveillance cameras will be watching, and tell her to go in to get help. Then drive away and follow us again, okay?'

'Yep, all good.' She paused. 'I just wish we could do more for her.'

'I know, babe. But at least she's alive. If we hadn't rolled in, she would have been another Orla.'

Tanya placed her hand on top of Harry's, which was on the sill of the car window. 'I know. It's just all so screwed.'

'Yeah, as is much of life. At least we well and truly fucked up three peds.'

'I don't think I'll be able to eat pork again,' said Tanya.

'What? So no black pudding and bacon for your breakfast tomorrow?' Harry grinned at her.

'Gross!' She turned up her nose.

The three vehicles drove slowly in convoy up the wooded driveway, like three conspirators slinking back into the shadows. Dark it certainly was. Silent it certainly wasn't. The ravenous herd of swine were squealing and grunting louder than a hundred politicians in a particularly puerile parliamentary question time. But, thought Harry as he drove, at least here something useful was occurring: three dead paedophiles were being masticated into pig shit.

– 14 –

Outside Swan District Hospital that night, Tanya gave the young girl a hug as she got out of the car. 'Believe me, sweetie, I do understand what you've been through.'

The girl looked at her silently.

Tanya was still holding her by her shoulders. 'Our stepfather raped me and my sister for years.'

There was a spark of light in the child's eyes. She put her arms around Tanya's neck and kissed her on the cheek.

Tanya hugged the little girl.

Still she said nothing, but simply clung to Tanya.

Part of Tanya wanted to do more, but she hauled herself back, remembering Harry's advice that they simply couldn't get involved. She gently moved the child off her neck.

Tanya choked back tears. 'I would so like to look after you, sweetie, but I just can't.'

The faint light in the little eyes went out, and she turned away.

Shit, life was awful, Tanya thought. Tears were now running down her cheeks, as the child trudged away from the car, towards the bright lights of the hospital's emergency entrance.

And Tanya didn't even know her name.

'Fuck!' she yelled at the windscreen of the car.

After the hospital drop-off, they parked the old Toyota outside the bikie's car-hire joint. They left Slade's Jaguar next to it. Trev, after driving the superb machine, grinned wistfully as he slipped the keys to both cars through the after-hours return chute. The bikies wouldn't hesitate to profit from untraceably disposing of a $300k Jaguar XJ Supersport. It tidied up that loose end nicely.

Then it was up the hill again to clear out the motel room, and back down the hill to the city.

They parked near Royal Perth Hospital this time, whilst Tanya walked into emergency, used a false name, and got her face stitched up. After that was finally done – Tanya waited over two hours – they headed for the dodgiest looking caravan park they could find online.

Serenity Grove Travellers Park looked at a cursory glance as calm as its name, but only because it was one of those places where no one enquired into each other and everyone was discreetly on edge, if they weren't out of it on booze, drugs, or both. One of those struggle-street locales where the repressed tension and uneasy quiet were palpable, even to the half-sober. It was a vicinity where sudden and brutal violence were only one misinterpreted glance away.

It suited their purpose perfectly and Trev booked in using Dieter Schwarz's credit card. Aside from enjoying both the cash and the irony of Dieter's generous contribution to the ped hunting, using his cash card and credit card in WA would help no end in muddying the trail should Dieter ever be listed as a missing person.

Tanya took one look at the communal bathrooms and promptly announced she wanted to go back to the Shangri-La fleapit in Mundaring. Harry laughed and told her this would make her appreciate the luxury sleeper cabin on the three-day train ride back east. But he did offer to stand guard outside whilst she did her ablutions.

Now it was Saturday, the sleuths' last full day in Perth before the morning train back to Sydney. It was late afternoon and they were sitting on a quiet stretch of beach eating barbecued chicken and salad, and enjoying a bottle of chilled Sancerre – the local bottle shop had carried an unexpectedly fine range of wines. Tanya had never seen the sun set over water, having always been on the eastern seaboard in Sydney, so Harry had suggested this jaunt to the coast near the caravan dump, where they had been lying low. And now, as Trev opened a second bottle of wine and refilled their glasses, the threesome gazed out at the water, the blazing grapefruit of a sun turning into a glowing pink, tinging the scattered clouds with subtle hues of peach and apricot. Soon it would become a burning blood orange as it hit the horizon.

The slanting rays were causing the highlights in Tanya's hair to sparkle. She lightly touched the stitched gash on her face – she'd taken off the hospital bandage the day before.

'Don't worry, babe,' said Harry. 'We'll get you as good as new back home. I promise you.'

Her reluctant smile was a little lopsided as she favoured her injured cheek.

'You'll always be a beautiful, hot woman, Tan,' said Trev. 'And that's coming from a gay guy.'

She blew him a kiss. 'Thanks, Trev.'

'Let's make that the most drop-dead-gorgeous woman on the planet,' added Harry.

Tanya blew him a kiss as well. 'Don't let Tessa hear you saying that, she might get jealous.'

'I doubt that envy is her style,' said Harry. 'And it's completely casual, anyway.'

'I haven't heard you mention her in a while, mate,' said Trev.

'She's been flat out with her business, lots of trips, and not much social time,' replied Harry.

'In reality,' said Tanya, 'Harry's so exhausted from keeping me satisfied that he hasn't got the energy for Tessa as well.'

'I have so!' said Harry.

'We need to get you fitter, big boy,' said Trev, enjoying the opportunity to join in the ribbing.

'Bugger off, the pair of you.'

Tanya leant over and poked Harry in the ribs.

'Actually, I think Harry's desperately hoping to get me and Tessa over at the same time.'

'Ooh!' said Trev. 'The old *ménage à trois*!'

Harry went slightly red, and it wasn't the evening light.

'Yes,' continued Tanya. 'Some filthy girl-on-girl action followed by you joining in, eh?' She poked him again.

Harry was blushing fully now. 'Well … um …'

'Bloody hell, not like the big Kenmare to be stuck for words.' Trev jabbed him from the other side.

Harry opened his mouth, but nothing emerged. He sheepishly shook his head.

Trev couldn't help himself. 'So, Tan, you and Tessa ever got it on?' He was smiling at her.

Tanya caught on immediately. She grinned back at Trev.

'Not yet, but there's definitely sexual tension there, especially when she gets close to me at the studio. You know, when we're close enough to smell each other, bit of skin brushing against skin.'

Harry groaned.

Tanya winked at Trev. 'And I so want to do a sixty-niner with her.'

Harry wailed as he covered his head with his hands.

'Tan, I reckon our mate Harry here has a serious chubby right now.'

They both laughed.

Harry, still a shade of red to compete with the sunset, emptied his glass. Trev refilled it.

Now they all laughed.

'So, Trev,' said Tanya, 'you said last night that the address you had for that Father Barwick was now a building site. Any other leads?'

'Potentially, yeah. I caught up with a local PI this morning. He used to be in the job here, that's how I knew him. He actually used to be on the police paedophile squad until it got closed down. He left the force in disgust. That was back in the late nineties.'

'Shut it down? How can they shut down a paedophile squad?' asked Tanya.

'Well, the police hierarchy can do whatever they please, really.'

'Okay, not how then, but why? Why the hell would you want to shut down a squad like that?'

'A burningly good and utterly reasonable question, Tan,' replied Trev.

Harry regained his voice. 'That sort of decision is usually made when detectives are a little too successful and are getting close to unearthing the Establishment's really dirty secrets.'

'But that's so fucked.'

Trev continued. 'So, Chris, this PI, said that they'd had investigation after investigation into Catholic priests and brothers, which had gone nowhere. The suspects were always tipped off, and the squad was starved of resources for their enquiries.'

'Tipped off by the senior cops?' asked Tanya.

'Possibly,' said Harry, 'but probably not directly. These things usually work with high-level contacts talking discreetly with other contacts, who then pass the message on, so it gets to the suspects. Especially so in the Catholic establishment.'

Tanya looked gobsmacked and shook her head.

'And there's no shortage of good Catholics in the upper levels of the police,' added Harry.

'Anyway,' said Trev, 'Chris has done a lot of private work for victims' groups, tracking down various priests and the like. He said he's got an extensive network of contacts, including a couple of insiders, and he's happy to fish around for me, and free of charge.'

'So does he think he can find Barwick?' asked Harry.

'Yeah. He said in all likelihood he's been moved interstate again, given the recent police enquiry. But he's confident he can locate him. Might take several weeks or even months.'

'A brief reprieve for the priest then,' said Harry.

'I've waited this long, so a bit longer is no drama. I'll get to front him soon enough.'

Harry topped up the three glasses this time. He held his up and the others followed.

'Here's to getting back to Sydney and to our fantastic little team,' toasted Harry.

They chinked glasses.

'Team,' said Tanya and Trev together.

'And to having Sasha back on board with us,' added Harry.

'To my sis,' said Tanya.

'To Sash,' said Trev.

They all drank and then sat in silence, gazing out over the Indian Ocean and the dying sunrays.

The sun, now a deep tangerine, floated above the horizon, spraying its last shafts of light across the vista. At sea level, the tops of the gentle waves were touched with warm sparkles, providing a kaleidoscopic effect across the vast expanse of cerulean water. Up in the sky, the scattered white clouds had their undersides brilliantly highlighted in red, like balls of cotton wool dipped in cochineal.

At land level, the three sleuths were bathed in the warm, coppery light. The two guys looked uncharacteristically bronzed, whilst Tanya resembled a goddess hewn from amber, despite her wounded cheek.

Harry thought about Orla. He tried to picture her running on the sand in front of him. She'd always loved the beach. He had a photo on his dresser of her in her little red swimsuit with a bucket and spade, taken at Avalon Beach a year before she died. He stared at the horizon and considered the vengeance yet to be sated.

Trev pictured Jean-Louis, and imagined sitting beside him now. They'd shared many sunsets, but none was more etched in his memory than one night lazing on the beach at Biarritz that summer they'd gone to France for him to meet Jean-Louis's family. It was during that sunset over the Bay of Biscay that they'd talked about spending the rest of their lives together. Trev longed to feel that loving arm around his shoulders.

Tanya focused on Sasha, the peachy light and gentle onshore breeze only partly assuaging her anxiety. She wanted to be an optimist, but their path together so far hadn't exactly leant itself to a positive outlook. Inside her lurked a bad feeling, and it fed her growing despair at the injustice of it all. She wished Sash was cuddled up to her now sharing the sunset with her.

Three humans, each dealt an ugly hand by life, gazed westwards at one of nature's most beautiful displays.

The now vermillion sun lowered itself into the twilight, crossing the horizon as if sinking into the ultramarine depths of the ocean. The spangled waves regained their heavy shade and the clouds enjoyed a final radiant stroke of magenta blush as the sun was swallowed up.

*   *   *   *   *

PART 3

HARRY'S FAT CATS

It was a blonde. A blonde to make a bishop kick a hole in a stained-glass window.

> \- Raymond Chandler

There were women you failed ever to sleep with; these, in retrospect, have a perverse vividness ...

> \- John Updike

– 1 –

Late October was hot for spring. The sun blazed down from a clear, powder-blue sky over western Sydney. The brilliant afternoon sunshine lit up the top-floor offices of the Perfect Plains Municipal Council, facing the imposing Blue Mountains in the near distance.

The largest office, and the one with the most commanding view, was that of the Council CEO, Johann Van Dijk. He was in his late fifties and a veteran of the ratepayer-funded trough of offensively inflated management salaries. His investment portfolio and asset collection were approaching parity with a few small nations. And his legendary meanness had assisted no end: despite his $520k annual salary, he made his executive staff pay their own way when he took them to their executive lunch functions. Having jumped from the sinking ship of white South Africa when the death knell of apartheid was sounding, like many of his compatriots he'd settled for Australia. However, he remained uncomfortable with multiculturalism even after more than twenty years in the country.

Van Dijk had adorned his office to reflect his view of himself – his excellence and status. The windows ran the entire length of the western side, with the solid timber door set in the opposite wall. On either side of the door were two poster-size framed photographs of Van Dijk receiving public service awards. Flanking these were massively enlarged and framed copies of the accompanying newspaper articles. From his grandiose mahogany desk and throne-like, leather executive chair, he could gaze to his right and take in the view, or he could turn to his left and reflect on his public recognition.

Behind his desk was a mosaic of a dozen large photographs of his vintage car collection, his two yachts, and his real estate holdings. He wanted his underlings, as they sat across the desk in front of him, to be forced to contemplate how successful he was. A vast mirror almost totally filled the last wall, opposite his treasure display. From an interior design perspective, it opened the room up enormously, not that the palatial office needed it. More accurately, it was in place so Van Dijk could gaze at himself from his desk at regular intervals. He found it so uplifting. At the start of each working day, he stood in front of the expansive mirror, striking a smile, and repeating his life-force mantra: 'Fuck *I'm* good. Fuck I'm *good. Fuck* I'm good.' Then it was down to business.

This glorious Monday afternoon, with the office door locked, Van Dijk was reclining in his throne, hands clasped behind his head and the smile on his face lit up by the sunrays now angling directly into the room.

Council's senior manager for human resources was with him in his office. More specifically, Agnes Stoul was under the CEO's desk, mouthful of executive member, and sucking hard. Well, naturally she was: it was, after all, her annual performance review meeting, and she knew a healthy bonus was up for grabs. If she'd had any self-respect, she would have had to swallow it in exchange for cash. However, having a copious reserve of greed, bugger all pride, and even less talent, she happily settled for swallowing the CEO's load instead.

As she gulped the last dregs down and wiped the sacred member with tissues, as Van Dijk liked, she reflected on her own career progression, amazing in the absence of any work-related skills or qualifications. She did, however, give absolutely phenomenal head, and that was definitely a talent in her view. But unfortunately you couldn't get a degree in that. Whilst hell would freeze over before Stoul got close to university admission, not even a postal-order one from the US, she'd often thought that at least TAFE could offer a Cert III in Oral Relief, or similar, but alas, no. Still, despite the lack of certificates to hang on the wall, she'd just about earned her doctorate in fellatio, and it had done her splendidly indeed. She emerged from beneath the desk and smiled moistly at Van Dijk.

'As always, Aggy, your performance is outstanding.'

'Thanks, Johann. I just love working for such a fantastic boss.'

She, along with a few other senior managers, had learnt the art of sycophancy quickly and perfectly. For her, sucking cock needed to be figurative and literal. If ever an alpha male needed his ego rubbing – and which of them didn't? – it was Van Dijk. And if you did so wholeheartedly and unreservedly, then you ended up on what less-favoured parties in the Council referred to as the A-Team. Those who didn't sit in that camp either kept their heads down or frantically job-hunted.

Van Dijk pulled some papers in front of him as Stoul took her seat opposite. He signed a form with a post-ejaculatory flourish. 'There you go, Aggy, maximum bonus. And I expect you'll be putting in extra effort on finessing my annual salary review to Council.'

'Boss, I'm all over it already.'

'Excellent. The brain-dead Mayor should be a pushover, with his faction following him, but as bloody usual, that bitch from the Greens and the wanker kaffir independent will want to put flies in the ointment.'

'We're working on strategies to deal with them, rest assured, boss.' She discreetly removed a pube from between her pre-molars and disposed of it on the floor.

'Good stuff,' said Van Dijk. 'See you at the exec meeting in the morning then, Aggy.'

'Absolutely. One more thing, boss …'

Van Dijk looked at her enquiringly.

'I was wondering about upgrading my council car.'

'And why not? I do every six months at least, and a couple of lovely new Merc models have come out recently.'

'Actually, I was keen on an Audi TT.'

Van Dijk laughed. 'A matching pair with your girlfriend then?'

Stoul blushed slightly. Her relationship with the Council's chief lawyer, Judith Albion, was not exactly well-known. And, given they were both married, they wanted to keep it that way.

She smiled obsequiously at Van Dijk. 'Boss, I was just keen to look part of the team.'

'I wholeheartedly agree, Aggy. Get yourself over to the CFO and he'll do all the necessaries.' Van Dijk used the finger speech marks with the last word. 'You'll be in your new Audi in a couple of days.'

'Oh, thank you, boss.'

Van Dijk nodded regally as Stoul hoisted herself out of the chair and headed for the door.

– 2 –

Three days later, Councillor Samuel Akobo pulled into the car park at Perfect Plains Council. He was an hour early for the council meeting, but he wanted to go through briefing papers that had been given to him at the last minute, a not irregular occurrence for him. He parked his faded blue Mitsubishi Colt, missing two hubcaps and with a cracked windscreen and numerous dented panels. He turned off the engine and waited for the tremble of the after-ignition to fade and die.

Must get that fixed, he thought. But it was an expense he couldn't manage, and the wheels still moved. Any spare cash he earned went to the refugee hostel he supervised on a voluntary basis. He knew all too well how difficult it was arriving here in Australia as an African refugee. The recent groups of Somalis being accepted into the country needed all the support they could get.

It was his much-lauded community work that had gained him sufficient support to get elected two years previously as an independent councillor. Given his own experience of corrupt military dictatorships in Africa, the whole democracy concept was something he had quickly grown to love. Inebriated on freedom was how he viewed his new life, much as he missed the smell of the African air and his relatives in and around Lagos.

As he strode across the car park towards the side door for staff and councillors, he stopped in his tracks at the sight of yet another new luxury car in the CEO's parking bay. The gleaming silver Mercedes coupé sat there looking as if it were a feudal lord surveying the peasants beyond the moat.

Bloody hell, he thought, that must be at least a hundred and fifty grand's worth of car. And paid for by the long-suffering ratepayers, many of whom were far closer to mortgage default and bankruptcy than they were to the mythical Australian dream. Many of the families he knew in his council ward were struggling with barely enough to feed their kids, let alone any cash to enjoy life with.

He looked along the line of managerial car bays. They were all luxury models. And there was a brand-new Audi TT, almost identical to the council lawyer's car. He walked closer to see the signage on the bay: 'Senior Manager HR'.

Akobo started to fume. It was bloody outrageous. He had raised the issue of luxury cars before, but the CEO had abruptly informed him, his South African accent laced with its usual condescending arrogance, that all the cars were within the financial parameters allowed under the managerial car policy.

Akobo, legally qualified himself, had read all the council policies on cars, and couldn't for the life of him see how the pride of the German automotive industry lined up outside could possibly fall under the luxury-car cut-off point for council-funded vehicles.

The loathsome Van Dijk had sneered at him, and told him to verify it with the CFO if he wanted. As he had turned to walk away, Akobo was sure that Van Dijk had muttered 'kaffir faggot' under his breath, but not loud enough to be caught out.

Akobo assumed that much of Van Dijk's disdain for him was the typical hatred a certain class of South Africans had for black people. But more relevant, no doubt, was Akobo constantly trying to hold the Council's fat cats accountable. And most troublesome of all for Van Dijk was that Akobo was a gay man. Van Dijk had been overheard saying that the Muslim extremists weren't all bad, given their penchant for throwing homosexuals off tall buildings.

Akobo shook his head. Something had to be done about this. And nothing official seemed to work. No, a new strategy was needed.

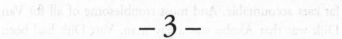

— 3 —

Tanya put her phone down on her desk and turned to Harry who was tidying up paperwork, or 'bureaucratic toilet paper' as he usually referred to it. 'I'm going to have to take off, Mr PI.'

Harry looked at her. 'All okay?'

'Sasha's doctor just called her and asked her to come in today to discuss her new test results. It sounded urgent. I want to go with her.'

'Of course, babe, absolutely you go. Any hints?'

'No, but I'm worried. The earlier ones she had when we were in Perth, they didn't tell her like this, seemed more routine.'

Trev came over from the couch where he'd been scanning the online *Sydney Morning Herald*. He gave Tanya a hug. 'Hang in there, Tan, and give Sasha our love.'

'Thanks, Trev.'

'Let us know how it goes, and if we can do anything,' said Harry. 'We're here for the next couple of hours to see our new client.'

'Yeah, he's bloody lucky you're prepared to do a Friday afternoon meeting. That's sacred pub time for you two,' said Tanya, forcing a smile.

'Damned right, but he sounded keen and couldn't make Monday. Business is business; we don't need him shopping around.'

'In this game you can never have enough coming in the door,' added Trev.

'Ain't that the truth, brother.'

'And what about getting on with the hunt?' asked Tanya, lowering her voice like a conspirator.

'Herbert Farr is banged up, so there's nothing we could do in a hurry anyway, as much as I'd like to,' said Harry. 'So, we may as well take a new client or two and boost the bank balance.'

'After that we'll be down the Emerald,' added Trev.

Harry got up as well and gave Tanya a kiss and a hug. Then she was out the door.

Harry turned to Trev. 'Fingers crossed for Sash, but I'm worried, too.'

'Yeah. She didn't seem her normal self last week when she was in here. You seen her since then?'

'No, she's been busy with the fashion work. But it's definitely getting to Tanya, big time.'

'To be expected. It's that special twin bond, mate.'

Harry nodded gravely. 'Back to sodding paperwork, I suppose, and to wait for this councillor from Perfect Plains.'

Trev chuckled. 'Hope he's not another breast-feeding alderman.'

Harry snorted. 'Bloody hell, there couldn't possibly be two of them.' He opened a bottle of mineral water.

'Careful, mate. Never say never in this game,' said Trev.

'Too true. But as he's called us and therefore is looking for help, perhaps he's one of the good guys.'

'If so, we might have to take him captive and bottle him. Oh, and by the way, still nothing in any of the news feeds about either Schwarz.'

'Excellent,' said Harry. 'And it can stay that way as far as we're concerned.'

'No updates from the Feds?'

'None. I don't think Tom's replacement is doing too much on this. So, no news is good news,' replied Harry.

Trev was now back on the couch with his laptop. 'Beautiful!'

'What?' asked Harry.

'Mate, breaking news. ICAC have announced public hearings into First State Transit and the tendering process. Names all the players. Starts end of next month.'

'Oh, that will be compulsive viewing. It'll be the top news item every single day it runs. How long's it listed for?'

'Two weeks. Bloody fantastic.'

'Can't wait to see it.' Harry looked over at Trev. 'And, I meant to tell you that union thug Stoddart rang me yesterday.'

'What did that wanker want?'

'Trev, he was smugger than a fat rat in a plague outbreak. He said he'd just taken over as the union boss. With the ICAC developments, now I know why.'

Trev chuckled. 'It'll just be different wallets getting lined now. It's a never-ending circle with these corrupt arseholes.'

'Abso-fucking-lutely. Still, the ICAC hearings will be a ball-tearer.'

'Yep, that they will.' Trev kept reading and chortling away.

Harry resumed his paperwork.

About forty minutes later, the buzzer sounded. Harry pressed the intercom.

'Councillor Samuel Akobo, I have an appointment.'

'Ah, yes. Come in.' Harry released the door.

An African man in an immaculate maroon business suit, leather briefcase and matching shoes stepped in rather cautiously, as if unsure whether to proceed or run away.

Harry stood up and smiled at the new client. 'Come in, come in, we don't bite.'

Trev, getting off the couch, smiled, too. 'Well, only on a bad day, and then only bad people.'

He held out his hand. 'Trevor Matson, I'm Harry's offsider.'

'Pleased to meet you.' The voice was that crisp and clearly enunciated English that educated Africans make sound so beautiful. He then walked over to the main desk and shook Harry's outstretched hand.

'Harry Kenmare. Have a seat.'

Akobo nodded, smiling, and settled himself in the client chair, briefcase on his lap. 'Thank you, Mr Kenmare.'

'Please, first names are fine. How can we be of service?'

'I think we have a serious corruption issue at our council. You've been recommended to me by a lawyer friend. He says you are a man who gets results.'

Harry chuckled. 'Corruption in a council? Whatever next?'

Akobo smiled. 'Yes, I guess you have seen enough to be cynical.'

'Understatement. So, tell me what's going down at Perfect Plains?'

Akobo proceeded to tell Harry about the fleet of luxury cars for senior managers, all funded by the Council, courtesy of the ratepayers. He relayed that he had requested all the relevant documents, convinced that the staff vehicle policy was being flagrantly flouted, but all the paperwork seemed to be in order. There was no smoking gun to be found. He'd even approached the ICAC. They'd made preliminary enquiries of the Council, and then informed him that there didn't appear to be anything for them to investigate.

Harry nodded. 'So, you want to see what we can find?'

'Exactly, Mr … uh Harry.' Akobo pulled an iPad out of his briefcase. 'Let me show you the cars, then you'll understand why I am sure it is corruption.'

Trev came over and joined them. They gathered around the tablet screen and watched the footage of the senior management car park Akobo had carefully filmed. There was a gleaming parade of luxurious German engineering: two Audi TT sports, two BMW 6-series, three BMW 5-series, two Mercedes SL class, and two Mercedes CL class, including the *pièce de résistance*, a CL65 coupé in the CEO's parking bay.

Trev whistled.

'Bugger me,' said Harry. 'Didn't know the Frankfurt Motor Show had relocated to Perfect Plains.'

'I know a bit about cars,' said Trev. 'There's well over a million bucks' worth of fine German machinery there.'

'Yes, I have done some research,' said Akobo. 'The cheapest model there is about seventy thousand dollars, the most expensive about two hundred thousand. And the cut-off value in the car policy is fifty thousand.'

'Bloody hell,' said Trev.

Akobo continued. 'They're not allowed to have council cars above that figure. They are deemed luxury cars.'

'Well, so they bloody should be, and that lot are certainly luxury. In fact, we haven't seen that much luxury since Marie Antoinette ordered her anal beads in twenty-four carat,' said Harry.

Akobo laughed.

'But you say the paperwork checked out?' continued Harry.

'Yes, here you are.' Akobo fished a wad of papers out of his case and then talked the sleuths through them.

Ten minutes later, Harry leaned back in his chair, placing his hands on the edge of his desk. 'Well, something definitely stinks. But how do we crack this one?'

'Surveillance won't get us anything,' said Trev. 'And whatever scam is going on, there's hardly likely to be any record of it.'

'I agree,' said Harry. 'It'll all be verbal exchanges and then carefully falsified paperwork. And we can't prove the papers to be crooked unless someone tells us the scam. There has to be some bent arrangement between the council managers and this car dealership, Palace Motors.'

'Neither side to the sweetheart deal is likely to talk to us,' said Trev.

Akobo shuffled a little uncomfortably in his chair. 'Ah, there might be a way. But it wouldn't be ethical.'

'Really?' Harry raised his eyebrows. 'Try us.'

'One of the key players leads a double life. Maybe you could use it to encourage him to talk. But, as I said, I think it is not ethical.'

'Double life? Excellent, we are listening,' said Harry, smiling. 'And don't worry about the ethics, you leave that to us.'

Akobo cleared his throat and looked at each of the guys in turn, hesitating.

'Come on, Sam, don't get shy now,' said Trev.

'All right. The CFO at Council, Colin Lodge, is a family man, but likes young men on the side.'

Harry chuckled. 'Ah, the classic blackmail formula.'

'And how do you know this?' asked Trev.

'Well ...' Akobo looked as if he needed help.

Trev cottoned on. 'Mate, no need to be nervous. I'm gay, too.'

Akobo let out his breath and relaxed visibly.

Harry helped out. 'It's all cool here, Sam. No judgement.'

'Thank you, both of you. I get a bit paranoid here sometimes.'

'Understandable,' said Trev. 'It can be tough enough being white and gay. So, tell us about this CFO.'

'I saw him at a place in Epping called the Steam Engine.'

Harry frowned.

Trev nodded. 'Yeah, I know the owner there.' He looked at Harry, who appeared lost. 'It's a gay sauna.'

Akobo continued. 'So, I was leaving one evening when Colin Lodge walked in. He didn't see me.'

'You're sure about that?' asked Harry.

'Yes, I am sure. But then it got me thinking, he might be a regular. So, I did a bit of hanging around over the next few weeks, and he is there every single Tuesday evening.'

Harry and Trev exchanged glances.

'Sam, I think we might be able to work with this,' said Harry. 'Let's talk business.'

'Thank you, Harry.'

'First things first, our fees. This sort of work doesn't come cheap, and I always ask for a down payment to kick things off.'

'That is okay.'

'You haven't heard the prices yet, Sam. I'd want a five-grand retainer, and then hourly rates after that. And they're two hundred an hour, plus expenses.'

Akobo nodded. 'I have some financial backing on this. Not everyone likes the Council or the car dealer. I can't say any more than that, but your bills will be paid, no problems.'

'Fair enough. If I was bankrolling something like this, I'd want it bloody discreet, too.'

'Damned right,' added Trev.

'All right, Sam. Are you able to transfer the five grand today?'

'Of course.'

'Excellent, we'll get started pronto,' said Harry, reaching out his hand. They shook.

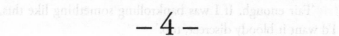

— 4 —

L ater that evening, Harry and Trev were sitting in the beer garden of the Emerald Bar, having consumed a fine steak dinner with Harry's friend, Liam. They had enjoyed a couple of bottles of the pub's latest red wine addition, a French merlot, and were now slipping into the Jameson.

Harry and Trev had updated His Eminence on their latest corruption tales, but said nothing about their other, bloodier activities.

Liam had finished another rant about corrupt councillors and politicians in Australia, when he suddenly changed tack. 'Oh, by the way, last night on the telly, I saw that bloody social services woman, Savage.'

Harry grimaced as if someone had farted in his face. 'That fucking power-hungry psychopath.'

'Oh, yeah, head like a battered pit bull and a soul of pure dog shit,' added Trev.

'She so badly needs karma to come get her,' Harry said, lighting another smoke. Harry thought back bitterly to the cover-up by Human Services boss Porcia Savage of the truth around the death of little Beau Jacobs, supposedly under departmental guardianship. Then Savage's monstrous campaign of psychological warfare that resulted in the tragic suicide of the one decent departmental officer, the ex-cop Stavros McMahon, who had tried to shine a light on the case. And the miserable death in an alleyway of the toddler's young mother, Lara Jacobs. Harry pictured Savage's arrogant face. He hated that bitch with a passion, and had promised himself that one day he'd exact some form of justice. He'd also made a similar promise to McMahon's only living relative, a sister he'd tracked down in Adelaide several weeks after Stavros's death. She'd lost contact with Stavros after his nervous breakdown and hospitalization in the psych ward. Yeah, Harry would give his left nut to see Savage brought down.

'Yes, I was thinking about that,' said Liam. 'I've an idea. Interested?'

'Are the Kennedys gun-shy?' drawled Harry.

Liam leant into the table, lowered his voice, and proceeded to spell out his scheme. He had the undivided attention of the sleuths. When he finished, Harry and Trev were both smiling.

Harry nodded. 'I like it, Your Eminence. And my Irish genes are truly proud of you.'

'Could definitely work,' added Trev. 'As long as we can find the connection. Mind you, rather unethical. By comparison Richard Nixon would look like a saint.'

'Fight fire with fire, gentlemen, as a cousin of mine back in old Belfast used to say. That was after Bloody Sunday, for sure, but all abuses of power are evil and deserve to be treated that way.'

Harry raised his glass and the others followed. 'Here's to the scheme. Operation Bloody Sunday, perhaps?'

'Definitely,' said Trev.

They toasted. Then they got more drinks.

Their upbeat soirée came to an abrupt end when Tanya walked in. Her stricken look and red, puffy eyes heralded a grim change in mood as she silently kissed all three men on the cheek and sat down with her vodka.

Harry touched her hand. 'Babe, what's up?'

Tears started running down her cheeks. 'Sasha's got cancer. She's in hospital.'

'Oh, shit,' said Liam.

'But I thought she was only seeing the doctor today for the results?' said Harry.

'She was. And then went straight to hospital. I've just come from there, as she's asleep now with the drugs. She starts chemo tomorrow.'

'Shit. Just how bad is it, Tan?' asked Trev.

Tanya burst out crying.

Harry leaned over and put his arm around her.

After a minute she regained her composure. 'It's pancreatic cancer.'

'Oh, fuck,' said Harry and Trev in unison.

'It's late stage and really aggressive.' She buried her face in Harry's chest and started sobbing uncontrollably. There were a few uncomfortable looks in their direction.

Harry wanted to tell everyone to go fuck themselves, but he restrained himself. 'I think we need to take you home, Tan.'

She got her tears under control enough to speak. 'I don't want to be at our place alone.'

'No worries. We'll take you back to mine. Okay?'

'Yeah.'

Harry swallowed his whiskey and stood up. He still had his arm across Tanya's shoulders. Trev stubbed out a smoke, downed his drink, and got up from his chair.

'Until next time, Your Eminence,' said Harry.

Liam nodded grimly. He stood up as well, and put his hand on Tanya's face. 'Be strong, young lady.' He turned to Harry. 'Look after her, man.'

Five minutes later, the two men and Tanya were back at Harry's apartment.

Harry took Tanya into his bedroom. Trev went over to the sideboard and poured two large glasses of Jameson, adding ice cubes from the kitchen freezer.

Ten minutes went past, and Harry came back into the lounge area. 'She's asleep now. I've given her a sedative.'

'Yeah, best thing. She needs rest.' Trev took a swig of his whiskey. 'I still can't believe it, Harry. Sasha is so young, and so vibrant, so alive.'

'Life's fucked, Trev.' Harry took the Jameson Trev handed him and drank almost half of it. 'All these total arseholes out there who frankly deserve to die, and yet thrive and prosper. And then Sash cops this. It's a great argument for atheism.'

'Yeah. Although neither of us needs any convincing on that point.'

'Bloody oath,' said Harry.

'Mate, let's do a bit of research for this new job, take our mind off things.'

'Roger that.'

They clinked glasses, then sat down at the dining table and Trev opened up his MacBook.

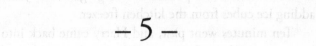

— 5 —

It was late Saturday morning before they could see Sasha. Tanya sat close on one side of the bed, holding Sasha's hand in both of hers. Harry and Trev sat on the other side. There was an array of machines to which Sasha was connected via wires and tubes. The room was bright, with a large window, but maintained a sterile hospital ambience, backed up by the tinge of disinfectant.

Sasha, propped up on pillows, wasn't exactly talkative following her chemo session. Harry and Trev were a bit lost for anything to say that didn't sound trite.

Sasha moved slightly. 'Gonna be sick,' she said to Tanya, who grabbed a plastic bowl from the bedside cabinet. Sasha dry retched a few times, then flopped back and wiped some spittle from her mouth with the tissues Tanya gave her.

Harry looked at Sasha's pallid face. It was the look of fear in her exhausted eyes that struck Harry the most. He'd never seen Sasha look like that before. In fact, he'd never seen any young person look as terrified as this.

Tanya had, of course, when they were kids. They'd both worn that expression regularly when, clinging to each other, they heard their stepfather drunkenly staggering towards their bedroom door.

Harry gently took Sasha's hand. He tried to smile when she turned to look at him. Fuck, he thought, it was so unfair.

She gave him an attempt at a smile. Then she spoke. 'I'm gonna have a sleep, guys. Thanks for coming. I love you.'

Harry fought back his tears. Trev let them flow.

'We'll come back tomorrow, Sash,' said Harry. 'You let us know if you need anything, and I mean anything.'

'Yep, absolutely anything at all,' added Trev, wiping the tears from his cheeks.

Sasha smiled weakly, and tried to blow a kiss in their direction.

'I'm going to stay here,' said Tanya.

'You belong here, babe. Call you later.'

The two guys kissed Sasha goodbye, then Tanya, and headed out. They walked down the corridor to the lifts to escape the morose place.

'It's unbearable seeing Sasha looking that scared,' said Harry.

'Yeah, as tough as she is, this will be the fight of her young life.'

'It doesn't look … ' started Harry, before Trev cut him off.

'Let's not even put that awful contemplation into words, mate.'

'Yeah, fair call. Fuck, I hate hospitals,' said Harry.

'You and me both, mate,' said Trev, as they stood outside the lift door. 'Five years ago I sat in one as my boyfriend died.'

'You've never told me about that, mate.'

'Still don't find it easy to discuss. Maybe over a drink later.'

Harry put his hand on Trev's shoulder. 'Mate, as long as you want to, I'll be here to listen.'

'Cheers, Harry.'

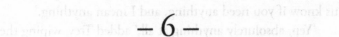

— 6 —

After grabbing lunch, Harry and Trev headed for the Lodge household in Bushlands Avenue, Hornsby Heights, where they propped the VW van slightly down the road, but with a clear camera shot.

About an hour later, a woman in her early forties, well-coiffured and trim, emerged from the McMansion-style house with two sulky teenagers in tow, doing their best to annoy each other. The mother stopped to remonstrate with them.

Trev meanwhile was snapping away with his Pentax – family portraits the Lodge clan had never contemplated. Mother Lodge and the aggravating adolescents got into a Mazda SUV. They drove past the van, but with the kids tormenting each other in the back seat, and the mother juggling driving and chastising, they were never going to take any notice of their observers.

'Looks like our boy's at home,' said Harry. 'That's his council Mercedes.'

'Yep, all one hundred and fifty grand of it,' replied Trev. 'Talk about snouts in the trough. Fucking pigs, the lot of them.'

'I was thinking, mate …'

'Ooh, did it hurt?' Trev grinned over at Harry.

'Piss off. No, I was thinking that once upon a time, all government agencies had to buy Australian-made cars.'

'Yeah, I remember. The way it bloody should be.'

'Exactly. With the last of our Aussie car factories closing down, you gotta wonder if things could have been different.'

'Shit, Harry, you'd be expecting these government wankers to actually care about Aussie jobs.'

'Yeah, stupid me. Still, I think I have a point.'

'No argument from me, mate.'

Trev took a few more shots of the house and the Merc. 'Wonder if Lodge is coming out today?'

'Let's give it another hour or so,' said Harry. 'If he doesn't show, then we could head over to your bath club.'

'Sauna, Harry.' Trev smiled.

'Whatever, smart-arse.'

They didn't have to wait long. About twenty minutes later, Lodge emerged, in casual clothes and a sports jacket, and jumped in his car. Trev grabbed several shots and Harry started the van. Ten minutes more and they watched as Lodge parked the car near the Hornsby Inn. He strode purposefully into the TAB that was part of the pub.

'So our CFO enjoys a flutter, it would seem,' said Harry.

'We going in?' asked Trev.

'I don't see much value, plus I think we're better not getting too close. Not yet, anyway.'

'Cool. In that case, fancy joining me in a gay sauna?' Trev was smirking.

Harry groaned. 'You're bloody enjoying this, aren't you?'

'Mate, it's priceless.'

'Bugger off.'

'Well …' Trev laughed. 'Let's get going then.'

'I need a drink,' said Harry. 'In fact, several.' He grinned ruefully. 'Mate, believe me I've got no problem with gay saunas. I just never thought I'd be visiting one, that's all.'

Trev kept laughing as Harry restarted the van and they headed off to Epping.

The pair were sitting next to each other in a dimly lit steam room with only towels wrapped around their waists, and the perspiration beading profusely.

Trev was entirely relaxed. Harry, however, was fidgeting, doing his best not to make eye contact with any of the other men. Trev acknowledged a pair of young guys who walked past holding hands.

Harry leant in slightly to Trev. 'Mate, I am *not* going to be holding your hand in here.'

Trev chuckled. 'You've no sense of adventure, Harry.'

'I just like a different style of adventure.'

'Relax, mate. If anyone looks keen, just make it clear you're not interested. Make them think we're together. Try to pretend it's a crowd of naked, busty Scandinavian girls instead.'

'Shit, don't give me that mental image. I might get a raging boner, and that's not the message I want to be giving out right now. I might get an offer I can't fulfil.'

Trev laughed. 'Ah, the things we have to do for the job.' He turned and winked at Harry.

'Bloody hell, how much longer?'

'We've got the next booking for the Sling Room, so about twenty minutes I reckon.'

'Can't wait.' Harry closed his eyes as beads of sweat ran down his face. He tried to think of naked Scandinavian girls without getting an erection. No, it couldn't be done, so he went back to fixating on the current work project.

An attendant came past and handed Trev a key. He stood up, adjusted his towel, and picked up the washbag on the bench next to him.

'Come on, big boy,' he teased Harry. 'Time for your education to continue.'

'Swell,' said a reluctant Harry, who stood up, grabbing desperately as he nearly lost his towel, and followed Trev down a carpeted corridor with burgundy-coloured walls and ceiling. Framed black-and-white photographs of well-buffed naked men adorned the walls.

Trev opened a varnished wooden door labelled 'The Sling Room', and they went inside, Trev locking the door behind them.

Harry took in his surroundings. The room, like the rest of the establishment, was bathed in subdued lighting. There was a smell of incense in the air – sandalwood, he thought – and candles burning on shelves. But the centrepiece of the chamber was a thick, black rubber sheet, shaped a bit like a cowhide. It was suspended by chains from its four corners. Off to the side was a stand with a bowl and tubes on the top. Harry peered closer and could see a large selection of condoms in the bowl, and the tubes were assorted lubricating gels. He looked back at the suspended rubber contraption.

'And what the hell is that?' he asked.

'That, big boy, is the sling.'

'Um … how …'

Trev smiled. 'One guy lies down on the sling, his friend stands behind him, and …'

'Okay, okay, I get the idea.'

'Live and let live, Harry, that's what you always say.'

'Yeah, of course. I just haven't seen anything quite like this before. Need to adjust.'

'Right, then, to work.' Trev grinned at Harry. 'And you can keep your towel on, mate.'

'Funny, ha-ha. So, what have you got in mind?'

Trev opened his bag and pulled out his iPhone. 'What we need is footage, or perhaps I should say "inch-age", of our friend Lodge *in flagrante delicto*. We need to suss out how we can do that.'

Harry was examining the condom and lube stand. 'Might be a bit obvious trying a hidden camera on this. Plus it's not fixed to the floor, so it could get moved.'

'Yeah, especially if they get really vigorous.' Trev walked around the room. 'Actually, I'm thinking of Buddha.'

'What?' said Harry.

Trev stepped over to the corner, where on a triangular shelf sat a large ceramic Buddha, which served as an incense holder, four smouldering sticks stuck in the statuette's head.

Harry moved over to join Trev.

'One of these with a camera inside would be perfect,' said Trev. He took several photos of it from different angles, then turned it around and did the same again. 'Lift it up a minute, Harry, will you?' He photographed the underside as well.

'And it's hollow,' said Harry.

'Yep. Plenty of room for the electronics. I'm sure we'll find the same ones in Chinatown.'

'Ah, now I'm with you. Build an imposter.'

'Exactly. We know Lodge's routine here, thanks to the Councillor. We'll make a Tuesday booking for the room before his visit, and then another one afterwards.'

'We?'

'Yes, mate. It's going to look a bit strange me coming in here on my own. You don't exactly book the Sling Room so you can have a wank on your lonesome.'

'Shit, all right, if I have to. Won't it look suspicious us having two bookings like that?'

'No. Happens frequently. There are some randy gentlemen in this joint.'

'Matson, you owe me some serious drinks for this.'

'Sure I can arrange that,' grinned Trev.

'In fact, are we done here? I could use a stiff drink now.'

'Yep, all good. Let's get our gear and then head for home.'

Fifteen minutes later, the pair left the Steam Engine in their wake and headed for familiar territory.

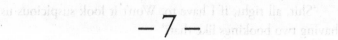

— 7 —

Harry and Trev chatted about the job on Colin Lodge as they drove back to Harry's place in Ultimo, both of them getting on their soapboxes about corrupt public officials, and how the senior bureaucrats all seemed to be purely interested in serving themselves rather than the long-suffering public. Harry did, twice, point out that all the badness kept business rolling in the door. Their only difference of opinion was that Trev reckoned the politicians were the most bent, whereas Harry voted for the bureaucrats being worse. They agreed to disagree, but concurred that it all boiled down to much the same thing: rotten governments for the community.

Back at Harry's, they garaged the van, and sauntered the short distance to the Emerald Bar. Over dinner they talked about Sasha, and Harry called Tanya at the hospital. Food and wine consumed, Harry came back from the bar with two double Jameson whiskies.

'Cheers, Trev. Here's to the demise of Lodge and his council cohorts.'

'Cheers, Harry. Here's to the sling.' He grinned.

Harry shook his head, smiling. 'Just goes to prove that every day's a learning day.'

'Indeed.' Trev lit a cigarette and offered Harry one. He accepted and lit up.

As he exhaled smoke, Harry said, 'Mate, feel like telling me about your boyfriend?'

Trev nodded slowly.

'Only if you want to, mate,' added Harry.

'No, no, that's cool.' Trev took a slug of his whiskey. 'Jean-Louis and I had been together for nearly four years up in Brizzie. Shit, we were even talking about getting married.'

'What, overseas?'

'Yeah, of course. This country's way too backwards. Here we are in twenty thirteen, and I can't see it changing anytime soon.'

'Sadly, you're right, I reckon. But go on, mate.'

'Well, one night Jean-Louis didn't come home. He'd been on shift at the wine bar he managed and should've been home by one. Bar shut at midnight. After a couple of hours I tried calling him.' Trev paused, and swallowed his Jameson. 'I need another, Harry.'

'Course.' Harry headed for the bar and returned a couple of minutes later.

Trev took a sip. 'Thanks, mate.' He smiled morosely and continued. 'So, I called him. Some bloke answered the phone. I could hear shouting and what sounded like crying. Then this voice says, "You another faggot?" I knew straightaway Jean-Louis was in serious trouble.'

'Shit,' said Harry.

'There'd been a spate of gay bashings. So, this guy says, "Wanna talk to your boyfriend, faggot? Before we kill him? Wanna blow him a kiss goodbye?" The crying got louder until I knew it was Jean-Louis next to the phone. I called his name and he said, "I love you, Trevor." He always called me by my full name, but he had that French rolling R when he said it. That was the last time I heard his voice.' Trev looked into his glass.

'Mate, you mentioned the hospital?'

'Yeah. After that, the thug came back on the phone, called me a "faggot cunt" and killed the line. I rang the local cops, but for a missing gay lover they showed as much interest as a politician in an ethics class. Didn't make any difference that I was a copper, either. Gay first, badge second, that's the way it was.'

'I remember that culture.'

'So, then I rang around the hospitals. A couple of hours later, I found him in Royal Brisbane.' Trev took a deep breath, then continued. 'He was in a coma. Doctors said with the kickings and stompings he'd had, plus what looked like wounds from a metal fencing picket, they were surprised he was still hanging in there. But he didn't for long. On the second day of me sitting there, whatever drive was keeping him alive finally gave up and he died. He never regained consciousness, not even for a second. And I stayed awake for over forty hours next to him.' Trev paused.

'Since he didn't have any next of kin here, and his parents weren't going to arrive in time from France, the head doctor was sympathetic enough to bend the rules and let me sit in with him. About ten minutes before the machines flat-lined, I'm sure there was a slight squeeze of his hand in mine, as if he was saying goodbye. Anyway, that's how I'm hanging on to that memory.'

Harry put his hand on Trev's. 'I'm so sorry, mate.'

Trev took a drink and lit another smoke. 'And just after that, in late two thousand and eight, I decided to pack it all up and come down here. I needed a clean start. What with my bitterness at the bloody police force, and the manner of my leaving it, plus Jean-Louis's murder, I couldn't stand Brizzie any more.'

'Yeah, fair enough.'

'Anyhow, life had to go on. For me, anyway. And I'm happy enough down here. Plus we're good mates now, which is a bonus.' He paused and smiled. 'Even if we can't go out playing the scene together.'

Harry raised his glass. 'Cheers to mateship.'

'Cheers.'

'So, did they ever nail anyone for murdering Jean-Louis?' asked Harry.

'Not exactly. The local detectives didn't give a stuff: just another poofter who deserved what he got in their eyes.'

'Same attitude down here, too,' said Harry.

'But Lady Fate exacted justice.' Trev smiled into the distance.

Harry looked at him enquiringly.

'My contacts in the job filled me in. There was CCTV from the laneway, next to the bar, where Jean-Louis was bashed. And like I said, there had been a series of them. So, they identified the two thugs from the footage: some pair who had done three other bashings over six weeks and were known to the police. Just nobody had bothered trying to lock them up.'

'Fucking typical,' said Harry.

'Yeah. Anyway, Uncle Providence decided to deliver the justice the bloody cops wouldn't. Turns out both the thugs were ice addicts and did soft-target stick-ups to finance their habits.'

'Like servos, Seven-Elevens, that sort of thing?'

'Exactly. A couple of months after I lobbed in Sydney, my mate at Headquarters gives me a call. Our pair of homophobic heroes had tried a stick-up on a Vietnamese corner store one evening. Thug A goes in with a machete,

Thug B keeps the stolen car running outside. Turns out the target wasn't so soft.'

'Really? I'm listening.'

'Yep. The shopkeeper, one Mr Nguyen – we'll call him Clint and forever more worship him – decides he's had a gutful of being robbed by worthless scumbuckets. He looks at the machete, looks at the bandit, pulls out a cut-down double-barrel shotty from under the counter, and gives both barrels to the arsehole. Blows him straight through the front of the ice cream cabinet.'

Harry whistled. 'Nice bloody work, Mr Clint Nguyen. Possibility of a new flavour of Magnum there.'

Trev chuckled. 'Good one. So, that's thug A done, died within minutes. Anyway, thug B sees the shooting of his mate, decides to leave in a hurry. Burns rubber all the way up the street in his haste. That draws the attention of a highway patrol unit cruising down the adjoining main road. They go to pull the idiot over, obviously thinking they'll get an easy addition to their ticket quota for the shift.'

Harry snorted. 'Good old traffic coppers.'

'Needless to say, thug B floors it, tries to outrun the patrol boys. The chase goes on for about ten klicks before the fuckwit loses it on a sharp bend, doing about one-twenty, and goes airborne into a concrete power pole.'

'Whammo,' said Harry.

'Exactly. He was probably dead before the fire, but by the time they got his barbecued body out, they needed dental records to identify him,' said Trev.

'That is an unusually pleasing dose of karma,' said Harry. 'It doesn't happen often enough.'

'Absolutely. Two complete fucktards the gene pool did not need. So, Lady Fate got my vengeance for me.' Trev looked at his empty glass. 'It's a dry argument, Harry, so my buy.' He headed for the bar, patting Harry on the shoulder as he moved past.

He returned a few minutes later. They chinked glasses.

'So, Harry, aside from finding Father Barwick in due course, my efforts on the hunting front are all at your disposal.'

'Thanks, mate, much appreciated. Once we've got the three of them, then I can be at peace with myself.'

'Fully at peace, mate, or just an armistice of sorts?'

'Yeah, fair point. Of course something will gnaw at me until the day I depart. But at least I'll be able to visit Orla's grave and tell her it's done.'

'Where's Orla buried?'

'Out at Rookwood Cemetery. Personally, I prefer cremation, but when it came to laying Orla to rest, I needed somewhere to go to visit her, a piece of ground.'

'I get that.'

'So,' said Harry, 'it's one down, two to go.'

'Well, brother, it's one down, plus one collateral.'

Harry nodded silently.

'You all right with it?' asked Trev.

'What, the vengeance for Orla? Or the extra dead ped?'

'The whole thing, I guess. I know I get through it mentally by constantly thinking about what Barwick did to me.'

'I have bad moments, sure. I'm fine with hunting down Orla's killers, of course. I only have to close my eyes and picture her little face.' Harry took a mouthful of his drink. 'I'm not actually enjoying it, but I do owe it to her. And they've hurt so many other kids.'

'The only good ped is a dead ped,' said Trev.

'True, although I wasn't okay with the idea of us executing Dieter Schwarz when we found out we had the wrong bloke. That's why it was such a bloody dilemma, remember?'

'Certainly do, and I wasn't ready with any answers on that score either. Then that Lady Fate again.'

'Yes,' said Harry. 'The divine Ms Tanya solved the dilemma in a millisecond. I'll always be in her debt for that one, 'cos I didn't know what the fuck we were going to do.'

Trev raised his glass. 'To Lady Fate, and all her angels. Excuse the religious reference.'

'To the good lady and all her crew. Tough girls who come straight off the page of a Christa Faust novel.'

'Haven't read any of hers. Recommend them?'

'Shit, yes. Great reads.' Harry lit a smoke. 'Nothing more on our next target, Herbert Farr?'

'Nope. Haven't been able to tap into any sources in the system in Melbourne yet.'

'Me neither.'

'I might shoot down there for a few days when we're done with Lodge,' said Trev. 'I'm still watching Bernhard's and Dieter's email accounts, just in case something pops up, or something from Reggie Wheeler over in Laos.'

'With Farr in the slammer, there's only a slim chance of anything on him.'

'Exactly. But I think a few quiet face-to-face chats in Melbourne might help. Some contacts don't like to be helpful on the phone. Never know who's listening in.'

'Too bloody true,' said Harry.

'Plus there's an Edward Steichen photographic exhibition showing at the National Gallery for a little while, which I'd love to see. So, another reason to visit Melbourne.'

'Sounds lovely,' said Harry. 'Might take us a while to work up an opportunity with Farr. Good job we're patient men.'

'We both know it'll be worth the wait.'

'Yep. Let's head back to mine. Tanya should be coming back from the hospital pretty soon. She said she didn't feel like the pub tonight. Be good to give her some company.'

'Cool. So long as there's plenty of refreshment available.' Trev winked at Harry.

'Mate, seriously, do bears shit in the woods?'

– 8 –

Tanya was sitting by the bed, holding Sasha's hand. Sasha's eyes slowly opened, their blueness adding the only colour to her pale, drawn face.

'Hey, Sis,' said Sasha. 'What day is it?'

'Sunday.' Tanya leaned over and kissed her cheek. 'How you feeling this morning?'

'Pretty tired, and doped, but at least the pain is down a bit.'

'Anything you feel like at the moment?'

'No. Just make sure they keep up the morphine.'

Tanya tried to smile, but a tear ran down her face instead. They looked at each other, saying nothing.

After a couple of minutes, Sasha reached for the glass of water on the other side of the bed and took a mouthful. She put it back down on the table and looked at Tanya. She squeezed Tanya's hand even harder. 'I don't want to die, Sis. It's not my time.'

Tanya's tears flowed. 'It's so, so unfair. There's nothing else the doctors have said that's even slightly hopeful?' Tanya sounded as if she was begging.

Sasha's eyes welled up. 'No. It's just what they said when you were with me yesterday. Might be six months, might be six weeks.'

'Oh, Sash.'

Tanya leaned onto the bed and the twins hugged and cried. After a few minutes, their sobbing subsided and they clung to each other.

A nurse came into the room, greeted Sasha, and introduced herself to Tanya. She changed the IV bag, took Sasha's temperature and blood pressure, and gave her a shot of morphine. She smiled at Sasha and put her hand on her cheek.

'Anything at all, Sasha, just buzz me. I'm on until ten this evening.'

'Thanks, Keira.'

'And the doctor said tomorrow we'll start the morphine drip, which will make it more comfortable for you.'

Sasha nodded weakly.

The nurse left the room.

'Another lovely nurse,' said Tanya.

'They're all really great,' replied Sasha. She looked back at Tanya. 'Sis, I want you to promise me two things.'

'Anything,' said Tanya.

'Number one. Avenge us and kill our arsewipe stepfather.'

'Believe me, that's already in my plans.'

'Thank you.'

There was a moment's silence and Tanya stared into space. Tanya had told Sasha nothing about the ped hunting with the guys, nor that she had actually killed one of them. She had wanted to say something, as she and Sasha shared everything. But Harry had been adamantly against it, given Sasha had had zero involvement. Harry said what she didn't know couldn't possibly be used against her in any way, and that's how things should stay, unless Sasha was to join them in the hunt. Then the cancer came out. That put paid to Sasha doing any PI work, plus Tanya then didn't want to burden her with anything dramatic. No, girl, stick to the script.

She looked back at her sister. 'You said two things?'

'Yeah.' Sasha held Tanya's hand in both of hers. 'I don't want to lie here suffering as it gets worse. When it gets really unbearable, I want you to help me go.'

Tanya stared at her. 'But Sash ...'

'There's no cure and the pain will just get worse.'

'Sis ...'

'Tan, I've thought this through. I'm just lying here waiting to die. At the moment I can manage a conversation with you, but that'll slip away. Then it's only pain and more pain. There'll be absolutely nothing to live for each day.'

'What about the doctors?'

'I've already asked. They're sympathetic, but said it's illegal to help someone die. Which is so completely fucked.'

'Yeah, true. But what can I do?'

Sasha gripped both her hands now. 'Promise me, Tan, please. I can't do this for months.'

'But how?'

'Talk to Harry. Him or Trev will be able to get something.'

Tanya opened her mouth, but was silent.

'Tan, promise me.'

Tanya swallowed hard as her tears started again. 'Okay. Okay, I promise.'

As Sasha drifted off into a morphine-fuelled sleep, Tanya watched her, wondering if life could get any more unfair. She closed her eyes. She saw their dad, in his smart army uniform. He was playing with them under the twin jacaranda trees that last day before he left, never to return. The jacaranda trees he had planted in their back yard the week they were born, to celebrate their arrival.

Then she fast-forwarded and saw their stepfather moving in, the trees being murdered with a chainsaw the same night their innocence was despoiled.

Then she saw the fading image of their dad.

Now Sasha was going, and so horribly. The world was really fucked.

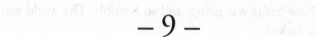

– 9 –

On Monday morning, Trev woke up in his own bed in Darlinghurst. It was a damned sight more comfortable than Harry's couch, his mattress of convenience too many nights of late. He'd even got in a well-overdue gym visit on Sunday afternoon, persuading Harry to join him, although encouraging a fitter lifestyle for Harry was one Herculean work in progress. After an hour of sweating, he'd left Harry to his own devices.

Trev had found, in the first Chinatown shop he visited, as it turned out, a Buddha statuette identical to the incense-burning version in the Steam Engine's Sling Room. He'd bought two, just in case.

After making himself a jug of black coffee, he sat down in his little workshop. The room was tiny and the real estate agent who described it as a second bedroom should have been charged with fraud. However, he didn't need another bedroom, and a workbench fitted in there perfectly. He sat down, put on Pink Floyd, and smiled at the photo of Jean-Louis that overlooked the benchtop. Then he settled into a morning of drilling and soldering. By lunchtime, he had an all-seeing miniature Buddha, ready to observe and record Colin Lodge chock-a-block up some guy in the sling. It'd certainly be one for the family album. He was singing along to 'Us and Them', doing a fair effort at accompanying Roger Waters, as he packed up his work gear and headed for the bathroom.

An hour later, he walked into Harry's office to show off his latest gadgetry.

By late afternoon, the guys were back in the grey van propped not far from the entrance to the Council's car park. Lodge's council limousine was in its allocated undercover car space. In a bogus call to the Council's finance department, Harry had been told that the CFO was in a meeting until 5 p.m., so they'd got in position before then. At a quarter past five, Lodge's Mercedes slid into the street. The van latched on and followed at a discreet distance.

Twenty-five minutes later, they were back in Hornsby Heights watching the Lodge residence. They didn't have to loiter down the street for long before Lodge emerged from his front door in a track-suit, with two poodles straining on their leashes. The dogs and their master turned onto the footpath and headed towards the van, about fifty metres away.

'Shit,' said Trev. 'In the back, quick.' He climbed through the gap between the seats, followed rapidly by Harry. They sat quietly until they heard the yapping increase, and then subside as Lodge passed the van. Through the heavily tinted back windows they watched as Lodge turned the corner.

'Let's follow,' said Harry, and the pair clambered back into the front seats. Trev started the engine and turned the van around.

Harry looked at the GPS screen. 'Mate, there's a large park a couple of streets away. Reckon he might be heading there.'

'Fair chance, let's go see.'

As they slowly turned the first corner, they could see their target approaching the next street. They gave him a couple of minutes' start, then cruised that way themselves. After the next turn, they saw Lodge entering the park a couple of hundred metres away. He bent down, unleashed the poodles that ran like the clappers onto the grass expanse, and took himself over to a bench, facing into the park.

Trev pulled the van over, still well short of the park, but keeping a visual on Lodge. 'Wouldn't mind betting this is his usual early-evening routine. Except steamy Tuesdays, of course. What do you reckon, Harry?'

'Yep, agreed. He probably stays here while the good little wifey is cooking dinner and dealing with the teenagers. Reckon he'd be that sort of bloke,' said Harry.

'Oh, yeah, the good old alpha male. Fucking dinosaurs, that hideous mixture of misogyny and power lust.'

'Brother,' said Harry, 'as we both know, the need for power is the most basic human trait. The driving force for so many people, I've always believed.'

'Yeah, so you've said many times. And I tend to agree. But it gets me that so many women still put up with it,' replied Trev.

'Things are slow to change. Mind you, I've also met quite a few females in senior positions who are just as much power-obsessed fucktards as the men.'

'True, mate, very true. That Porcia Savage from Human Services being a case in point,' said Trev.

'Oh, yeah, there's a sociopathic bitch of the first order. Let's just hope that scheme of Liam's grows some legs. She really needs to be brought down.'

'Hear, hear,' said Trev. 'Anyway, back to the task at hand, mate. If Lodge does come here every arvo, might give us a nice little venue to introduce ourselves, after we've got the salacious footage from the sling chamber.'

'Absolutely. Chance to get him whilst he's away from his loving family.'

An hour later, Lodge stood up from the park bench, whistling the dogs back to him. He put them back on their leashes and walked out of the park.

Harry and Trev hid in the rear of the van again until Lodge had disappeared. Then they headed back to Harry's office in the city.

– 10 –

Late Tuesday afternoon saw Harry and Trev, wrapped in towels again, entering the Sling Room for Trev's first booking of the day. As soon as they had locked the door, they got busy swapping the Buddhas over and putting the incense sticks into the new Buddha's ceramic head.

Feigning a lascivious interest in meeting Lodge, Trev had cajoled the establishment's manager, Jorge, to let on about Lodge's precise booking time. He'd then booked the session times either side for himself and Harry.

Out on the street, Tanya was sitting in the back of the VW van, looking at a MacBook screen. Her phone rang.

'Looking good, Trev. The vision is as clear as crystal.'

'Okay, Tan, press record now, like I showed you, and then leave it running until we return to collect Mr Buddha.'

'Cool. Hey, put me on speaker so Harry can hear.' Tanya could see Trev move over next to Harry. Despite her glum mood, she managed a smile to herself. 'So, boys, who's going in the sling?'

Trev laughed.

Harry shook his head. 'Yeah, very bloody funny.'

'Okay, Tan, we'll see you in about an hour. We'll be in a steam room. Text me when you can see Lodge in action.'

'Will do. Or is that "roger"?'

Trev laughed again. 'Yeah, pay that. And there'll certainly be some rogering in here shortly,' he replied. 'Happy viewing, Tan.'

'Gee, thanks. Not quite the genre of porn I like to watch.'

Harry's ears pricked up. 'We must discuss that one further, babe.'

'We'll see,' she teased.

Trev ended the call. He turned to Harry. 'So, we'll give it about fifteen minutes before we exit here to let the real action begin.'

'Cool. And it'll all be recorded in glorious colour by the Buddha in here, as well as out on the laptop with Tanya. Sensational idea, mate, I do like it.'

'Yeah. Record and transmit. Always best to have both. Bit more tech involved, but I prefer to be on the safe side.'

'I totally agree. I couldn't bear the thought of coming back here next Tuesday.'

'Harry, where's your sense of adventure?' laughed Trev.

Harry looked around the dimly lit room and shook his head.

'Mate, given that I don't imagine there's ever been a lusty woman spreadeagled on that sling, again, my adventurism remains firmly elsewhere.'

'Fair enough. I'm keen to see who comes in here with Lodge. Wondering if he has a particular sort or not.'

'I'd rather not wonder,' said Harry.

Twenty minutes later, they were sitting next to each other on a bench in the otherwise deserted steam room. Trev had an earphone in so he could hear Tanya's running commentary. Harry had the other earpiece, so it looked like a pair of guys sharing music. Trev's phone flashed, and he pressed 'Accept'.

'He just walked in,' said Tanya. 'Got a young Asian guy with him.'

'Ah, seems our friendly CFO is a rice queen,' said Trev quietly to Harry.

'It looks like he's giving the guy money,' continued Tanya.

'I know who that'll be then,' said Trev.

'Really?' said Harry.

'There's a young Korean dude who works the joint for the wealthy older men who are here on the sly leading their double lives. I chatted to him a few weeks ago. He's doing rather well out of it, paying his uni fees and drives a brand-new Nissan Sports. Hey, Tan, has he got shaved side patches under a blonde-tipped hairdo?'

'Sure has.'

'That's him then,' said Trev. 'His nickname here is Kumchi.'

'I don't even want to think about how he earned that one,' said Harry under his breath.

'He's dropped his towel and they're fondling each other, kissing,' said Tanya. 'Now Lodge is pushing him over a chair. Ouch! Lodge is spanking the hell out of him.'

'Sounds like Lodge is the dominant here,' said Trev.

'That's stopped. Kumchi's now having a sniff of something, must be the amyl.'

'Will be,' said Trev.

'Now he's climbing onto the sling. Lodge has dropped his towel and he's turning around. Fuck me!' exclaimed Tanya.

'What?' asked Trev, somewhat startled.

'You should see Lodge. He's hung like a fucking donkey. No wonder Kumchi's on the amyl, he's going to need all the loosening up he can get.'

'Thanks for that,' said Harry.

Tanya heard him. 'Mr PI, you're just jealous. He's got about three inches on you, plus girth.'

Harry defaulted to male defensiveness of all things personally penile. 'Yeah, fine, whatever. With my tongue work I don't need the extra size, and you should know that.'

'Oh, I'm not complaining, Mr PI. Believe me I'm not. But this guy is seriously hung. Oh, he's rubbered and lubed and … in he goes. There's a lot of groaning. You should see Kumchi's face, looks as though his eyes are about to pop out.'

Ten minutes later, it was all done. Tanya had given live commentary of Lodge climaxing and giving Kumchi a handjob. Then Lodge left the Sling Room.

Harry and Trev, the Buddhas swapped back, climbed into the back of the van. Tanya was still reeling from the vision of Lodge's endowment.

'So we have a great film for the Lodge family?' asked Trev. 'Something to put on after Sunday lunch?'

Tanya giggled. 'You bet. But that young man won't be walking properly for a week. Seriously, that beast of a thing. I would *not* want that up my arse, no matter how much money was involved.'

'Babe, somehow I don't think our friend Lodge would be remotely interested in your arse, as magnificent as it is.'

'Phew,' said Tanya, smiling at Harry.

The three of them watched a replay of the CFO and the Korean rent boy's sling soirée.

'I think that will do the job perfectly,' said Trev, closing the laptop.

'Yep, priceless,' added Harry. 'Can't wait to meet the man and have a little chat.'

'You won't need me for that, will you?' asked Tanya. 'I want to go back to the hospital, be with Sash.'

'That's all good, babe,' said Harry. 'Thank you so much for taking the time away from Sash to help us out, we needed you.'

'No worries. Getting away for a little while has been good. It's a headfuck sitting in that hospital the whole time.'

Harry gave her a hug. 'Hang tough, babe.'

Trev put a hand on her shoulder.

Harry continued. 'We'll deal with Lodge tomorrow when he's out for his dog walking. And we'll come for a visit with Sasha before that.'

'Cool, thanks,' said Tanya.

'I think we've earned a drink,' said Trev.

'After what you've put me through, mate, you're buying,' said Harry. 'To the Emerald Bar, chariot driver.'

— 11 —

Harry and Trev were cruising towards Hornsby Heights in the grey van on late Wednesday afternoon, aiming for an introduction to Colin Lodge. Despite their enthusiasm for the task at hand, and the usual pre-operation copper adrenalin surge, the pair were subdued, smoking in near silence. They'd spent an hour at the hospital with Sasha and Tanya. They'd got a hint of a smile from Sasha courtesy of a large bunch of tulips and daffodils, two of her favourites. And the flowers had certainly brightened up the hospital room.

'I can't believe how pale and drawn she looks already,' said Harry.

'Fucking cruel disease, mate. And it's advancing on her so quickly.'

'Tell you, mate, if one of those religious types came along now and gave me some drivel about everything having some loftier purpose, I would literally beat them to death with my bare hands.'

'You'd have a ready accomplice. Purpose, my arse,' said Trev. He blasted the horn at a P-plate driver who'd cut in front of them.

'Even without all the shit those twins have had to put up with in their lives, it's just so bloody wrong,' said Harry.

'Yep. I could nominate a few oxygen-stealing maggots to swap places with Sasha.'

'I might have a longer list.'

And as a distraction from their glumness, they spent the remainder of the drive north competing to list the most death-deserving arseholes they'd come across during their lives. By the time they got to the dog-walking park, they'd both lost count and called it a draw.

Trev parked the van by the kerb, close to the park bench on which they'd observed Lodge sitting on Monday afternoon whilst his poodles frolicked.

Harry turned up the music, ELO as usual, to fill the void as they waited. He'd picked the album *Out of the Blue* for a little ironic touch. Trev had suggested that *Discovery*, *Secret Messages* or *Face the Music* could all be equally apt, but Harry wanted the double album. And he reckoned Trev's third choice would be better as background music if Mrs Lodge ever happened to see the video from the Sling Room. Trev conceded that point.

Colin Lodge was a contented man as he strolled along Galston Road to the dog-friendly Rofe Park. The poodles were straining on their leashes, at least as much as poodles could strain. The late sun and warm breeze had turned a great day into a sublime evening.

All in all it had been a bloody good week so far. On Monday his wife had announced she'd decided to take the kids away to visit her parents at the beginning of the school holidays, meaning free rein for his libido for a fortnight. Then yesterday evening he'd had one of the best shags in recent memory – note to self, more petite Asian men on the menu. And today he'd pulled off a masterful accounting subterfuge to hide half a million dollars of hush-hush expenditure from two nosey bloody councillors. The CEO had been so impressed he'd signed off on an ex-gratia bonus of $10,000 on the spot. Ah, yes, life was truly beautiful.

He got to the park, unleashed his beasts, and ambled over to the bench, plonking himself down in the middle, and relaxing in the sunset. His eyelids lowered and his thoughts drifted to the spreadeagled Kumchi as he slammed him on the sling last night. Life was even better than beautiful: it was nigh on perfect.

'Hello, arsehole.'

A deep voice broke Lodge's dreaming. His eyes opened in a panic and he immediately realized two men were sitting either side of him on the bench. He made a slight involuntary movement as if to get up.

'If you even think about moving, I'm going to fucking hurt you,' said the stocky one to his left, slapping his thigh.

'We need to talk, matey,' said the other one.

Lodge looked at them, back and forth. This didn't happen in his world, his civilized realm of spreadsheets and ledgers. These two aggressive strangers, encroaching menacingly into his personal space, were scaring him shitless. Why hadn't he chosen Rottweilers rather than poodles?

His mind tried to scramble past his fear to find clear ground to figure out a defence against these guys.

All he could muster was, 'What do you want?'

Trev and Harry were both grinning.

Trev leant into Lodge. 'Like I said, we need to talk.'

'Yes, you've been a very bad boy, Colin Lodge,' said Harry.

Lodge started at the sound of his own name. 'Leave me alone, please. I need to get home,' he said. He made to move.

Harry moved in closer, gripping Lodge's thigh firmly. Lodge winced in pain. 'I will really fucking hurt you, Colin. You want that?' Harry dug his fingers harder into the soft inside of Lodge's thigh.

'No, please, no.'

'Okay, so shut up, sit still, and listen,' grated Harry. He released his grip on Lodge's leg.

'Lead an interesting life, don't you, Colin?' said Trev.

'Respectable government CFO, then good family man with the nice house in the 'burbs, with the lovely wife and two kids, then rampant arse-fucker in a gay sauna,' added Harry.

Trev activated his iPad.

Lodge looked at the screen with an expression of horror.

'That young Korean dude looks like you're about to split him open,' said Trev. 'Mate, you certainly got more than your fair share when the schlongs were handed out, didn't you?'

Lodge, mouth agape, watched himself ramming his massive member into Kumchi on the sling.

Harry opened another iPad. Up came a photo of Mrs Lodge and children in the driveway of the Lodge residence. 'Wonder what your good, wholesome family will think after they've watched you fucking your little Korean friend?' asked Harry.

Lodge looked as if he was going to throw up.

Harry brought up more photos of the Lodge children. 'Nice-looking kids, Colin. Wonder how they'll go at school when the other kids see you and your lover boy on the Internet?'

'No … please …' stammered Lodge, all colour now emptied from his face.

'So, Colin *mate*, today is one of those life-changing days,' said Trev. He closed off the video, putting an end to the gasping noises emanating from Kumchi and the blissful grunting of Lodge. 'Keep looking at my screen, Colin,' he said, flicking through photos of the Council collection of German luxury cars and then the car dealership, Palace Motors.

'I don't understand,' whimpered Lodge.

'Yep, there's no immediately apparent connection, is there?' said Trev.

Lodge said nothing.

'Let's think outside the square,' said Harry.

Trev laughed. 'I think our mate Colin here is pretty good "outside the square".'

Harry chuckled. 'Yeah, should be easy for him.' Harry slapped Lodge's thigh again. 'Colin, we know there's a scam going on with the luxury cars at Council.'

'I don't know anything ...'

'Uh, uh. Don't start playing silly buggers, excuse the pun,' said Trev. He opened up his email. 'Silly buggers end up with the video being emailed to their wife, right now.'

Lodge looked on like a stunned mullet as Trev typed Mary Lodge's email address into the recipient line on a blank email.

'No, no, no ...'

'Okay then, Colin, matey! Start telling us about the scam.'

Lodge hesitated.

Trev attached the video file to the draft email. His finger hovered over the send button, as the file loaded. Lodge made a slight choking noise.

'Okay, I'll tell you,' he whined.

Harry pulled a digital voice recorder out of his pocket and activated it.

Lodge spent the next ten minutes detailing exactly how the council scam worked, all the while nervously watching Trev's finger over the email screen.

The rort was quite basic, albeit outrageously brazen. Council's car policy did allow for any make of car, but the value had to be below $50,000, which certainly counted out the higher-end German autos. The CEO and CFO had persuaded the owner of the local major car showroom, Des Shine, to get on board with them. His dealership, Palace Motors, was traditionally the supplier for the Council's vehicle fleet. Shine's role was to fictionalize the vehicle values, so even $200,000 cars were supplied at $49,000. That was on paper, at least, and the car model numbers were altered to indicate a much cheaper version. So, all looked hunky dory, with Shine selling a heap of expensive models, rotated on a regular basis, raking in a fortune from the Council. And the Council's fat cats motored around in luxury cars that their ratepayers couldn't even envisage in a rev-head's wet dream.

Lodge paused for breath. He looked at Harry's voice recorder.

'That seems pretty simple, Colin,' said Harry.

'It is straightforward, but it works,' replied the downcast CFO.

Trev joined in. 'But how does Palace Motors get any extra benefit out of this, apart from selling the expensive cars?'

Lodge continued with his tale. Shine's pay-off for his collusion was exquisite in its simplicity. Council had a disused depot warehouse. Every three months, Palace Motors would deliver 100 brand-new vehicles for storage. Three months later, they'd be replaced by another batch. The existing 100 units would be sold off from the dealership. On the face of it, there didn't seem much point. Council officially bought the cars, although didn't actually pay for them, and then, on paper, sold them back to Shine. The car dealer got the usual retail price for them, when they were eventually sold to real customers. The true benefit to Des Shine, however, was the value of orders from the manufacturers. The extra 400 units a year meant he got a healthy discount on the wholesale price of all the cars that went through the dealership. Annually, it represented over a million dollars in extra net profit for Des Shine, and all in his own personal pocket.

'There you have it. It's a win-win,' said Lodge, trying not to sound, in his circumstances, proud of the scam that he'd designed.

'So, those poor schmucks, the ratepayers of Perfect Plains, are paying hundreds of thousands of dollars from their rates for you wankers to cruise around like rich aristocrats. It's not a fucking win for them, is it?' hissed Trev.

'No,' murmured Lodge.

Harry stopped the recorder. He turned to look at Lodge, who was staring at his lap. 'You bunch of greedy cunts.'

'Cunts, indeed,' added Trev. 'And now this cunt is ours. You're working for us now, Colin, *mate*.' It was Trev's turn to slap Lodge's other thigh.

'I've told you everything. What else do I have to do?' asked Lodge, still staring down at his lap.

'Colin, that was just the entrée, so to speak. We've got main course and dessert to go yet,' said Trev.

'And all the while, Colin, you're going to be hoping your wife and kids don't get to see you chock-a-block up Kumchi's arse,' added Harry.

Lodge started to sob. 'No ... please ...'

'So, Colin, this is what's going to happen next,' continued Harry. 'You're going to man up, and have a meeting with your CEO to discuss the whole car arrangement. You'll be wired for sound, naturally. After that, you'll do a phone hook-up, again recorded, to Des Shine and get him talking. Then, my friend, you are going to become the white knight with a conscience and volunteer yourself to ICAC to roll over on all this heinous corruption that you just can't live with any more.'

'But ... but ... I could go to prison,' snivelled Lodge.

'Possible,' said Trev. 'But there are two incentives for you here, Colin.' He slapped his thigh again and gripped it hard. Lodge whimpered.

'First, and most important, of course, is that your good wife and lovely innocent kids don't need to see Daddy doing Asian anal. Second, this *will* get to ICAC one way or another. And if you get in there at the outset, the first deserting rat, so to speak, you'll get the benefits of being the roll-over man. All that credit for helping ICAC to uncover this sordid corruption.'

'And that, mate,' added Harry gripping Lodge's other leg, 'is your best bet, and we know you're a betting man, of minimizing the penalty for yourself. Perhaps even avoiding prison altogether.'

Lodge looked from one to the other, desperately.

'Do you think ...' Lodge coughed as he tried to clear his throat. 'Do you think I can avoid going to jail? If I tell everything?'

Trev smiled at him. 'Colin, mate, you need to start doing everything you can to look after number one. Because if you go to prison, you are in for a rather different sex life to either of the ones you've enjoyed to date.'

'Oh, yes,' said Harry. 'You'll have a huge, sweaty, tattooed cell-mate who'll take to calling you Colleen, and make you play mummy bear, with just some spit for lube. And then before you know it, you'll be getting passed around the cellblock as slutty mummy bear who just can't get enough daddy bear cock. And you'll never walk quite the same again.'

Lodge started sobbing audibly.

'So, Colin, you're working for us, yes?' said Trev.

Lodge nodded miserably.

'Can't hear you,' said Harry.

'Yes,' whispered Lodge.

'Good man,' said Trev. 'You really don't want to meet your mystery cell-mate. So, let's discuss how tomorrow is going to go down at Council. You listening?'

'Yes,' said Lodge. He pulled out a hankie and blew his nose wetly and loudly.

Trev and Harry proceeded to set down the events for the next day.

– 12 –

Colin Lodge was sitting in his office on Thursday morning feeling decidedly sick. He'd spoken to the CEO's executive assistant and made an appointment to see Van Dijk. It was in an hour's time and Lodge wondered – hoped, in a way – if he would have a heart attack beforehand.

How had it come to this? And all in less than twenty-four hours. This time yesterday he'd been relaxing in this very office, contemplating a new car, a fat bonus, and an overseas holiday. Not to mention savouring the memory of rooting Kumchi the previous evening with promises for next Tuesday to boot. Now, his life had unravelled, spectacularly.

How? Why? He felt as if he was going to burst out crying. He was supposed to meet with the investigator men to get wired up for the CEO meeting, but he sat immobile, rendered useless by a fug of disbelief and depression.

He didn't get to ponder for long. His mobile phone rang. He looked at it, wanting to ignore it, but it kept ringing, 'No Caller ID' displayed on the screen. He was still vacillating when the ringing stopped. There was a ping as an SMS arrived.

Pick up the phone Lodge NOW!

He started to shake. The phone rang again. He pressed 'Accept'.

'Don't start playing games, Colin,' said Harry. 'When we ring, you answer. Got it?'

'Yes,' he replied, close to tears.

'Now, get your arse out to the van. We're in the public car park around the first corner. Know it?'

'Yes.'

'If you're not here in five minutes, there's going to be trouble: family trouble in the Lodge household.'

'No, please. I'm on my way now.'

Lodge composed himself, exited his office and went down the corridor to a little-used side entrance to the Council building. Three minutes later he was in the back of the VW van.

'Cardigan and shirt off, Colin,' commanded Trev.

'But …'

Harry leant in close to Lodge's face. 'Listen, fuckstain, I've had just about a gutful of your umming and ahing. Weren't hesitating when you were ramming Kumchi the other night, were you? Now, cut the crap and do as you're fucking well told.'

Lodge said nothing, and stripped off the top half of his clothing.

Within ten minutes, Trev had taped Lodge's pale and flabby torso with not one but two record-and-transmit devices, plus a battery pack, and had tested them. As Lodge put his shirt and cardigan back on, Trev carefully arranged the wires and tiny microphones to sit inconspicuously around Lodge's chest.

'There you are, Colin, mate. Wired for glorious stereo. And we can track these babies, Colin, so don't deviate from the plan.'

'Got it?' growled Harry.

'Yes, yes, I'll do it.'

'Damned right you will, or the lovely Mrs Lodge will be finding out who she's sharing your dick with. And I don't think she'd be the sharing type in that way, do you?'

Lodge didn't tell them he hadn't had sex with his wife since the second kid had been born.

Harry didn't let on that during one of their snooping sessions whilst Lodge was at work, they'd seen the local lawn-mowing contractor stop in for more than a mere cuppa with Mrs Lodge. In fact, peeking in the bedroom window, Harry had considered Mrs Lodge's lawn to be immaculately trimmed indeed, until the gardener plunging between her parted thighs had obscured his view.

And Trev didn't disclose that the tracking was a bit of a lie. They'd gone one better than that: one of the microphones was a miniature fibre-optic camera lens. As he deftly threaded the fibre-optic through the shirt fabric and into a button, Trev smiled to himself at the poetic efficiency of re-using the pussycam gear from the harbour job back in August.

Trev slapped Lodge lightly on the shoulder. 'Righto, Colin, into battle my son. Off you go. Do exactly what we agreed, and then back here as soon as the meeting is done. All clear?'

Lodge nodded insipidly.

'All fucking clear?' grated Harry.

'Yes, yes.' And with that he got out of the van looking like a defeated man. With his head down and shoulders sagging, he started walking slowly back to his office.

Trev got into the driver's seat and started the engine.

'We moving?' asked Harry.

'Yeah. This bastard's as weak as piss, so we need to be able to watch him all the way into the building, and keep an eye on his car.'

'Sounds reasonable.' Harry climbed into the passenger seat and the van moved off as Lodge went around the corner. Trev pulled the van up with a clear visual of the side of the building just as Lodge was approaching the door.

Lodge slowed down and then stopped, looking at the door. He suddenly turned on his heels and walked back out into the street. He looked lost as he wandered down the pavement.

Harry climbed into the back of the van and prepared to open the side door.

'I'll just reverse a bit so we're out of line of sight,' said Trev.

Lodge, in a daze, walked closer without seeming to notice them. As he got alongside, Harry slid the door open.

'Colin, get the fuck in here,' he hissed.

Lodge jumped. There was no fight in his eyes. He stepped docilely into the van, the door closing behind him.

'What the fuck?' asked Trev.

'I ... I ... I lost my nerve.'

'Well, let's give you a little tonic then, dipshit,' said Harry menacingly.

He grabbed his phone and tapped a number.

'Hey, babe. We need Plan B.'

'On it, Harry,' replied Tanya.

'Watch the screen, Colin.'

Harry held the iPhone so Lodge could see the screen clearly. It showed a suburban street, then jerky movement as Tanya started walking. The Lodge residence in Hornsby Heights came into view.

'And we know from our agent there, the one doing the camera-work at your place, that your good wife is at home.'

'No … please,' begged Lodge.

'Tan, just walk straight on up and knock. Show Mrs Lodge the footage on your iPad, and leave her the version on the USB. Then walk away. Got it?'

'Sure do, Mr PI.'

'No! Stop her, please,' Lodge wailed.

'So, you've got work to do, Colin,' said Trev.

'Otherwise it's all over red rover,' added Harry, sliding the van door open again. 'Now get your greasy, corrupt little arse back out there and do the job. And stop fucking blubbing. It's pathetic.'

Lodge blew his nose into a hankie and got out of the van.

'Okay, Tan,' said Harry into his phone. 'We're back on track so don't go knocking just yet.'

This time Lodge headed straight, albeit slowly, into the Council building.

Lodge walked into the CEO's office bang on his allotted time. He looked composed, but he felt as if he was going to vomit.

Van Dijk motioned to the empty seat in front of the grand desk. The Council's lawyer, Judith Albion, and the HR manager, Agnes Stoul, occupied the other two chairs.

'Just have some other business running over, Colin, so bear with us,' said Van Dijk, in his usual abrupt way.

'No problems, boss.'

Lodge sat down as Albion and Stoul sold the CEO on yet another scheme to sack staff through the pretence of an efficiency restructure. The Council certainly didn't need to shed staff: it was flush with money. But Lodge knew that Stoul and Albion got off on the sport of screwing underlings over, and they were so practised in their sycophancy to the CEO that Van Dijk always gave them the go-ahead. It wasn't for nothing that the corporate power trio were known by the staff as 'the dick with two cunts'.

They finished their chatter, victims marked for redundancy, and Van Dijk turned to Lodge. 'You all right, Colin? You look a bit sweaty there, my friend.'

'Yes, I'm fine, boss. Just feeling the humidity a bit.'

'Now, what was it you needed to see me about?'

Albion and Stoul got up to leave.

'Well, boss, it's about the car arrangement.' Lodge paused. 'We may have a problem.'

Albion and Stoul both promptly sat back down.

'How so?' Van Dijk's eyes narrowed and he leant over his desk.

Lodge scrabbled to remember all the script he had been given. 'Shine is asking for more. He wants us to double our phantom fleet order.'

'The greedy bastard,' said Van Dijk. 'He does very nicely out of the arrangement as it stands, and so do we. It's the best win-win I've enjoyed in many years. I hope you put him in his place.'

'Yes, I wouldn't want to miss out on the next Audi release,' added Albion, with a hyena-like cackle.

'Me, neither,' echoed Stoul, doing her best to imitate Albion's laugh.

Van Dijk held up his hand to silence them.

Lodge cleared his throat. 'Well, I did tell him he was on a bloody good deal, and that there was no need to rock the boat and maybe raise eyebrows.'

'So, what exactly are the figures for what this greedy wanker wants, Colin?'

And they proceeded to dissect the scam in explicit detail.

For Harry and Trev listening and watching in the van outside, it was like a bunch of conspirators filling in a spreadsheet entitled 'A Dummy's Guide to Corruption'.

'Bloody perfect,' said Harry.

'Yep. Now we'll just get Lodge back here and he can make a call to Shine telling him the council scum want to get greedier on the deal, getting his side of it, and the package is complete,' replied Trev.

Harry was smiling as he pointed at the computer. 'Outstanding, mate.'

'They're certainly not shy about blabbing, are they?' said Trev.

'That's arrogance, mate. Seen it plenty of times with these politicians and bureaucrat fat cats. They think they're entitled, better than the rest of us, and entirely untouchable. This particular bunch of wankers are about to find out different.'

– 13 –

Harry pressed 'Call' on his iPhone. It connected. 'So, Colin, how did it go?'

Ten minutes had passed since they'd heard and seen Lodge leaving the CEO's office, with all the trough-feeders creaming themselves over their car choices.

'We talked a lot, a real lot, and I did exactly as you said, I promise.'

'I really bloody hope so, Colin, or it's going to be big trouble in Hornsby Heights this evening. See you in an hour, as planned.'

They neglected to tell Lodge they had been listening live as well as recording the meeting, but Harry enjoyed his sport.

So, too, it seemed did Mrs Lodge.

Tanya had not been able to resist the temptation to sneak down the side of the Lodge residence upon hearing loud, carnal noises coming from the house.

When she peered into the bedroom window, she saw the two tradesmen she'd observed going into the house about an hour earlier. They were now butt naked and spit-roasting the groaning Mrs Lodge on all fours.

'Wild little minx!' exclaimed Harry when Tanya called him.

'It's these housewives who get bored, feel neglected, and need some action,' said Trev. 'I certainly had some offers when I was in GDs out in the suburbs. Not that it was my thing, of course. And there never seemed to be any bored men at home, damn it.'

Harry laughed. 'Yeah, so did I as a young uniformed copper.' He grinned at Trev. 'And a couple of times it was my thing. Made for an excellent shift at work.'

Trev laughed. 'You rascal.'

An hour later, the VW van was parked next to the dog park at Hornsby Heights. Lodge's council Mercedes pulled in slowly behind the van, and Harry watched through the rear windows as Lodge trudged towards them, head down and looking like a dead man walking.

Harry slid open the side door and Lodge stepped in. Trev joined them in the back.

'Wasn't that hard, was it, Colin, mate?' said Harry, slapping the stricken CFO on the shoulder.

'Yeah, a bit of ethical cleansing, so good for the soul, Colin,' added Trev, motioning Lodge to sit on a stool.

Lodge started tearing up. 'My life's over,' he whined.

'Well, matey, you can either change your life by our plan, or you can let us throw you to the wolves. And don't forget the mummy bear scenario,' said Harry, throwing in a bit of pelvic thrusting for effect.

'And the lovely Lodge family getting to see Daddy enjoying some Asian arse,' added Trev.

'So really, Colin, we're offering a much, much better deal. You've already done the hardest bit back at the Council today.'

'Right,' he stammered. 'Now, I've got to phone Des Shine?'

'Absolutely,' replied Trev. 'Then we'll take you into ICAC so you can spill your guts to them.'

'Making quite clear to them that you want maximum credit, even immunity, in return for rolling over,' added Harry.

'You … you think they'll give me immunity?' asked Lodge, looking as desperate as an alcoholic on Good Friday.

'I reckon you've got a good chance. They'll want to see the evidence first, but if you're prepared to do the roll-over for them, and bring all the others down, you might just save yourself.'

Trev handed Lodge an iPhone. 'Number's ready to go and it's on speaker so we'll record it.' Trev held a digital recorder near Lodge's face.

'Call him, Colin, and remember the script,' said Harry firmly.

Lodge swallowed and coughed. 'Have you got some water, please?'

'No worries.' Harry passed him a plastic bottle.

Lodge took a mouthful. 'Thank you.' He picked up the iPhone again and pressed the green button.

'Palace Motors. How can we help you?' said a far-too-chirpy female voice.

'Mr Shine, please.'

'Who can I say is calling?'

'Colin Lodge from Perfect Plains Council.'

'No problems, Mr Lodge. Putting you through right now.'

There was a slight pause.

'Colin, you old bastard, how's it hanging?' said a deep, syrupy voice, pitch-perfect for a car salesman, and with a broad Australian accent.

'Not bad, Des, not bad, thanks. Mate, we need to talk some more details on the deal. The CEO is wanting a couple of special favours, and we can increase your phantom fleet in return.'

'Colin, I'm all ears, as the fucking Easter bunny said. Let's talk the figures, mate. It's all in the figures.' There was a whistle. 'Talking of figures, fuck me drunk, will you look at that. My new receptionist, Colin, body like the hottest Kardashian and badly in need of my cock. She just doesn't know it yet. Fucking sensational. Now, Colin, where were we? Some new arrangement, was it?'

'A new deal the CEO is proposing.'

'Ah, yes, hit me with it.'

They discussed the proposal that Van Dijk supposedly wanted, encompassing the figures from the current scam and venturing into the new arrangement, plotted out by Harry and Trev.

Nearly ten minutes later, with the sleuths barely able to contain their smiles, the revelations were complete and recorded for posterity.

'Okay, thanks, Des. I'll be back in touch early next week to finalize the payments and the new vehicles.'

'Sweet. Always a pleasure doing business with my favourite council, Colin. Give my regards to Johann and tell him I want a day out fishing on that monster fucking boat of his very soon.'

'Sure, Des, I'll let him know.'

'Okay, see you, Colin. Must fly. I've got a young girlie to go and sexually harass.' Shine's boorish laughter reverberated down the line. Then he hung up.

Lodge handed the phone to Trev.

Harry patted Lodge on the shoulder. 'Colin, that was worthy of an Oscar.'

'Brilliant, Colin, red-hot brilliant,' said Trev. 'Now we'll copy everything onto USBs and give you a lift into ICAC.'

In contrast to the grins of the two sleuths, Colin started blubbing again. 'What am I going to tell my wife?'

'Perhaps you can embellish your sudden surge of honesty. Pretend it was your idea to run off to ICAC and roll over,' said Trev.

'But I'd leave out the soirées at the sauna, mate. She might deal with the corruption: you know, you wanted some extra money for the family, all that, but she sure as hell won't cop your anal games at the Steam Engine.' Harry winked at him.

'Yeah, looking at the lovely Mrs Lodge, I don't reckon she'd like anal at all,' said Trev.

Just then Tanya pulled up in her hire-car and parked in front of the van. She joined them inside.

'Hey, babe, all good?'

'Oh, yes, Harry.' She was smiling, a rare sight in recent days.

'Colin, this is a team member. She's rather familiar with your house,' said Harry.

Lodge buried his face in his hands, still blubbing. Tanya signalled to the two guys to gather around her iPad. She pressed play and turned the volume down. She'd filmed a short clip at the Lodge residence as Mrs Lodge was getting serviced by her tradesmen.

'Yeah, that is one good spit-roasting,' murmured Harry, as they watched two large penises sliding in and out of Mrs Lodge's pussy and mouth. Then there were faint voices as the tradies exchanged words and both withdrew from the wanton Mrs Lodge, who started to protest. But it was only temporary as one of the men grabbed a tube of lube. Then one lay on his back and, holding Mrs Lodge by her hips, manoeuvred her onto his cock.

'They are big boys,' said Tanya.

'I reckon we're about to get the classic Malachi Crunch,' said Harry. He looked over at Lodge, who was still head down blubbing.

Then the second tradie, having smeared himself and the fair lady with lube, came in behind her and slowly drove his cock into her arse. As Mrs Lodge's groaning threatened to shatter the bedroom window, Tanya quickly muted the volume. The clip finished a few seconds later when Tanya decided she'd risked being at the window long enough. However, in that closing scene, enough was clearly not what Mrs Lodge had had.

Trev looked at Harry and whispered, 'First drink's on me, I was wrong about the anal.'

'And how,' grinned Harry. He turned to look at Tanya. 'Naughty, babe, and risky. But totally priceless.'

'All right, time to rock and roll,' said Trev. 'Chop-chop, Colin, snap out of it.'

He looked back to Tanya. 'Ms Porno Sleuth, we'll see you back at the office. You good with where to park the car?'

'Yep, see you there.' She kissed both of them and hopped out of the van.

Harry turned to Lodge. 'Colin, anything valuable in your car?'

'No, I've got my wallet and phone here,' he sniffed.

'Good,' said Trev, climbing into the driver's seat. 'ICAC, here we come.'

An hour and a quarter later, a shaking Lodge was let out of the van on Elizabeth Street in the city. The PIs drew away slowly from the kerb, still watching Lodge.

'Not much resistance, was there?' said Trev. 'Thought we might get a bit more of a fight.'

'No, complete soft cock, that one,' said Harry. 'In my experience, most of the corrupt ones are as weak as piss when the chips are down.'

Trev chuckled. 'Yeah, and how fast they are to shaft their mates if it's going to suit them.'

'Brother, these wankers lead their whole lives like that. Can't even spell loyalty.'

'Yeah, fuck them. I don't have many friends, but at least mine are genuine.'

'And,' said Harry, smiling, 'genuine mates buy each other drinks. So, let's go, brother. A watering hole awaits us.'

'Roger that.'

They accelerated down the street.

Lodge had been told exactly what to do, and had been reminded about the video of the Sling Room. He walked straight into the ICAC building. He had two USBs, although he didn't know exactly what was on them. He got through the security door and walked up to two special constables standing at the reception desk. He didn't know if he felt more like pissing, shitting or vomiting.

'Can I help you?' asked one of the officers.

Lodge paused.

'I said, can I help you?' repeated the officer, his eyes narrowing. The other one discreetly moved his hand to his holster.

'I want to hand myself in … in for corruption. I'm with a council. But I want to cut a deal. Please?'

The two constables looked at each other with 'Here's another whack job' expressions.

'Okay, sir, come into the room here and we'll get someone to speak to you.'

And so Colin Lodge, escorted by an armed constable, walked into the next chapter of his sordid life.

– 14 –

More than two weeks had passed since Harry and Trev left Colin Lodge to his life-changing introduction to the ICAC. They'd called him a couple of days later to remind him to stick to the plan or else Mrs Lodge would be getting a visit. Harry and Trev had privately joked about Mrs Lodge not being short of a visit or two, but they didn't share that with Mr Lodge. The latter had been fairly tight-lipped due to the corruption investigators putting the fear of God into him about confidentiality, but he had revealed to the sleuths that he had been granted immunity from prosecution in return for his full cooperation. Now they were simply waiting for the case to explode into the public arena.

They'd hit a hiatus in their detective activities after their work on the luxury car fraud, with no new clients charging through the door and no developments in relation to the peds Harry was hunting. Trev had taken a few days R and R in Melbourne, during which he was also sniffing around old police associates for any intel he could get on Herbert Farr.

Harry wasn't too worried about the client side of things, as recent jobs had left him with a healthy bank balance. But he was itching to pursue Farr. Still, he thought, nothing for it but to be patient. Figuring a way to get Farr from prison was an involved matter, and rushing the hunt at this tricky stage could potentially lead to mistakes. And on this quest for justice, errors were not on the allowable list.

Tanya was at the hospital as often as she could be, which, given the quiet patch at work with Harry, was most of the time.

Harry had been catching up on reading and movies. As today was Monday, lying on the couch for the afternoon watching a couple of his favourite films felt spectacularly decadent. His second movie was one of his frequent choices, Chabrol's *Les Innocents aux Mains Sales*. He had been savouring the scene, replaying it twice, in which the delectable Romy Schneider was sunbathing butt naked. Well, almost naked: she was wearing sunglasses. The intercom went. Harry frowned. He certainly wasn't expecting anyone. He hauled his sarong-clad body off the couch and picked up the intercom.

'Hello.'

'Is that Mr Kenmare who reputedly eats pussy better than a dozen lesbians?' enquired a teasing English female voice.

Harry laughed. 'My English rose, it feels like months. Come on up. And, for the record, it's two dozen lesbians, of the cannibal variety.'

'I'm coming,' she replied saucily, and Harry clicked the switch to open the main lobby door. He thought about throwing on shorts and a T-shirt, but then considered they would, hopefully, be coming off again imminently, so he didn't bother.

A minute later, Tessa walked into his apartment, radiating class, sex appeal, and expensive perfume, the floral notes of Poison wafting over Harry. She kissed him, wetly, then stood back and looked at him. 'You've lost weight, Harry.'

'Yep. Believe it or not, I've been getting into the gym.'

She grinned. 'Tanya's or Trev's influence?'

Harry tried to look indignant. 'Maybe it's my idea.'

'Nice try, handsome, but I wasn't born yesterday. Whose influence?'

Harry grinned. 'Okay, both, but mainly Trev.'

'Good on him.'

'Yeah, I'm not the most enthusiastic gym buddy, that's for sure.'

'Keep it up, handsome, the fitter you are, the better I get it in bed.'

Harry grinned. 'And I've been cutting down on the grog.'

'Bloody hell, you're not giving it up, are you?' She looked horrified.

Harry's grimace made it clear he was equally perturbed by the suggestion. 'Fuck no, I'd rather be dead than teetotal,' he replied.

She ran her index finger down through his chest hair. Harry's loins moved into second gear.

'Successful trip?' he asked.

'Very, but exhausting. I get so sick of living out of a suitcase, and it was about eight weeks.'

'Seemed longer. Mind you, it was June, I think, when we last caught up. And I mean properly caught up.'

'Yep,' she smiled. 'I remember it well.'

'I was wondering when you'd be back.'

'Flew in this morning. First priority was to spend some time at the hospital with Sash and Tan. I still can't quite believe it. I just cried when I saw her.'

Harry winced. 'Yeah, she's going downhill pretty fast. Bastard disease. So bloody unfair.'

'Yeah.' Tessa looked around. 'So what's this lazing around on a Monday afternoon?'

'We've just wrapped up a particularly successful investigation, so taking it a bit easy. Plus I need to take my mind off Sasha when I can.'

'And what's Trev up to?'

'He's been taking a few days down in Melbourne. He's back this afternoon.'

'Nice.' She wiped a tear away from her eye. 'Yeah, after seeing Sash today, I can see why one needs to seek out a distraction. It's still such a shock. Before I left she was fine, and now she's …'

Harry put his arms around Tessa and hugged her. 'Can I get you a drink?'

'No, just distract me.' She looked up into his eyes. 'Perhaps something so shatteringly alive that it pushes the sadness away.'

'Well, Philip Roth did say something about "never feeling so alive as when we fuck". Can I get you in the mood?'

'Mmm, yeah. Probably do us both good, wouldn't it?'

'Yes, ma'am. Some oblivion through steamy passion before we need to come back to reality.'

'Reality's overrated, but you know that already. And I've been severely under-serviced on the male-action front. Two months travelling on business with only a dildo for company.' She grinned. 'Mind you, I had to change the batteries twice.'

Harry raised his eyebrows. 'So, not even one gentleman to be found? I'm surprised. Millions of men would crawl over a field of barbed wire just to suck your toes.'

'You're too kind.' She kissed him, sliding her tongue in. 'Too much work, and I'm too fussy. One of my very few lazy evenings, I did get talking to a guy in the hotel bar in Hong Kong. Younger than me and buffed. He looked rather appetizing.'

'And?'

'And then he let slip that he thought eating pussy was unhygienic.'

Harry smiled. 'Crashed and burned then?'

'Shit yes. I finished my drink and walked. Men who won't eat pussy aren't worth feeding. Better off with a girlfriend and two vibrators. I'll take a battery-assisted sixty-niner with a chick over a man like that anytime.'

'Now that image does it for me,' grinned Harry.

She pushed him into the bedroom and ripped his sarong off. He had an impressive erection.

'Now your turn, detective.'

'Don't mind if I do,' said the naked Harry, sliding her blouse off and deftly unhooking her bra. He cupped her snow-white breasts in his hands as if they were precious ornaments made of alabaster. He kissed her deeply, guiding her to the bed and gently lowering her onto the sheets. He undid her belt whilst she flicked off her heels. Then he slid her jeans and knickers down, with her wriggling her bottom to assist. He tossed the garments over his shoulder and ran his hand up into her crotch. 'Mmm, you are positively dripping, my English rose.'

'So get lapping,' she replied, lying back and putting her hands behind his head as he nosedived into her wet vagina.

She moaned, loudly. Harry went at it with more tongue activity than a hundred kittens in a milking shed. It only took a few minutes and Tessa screamed as she came.

Harry raised his face from paradise. 'Up to standard, your ladyship?'

'It'll do for starters.'

Harry leant over and opened a bedside drawer. A set of handcuffs came out. She frowned.

'You did ask once,' he said, dangling them in front of her.

She laughed. 'You've got a good memory. I seem to recall it *was* on my bucket list.' She sat up, kissed him, and then started licking his face.

Harry dragged himself from his ecstatic musing. 'Well, madam, consider yourself under arrest.'

'Ooh, my big detective. Read me my rights and then fucking fuck me!'

Harry proceeded to handcuff Tessa to the bed-head. Then he pushed her legs apart. As he and his straining cock towered over her, he smiled and delicately ran his finger over her soaked clitoris. 'Now, babe, you just lie there and do everything, and I mean everything, the nice policeman tells you to.'

'Yes, detective, yes, yes!'

Two hours later, they fell apart, Harry claiming his dick was too sore to go again, Tessa protesting she wouldn't walk properly for a fortnight. And if the sheets could have spoken, they would have screamed brutality and demanded a steam-clean.

Harry went out to the kitchen and came back with two large glasses of white wine.

Tessa took a sip. 'I really, really needed that, detective. I had to feel human again. And alive.'

Harry lay back next to her, wine in one hand, other hand resting on hers. 'Yes, the solace of sex. Can't beat it, and yet can't put it into words either.'

'Who needs words? That tongue of yours is far better employed in silent mode.'

'On that note, are you planning on being around for a while, or is business going to drag you away again?'

'No. No more travel for a while. Lots to do for the business here, plus I'd like to spend some time with Sasha and Tanya.'

'Good. They'll appreciate that, especially Tanya. I'd like to see a bit more of you, too.'

She poked him in the ribs. 'Surprised you can find the energy for me and Tanya.'

Harry laughed. 'Hence the gym!'

Tessa laughed as well.

'Anyway, I'm not a "settle down with one woman" sort of guy. So, I need to find the energy.'

'Suits me, and I know Tanya's happy with it.'

Harry raised his eyebrows at her.

'We do talk about you, you know,' she said, grinning mischievously.

'Really? Tell me more.'

'Nope, it's secret women's business.'

Harry put his wine down and leant in and started tickling Tessa's ribs. She giggled, jerking around, sauvignon blanc splashing all over her.

'Tell me!' commanded Harry.

'Nooooo!' giggled Tessa.

Harry stopped tickling and started to lick the spilt wine off her breasts.

'Ooh, that's nice. Well, we do both reckon you want to have the two of us in here together.'

Harry looked up from his lapping and grinned at her. 'Couldn't possibly deny that. Feel free anytime.'

'Dream on, big boy.' She poured wine over her crotch. 'Get down there now!'

'Thought you'd had enough?'

'I've changed my mind. Female prerogative.'

'Yes, ma'am.' Harry smiled and buried his face in her wine-drenched sex.

– 15 –

The light breeze in the late afternoon was fuelling the lavender cascade from the jacaranda trees along Kelly Street as Harry, whistling in post-orgasmic bliss, strolled towards the Emerald Bar. He loved November in Sydney with the abundance of flowering jacarandas, mingled with the flame trees and the bougainvillea: stunning pastiches of purple, red and magenta. Aside from his innate love of flowers, the colour and the beauty of nature always made life seem a little less dark, thought Harry. He had a flash of Orla playing in their garden years ago, surrounded by daffodils the spring before she died.

He caught a jacaranda flower as it floated down in front of him. He admired its delicate, pale purple beauty and dropped it into his shirt pocket. He crossed Bay Street and stepped into his favourite watering hole. He found Trev and Liam at the bar. 'Thought you blokes would be out in the garden smoking,' said Harry.

'We were,' said Trev, 'but the news is about to come on and Perfect Plains Council should be top bill. You not see the earlier headline?'

'Ah, no. I've been otherwise occupied all afternoon.' Harry couldn't help a little smug smirk.

'Oh, I see. And who was the horizontal-tango partner today? I know it wasn't Tanya, she's at the hospital,' said Trev.

'Tessa got back today.'

'Ah, the English filly,' said Liam. 'You're a scoundrel, Kenmare. I'm fucking proud of you, lad.'

'And here's the news,' said Trev. 'Can we have a bit more volume, please, Shaun?'

'Certainly, gentlemen.'

Sure enough, the Council was lead story, following a joint operation between the NSW Police Major Fraud Squad and the ICAC. Harry and Trev couldn't contain their mirth as the footage rolled of the Council's CEO Van Dijk, the Council's lawyer, the HR manager, and three other senior staff all being put into the back of police cars. And separate footage showed the car dealer, Des Shine, being arrested at his showroom.

'This the one you were telling me about with the luxury-car scam?' asked Liam quietly, looking around to make sure no one else was close by.

'The one and only,' replied Harry.

'I doubt it would be the only one,' said Liam.

Trev chuckled. 'Yeah, too right. Power and greed equal corruption.'

'Don't we know it,' said Harry.

'Well, nice bloody job, you two,' said Liam. 'Drinks on me.' He pulled out his wallet.

'Pass the Baygon someone!' said Harry. 'Moth swarm incoming!'

'Fuck you, Kenmare,' said Liam, grinning and pulling out a fifty-dollar note.

'You sure the ink's dry?' said Trev.

'Oh, and fuck you, too, Matson. I'll get us three doubles and then I vote we retire out back for a smoke.'

'Sweet,' said Harry.

Out in the beer garden they occupied a table in the far corner. There wasn't much of a crowd at this time on a Monday, despite the balmy evening air.

After a bit more ribbing and banter, Liam suddenly leant in and assumed a conspiratorial mien. He looked at Harry. 'So, you bring what I asked for?'

'Sure did, Your Eminence.' Harry pulled a folded envelope out of his trouser pocket and passed it over the table. 'But we're intrigued to know what you're up to with this scheme of yours.'

'Yeah. All we know is what you said a couple of weeks back about your idea to try and find Lara Jacobs's father,' added Trev.

'I really would like to see some justice for Stavros McMahon,' said Harry. 'Not to mention all the other poor bastards that Porcia Savage would have destroyed in her career. There have been a lot of cover-ups under her watch. That's how she's risen so far.'

'Combined with her complete ruthlessness and lack of ethics,' said Trev. 'She is a complete monster.'

'Well, gentlemen, on a positive, anti-monster note, I've hit the jackpot,' said Liam, with a sly grin on his craggy face. 'You remember I mentioned that I'd heard some passing remark at the Gaelic Club after Lara's death?'

'Yep,' said Harry, as Trev nodded.

'Well, I put word out after we chatted before. And bugger me, word comes back that Lara Jacobs's old man is not called Jacobs, but O'Reilly. None other than Connor O'Reilly, former Provo.'

Trev frowned. 'Provo?'

'Provisional IRA, Belfast,' continued Liam. 'He and Lara's mother, Edie Jacobs, split up when Lara was a toddler. The girl always used her mum's name, not her dad's.'

'Nice work, Your Eminence, we'll make a detective of you yet.'

'Fuck off, Harry, I'm way too anti-Establishment, a Fenian to my very core.'

'Okay, so Connor O'Reilly?' asked Trev.

'Now, I hadn't met Connor myself. In our Irish circles, he's one of those legends you hear about, but you're never sure if he exists or not. Well, he certainly does. I was having lunch at the Club last Thursday and the man himself suddenly sits at my table. Introduces himself. Eyes like fucking green ice-picks. Man's so hard he'd cut diamonds. Told me he'd heard I was asking around for Lara's father. So, I told him the story.'

'Bet his blood was boiling by the end,' said Harry.

'You've no idea,' said Liam. 'Lara was his only surviving daughter. He'd had two kids in Belfast, but both died in the Troubles. His first daughter and her mum were killed when British paratroopers opened fire at a roadblock. His only son got old enough to want revenge, but was blown to bits when a car bomb went off prematurely. Connor had been to and from here, fathered Lara, and then settled here permanently after his boy died. And so, of course, Lara's little lad was his only grandchild. Now he's got nothing as a legacy, except a deep, dark cesspit of hatred.'

'I sure would *not* want to cross him,' said Harry.

'Not wrong there,' added Trev.

'Anyway,' said Liam, 'he wants this Human Services bitch big time. Now that I've told him the whole story, he is on a mission. He even talked about taking out the Minister who covered for bitchface Savage.'

Harry whistled. 'Shit, that's A-league.'

'Exactly, so best you don't get too close, if possible. That's why I asked for the items to pass on to him.'

'It's all in there,' said Harry. 'Photos, addresses, car plate numbers, new job details since her promotion, anything he'd need, really.'

'He did say he wants to read the actual reports, so he might drop into your office.'

'Liam, it might be best if we didn't have any direct dealings with him,' said Harry.

'Not much I could do to dissuade him there. But that's the only contact you might have. And that won't ever come to light, believe me. O'Reilly's idea of secrecy is tighter than the Vatican's treasury.'

Harry swallowed some whiskey. 'We'll be on our best behaviour if he does visit.' He pulled the jacaranda flower out of his pocket. 'And give him this. Tell him it's my local take on a shamrock. I wish him well. And so does Stavros McMahon, the last man who tried to take on Savage. And paid for it with his life, the poor bastard.'

The three of them raised their glasses.

'To Stavros, rest in peace, brother,' said Harry.

'To Stavros,' echoed the others.

'Wish I could watch him deal with Porcia Savage,' said Trev. 'As unethical as this scheme might be, it is bloody justice.'

'Bloody oath,' said Harry. 'Reckon he'll kill them or just inflict appalling injuries?'

'Frankly, I don't care,' said Liam. 'All I'd put money on is that it'll be professional, Provo-style, mark my words.'

'I won't be losing any sleep over it, that's for sure,' said Harry.

'Nor me, brother,' added Trev.

Liam took a mouthful of whiskey. 'That pair of corrupt bitches won't know what hit them.' He paused. 'Although he will probably get hands-on with Savage: he won't be able to contain himself. It'll be horrendous, but also just, in its own way. Anarchic justice, true, and inherently satisfying.'

'Here's to justice, whatever outfit it's wearing,' said Harry.

* * * * *

PART 4

HARRY'S JIHADIS

Passionate legs. All that was left were the transparent
panties. And she was a real blonde.

> \- Mickey Spillane

... seductive, rapacious, brazen, with a hunger in her
womb that would have satisfied an entire barracks.

> \- Gabriel García Márquez

– 1 –

The summer heat and shirt-wetting humidity had arrived early in Sydney. It was late November and, on this steamy Monday morning, the temperature was already licking thirty degrees.

Harry's battered old office, even with the additions courtesy of the twins, still didn't exactly boast five-star air-conditioning. Harry was behind his desk, Trev on the couch using his laptop. They were both sweating, faces glistening, as Harry looked through paperwork and Trev trawled online.

'Shit, I hate this weather,' said Harry. 'It's not even eleven and I'm sweatier than a sumo wrestler's arsecrack.'

'Mate, this is minor league. You should try Brizzie.'

'No offence, but no thanks.'

'None taken. I'm never planning on going back there.'

'The Emerald Bar opens at eleven. We could head down for an early lunch and a couple of coldies. At least their air-con works,' suggested Harry.

'Got my vote.'

'Cool. Head off in about half an hour then.'

'Sweet.'

Fifteen minutes later, the buzzer went. Harry pressed the intercom. 'Kenmare and Associates.'

'Yeah, hi, um … Mr Kenmare, my name's Debbie Shaw. I need a private detective.'

Harry frowned. Usually clients made an appointment before turning up. He could make out a female silhouette through the frosted-glass panel of the door. 'Okay, come in.' He pressed the release.

A youngish woman, with quite a pretty face, high cheek-bones and a slender nose, stepped in. Late twenties, Harry guessed. As he was sizing her up, a large male figure stepped in behind her.

'Fuck!' yelled Harry, reaching hurriedly for the .38 Smith & Wesson in his desk drawer. The revolver came out above the desk. Trev, reacting to Harry's shout, had grabbed his .357 Ruger from his bag as he rolled off the end of the couch leaving his laptop behind.

The woman froze in her tracks looking at both guns, her jaw hanging down.

'Fucking chill out, Kenmare. If I wanted to do anything to you, you'd never see it coming.' The male voice sounded like a concrete crusher.

Harry looked at the rough, bearded face, and considered this was probably true. He knew the big, tattooed man, dressed in black leather. And rather too well. 'What the fuck do you want, Longman? And why use her as a decoy?'

'She's not a decoy. She does want a private detective. Well, more exactly I do, but it's for her. She's my niece. Now, can we put the fucking gats away?'

Harry considered for a moment, then slid his .38 back in the drawer.

'So you two know each other?' Trev asked Harry, only half lowering his gun.

'Trev, this is Archie Longman. Career criminal and old-school armed robber. And one of the more successful until we ended his run. Ninety-five, wasn't it?'

304

'Yeah,' growled Longman. 'Did twelve years in Long Bay. Used to think you were a right cunt, Kenmare. But then I saw the news about your kid being raped and killed, and you bashing that rock spider, and getting chucked out of the coppers. So, I figured you weren't such a cunt after all. And sorry about your kid.'

By now Longman and Debbie were in front of Harry's desk. He held out his hand and they shook. 'As I said, this is my niece.'

Harry nodded at her, shook her hand, and motioned to them to sit. He looked at Debbie. She'd probably been even prettier as a teenager, but now a combination of drugs, booze and smokes, at Harry's educated guess, had left her skin sallow, blemished and tired. Her hazel eyes had lost any sparkle they might have had, and her mousey hair was flat and lifeless. 'So, Debbie, what can I do for you?'

'Um ...' She looked at the chunky, cobalt blue ashtray. She was sweating. Not that Harry was surprised given the heat and the amount of clothing she was wearing: barring her face and hands she was completely covered. It was a bit hard to discern, but Harry thought she had a rather good figure and she was certainly well-stacked up top. Didn't seem to be one to show it off, though. Unusual. Especially for someone from her side of the tracks.

'Can I smoke, please?'

'Sure.'

Longman produced a packet from his pocket, gave Debbie one, and lit it. He then lit one himself. He put the packet on the edge of the desk.

Harry joined them. 'So, Debbie?'

'Um ...' She nervously drew on her smoke. 'Well ...'

'You can do it, love,' said Longman, a gentleness to his voice that Harry wouldn't have thought him capable of.

'There was these four guys.' She stopped and started sobbing.

'Okay, love,' said Longman, putting his huge, scarred hand on her shoulder. 'Want me to tell him?'

She nodded dolefully and then looked down into her lap.

Longman took a long drag of his cigarette. His was one of those steely stares that sent a chill down the spine of the toughest or most experienced of men. Harry held the stare.

'You remember the Muslim gang rapes back around two thousand?'

'Yeah, I was still in the job then. Couple of my mates worked on that task force.'

'Debbie was one of the victims.'

'Shit, I'm sorry.'

Debbie looked up at Harry. 'Those arseholes. They ruined my life.' She looked back down.

Longman continued. 'She was sixteen. There were four of them. Fucking scum. Won't go into the details 'cos it upsets Deb.'

'Of course,' said Harry. He looked at her again and realized the overdone covering up was a sad consequence for her: she'd never want to show herself off again for fear of unwanted attention.

Debbie suddenly looked up. 'Nah, tell him. Tell him everything. I want him to know what the scum did to me.' She looked down again, took another smoke out of the packet in front of her, and lit it from the one she was finishing.

'Anything to drink in here, Kenmare?' asked Longman.

'Do bears shit in the woods? What's your poison?'

306

'Any vodka going?'

'Sure. My two assistants sometimes prefer that option.

'Don't suppose that young, blonde good sort I saw in the corridor as we were coming in was one of your assistants, Kenmare?'

'Yeah, that was Tanya, just on her way out.'

'She's smoking hot, mate.'

'And smart, and tough, and off limits, Longman.'

'Just admiring. Chill out.'

Harry got up and poured two vodkas from the drinks cabinet in the corner of the room. He brought them, and the bottle, back to the desk.

'Ta,' said Debbie.

Longman nodded his appreciation. Harry sat back down. Longman looked at him with raised eyebrows. 'Not joining us, mate? You turned into a soft prick now?'

Harry reached into his bottom drawer and pulled out the Jameson. 'Don't drink vodka, mate.' He smiled slightly at Longman, only dropping eye contact to pour himself a whiskey. He didn't feel like one, but he wasn't going to display any hesitation in front of Longman.

The bearded man took a decent gulp of vodka, lit another smoke, and started to talk. 'Debbie was on her way home from netball practice. It was just getting dark. A car full of Middle-Eastern wankers pulled up in a driveway and started chatting to her. She was a bit wilful as a teenager.'

Longman touched Debbie's arm. 'Anyway, she fell into talking with them, enjoying the attention. Had a smoke with them.'

Longman put his hand back on Debbie's shoulder. 'It was never your fault, love.'

His niece nodded without looking up.

Longman continued the story. Debbie was grabbed from behind and pushed into the car's back seat. There was a guy either side of her before she knew it, and two in the front. They drove off with one of the guys holding her head down out of view. Before she could even think about trying to scream, the other one in the back produced a large knife and told her to keep quiet. She complied. They drove for a while. It was dark when they pulled into the back of a house. She was threatened again with the knife and taken inside. It was an old fibro place that seemed deserted.

Debbie interjected. 'It was like a dero house, stank of piss and mould, rubbish everywhere.'

'Then one of them lit a camping lamp and they took her to a room with a mattress on the floor,' said Longman.

He looked over at Debbie. 'Okay for me to go on?'

She nodded slowly. She held up her empty glass and looked timidly at Harry.

Harry poured her another drink. Then he refilled Longman's glass.

The bikie resumed the awful tale. The guy who seemed to be the ringleader boasted loudly of his Lebanese heritage and superiority. He then slapped Debbie several times, called her an 'Aussie slut', and ordered her to undress. She pleaded with them to let her go, but then one of them punched her. She fell onto the mattress and two of them stripped her naked. For hours they raped her, every way possible. They kept telling her she was an 'infidel bitch' and that Allah provided 'Aussie whores' for their pleasure. When they'd finished the rapes, they all stood around the mattress and urinated on her. Then they left.

Debbie was found later, wandering naked and dazed in the street.

Longman paused and lit another smoke. He looked through the grey cloud at Harry. 'There you have it, Kenmare. One minute Debbie's playing netball with her friends, the next her life is destroyed.'

Harry snarled, 'I remember the case and reading about the trial. All four went inside for a while, but it was never going to be long enough in my view. Should have been for life.'

'Even that's too good for these mongrel dogs.'

'Won't argue with you there.'

Longman slowly drew his finger across his own throat. 'Death is the only fit punishment, Kenmare.'

Harry didn't feel any inclination to debate the death penalty as a judicial option, and if Longman wanted to exact his own lethal justice, Harry wasn't exactly in a position to challenge that approach. In fact, he understood it all too well; he wasn't in a rush to become known as Harry the hypocrite.

'You didn't have any avenues to get them on the inside? You were in yourself when they went down,' said Harry.

'In a different prison, mate. But I put word out and over the next couple of years we got two of them. The official reports said suicide, but I don't think the screws were particularly careful about preserving the nooses used, if you know what I mean.'

'I could take a knowing stab at that one.'

'So, that leaves the ringleader, Hakim Bakhash, and his brother, Rashid. The younger one got out on parole last month. Hakim got out last week. I've been waiting for this, Kenmare.'

'Well, don't let me hold you back, mate. You should know I won't be saying anything. The scum deserve whatever you've got in store for them.'

'Yeah. But I need them found.'

'You need me for that? With your resources?'

Harry had heard that Archie Longman was now the top boss of the Sydney chapter of the Satan's Hogs outlaw motorcycle gang.

'Blokes like me and the club boys can't exactly hang around the Lakemba area without raising alarm bells: those areas are like downtown Baghdad these days. I don't want these fuckers disappearing. If they got wind, before you know it the families would have them safely back in Lebanon or Iraq or whichever shit-box country they come from.'

'Point taken. They probably would be on the next plane out if they knew you were hunting them.'

'So, you've got the means to get all the info I need, and do some shadowing. Then you give me all the details, and we'll do the rest. The Hogs' special way.'

Longman pulled a brown sandwich bag out of his inside pocket and slapped it on the desk. 'There's ten large, Kenmare. Cover it?'

Harry pondered doing a job for Longman. He looked over at Trev, who gave him a 'Your call, mate' face. Harry looked back at Longman. 'I haven't said "yes" yet.'

'No, but you will. I can see it in your eyes when you look at Debbie here. Part of you sees your own little girl.'

Harry looked at him. Well, Longman, he thought to himself, you got me there, you bastard. Never thought I'd get psychoanalyzed by an ex-armed-robber bikie boss.

'Okay, that will cover it. What details do you have so far?'

'Just their names, and their suburb at the time they were arrested. Got all the news clippings, too.' He handed over another, slimmer envelope. 'That's my mobile number and email.' Longman pointed to the envelope. 'To be completely honest, I wasn't sure you'd entertain me, Kenmare.'

Harry smiled at him. 'No, mate, nor was I. But we've got plenty in common when it comes to sexual predators, so happy to help Debbie, and your project.'

Longman held out his hand across the desk. 'So, bygones?'

Harry nodded at him and shook his hand. 'Yeah, deal. Bygones.'

Harry gave him a business card from the holder on the desk. 'We'll let you know as soon as we have the info, and we'll update you over the next few days, whatever the status is.'

'Cool, thanks. Let's go, Deb.'

Debbie looked up finally. 'Thanks, Mr Kenmare.'

The pair got up and left the office.

Harry stared at the door, let out a deep breath and looked over at Trev. 'Well, fuck, that was a blast from the past.'

'Funny how life turns, isn't it?'

'Not wrong, Trev. He's a bloody legend in crime circles, that bloke. Harder than a Roman gladiator and more cunning than a two-legged weasel in Parliament.'

'He ended up getting caught, though?'

'Yeah, not everyone's trustworthy, especially in his world. And blokes always let their cocks get them in the shit.'

'Pray tell.'

Harry smiled. 'Longman banged his cousin's girlfriend. She wanted it, but the cousin wasn't too happy. Made a call to the squad, and so we got Longman. I did hear that the cousin subsequently became subject of a missing person report. And still is.'

'He'll be worm food somewhere.'

'For sure. But Longman's a survivor. With his ruthless hardness and his brains I reckon he'll be doing rather well in his newer line of work.'

Harry counted the money from the brown bag. He put it back in the bag. 'Dread to think where this came from, but it is ten large, and business is business.'

Trev chuckled. 'Since he's in the Hogs, my guess would be drugs or molls.'

'Or maybe rebirthed motors. Remember our hire-car establishment in Perth?'

'True. Wonder if he's seen a "new" Jaguar on the market?'

Harry laughed. 'Yeah, bet someone's enjoying that car.'

'So, we going to start on the job today?'

'May as well do our background research. Let's have a look at the newspaper stuff he gave us, and online. Then we'll hit the streets tomorrow.'

'Cool. I'll head off to the gym after we're done here. Joining me?' asked Trev.

'I'll pass, mate.'

'Come on. You need the exercise, brother.'

'Yeah, I know. But I promised Sasha I would drop in again. She wanted a chat.'

'Oh, okay. No worries.'

Harry put the cash in the safe and then spread the yellowed newspaper clippings across his desk as Trev came over.

'I vaguely remember some of this in the news around the time,' said Trev.

'Mate, it was huge news down here. There were a few gangs of Muslim men getting around raping young Aussie girls and women. Went on for a couple of years. It was horrendous. Most of them got caught eventually, I think.'

'Well, your mate Longman and his crew will certainly dispatch the two that he's after. Reckon he'll make them suffer, too.'

'The scum deserve plenty of pain,' said Harry.

'Yep, I agree. But it's a bit like trading with the devil, don't you think?'

Harry pondered, although not for long. 'In a way. But then there are different degrees of devil, I guess. I wouldn't rush out drinking with Longman, but by the same token I wouldn't wish him ill. The rapists on the other hand …'

'A devilish distinction I can certainly live with,' added Trev. 'And I don't think we're going to be wishing for long.'

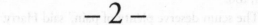

— 2 —

Sasha was looking into Zanza's eyes. Another tragedy of her awful illness was that she wouldn't get to grow her relationship with the big guy. Even seated, he towered over her. And he was big, everywhere. She'd enjoyed the look on Tanya's face when she'd demonstrated precisely how big. What she hadn't been able to indicate to Tanya was how big his heart was. It was one of the reasons she'd become so keen on him. For such a giant, muscled man, and considering the terrors he had endured in his earlier life, he was so incredibly gentle. As gentle as he was now, one of his enormous hands holding hers and the other caressing her face. Sasha was exhausted, mentally as much as physically.

'Thank you for being my friend. Please just hold me,' she whispered to him.

He picked up the writing pad and pen on the bedside cabinet. He tore off the top sheet, which read, 'Hello, baby. I'm missing you.' He'd written that when he arrived half an hour before. He scribbled a fresh note and showed it to Sasha. 'I will always think of you.' As she started to cry, Zanza cradled her to him.

Twenty minutes later, Harry tapped on the metal door-frame. 'Would you like me to wait a while, guys?'

Zanza shook his head and gestured Harry into the room. They shook hands.

Harry put one hand up on Zanza's shoulder. 'Thanks for being here, big fella. Life's a bastard. But you learnt that one a long time ago.'

Zanza nodded ruefully. He pointed at himself and then at the doorway, raising his eyebrows.

'No, mate, I'm happy for you to stay, and I'm sure Sasha is.'

Sasha nodded and whispered, 'Please, yes.'

Zanza sat back in his chair and Harry pulled a second one over next to him. He leant over and kissed Sasha before he sat down. 'Divine One, Tanya messaged that you wanted to see me.'

'I've told Tan, and Zanza knows. Harry, I'm about at the end of what I can take. I want to end it.'

Harry stared at her. He glanced to his left and saw a tear rolling down Zanza's cheek. 'Babe, I don't know what to say. Can't we just make sure you've got more pain relief?'

'Harry, I can't do this. I'm just waiting to die, and it's fucking awful.'

Harry wanted to say something like he could imagine, but he knew he didn't have a clue what it was like right now for Sasha. He put his hand on top of hers resting in Zanza's palm.

'I told Tan to ask you and Trev to get whatever's needed. Harry, you've always been good to me, to us. Please help me out now.'

Harry, in a scarce occasion, was speechless. He looked at Zanza, as if another face might reinstate his voice.

Zanza was busily writing on the pad. He passed it to Harry. 'It has taken me a long time to find this girl. She already means much to me and I can't stand to lose her.

315

But I can't stand to watch her suffer like this. There is no happy end to this. Harry, please help her with what she wishes for.'

Harry burst out crying. He leant over Sasha and hugged her. 'Okay, babe, I'll talk to Tanya and Trev and we'll sort something.'

He kissed Sasha on the cheek, hugged Zanza, and traipsed sadly from the room.

— 3 —

Lakemba and Belmore were not suburbs that Harry or Trev spent much time in. None, in fact. Forty or fifty years ago, either of the guys, with their Australian working-class backgrounds, could easily have grown up around these areas, back then being the typical grid of quarter-acre blocks with brick or fibro bungalows on them. Now, these localities were predominantly, almost exclusively in many streets, populated by Middle-Eastern immigrants and their locally born kids. Garish two-storey mansions with their concrete curtilages were filling the old blocks, at least the ones that hadn't been grabbed by developers for apartment buildings. The occasional original Aussie bungalow with a front lawn remained, resisting the bulldozers, but they were looking like the last girls left in the nightclub at 2 a.m.

Doing surveillance for three days straight in these almost alien landscapes had Harry and Trev climbing the walls of the two VW vans they were alternating from day to day. The magnetic business signs changed every day as well. Trev enjoyed a bit of humour by adding 'The Halal Meat Emporium' and 'Turkish Delight Bakery' to his confected collection. They had pinned the two paroled gang rapists down to the Bakhash family home in Moreton Street, Belmore, but hadn't yet established any regular routine.

On Thursday, the brothers finally emerged further than the letterbox, and drove a white Subaru WRX to a local gym in Lakemba. They were out fifteen minutes later.

'Just joining up, I reckon,' said Harry. 'Don't want to lose all that beef they've put on in the prison gym.'

'Yeah, they look pretty buffed,' said Trev, snapping away with a camera.

They tailed the pair back to the family home. Then they waited, again.

Late afternoon arrived and the PIs were contemplating pulling the pin for the day when the brothers resurfaced, hopped into the same Subaru, and pulled out of the driveway. Harry started the van and they followed at a respectable distance.

Ten minutes later the Subaru pulled into the driveway of an old weatherboard house in Augusta Street, Punchbowl. The place had a derelict air, but there was a light showing from a front room. As the brothers got out of their car, another swarthy-looking male appeared on the timber porch. After exaggerated greetings, arms everywhere and high-fives, the three went inside. The front door closed.

Twenty minutes went by before a souped-up, orange Honda Prelude, with mag wheels and a rear spoiler that would put an F1 machine to shame, roared past the VW van and screeched to a halt in the driveway behind the WRX.

'Another bloke with an oversized ego and undersized penis,' said Trev.

'This bloody suburb's full of them,' said Harry.

A guy in his twenties, dripping with gold bling, jumped out of the driver's seat. Two bottle-blonde girls got out of the other side of the car. They were both heavily made up and in skin-tight clothing that left little to the imagination. The taller one was wearing a pink crop top with 'Roxy' emblazoned between the two massive mounds created by her outlandish breasts, evidently silicone-assisted. The shorter girl had her prime assets below the waist, showing off her perfect buttocks in her active-wear pants. As she turned around, her front revealed a camel-toe so blatantly bulbous that it would have started a riot in any souk in her country of origin.

'Bloody hell,' said Harry. 'Her tits are about to pop out of that excuse for a top. And the other one's at risk of her arsecrack swallowing those tights.'

'Mate, if we were watching the contest for the sluttiest slut in Slutsville, we'd be looking at gold and silver right here.'

'Yep. And you, Matson, get gold for political incorrectness.' Harry grinned at him.

'Ooh, smack me now, Kenmare, you big boy, you.' Trev smiled. 'And fuck political correctness.'

'I'm with you, brother, one hundred percent.' Harry turned back to the house. 'I reckon the other lads have organized a couple of tarts to let the brothers unload their ball sacks after all those years inside.'

'Well, unload in a female, anyway,' said Trev.

Harry chuckled. 'Yeah, they probably learnt all about being mummy bear inside. Now they're desperate to play daddy bear again.'

As Harry said this, the front door opened and the brothers and their host appeared.

The Honda driver threw up his arms. 'Habibi! Look what I have for you,' he yelled. He indicated the girls, who were standing akimbo next to the car, chewing gum. As the brothers looked hungrily at them, the girls leant into each other, fondled each other's breasts, and locked faces in a tongue-kissing marathon.

'Wonder where the chewing gum goes?' said Harry.

'I'm sure they swallow much worse,' replied Trev.

The driver walked over to the girls, slapped their arses, and ushered them up the steps into the house.

Two hours later, Harry and Trev were extremely bored. Then the front door reopened. The two young women, now quite dishevelled, and their driver left the scene in the Honda.

Shortly after, Hakim and Rashid Bakhash came out, hopped into their WRX, and headed off. After that, the PIs decided to call it quits.

As they drove back towards the city, Trev was searching databases. 'Mate, that house the brothers went to, looks like it's owned by the family of another of the gang rapists from back then. But different from the gang that raped Debbie.'

'Interesting. I've no doubt they probably all know each other, all with their bastardized, medieval version of Islam. Probably get together for coffee to reaffirm their right to rape western women. Primitive scum.'

'I'm with you on that one, partner,' said Trev. 'And you can have a medal for political incorrectness, too, mate.'

'I'll wear it with pride,' replied Harry, smiling.

Trev brought up an old newspaper photo on his screen. 'Well, it's twelve years old, but I reckon that's our bloke at that house: one Mustafa Ahmad.'

Harry looked over quickly. 'I think you're right. We'll make a detective of you yet.'

'Funny, ha-ha.'

'So, now we have to figure out how to get the brothers back there, or somewhere else, away from the family home,' said Harry. 'And at a given time, so Longman and his crew can be ready to rock and roll.'

'Yep. Maybe thinking about that problem over dinner would work better?'

'Excellent idea. We'll ditch the van at my place then,' said Harry.

Trev kept tapping on his keyboard.

'Hey, Harry?' he said a couple of minutes later. 'Think I might be on to something here.'

'Don't tell me, smart-arse, another sling establishment for me to visit?'

Trev laughed. 'You wish, big boy. No, it's about our paedophile friend, Herbert Farr, our next molester off the rank, so to speak.'

Harry swerved the van over to the kerb. He leant over to Trev, looking at the laptop screen. 'What you got?'

'News item from Melbourne. Some trouble at Ararat Prison. Two inmates taken to the local hospital. One of them is our Mr Farr. Expected to be there for quite some time.'

'Mate, that presents us with an ideal bloody opportunity.'

'Not wrong. We can get into a hospital. Plus it's a damned sight easier than trying to grab him whilst he's being transferred between prisons.'

'And we still don't know that's a definite, do we?'

'No. My contact said that it was still up in the air. Reckon we plan a trip to Ararat.'

'Oh, yes,' said Harry. 'We need to crack on with this job then to free us up for a hunting trip down south.'

'Well, we should have everything we need on these wankers to give to Longman by the end of the weekend, I reckon.'

'Agreed, and we can get our job planned in the meantime.' Harry gently smacked his right fist into the palm of his other hand and smiled over at Trev. 'It's time for the next episode in our game of vengeance, mate.'

— 4 —

By lunchtime the next day, the mood in Harry's office was bleaker than a nuclear winter. Harry and Trev had been to the hospital and both wished they hadn't. Harry had also had a chat with Tanya about her sister's request. Sasha had seemed to wither overnight. In actuality, it had been several weeks. She was in a lot of pain, on and off, despite the morphine. She was having trouble keeping her eyes open, she was so drugged, and her conversation was sparser than desert grass.

They'd spoken to Tanya outside Sasha's room before they'd left.

'Hell, she's looking even worse than the other day when I popped in,' Harry said.

'As much as I'm hating it, I do support her decision,' said Tanya.

'Shit, this is awful,' said Trev.

'So, you will help, won't you, my Mr PI? Please?' Tanya put her arm around Harry, resting her face on his chest.

'Yeah,' he whispered into her hair. 'Zanza was supportive, too, when I saw him here the other day.'

'Yeah, poor guy. They were looking ecstatic together the few times I saw them at our place.'

'Why is it that such awful things happen to such decent people?' said Trev to no one in particular.

'Because life sucks,' said Tanya. 'Harry, there won't be any investigation with Sasha, you know, leaving?' She couldn't handle the death word.

'No, it'll just accelerate what would have happened, so it'll seem as if she went naturally. No investigation.'

'Nothing too fucking natural at her age,' said Trev.

Now, at the office, Harry and Trev were facing the practical ramifications of Sasha's decision.

'Is morphine the best option?' asked Harry.

'I know that would do it with a big enough shot. And it'll be totally painless for her, she'll just drift off to sleep.' Trev looked down. 'Forever.'

'Fuck, I hate this. Just want to shake my fist at Mother Nature and shout, "You bitch!" You know?'

'Yeah, I'm with you,' said Trev. 'I've still got that list of candidates I'd happily shove into Sasha's place.'

'Likewise, brother. So, can you get the gear?' asked Harry.

'Yeah, no problems there. Probably be a few grand, though.'

'Covered. Plenty in the safe. And all used notes.' Harry held up his hand, thumb and forefinger imitating their hold on a large wad of banknotes.

'Okay, I'll make the call. Just pop down to the payphone outside.'

'That's old school.'

'Yep, and still the best anonymous number you can get.'

'What about your chuck-away mobiles?'

'Not going to burn one of them up for just one call.'

'Fair enough. See you shortly.'

Trev nodded grimly, stood up, and headed out of the office.

Harry sat there staring at the door. He looked down at his bottom drawer where Brother Jameson dwelt. No, you don't need one, he thought. He lit a smoke. He looked back at the bottom drawer. Yes, I bloody do. 'Fuck it,' he said out loud.

He pulled out the bottle of Irish nectar and two of his favourite chipped Cavan crystal tumblers. He poured two generous serves, pushed one over to the far edge of his desk, and took a long swig from the other. Then he drew back hard on his cigarette. He closed his eyes, and saw Sasha's ravaged face and her exhausted, pleading look. No, he couldn't handle more of that. He opened his eyes. He scowled at his own reflection in his computer screen.

How could life be such a vile, capricious bastard? The fact that it was didn't come as any surprise: he hadn't exactly had a charmed existence himself. But he could never grasp the how of it. For Harry, injustice stung more than a bull ant sampling your scrotum. And Sasha's tragedy made injustice look mild as a label. So many people, really shit people, he could put into her place. Before his moroseness deepened any further, Trev came back in. He spotted the full whiskey sitting on the client side of Harry's desk and he strode up to it. He took a slug.

'Thanks, mate, you read my mind. Okay, job's done.'

'Thanks, Trev.'

They chinked glasses. 'Four grand. Got a meet in two hours,' continued Trev.

Harry went over and opened the safe. He pulled out a thick bundle of twenty-dollar notes and handed it to Trev. 'There's five, just in case.'

Trev stuck the wad in his pocket and was about to sit down when the intercom buzzed. Harry went quickly back to his chair, opening the drawer with his .38 sitting in it. Trev stepped over to the couch where his bag of tricks was perched. He rested his hand on his .357 Magnum inside the bag. They nodded at each other. Harry pressed the intercom button.

'Kenmare and Associates.'

A thick Irish accent blasted into the room like a Hibernian hurricane. 'I'm here for Harry Kenmare. Liam Doolan is my referral.'

'Come on in.' Harry pressed the door release.

The door was thrust open and in stepped a squat, gnarled and muscle-packed man. The 160 centimetres of Homo bulldog flicked the door closed, looked at Harry and Trev in one smooth survey, and took four swift steps up to Harry's desk. A hand shot out. Harry took it. The grip was pure brutality.

'O'Reilly.'

'Ah, yes, Mr O'Reilly. Liam said you might drop in.'

Connor O'Reilly pointed at Harry's drink, and said, 'I'll be having a large one.'

'Of course,' replied Harry, finding another crystal tumbler in a desk drawer. He poured a full drink and passed it across, as the visitor sat down. 'I, and Trev there, are both very sorry for your losses, Mr O'Reilly. I got to meet Lara before she died.'

'Murdered, not "died". Fucking murdered, Kenmare. Just like my only grandson, young Beau.'

He caught Harry glancing at the two long, trench-like scars down the side of his shaved head. One of the wounds cut a gap through where most of his ear had once been. 'Derry, nineteen seventy-eight. Two fucking seven-point-six-two bullets from a Scottish squaddie in the British Army.'

'Close call,' said Harry looking at the vivid bullet wounds.

'At least I survived. The Scottish fuck who did it wasn't so lucky. We hunted him down. Got him on R and R one weekend. Yes, Ian McPhail, known as Jock to his mates. Won't forget him. Tortured the cunt for hours. Cut his nuts off and fed them to him. Then cut his throat and dumped his body outside the pub they all used to drink at. Payback's a bitch where I come from, Kenmare.'

Harry swallowed. Yep, he didn't doubt a word of it. Still, the thought of that evil Porcia Savage meeting O'Reilly brightened his day immensely. He would never forget poor Stavros McMahon being driven to his death by that bitch. He smiled. 'So you've got the photos and addresses of the department head, Savage, and the Minister, Steele. What else can we help with?'

'Liam told me what he knew. I always knew the official version was bullshit. But Liam mentioned you had a copy of the real report about Beau, one written by some ex-copper who necked himself.'

'Stavros McMahon,' murmured Harry. He had a visual of the covered stretcher being carted out of the boarding house in Chippendale all those months ago.

'I'd like a read,' growled O'Reilly. 'Please.'

'Of course. But it's not pretty.'

'Do I fucking look like I'm into pretty?'

'Fair point. Let me pour you another Jameson to smooth things a touch.'

'Ta.'

'I'll get the report,' said Trev, moving towards the safe. He brought a file over, handed it to O'Reilly, and sat down in Tanya's usual chair at the twins' desk.

O'Reilly proved a fast reader, with growing tension in his neck and face.

Harry looked at him as he finished.

The Irishman carefully placed the report on the desk. His eyes narrowed. 'She's fucking dead meat. And the minister bitch,' he hissed. He threw his remaining whiskey down his throat, stood up, and shook hands with the pair of PIs. 'Thank you, gentlemen, you'll never see me again. But I'll always owe you one.' He turned and walked out of the office without another word.

Harry let out a sigh of relief.

'Fuck,' said Trev. 'He's hell on legs.'

'Oh, yeah. I wouldn't want to be on the wrong side of him for anything in the world. But that Porcia Savage bitch is heading for her day of reckoning. Nothing will save her from O'Reilly's brand of justice.'

'Good riddance to her. I'm almost apologetic, given the violence that we know will be used, but I can't quite get there. Not with all the evil that she's done,' said Trev.

'With you one all the way, brother. I've never forgotten McMahon's face that day I saw him. He'd been utterly crushed as a human being. So, yeah, fuck Savage. But not in that way, of course.'

'Ugh. Even if I was straight, I wouldn't fuck her with yours. But do you reckon he'll do Steele as well? Taking out a government minister is top shelf.'

'Yeah, we haven't had a political assassination in donkey's years. But, you know, I really do think O'Reilly is the man who's about to change that.'

— 5 —

Tanya insisted on coming with them to Punchbowl that afternoon for the surveillance operation, saying she was desperate for a break from the hospital. She suggested she could lure the rapists somewhere if needed. That wasn't a winning approach with Harry, but she convinced Trev, and he persuaded Harry to let her work the afternoon with them.

The Bakhash brothers appeared to be home, given the presence of their hotted-up Subaru in the driveway of the Belmore house. Harry had spoken to Longman earlier in the day, letting him know everything they had, and in particular the house the brothers had visited for their post-custodial sex session the previous day. Longman and his crew were on standby in a shopping centre car park nearby, just in case an opportunity arose to finish the job.

Half an hour later, the brothers emerged in their gym gear, hopped in the WRX, and roared off down the street.

'Don't we need to get after them?' asked Tanya.

'No need,' said Harry. 'We know their gym.'

Trev started the VW van. 'Yep, a slow drive there and then wait and see what they do after.'

'Maybe I could hang around outside,' said Tanya. 'Get friendly when they come out. All I need is an address to send them to, on a promise of me.' She smiled impudently at Harry.

He considered for a moment. 'Well, yes, that could work. But we need an address.'

'Harry, you hop in here and drive,' said Trev, getting out of the driver's door. Harry slid across and Trev got back in through the passenger side.

'What you got in mind?' asked Harry.

'There was a derelict joint a couple of streets away from the place we dogged them to yesterday. I'll find it on Google maps and then we've got an address. And we'll let Longman know.'

'Okay, sounds like a start,' said Harry, putting the van into drive and heading down the street.

Within twenty minutes they were watching the gym car park and the white WRX. Tanya was sitting on a bench outside the gym having a smoke, and pretending to play with the phone that Trev had given her for the job.

An hour later, the Bakhash brothers emerged into the car park. The older one, Hakim, was on his phone, but Rashid wasted no time in eyeballing Tanya, flaunting her wares in tight jeans and an even tighter halter top that was struggling to contain her breasts. She had on more make-up than usual, deliberately looking painted and cheap. It did the job to the point where Harry had told her she could easily blend in with the working girls they'd passed walking their beats back up Canterbury Road. That had earned him a smack.

Tanya's cosmetic effort completely covered the faint, fine scar on her cheek from the piggery episode in WA back in September. As promised, Harry had facilitated her seeing a great plastic surgeon whose work had proved remarkable.

Trev was watching her and the brothers through binoculars. 'I reckon the little prick's got a boner already,' he remarked, as Rashid strutted over to Tanya.

Tanya drew on her cigarette as the younger brother walked over with a cocky smile on his face. He was thrusting his pelvis forward as he moved. It made his walk look ridiculous. Surely girls in Beirut didn't go for this? Mind you, they probably didn't get too much say in what they did or didn't go for. You fucking wanker, Tanya thought. But she smiled and pushed her chest outwards, not that it needed any assistance.

'Yo, girl, what's up?'

'Just waiting for a girlfriend.'

'And where's ya boyfriend at?'

'Don't have one.'

He whistled. 'Hot stuff like you and no man?'

She tried to look forlorn. 'Yeah, just the way it goes.'

'Well, girl, we could fix that for you. Me and my bro.' He indicated the older brother still on the phone.

'What? Both of you together?'

Rashid was feeling pretty good. He had this skippy slut on the hook. He flexed his arm muscles and pushed out his crotch in his brief gym shorts.

'Girl, we'll give you all the Leb cock you can handle. You'll love it.'

Tanya's immediate reaction was to want to vomit. She smiled seductively instead. She was going to ask Harry for a pay rise for this job.

'Mmm, I've never had a Leb boy before, let alone two.'

'So, you and your girlfriend, let's go back to our place.'

'She might not be into that, you know, going to a strange house.' Tanya thought she'd best not be too fast on the offer; make the fuckstain hunger for it a bit.

'Could get a motel room then, but our place is close by and much more comfortable.'

'Don't know she'd go for that either. She likes her own comfort zone.'

'What about you, girl? You want some Leb cock, don't you?'

'Yeah, you bet.'

'Well, you gotta play the game, girl.'

'Hey, maybe I talk to her and we can go to the place we're staying at, if you like. I reckon she'd be fine with that. She brought a couple of guys home there last week.'

'Cool. What's the address? I'll talk to my bro.'

Tanya gave him the derelict house address and Rashid punched it into his phone. 'We'll be going there as soon as she picks me up, but I promised I'd wait for her,' said Tanya.

'Cool. She as hot as you?'

'Yep, you bet. And she loves anal, that's her favourite.'

Rashid's eyes widened.

Tanya tried not to smile as she enjoyed laying it on thick. These arseholes were so predictable.

Rashid started to bar up, noticeably. He bent slightly, the budding erection difficult to hide in his shorts. At that point, Hakim walked over having finished his phone call.

'Hey, Bro,' said Rashid. 'Sex bomb here is up for a bit of fun when her friend picks her up.'

Hakim couldn't take his eyes off Tanya. 'Fully sick, little Bro. We'll show you girls what real men are like.'

Tanya looked at him, got an image of putting a gun against his head, and blowing him away. She smiled and fluttered her eyelashes at him. 'That's what I was hoping for. Told your brother here that I've always wanted to try some Leb.'

'I got their address, Bro,' said Rashid.

'Sick. Let's go, Bro, we've got that pick-up to do.' He turned back to Tanya. 'We'll see you in about an hour, girlie. And then it's party time.'

'Can't wait, stud,' said Tanya, running her tongue along her top lip.

The brothers high-fived each other and strutted off to their WRX. They got in, backed out of the car space, and then gunned the engine, burning rubber as they drove away.

You pair of total fucking losers, thought Tanya. She lit another smoke and continued sitting there in the pretence of waiting for her girlfriend.

Fifteen minutes later, Harry called her. 'Divine One, it should be well and truly clear now, so wander up the road to the van. You see us?'

'Yep. On my way, Mr PI. And you've no idea how fucking revolting those two are.'

'I can well imagine. I know the type. See you shortly, babe.' Harry ended the call.

He turned to Trev. 'Used to love locking up the real wankers like them, not to mention handing out a bit of summary jurisdiction in the interview room when they got the attitude going.'

'Nothing they didn't deserve, I'm sure,' replied Trev.

'Too much scum in the world, mate.'

'Yep.' Trev lit a smoke.

There was an approaching roar of an engine and a hotted-up black Nissan Skyline screamed past them, grabbing their attention.

'Talking of scum,' said Trev. 'Here's some more.'

As the sleuths watched, the driver of the Skyline slammed on his brakes about fifty metres in front of them. Then, in the middle of the road, he proceeded to do circle work, the doughnuts causing a pall of rubber smoke to billow into the still air.

'You fuckstain,' said Harry.

A few other young men standing near their machines at the edge of the car park started to holler their appreciation.

Harry and Trev shook their heads in utter contempt.

As Tanya was walking away from the bench, a Subaru WRX cruised into the side entrance to the car park and accelerated down to the front of the gym.

The WRX screeched to a stop next to her, and Hakim leapt from the back seat. Before Tanya could react, he grabbed her by her hair and pulled her totally off balance. As she fell, he took hold of her around the waist, put his knee in her back, and propelled her into the back seat of the Subaru.

Another set of hands grabbed her by her hair. Hakim climbed in behind her, and the door slammed. Rashid, who was behind the wheel, threw the car into gear and took off towards the exit onto the road, where the doughnut-chucking Skyline was almost completely shrouded in smoke.

Tanya tried to lash out with her arms, but the man holding her produced a nasty-looking knife and held it in front of her face. 'I'll hurt you, bitch. Bezam likes to hurt girls.'

Hakim smiled evilly at her. 'Cut just there, Bezam.' He pulled the halter strap on her top. Bezam moved in with the knife and she heard the fabric being slashed. Then

Hakim pulled down her top. He squeezed her breasts, and got his face close to hers. She could smell his breath, rancid with the odour of stale fried food.

'We're going to have a lot of fun with you, skippy slut.'

As the WRX approached the car park exit, the rubber-burning Nissan took off down the street.

Harry spotted the Subaru. 'Hang on, that's the brothers back again.'

Trev looked over to the gym and the empty bench. 'Shit, Tanya's gone,' he yelled. 'Think those burnouts were a distraction so nobody was looking at the gym.'

The WRX accelerated into the street. Through the clearing cloud of smoke, Harry caught a glimpse of blonde hair inside its back window. 'Jesus fuck! They've got Tanya!'

He rammed the van into drive, as the WRX disappeared around the corner.

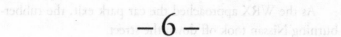

— 6 —

'Okay, the tracker's now live on that phone I gave her, I'm getting the signal,' said Trev. 'Left at the intersection, Harry. Looks as though they could be going back to that house we saw them visit yesterday.'

'I'll head there. Tell me if they change tack.' Harry dropped the automatic transmission into second and gunned the engine.

Trev got on his phone. 'Longman? Head for the Punchbowl address from their visit yesterday, not the new one we gave you. Repeat, not the new one. Things have changed. They've grabbed our girl, Tanya. The scum are heading for Punchbowl now, we think. We're about five minutes away.' He hung up.

'Make that three!' yelled Harry.

'Tracker is showing them turning into that street right now.'

There was a squeal of rubber as Harry threw the van around the next corner.

The Subaru pulled into a driveway. Tanya could see another swarthy guy holding open a garage door. The car slid inside and the guy pulled the door down behind it.

Tanya's sense of dread was snowballing. She had to hold it together until her guys got there. But she was scared. She could feel that same growing terror that used to surface every time she heard their stepfather lumbering lasciviously towards their bedroom. She fought to steady her mind. She was not going to become a victim of these scum, with their odours of sweat and cheap cologne, and their sense of entitlement to any woman's body at their whim. She absolutely loathed men like these.

Hakim got out of the car. 'Habibi! We bring a fine offering of Aussie *sharmouta*.'

The two guys hugged.

'Hakim, you champion.'

'Mustafa, it's time for some fun. Just like the old days.'

The pair started laughing as the knifeman, Bezam, pulled Tanya out of the car. Her top had been removed and finger marks were visible on her large, firm breasts.

Mustafa whistled. 'Habibi, this is a great piece of booty. We're going to gang-bang it for hours.'

Knifeman slapped Tanya's bottom as another guy appeared in the doorway into the garage from the house. He whistled, too.

'Thanks be to Allah. Great fucking tits.'

Rashid had got out of the driver's seat and come around the car. He grinned at Tanya and grabbed one of her breasts. 'Going to enjoy this, slut.'

Bezam, meanwhile, was groping her backside and pushing his fingers into her crotch. 'You got a hot arse, slut. I'm going to fuck it so hard,' he hissed in her ear.

'Bring her in,' ordered Mustafa.

Knifeman slapped her bum again and breathed garlic around her face. 'Inside, bitch. Move!' He waved the blade in front of her face. 'And any screaming or anything stupid like that, I'll cut this pretty face to pieces.'

Tanya felt nauseous at the thought of another knife wound to her face. She found herself herded through the door and pushed along a hallway. The house had a pungent chemical smell to it. The guy who'd commented on her breasts disappeared around a corner further along, but Mustafa stopped next to an open door.

'In there, slut.'

Tanya had to buy time. And she had to keep hold of her purse at all costs. She still had one surprise, but she wished like hell she'd taken the five-shot Smith & Wesson Harry had got for her. And she was desperate for Harry and Trev to arrive.

'I need to go to the toilet,' she pleaded.

They all laughed at her.

'Nice try, bitch,' said Hakim. 'If you want to piss before we fuck you, go squat in the corner over there. You can go to the bathroom when we're done with you.'

Rashid cackled and grabbed her breast again. Tanya recoiled, only to back into the knifeman. Rashid leant into her ear again. 'And you'll fucking need the bathroom then, bitch, 'cos you going to be dripping with good Muslim cum.'

'*Allahu akbar!*' cried Bezam, grabbing her by the hair and propelling her into the room.

She lost her balance and landed on her back on a stained double mattress on the floor, the only thing in the room. The chemical smell was overtaken by urine and what Tanya thought was shit. She gagged as she noticed a dried brown smear near her face.

Hakim laughed. 'See, the Aussie slut's straight onto the bed. Can't wait for all this great Lebanese cock.'

Knifeman grinned, showing two gold teeth. 'Bitch here is about to eat a whole lot of kebab.'

They all roared with laughter.

A weaker woman might have dissolved into a crying heap by now, but not Tanya. Her mind was racing, trying to pick the best strategy. There was no point lashing out and fighting like a cornered she-cat: there were four of them, plus at least one more in the house, and she wouldn't have a chance. Might injure one or two of them, but then she'd be fucked, in more ways than one.

Use your street smarts, girl, she thought, you've dealt with arsehole men before: just not captive in a room with four of them all intent on raping her. Subterfuge was the key to survival right now. Harry had said to her several times that you slide a lot further on bullshit than you do on gravel. She had believed him before, but now was the ultimate test case.

She kicked off her shoes and slid out of her jeans. The four guys started catcalling and hooting.

'See? These infidel sluts all want cock,' crowed Hakim. 'Rashid, my little brother, never believe them when they say "no". They exist for our enjoyment, praise be to Allah.'

'*Allahu akbar!*' they all chanted, and high-fived each other.

Tanya couldn't quite believe the macho, pious hypocrisy of them. But, more crucially, they failed to keep their eyes on her, and she made the most of it. No one saw her hand quickly dip into her purse and then behind her back for an instant.

Now she lay back against the wall in her lacy knickers, legs spread. She eyed them all with a pout on her face. She pulled the front of her knickers down and started fingering herself. She worked the whole length of her middle finger inside herself, and started slowly thrusting it in and out.

The guys went silent. She pulled her finger out of her vagina and sucked on it, making loud slurping noises for effect. She looked at them, her eyes roving between the four, and kept sucking and licking her finger, with plenty of tongue out.

'So, who's first, boys? Who's my main man? Who's going to break me in?'

'Mustafa, this is your house, so the right is yours,' said Hakim. Rashid and Bezam agreed. Mustafa stepped forward and started to undo his belt.

'Get naked, big boy, I want to see all your beautiful muscles when you fuck me,' purred Tanya.

Mustafa went into overdrive stripping off his clothes. The others all peeled off their shirts.

Hakim turned to Rashid. 'You see, my brother, all of them here for our pleasure.'

'Oh, yes,' replied Rashid, unbuckling his belt.

Bezam, meanwhile, had stuck his knife into the door-frame and had his erect cock out of his jeans, rubbing it.

Mustafa was now stark naked and he advanced, replete with an impressive erection, towards Tanya.

'Come on, big boy, I want that beautiful thing inside me,' she taunted him.

Two more steps and Mustafa was directly in front of Tanya. She came up onto her knees and grabbed his cock. With her other hand she was playing with her breasts.

There were howls of encouragement from the other blokes, all now eagerly stripping off their clothing.

'That is magnificent,' cooed Tanya, looking up at Mustafa and breathing hot air onto the head of his penis. He had a grin on his face to rival a circus clown.

Tanya started masturbating him. 'Feels good, doesn't it, big boy? So, you want to fuck my pussy or my arse with this beautiful rod?'

'Both, bitch, both,' said Mustafa, turning his eyes to the ceiling in rapture.

It was the final moment of pleasure in his life. As Tanya speeded up stroking his cock, her hand slid off her breasts and behind her back.

'Okay, bitch, get those lovely legs apart, I'm going to fuck your pussy the best you ever had.'

Not fucking likely, you cunt, thought Tanya.

Mustafa looked down at his conquest and impending fuck just in time to see a flash of steel as Tanya brought the flick-knife out from the back of her knickers and rammed it into the base of his scrotum.

The ensuing scream was worthy of a horror movie. Blood spurted over Tanya and Mustafa collapsed to his knees, trying to clutch at his manhood, still firmly gripped by Tanya. She jerked the knife, cutting him further. 'You move, fuckstain, and I'll slice your cock off. Won't be much of a man after that.'

The other three rapists were looking like stunned rabbits in a set of headlights.

Bezam stopped playing with his penis and grabbed hold of his knife again. The Bakhash brothers merely stared inanely at the unfolding catastrophe. Bezam moved forward.

'Back off, arsehole!' screamed Tanya. To reinforce her point, she twisted the knife in Mustafa's crotch, and pulled it around further, resulting in a fresh spray of blood onto the mattress. Mustafa shrieked again.

'No, Bezam, no!' pleaded Mustafa.

Bezam stopped in his tracks.

Tanya, looking at Bezam's face of dumb confusion, was quickly trying to figure out her next move. Whilst she'd secured a stand-off, for the moment, she couldn't get out of here either.

— 7 —

The grey VW van pulled up a few metres short of the house in Punchbowl.

'There's no WRX in the driveway,' said Harry.

'Signal's still coming from the house,' said Trev. 'Reckon the car's in that garage.'

Harry reached into the trunk behind the seats and pulled out two Remington pump-actions. He gave one to Trev and they both loaded shells into the magazines. They checked their revolvers and got out of the van.

As they did so, two black Ford F250 pick-ups pulled up in front of them. Four muscled bundles of tattooed, leather-clad violence spilled out of them. On the pavement, the two ex-cops joined forces with four ex-cons, all for the greater good. The bikies were even more heavily armed than the sleuths. All four had 9 mm automatics tucked in their beltlines, and between them they were holding a sawn-off double-barrelled shotgun, an M16, and two AK-47s.

'Kenmare,' nodded Longman.

'Longman,' replied Harry. 'Gents.' He looked at the others.

'How many?' asked Longman.

'There were three of them in the car that grabbed Tanya,' said Trev. 'And there's the guy from the house, unless he was number three in the car. So at least four, I reckon, but could be more.'

'So how about we do two teams?' said Harry. 'One of us with two of you. That way we can take out the door hinges with these pump-actions, hard and fast.'

'Good plan,' said Longman. He looked at his gang. 'Rocco, you and Joe with Kenmare's mate, Trev, here, and around the back. Sammy, you and me with Kenmare in the front.'

'And we have to move,' said Harry. 'Tanya's in there with these cunts.'

One of the other bikies chipped in. 'How we going to know this Tanya? So we don't knock her by mistake.'

Longman grinned. 'Oh, you'll know her, Sammy, when you see her. Blonde perfection, body to die for, and beautiful enough to make an angel weep tears of envy.'

Harry snorted. 'Fuck, Longman, that was almost poetic. Now can we get going?'

'Right, guys, let's go,' commanded Longman. 'Shoot anything that moves, except young blondie, but leave the two brothers for me. Unless you really have no choice.'

The small army split into two groups and headed for the house.

— 8 —

Harry and his two new leather-clad mates were either side of the front door, waiting for Trev's text from the rear of the house.

Go

The door was locked. Harry stood in front of it. Two rapid blasts from the Remington and the door fell inwards having lost both its hinges. Longman was in first, M16 at the ready. Harry followed, then Sammy.

At the rear, Rocco burst straight in, his AK-47 raised, with Trev and the fourth bikie, Joe, close behind him. The door opened straight into the kitchen, and the trio's sudden entry was met by stunned looks from two dudes weighing powder into deal bags at a table. One of the Lebanese reached for a Glock pistol sitting on the tabletop, but was permanently delayed by a burst of rounds from Rocco's AK. The other dealer, trying to stand up and reach for an AR-15 rifle propped up at the end of the table, took a blast to the side of his head at close range from the second bikie's sawn-off shotgun. The ensuing red rain of brain matter sprayed over his dead mate.

Trev and the bikies moved to the hallway, where Longman was leading the other trio down from the front door, clearing rooms on either side as they went.

'In here!' Tanya's shout was unmistakeable.

Longman rushed through the bedroom door, Harry and Trev close behind him. Rocco brought up the rear, having sent the other two bikies to check the rest of the house.

Harry looked at the surreal scene of sexual violence. Tanya, on a mattress in only her knickers, had a knife partially stuck into one petrified rapist's scrotum, with blood dripping out. Harry recognized him as the house owner, Mustafa Ahmad. The two Bakhash brothers and one other Lebanese-looking guy were standing at the end of the mattress in various latter stages of undress. It appeared Tanya's introduction of the steel blade had curtailed their shedding of clothes.

The rapists looked at their visitors in disbelief.

'Babe?' said Harry, walking over to Tanya.

'Bit shaken, but I'm not hurt. Except my pride.'

'On your knees, you fucks!' Longman shouted at the three standing rapists. Looking down the assorted gun barrels, they complied.

Harry grabbed Mustafa by his throat and dragged him off the bed, Tanya's knife sliding out of his flesh. Harry handed Tanya his .38 as she wiped her bloodied hands on the grimy mattress. He lowered the pump-action onto the floor. Harry hauled the now whimpering Mustafa up against a wall. Then he drove his fist into the rapist's gut so hard that the plasterboard of the wall gave way.

'Just shoot the cunt, Kenmare,' urged Longman.

'No!' said Tanya, standing up and stepping off the mattress.

'Want my jacket, babe?' asked Harry, peeling it off.

'No, not yet. I want this piece of garbage looking at my body when he dies. Because a woman is going to have the final say over him.'

The magnificent young lady, naked except for skimpy knickers, gripping a .38 revolver in a ruthlessly business-like fashion, was an image straight off the cover of a classic pulp novel: wet-dream stuff for the bikies and Harry alike. For the predatory jihadis, it was their worst nightmare: a woman in lethal control.

'This one is mine,' said Tanya, stepping in front of the now kneeling Mustafa.

'Okay with you, Longman?' asked Harry.

'That's cool, he's not one of the two here that I wanted. So, all yours, girl. And you are an image I will never forget.'

'Brings new meaning to Angel of Death,' remarked Rocco.

'No, please!' cried Mustafa. 'Not her!'

'No, don't let the girl kill him,' Hakim joined in. 'If he dies at the hands of a woman, he will go to hell.'

Longman stepped up to Hakim and drove his boot into his face, breaking his jaw.

'Shut up, motherfucker. On that basis, I'd let her kill all of you, but you and your little maggot brother here are mine. Remember Debbie Shaw?'

The two brothers looked at each other, then back at Longman.

'I'm her uncle, and it's time to pay for your crimes. We got your other two gang mates on the inside, but I've been waiting every day for twelve years for you two.'

At that point, the other two bikies entered the room.

'All clear,' said one of them to Rocco. They both stared at Tanya, just in time to see her pull the trigger and put a .38

hollow-point round into Mustafa's forehead. He collapsed back against the wall, and then slid down onto the floor, dead.

'Rocco, move that third fuck over to the bed. Little lady here can do him as well, if she likes.' Longman looked over at Tanya.

'Yes, please. Could never take out enough of these fuckers for all the shit they give to women.'

Rocco kicked Bezam in the guts, dragged him away from the brothers, and threw him onto the mattress. 'All yours, baby,' he said to Tanya.

Tanya stepped over to Bezam, cowering against the wall at the head of the mattress. 'Ironic,' she said. 'Exactly the spot where you were all going to fuck me. Tables turned now, aren't they?'

Bezam looked up at Rocco. 'Please! You kill me. Don't let her do it,' he pleaded.

Rocco laughed. He didn't bother replying. He simply stepped over and sunk his boot in again.

Tanya stepped next to him, and raised the .38 in both hands in front of Bezam's face. 'You wanker Muslim boys need to learn to respect women. Although it's too late for you, fucker.'

She blasted a third eye socket in his face, square between the other two. Bezam slumped down on the mattress.

Tanya stepped back, handed Harry the .38, and retrieved her jeans and shoes. She took Harry's jacket and put it on.

'Yep, the lady, and she is a lady, is spot on,' said Longman to Hakim and Rashid. 'You fucks definitely need to respect women. Too late for you two as well. I'd like to spend the whole afternoon making you suffer before you die, believe me I would, but we don't have time. More's the pity. Ciao, you jihadi cunts.'

He raised the M16 and put two rounds through Rashid's head. Hakim made a groaning noise through his swelling jaw and mouth. It was his last earthly utterance as two more bullets blew the back of his head away.

Harry looked around at the bedroom turned into a slaughterhouse. 'Time to go, team,' he said to the room.

Trev turned to Longman. 'Mate, you guys might want to take the gear that's in the kitchen. Must be at least five kilos of powder, plus some guns.'

'Sweet,' said Longman. 'Joe and Sammy, you get the gear. Rocco, you take the guns. Now let's move, before we have people coming out in the street for a look.'

'Mate, not very likely around here,' said Harry. 'In these salubrious suburbs, gunshots keep everyone well and truly inside. Too many drive-by shootings, plus none of them wants to be a potential witness when the cops eventually turn up.'

'Yeah, hadn't thought of it that way,' smiled Longman.

'I've worked these streets. Still, we had better move.' Harry smiled in return.

They left the four dead jihadi rapists in their pungent atmosphere of blood, piss and cordite.

Sammy picked up a sports bag lying next to the kitchen table. His mate, Joe, was busy putting all the heroin into a backpack.

Sammy whistled as he looked in the bag. 'Lot of fucking cash, Archie.'

'Tip it on the table, mate.'

A cascade of yellow and green, bundled fifty- and hundred-dollar notes, poured onto the table, replacing the mountain of hammer. Sammy dropped the empty bag next to the cash.

Longman looked at Harry. 'You might not be into the gear, mate, but this is a bit of a bonus. Wanna split it?'

'Does Dolly Parton sleep on her back? Sounds fair and reasonable to me,' replied Harry, grinning at him. 'Reckon there's at least three hundred grand there.'

Longman deftly halved the green bundles, then did the same for the yellow ones. He gave Harry the empty sports bag.

'For your share, Kenmare. Sammy, throw our half in with the gear.'

'Cheers, Longman.' Harry quickly piled their haul into the bag.

'And I'll be having some of that as back-paid danger money, Mr PI,' said Tanya, slapping the bag in Harry's hand.

'Yeah, we'll discuss that.'

Longman laughed. 'Kenmare, you couldn't possibly shower enough cash on this lovely lady, and she sure as hell earned it today.'

'Thanks, Archie,' said Tanya, smiling at him.

She turned to Harry. 'So, a third of that is mine, yes?'

Harry shook his head, grinning. 'Yes, of course, Divine One.'

'What?' asked Longman.

'Oh, don't start him,' replied Trev. 'Let's just get the fuck out of here.'

And then the seven of them were out the front door and on the street. The four bikies piled into their black Ford pick-ups. Harry, Trev and Tanya jumped in the grey VW van. All three vehicles sped away into the dusk.

Still not a single soul came out of any house to rubberneck.

Ten minutes later the sound of sirens gradually enveloped the neighbourhood.

– 9 –

Harry generally avoided his office on the weekends, but this Sunday was an exception. After Friday's bloody exploits, there had been a stiff drink or sixteen all round when they escaped the western Sydney neighbourhoods and got back to the city. Harry had been concerned for Tanya's aftershock, but she seemed surprisingly settled. Perhaps the pleasure of executing two of her captors had been therapeutic. Harry liked that hypothesis: it fitted well with how personally satisfying and cathartic he was finding the hunting down of Orla's killers. Harry also reminded himself that Tanya was one hell of a tough and resilient young lady. So, Saturday had been a dusty and very late wake-up, around lunchtime, and any thinking-type work had not really been on the radar. However, that left an important matter outstanding: the need to start planning how to extract the invalided Herbert Farr from hospitalized custody and into Harry's chamber of inquisition and vengeance. It wouldn't be as simple as lifting Dieter Schwarz from his home or hunting down Bernhard Schwarz in WA: there was the slight issue of prison guards. In addition to the work project, both Harry and Trev wanted the distraction from dwelling on Sasha. So, the office it was.

As Harry and Trev worked on ideas for Farr, in the background were the regular radio news updates on yet another drug-gang massacre at Punchbowl. It had dominated every bulletin since Friday afternoon. A police commander was now on air pontificating about the evils of the drug trade and appealing for public assistance.

'A futile waste of bloody time on both scores,' said Harry after the 11 a.m. bulletin had concluded.

Trev chuckled. 'Not wrong, mate. And never thought I'd see the day I worked *with* bikies rather than *on* bikies.'

'Yeah. But necessity can make strange bedfellows. It worked well, apart from the Tanya bit.'

'We dodged a bullet there, mate,' said Trev. Then he snorted. 'At least that's more than can be said for all those rapists.'

'True.'

'But seriously, Harry, we need to be more careful. Tan's great in so many ways, but she's just a bit too eager at times.'

Harry nodded. 'Yes, agreed. She needs more experience to temper her impetuousness. It will come.'

'Plus, I think with Sasha's illness, her judgement is off kilter.'

'Understandable, but you're right. I said we'd go in with her tomorrow. It's getting close.'

Trev sighed. 'I've been dreading it more each time.'

'Likewise, brother.' Harry lit a smoke. He went over to the window and looked out at the sun-drenched cityscape. The pair were silent.

Harry came back to his desk. 'So, Herbert Farr has a date with destiny. How best to give him his date?'

'Word from my source is that he'll be in Ararat Hospital for at least another several weeks, into the New Year. On top

351

of his serious injuries from the fight, he's got pneumonia, apparently.'

'Oh, poor prick. Must be terrible for him.'

'Minor compared to what we have in store,' said Trev, smiling. 'But, it does mean that this isn't going to be doable too soon. He'll be in intensive care for a while, so no possibility for us there.'

'No, that won't work. Staff near him the whole time.'

'Yeah. We need to wait for him to be moved into a room on his own, which is what he'll get being a prisoner.'

'I concur. So, the first big question is whether there'll be one guard or two at that stage.'

'Got that covered off,' replied Trev. 'There's just one guard each shift, three shifts around the clock, whenever a prisoner is in the hospital for care, except ICU, of course.'

'And it'll be a male guard since he's a male prisoner.'

'Correct. And prisoners are handcuffed to the bed at all times.'

'Was this your contact down there who found all this out?'

Trev grinned. 'Yeah. Well, actually a friend of a contact, who's now my friend, too. He's an ex-copper from back home and moved down south. Had the same problems I did with homophobic bosses.'

'Ah, I see,' said Harry, smirking. 'So your little jaunt down to Victoria the other week paid off?'

'Big time. Got all this info from Ararat, saw a fantastic Steichen photo exhibition in the city, and had a bit of fun.' Trev smiled at Harry and winked.

'You dirty stop-out, you.' Harry laughed.

'Anyway, back to my new friend. I've been talking to him casually since Farr went to hospital. Don't worry, I haven't let too much on. He knows some of the nurses in the town, and one in particular who was a victim of abuse herself. She's been very happy to help out.'

'Sweet. So, in theory we just need to distract the guard for long enough to wheel Herbert out to the van and off we go.'

'Yep. We can start getting things ready, and then head down when we get word that Farr is available for us, so to speak.'

'But sounds like at least two or three weeks away yet?'

'Yeah, I reckon. Bonus is that we can be here to give Tanya some support.'

Harry nodded. 'Yes, she's going to be needing us big time in the next couple of weeks, I think.'

'Shit, it's so unfair.' Trev banged his hand on the desk. 'Let's get back to our plans.'

'Yes. So, we need a decoy then?' Harry mused. He went back to look out the window for inspiration. He turned to Trev. 'Male guard. We need irresistible sex, mate.'

Trev nodded and laughed. 'An oldie but a goodie. Always rely on guys to follow their dicks.'

'And if we're unlucky and it turns out the guard is some bible-thumping chastity wanker who won't succumb to his cock?'

'We'd need a plan B. We could start a ruckus, have a female screaming for help, maybe? But that would be messier. I still think the sex angle has a better than even chance of success.'

'Okay, back to sexy plan A. We are *not* taking Tanya on this one,' said Harry.

'Agreed. She's got way too much on her mind.'

'And it's going to need to be genuine sex, anyway. Lure him off for a blow job in the bathroom, something like that.'

'Well, Tan definitely wouldn't be up for that assignment,' said Trev. 'She's made it clear that her sex-selling days are over.'

'Hey, what about those two girls we met from the Chinese guys on the boat, the union job? Carla and Lauren. We know they will do anything required for the right price.'

Trev nodded. 'Yeah, perfect.'

'We'll just need to get two nurses' uniforms.'

Trev laughed. 'Easily arranged, I'll talk to my friend down there.' He smiled at Harry and wagged his finger at him. 'Mate, you just want to see them dressed as saucy nurses, don't you?'

Harry grinned. 'True, but remember we've already seen them wearing considerably less.'

'Alas, that was wasted on me,' sighed Trev. 'Although, I can imagine from a straight perspective that they are both sex on legs.'

'You bet. Anyway, I reckon the two of them together, some story to the guard on duty about always having had a fantasy about a threesome with a man in uniform, and we are set.'

'Like your style, brother,' said Trev. 'I'll arrange the uniforms, and you organize the girls.'

'Will be my pleasure,' grinned Harry. 'I'll call them next week.' Then he frowned. 'I know it's a slim chance, brother, but what if the guard is gay?'

Trev winked at him. 'Well, I guess I'll need to improvise and become a hospital orderly to tempt him in the direction of the male toilets, whilst you and the girls get Farr out of there. But you'll need to work fast, because I won't be sucking his dick!'

– 10 –

Tanya gently stroked Sasha's face, her sister's once full and vibrant cheeks now sunken pits. Her blue eyes had lost their pale sapphire brilliance and now had the look of a bleached, dimming sky. The wavy blonde tresses, previously something to behold, had been cruelly devastated by the futile chemotherapy. Little hair or brows or lashes remained.

Tanya wanted to scream and punch the walls.

'Sis,' murmured Sasha.

Tanya leant in closer.

Sasha's words seeped out like the stealthy whisper of doom. 'Please, now.' Faded blue eyes looked desperately into their genetically identical bright blue, but weeping, counterparts. 'I love you, Sis,' said Sasha.

Tanya's emotions were savaging her insides like a pack of rabid dogs. Half an hour earlier she'd asked Harry and Trev to leave her to it. They'd both kissed Sasha and hugged her goodbye, for the last time. They were crying as they left, and made no effort to hide it from the staff.

Zanza and Liam had visited earlier, being the only other people privy to Sasha's wishes. They all cried in the room after the old Irishman's farewell words, which he'd put into a verse:

You beautiful young angel, so lovely of heart,
mind and deed,
During your short life, in so many ways cruelly
put to the sword,
Your tragic leaving renders farcical every single
creed,
May eternity, whatever that may be, render you
true reward.

And with that Liam had kissed Sasha, put his fatherly
hand on Tanya's face, and left. The Irishman's rant about
there clearly being no god echoed down the hallway as he
departed.

Zanza, tears streaming down his face, had balled up his
fists and looked as if he was going to punch someone or
something.

'I am so not going to try and stop him if he lashes out,'
said Harry.

'Mate, you couldn't if your life depended on it,' replied
Trev. 'And I'm not volunteering, either.'

As it transpired, Zanza, whilst having the physical
potential to wreak havoc, had a level of self-restraint that
most men would envy. His goodbye hug for Sasha nearly
obviated the need for final drugs, and then he moped out
of the room, his proud head hanging down. Both Harry
and Trev gave him a hug on his way out.

Tanya had been slowly psyching herself up, knowing
this was going to be the hardest day of her life. She'd
lost plenty before. She'd lost her innocence to their filthy
stepfather when she was eleven. She'd lost her dad in some
secret military mission before that. She'd lost no end of
dignity with a few of the clients she'd had to put up with
at the brothel. She'd lost girlfriends to their demons, via

the needle. But none of that could compare to losing Sash. Sash was her whole universe. How the hell was she going to live without her?

After Liam and Zanza had gone, Tanya had considered asking Harry to do the dreaded deed for her. But that weak moment passed. She couldn't ask anyone to do this. Sasha wanted her to do it, and, damn it, she was strong enough. She just had to get past the constant asking herself, 'Why?' There was no bloody answer, simple as that. And so she'd asked Harry and Trev to say their goodbyes. Without them there, there was no avenue for any weakness of resolve as her emotions ripped the living shit out of her.

Tanya leant in and kissed Sasha on her wan lips. 'I love you, Sis. Goodbye.' Tears streamed down her face.

Sasha gave the merest hint of a smile. 'Thank you, Sis. I love you, too.'

Tanya hesitated.

'Please, Sis, please,' implored Sasha.

Tanya took out the syringe of morphine Harry and Trev had given her. She thought back to her earlier conversations where the guys had reassured her that it would be a totally pain-free way for Sasha to go, and since she was terminally ill anyway, no one would be likely to suspect anything other than death from the cancer. Anyway, even if there was a risk for her, this is what Sash wanted; she'd made that abundantly clear. Right now, the only thing Tanya cared about was keeping her promise to her sister, as heart-rending as it was.

She kissed Sasha again, and then eased the needle into the cannula in Sasha's hand. She depressed the plunger fully. She quickly capped the needle and put it into her purse.

Sasha's face started to relax, her limpid eyes easing into relief.

Tanya put her face next to Sasha's and kissed her again. 'Thank you,' whispered Sasha.

A torrent of tears now washed down Tanya's cheeks as she laid her face against Sasha's, her hand stroking the other side of her head.

Sasha looked almost serene as she slipped away. Tanya kept holding her. Then the cardiac monitor flat-lined and the alarm went off. Tanya burst out crying uncontrollably and let out a howl of anguish. Two nurses came running into the room.

– 11 –

A sultry and sombre Monday evening at the Emerald Bar was in effect Sasha's unofficial wake, albeit for a small, select crowd.

Just for once it wasn't Harry or Trev who'd suggested the pub. Tanya had insisted, saying tearfully that she had to have the company and the distraction. Harry had called Tessa to let her know about Sasha's death. Tessa hadn't been at the hospital that day, as she wasn't privy to Sasha's wishes. Harry had wanted to say something to her, but Tanya requested it stay as quiet as possible. Liam had ended up there as Liam got wind of everything: he was one of those people. And, of course, Sasha had wanted Zanza in the inner circle.

Tanya had messaged Zanza about the pub, but he was on shift at Club Mammary. Tessa had, however, joined them at the pub for an early dinner in the restaurant, and then out to the beer garden.

The news bulletin came on the big screen and the crowd hushed, for snippets had been emerging online all day from the public hearing at the ICAC into the First State Transit corruption scandal. The first story at six o'clock was delicious in its salaciousness: excerpts of evidence from the main players, including being tripped up by their own lies, details of the harbour cruise orgy, and protestations from the transport union that corruption was not endemic to the labour movement.

'Bullshit!' added Trev, loudly at that point, unable to help himself.

Then came the cream on the cake: the glorious footage of the goings on, courtesy of 'pussycam'. Trev's handiwork had hidden the faces of the girls, of course, before the footage went anywhere near the ICAC. But the ICAC Commissioner had decided that their take on juicy didn't run as far as beautiful breasts bouncing around, so all the faceless fair maidens also had pixelated bosoms.

Then the news bulletin had the obligatory footage of the camera crews and reporters pursuing each scoundrel as they left the ICAC building.

'Always such a hoot to watch,' added Liam.

And then, as if that wasn't enough entertainment, breaking news reported the government in Beijing taking the Chinese rail executives into custody.

'That's big league,' said Harry. 'They'll execute them over there for official corruption.' His thought was immediately echoed by the TV correspondent on the live cross from Beijing.

'Well, as much as I disagree with the death penalty,' said Trev, 'they're no great loss.'

'Nor would the arseholes here be, either,' said Liam. 'But state executions are uncivilized. We'll make do with our crooked wankers getting several years in prison.'

Harry chuckled. 'At least it'll be hard time for them, very hard indeed.'

Then the story about the ongoing investigation into Friday's events at Punchbowl came on. Most of the rest of the beer garden clientele went back to their drinks and chats – another inter-gang killing between Middle-Eastern drug-dealers, as the media was still pronouncing it, was of little interest. Except to other drug-dealers, of course, but there didn't seem to be any of them at the Emerald Bar that night. There never were: it wasn't that sort of establishment.

The newsreader announced it was believed that at least two of the Punchbowl shooting victims were convicted participants of the infamous Muslim gang rapes around 2000 and 2001. Police were stating this was purely coincidental, and the significant traces of narcotics and related equipment in the house were all indicative that the killings were drug-related.

'And let's keep it that way,' said Harry under his breath.

'Drink to that,' added Trev.

'What's the story with those gang rapes?' asked Tessa. 'That was before I arrived in Sydney.'

Harry gave her a succinct synopsis.

'Ugh, total bloody scum,' said Tessa when he had finished. 'Rapists deserve the very worst; I would consider hanging them. Men can be such pigs. But these extreme religious types, I think their whole view of women leads to abuse.'

'Yeah, second-class citizens only good for cooking and screwing!' added Tanya forcefully. 'Shame there's not more honest discussion about it in our wonderful multicultural society.'

'Tsk, tsk,' said Liam. 'That would be devastatingly upsetting to the political-correctness brigade in this country.' He grinned mischievously at her.

Tessa downed the rest of her wine. 'To be fair, of course, there are abusive and misogynistic branches in most religions. Some Christian groups are definitely up there, too. Does that help on the political correctness front, Liam?'

Tanya smiled and joined in. 'Fuck correctness. I'm a woman and I deserve to be treated with respect.'

'We can all drink to that, young lady,' said Liam, raising his glass.

They all followed suit.

'And this is the problem,' said Trev. 'Some people come here and yet don't subscribe to our core principles of liberty and equality. Some of them even want to execute gays, so I'm a bit stuffed, too.'

'Yeah, I agree,' said Harry. 'Not with executing gays,' he added quickly. The others laughed. Harry continued. 'I mean I'm happy for anyone to come and live here, but only if they genuinely believe in our basic way of life.'

'Yeah, sorry to sound like a raving feminist again, but just look at the bloody face covering,' said Tessa.

'That should be banned,' said Tanya. 'It's so demeaning of women. As if we have to be hidden from view.'

'Exactly,' replied Tessa. 'Just chattels of the men. Was it France that banned the burqa?'

'*Mais oui!*' said Liam. 'Whatever their faults, you can usually rely on the good old French to stand up for *liberté*, *egalité*, and *fraternité*. And the Belgians banned it, too.'

'Part of me agrees,' said Trev. 'But I then think it's contradictory to civil liberties to ban people from wearing certain things.'

'I wrestle with that, too,' added Harry. 'But I do think things that directly undermine our democratic foundations do need to be confronted, as contradictory as that may seem.'

'Ah, the great paradox for liberal democracies when they try to do multiculturalism,' said Liam. 'The problem is, it's only really workable if we all have the same fundamental beliefs about running society. We can have all sorts of cultural variety, that's great, but the real basic building blocks need to match.'

'I think you're right, Your Eminence,' said Harry. 'I like the idea of a diverse society, but I agree that it can't work if we don't share the same essential values.'

'I just want to see women treated as equals,' said Tanya. 'And with bloody respect.'

'I'm with you, sister,' said Tessa.

Liam raised his glass. 'To respect, equality, and liberal democracy.'

The others lifted their drinks. They all chinked their glasses and drank.

Liam looked at them all. 'But to hell with politics. Most importantly, tonight, here's to Sasha, an angel taken from us far too young.'

'Yep,' said Harry. 'All the other shit pales into insignificance today. To Sasha.'

They drank.

Then they were remarkably silent, considering their previous voluble rant.

Tanya had tears running down both cheeks.

— 12 —

F riday morning was oppressively humid and already past thirty-three degrees at 11.30 a.m. as Sasha's funeral ceremony started at the Rookwood Crematorium.

Harry, Trev, Zanza and Liam sweated in their dark suits and ties. They were the only men in the small crowd of about thirty. Everyone was crying as they looked at the cedar coffin on its bier. Along with Tessa, Miss Andromeda, Sandrine, and Miss Trixy, the madam from the Scarlet Boudoir where the twins had worked, the guys were also in the older brigade of mourners. Most of the group were young women with whom Tanya and Sasha had worked, some from their modelling and fashion work with Tessa, the others from the sex industry.

Harry had acknowledged the two girls, Carla and Lauren, from the harbour cruise escapade. And he was sure he recognized at least a couple of the others, although now that they were fully dressed it was a bit hard to be sure.

Sasha had asked for one of her favourite songs as the tune for the occasion: Christina Aguilera's 'Beautiful'. The sweet melody played as each woman placed a single pink rose, Tanya's choice and request, on top of the casket, the singer's dulcet tones capturing the mood.

'She certainly was beautiful in every single way, as the song says,' said Harry under his breath.

'A tragedy that makes a mockery of life,' whispered Trev.

Everybody present, without exception, gave a brief eulogy.

Harry was in awe at the outpourings of heartfelt appreciation of Sasha. 'So much love for her,' he whispered to Trev.

'Don't think there'll be quite so much when my time comes,' murmured Trev in reply.

'You and me both, brother.'

'Mate, you're right into your flowers, which never ceases to surprise me, but what does a pink rose signify? I know all the colours are supposed to have meanings.'

Harry smiled wryly. 'Brother, it's my sensitive side. And a pink rose represents grace.'

Trev nodded slowly. 'Yeah, I can see that fits for Sash. That is beautiful.'

'Exactly,' murmured Harry.

When all had paid their tributes to Sasha, Tanya stood at the head of the casket for the final words. She spoke of their life together, without glossing over the tragedies, and thanked everyone for their love and support. Then she finished with her own take on Auden. As tears ran down her cheeks, she read from a card in her hand:

> Sash was my sister, my twin, my joy, and my daily zest,
> My loving soul mate and of all my friends, the best,
> My all the time, my anytime, my confidante so long,
> I hoped we would be together for life, but I was wrong.

She paused. The whole room was silent.

'I love you, Sis.' She bent down and kissed the casket lid.

Every eye in the room was streaming now, as the casket moved towards its fiery destiny. Everyone watched silently until Sasha was gone.

As mourners were hugging Tanya outside in the close, unpleasant air, Harry approached Carla and Lauren. 'Hi, girls. Sorry to see you on a day like this,' he said.

'I can't believe it,' said Carla.

'So, so sad, and so bloody unfair,' said Lauren.

'Yeah,' sighed Harry. 'Sasha was a truly wonderful human being. You joining us for her drinks this afternoon at the Emerald Bar?'

'Definitely,' said Carla. 'Tanya said you've booked an upstairs part called the Nude Bar.' She looked quizzical.

'Yeah, what is that?' asked Lauren.

'Well, we won't be getting naked, that's for sure. It's a reference to all the erotic artworks they've got on the walls. You'll be impressed, I think. Sasha wanted her proper wake to be held there. She was particularly fond of it.'

The two girls looked at each other. 'Cool,' said Carla. Lauren was nodding.

'Not the time or place now,' said Harry, 'but we want to talk business later.'

'Okay, always happy to work with you guys,' said Carla.

'See you at the wake, then. And thank you for coming today. It really means a lot for all of us, but especially Tanya.'

'We really wanted to be here. See you later, Harry,' said Lauren.

The girls walked off towards their car.

Trev wandered over. 'They in?'

'Yep.'

'Cool. Ready to go?'

'Not yet, Trev.'

Trev raised his eyebrows.

'A little visit to make first, brother.'

'Your Orla?'

'Yes, Orla's grave is not far. Will you walk with me?'

'Yeah, of course.' Trev put his hand on Harry's shoulder, then hugged him. The pair walked away together across the expanse of cemetery.

Ten minutes later, Harry was standing in front of a headstone. Trev loitered a respectful distance behind him.

Harry knelt in front of the grave. He gazed lovingly at the inscription on the stone. He spoke quietly to himself. 'My little angel, you are never forgotten. You are in my thoughts, always.'

Harry paused; looked down at the grave itself. 'My little Orla, I've got one of the bastards. And I won't rest until I've got the others. You have my promise, my little angel. I love you.'

Harry blew a kiss to Orla's grave, then stood up. He held his head down in respect for a minute, then turned to face Trev. They met eyes.

'You good, Harry?'

'Yeah. Now let's go get wasted. I've had enough of reality today.'

– 13 –

In the 1980s, three young Irishmen came together in the Maze Prison outside Belfast, courtesy of custodial terms for their IRA activities. Whilst they'd heard of each other on the outside, and pursued similar 'hobbies', including explosives, they hadn't worked together. That was the cellular nature of the organization.

Padraic Finnegan had been caught for his role in a rocket attack on a British Army checkpoint. Mickey O'Rourke was dobbed in by a turncoat for the car-bombing death of an RUC commander. Owen Driscoll, a chemist by training, was caught in his 'laboratory' when the same rat in the ranks found out the address.

That snitch for the British, however, didn't get to enjoy his reward money from London. Another Provo kneecapped him and then cut his throat as his young family, tied and gagged, watched on. That Provo was Connor O'Reilly.

O'Reilly then masterminded the escape of the incarcerated trio whilst they were being transferred to court for a hearing date. They profusely thanked O'Reilly, pledging him a lifelong debt, and then disappeared south of the border to hide out in the Republic and assume new identities.

Now, nearly three decades later, they were on the move again. With not quite as much youthful spring to their step, but still lethally dangerous indeed.

As Tanya and her mourning entourage were celebrating Sasha's life and memory at the Emerald Bar on Friday evening, a British Airways flight from Heathrow via Singapore touched down at Sydney's Kingsford Smith Airport.

Three Irish-passport holders went separately through Australian immigration control. The trio, whose official names meant nothing to law enforcement anywhere, were all ostensibly visiting the land down under for a holiday.

Finnegan, O'Rourke and Driscoll emerged from the international terminal into a dark and tropical Sydney night. They got three cabs to a house in Surry Hills. One after the other, they were greeted at the door by O'Reilly.

Sydney's heat was broken an hour later by a massive tropical thunderstorm.

* * * * *

PART 5

HARRY'S KARMA

The truth is, the biggest, hardest dick in the world is useless if you don't know how to eat pussy.

- Christa Faust

No past or future. Nothing but a fragile present, which we sipped and savored together. We feasted ourselves on little pleasures, on patterns of light and shade which we knew we should remember all our lives. As for our flesh, we tortured it with our desperate efforts to blend it into a single whole.

- Georges Simenon

— 1 —

Roger Allen's right hand moved rhythmically along his rigid penis, each stroke pulling the foreskin back over the glistening glans. His other hand held an A4 colour photo of two naked twin girls, aged eleven. They were posed on a bed, his bed, all those years ago, one afternoon whilst their mother, his wife, was out. He'd just finished raping them both, and the picture was a keepsake. Now he masturbated over his memories, his triumphs, his conquests. The photograph, his personal favourite from a large collection, was laminated.

Not that he didn't have more recent memories. The appearance of being a respectably married man brought with it lots of automatic trust. This was gold currency for a paedophile, and the reason he'd stayed with his wife. The marriage, or course, was entirely platonic. Even the thought of intimacy with an adult woman made Roger Allen feel queasy.

So, suburban life had yielded huge benefits. Years of voluntary work with various youth organizations, as well as at the local church Sunday school, not to mention a couple of babysitting gigs for needy neighbourhood single mothers, had presented him with many prepubescent trophies. But he still rated those twins above all others.

And, of course, moving in as their stepfather had given him total power over them. Ah, such great years, he thought.

His hand picked up speed.

Tanya stood in the darkness of the back patio. The early January evening was stiflingly humid and deathly still. Flashes of light on the western horizon heralded a tropical storm. She sweated in her jacket in the shadows. She watched through the open French doors as her stepfather ejaculated over a photo of her and Sasha.

His last orgasm, although he didn't know that, yet.

Tanya clicked open the golden heart dangling in her cleavage and kissed the little photo of her and Sasha. Her sister's death itself, as well as her promise to her, had spurred Tanya into taking action. It had now been a few weeks in the making. Then she looked at their dad in the opposite half of the locket. She closed it up and dropped it back between her breasts.

She stepped over the threshold of the Panania house where she and Sasha had grown up. A Christmas tree, the same mangy old plastic one she remembered, was still up. The December event wasn't something Tanya celebrated now, not since she'd escaped this hell-hole and the scene of her rapes. Harry and Trev didn't seem to take any notice of the festive season, either, except as an extra excuse to get on the sauce, so December had been and gone much like any other month. Except, of course, it was now her first New Year without Sasha.

She walked across the room to her stepfather. He jumped at the sight of her, and dropped the dripping photo on the carpet. He started to get up, but Tanya sent him reeling back into the armchair with a powerful heel kick to his gut. His now flaccid penis was hanging out of his Y-fronts, like a raw chipolata escaping the butcher's bag.

'Bet you never thought you'd see me again, you piece of shit. At least not in the flesh,' she said, nodding at the photo on the floor. She considered spitting on it, but didn't want to leave any easy DNA finds for the cops.

Allen's eyes widened as Tanya produced a Beretta 9 mm pistol from inside her jacket. It had a silencer attached to it.

'I've been thinking of this day for years, you cunt. You reckon an apology might be on the cards? For fucking up our lives?'

Some of the fear on Allen's face evaporated and was replaced with arrogant conceit. 'Your mother said I could do what I liked so long as she never knew anything and I kept paying for everything, especially her booze and pills.'

'Is that right? And that makes it all fucking okay, does it?' She kicked him again.

He grunted, then looked back up at her. He smiled malignantly, sitting up. 'You two were the best fucks of my life.'

'Take this, scum.'

There was a muffled crack as a bullet ripped into his forehead. Tanya felt a wave of elation rushing over her. A second crack. A second hole appeared in her stepfather's forehead. Damn, this feels good, she thought.

'Fuck you, arsehole,' she said to the man with two dribbles of blood running down his face. His grin remained even after the two bullets slammed into his head.

As he slumped back in the chair, Tanya fired one more round into his heart.

'That's for me and Sash. And one less filthy ped in the world.' Hey, Sis, she thought, first one down. She stood back and admired her handiwork. Then she strode off down the hallway. The noise of her mother's drunken snoring got louder as she made her way towards the master bedroom.

She stopped momentarily to look into their old room. It was now piled high with boxes and green plastic bin bags of junk.

She continued to her mother's room and stepped inside. The light was on and the air was rank with sour sweat and rotten flatulence. Megan Allen, formerly Roberts when she was married to the twins' father, was in her yellowed underwear, lying on top of the bed. An almost-empty bottle of McWilliams sweet sherry was on her bedside table. There was no glass. Another empty sherry bottle lay on the old carpet, half under the bed, as if trying to flee the crime scene to come.

Tanya slipped on a pair of latex gloves. She slapped her mother hard across the face, which brought a startled, semi-conscious response. Tanya hit her again. Her eyes opened more fully, took in Tanya, and adopted an alcohol-dulled gaze of astonishment mixed with fear.

'I want Dad's army photos, and that album with me and Sasha.'

'Wha ... what?' murmured the confused drunk.

Tanya slapped her again, twice. 'Get with it, bitch!' she hissed quietly. Tanya didn't want to draw attention from the neighbours, so she suppressed the urge to yell. 'Where are they?' She raised her hand to slap her mother again.

'In ... in that trunk over there.' Megan vaguely indicated a black lacquered chest against the wall.

'Stay on the bed and don't move.'

Tanya needn't have worried about that possibility: Megan Allen was having trouble even keeping her eyes open.

Tanya went over to the chest and opened it. She rummaged around and found the photos, plus her father's service medals. She placed them in a small fold-up bag she pulled out of her pocket. She closed the chest, slung the bag over her shoulder, and then went back over to the bed. She pulled out her gun.

Megan Allen barely registered the black object in front of her face, let alone recognized it as a gun and silencer.

'You're a fucking piss-weak excuse for a mother.'

'I don't understand,' murmured Megan.

Again Tanya resisted the strong temptation to spit, this time in her mother's face. 'This is for Sasha and me, and for you allowing our lives to be ruined, you fucking cow!'

There were the muted bangs as two bullets put Megan Allen back to sleep, permanently.

Tanya allowed herself a moment to look at her dead mother with satisfaction. 'That's both of them done, Sis,' she said quietly. Tanya felt as if a burden of years was rapidly lifting from her.

Feeling lighter on her feet and happier in her heart, she moved quickly back down the hallway, into the lounge room, and out into the darkness of the back yard, closing the patio door behind her. She crossed the lawn to the twin stumps of the jacaranda trees their dad had planted to celebrate their birth. The same beautiful trees that were then cut down by their stepfather in celebration of his carnal violation and dominance of them. Tanya kissed both the jacaranda remains, then turned and left the Panania property for the very last time. She wiped the gun of her prints and wrapped it in a cloth, putting it back inside her jacket. She walked out into the dimly lit street.

Two blocks away, a black Ford F250 was parked inconspicuously against the kerb. She stepped up to the open driver's window, a mist of cigarette smoke drifting out into the still night air.

'All go okay?' asked Archie Longman.

'Perfect, thanks.' Tanya pulled out the silenced Beretta in its cloth and handed it through the pick-up window to Longman. 'I really appreciate this, Archie. I didn't need Harry trying to talk me out of it.'

'No worries, blondie. Happy to help you out. And thank you for all the support you've been giving Debbie. You've made a very big difference for her. She thinks the world of you.'

'Cool. I'll be seeing her shortly. Got to drop the car back.'

'Sweet, see you 'round. Give my regards to Kenmare and his mate.'

She smiled. 'I won't be telling him anything just yet, okay?'

Longman grinned back at her. 'Got you. *Ciao, bella.*' The F250 engine growled throatily to life and Longman drove away.

Tanya got into the car Debbie had lent her and headed off into the night.

– 2 –

Tanya locked the car and left it in the parking lot at Debbie's apartment block in Marrickville. She walked up the stairs to the second floor. It was an older-style building with walkways running along each floor on the outside, and no lifts.

Tanya felt a weird exhilaration at having killed her paedophile stepfather, combined with a burning sense of justice and pleasure at having kept her promise. She thought of Sasha. *Fuck, I miss you, Sis, but I did us proud. Wish you could be here to enjoy it with me.*

But she was also experiencing other strange emotions. This wild, savage side of her had suddenly emerged, over and above her revenge mission. It was like a high that demanded still more satisfaction. So, she had killed her mother into the bargain, also justice in her view. And after that she felt sated. For a while. But now this feral urge was returning. And it wasn't a hunger that alcohol or drugs would sort out. The urge was entirely carnal. *I need to go and screw Harry half to death,* she thought. *That would give me the right sort of fix.* Having just killed two people, she had a desperate urge to feel alive. She looked at her watch. It was a touch after ten. Harry would still be up. Well, he certainly would be when she sat on his face.

She knocked on the door of the apartment.

'Who is it?' came Debbie's voice, along with the unmistakeable metallic sliding noise of a pistol being cocked. Longman had made sure Debbie was adequately armed in her own place.

'It's me, Deb.'

The wooden door opened. Then Debbie unlocked the first-grade security screen door, which looked tough enough to protect a bank vault. 'Hey, Tan. How did it go?'

Tanya stepped inside and Debbie resecured both doors behind her. Tanya had got used to that in the short time she had been friends with Debbie. Hardly surprising Debbie was so paranoid after her appalling ordeal all those years ago. The only male ever to come through the door was Uncle Archie.

'All done,' replied Tanya. She hugged Debbie. 'Thank you so much for the car. That was a huge help.' She kissed Debbie on the cheek.

'No worries. You've been so good to me with all your support, Tan.'

Tanya had visited regularly over the few weeks since the Punchbowl extermination. Deb needed more female friends, and Tanya felt she was able to empathize with her on a number of levels.

Debbie gave Tanya a kiss on her cheek, and then stood looking at her for a moment. She still had her hands behind Tanya's shoulders. She slowly moved her face back towards Tanya's. Debbie kissed Tanya on her mouth. She paused momentarily, but Tanya didn't move away or react badly. Debbie continued, sliding her tongue in slightly, hesitatingly.

Tanya opened her mouth wider, inviting Debbie in. Her tongue wasted no time; hesitation was gone. A few moments later, she withdrew, looking Tanya in her eyes. 'Tan, can I ask you a huge favour, please?' she said in a husky voice.

'Of course,' murmured Tanya, taken aback by the pash.

Debbie paused, then whispered, 'Will you sleep with me, Tan? I need to feel wanted, in that way. I trust you.' She kissed Tanya again, with more vigour this time, running her hands down Tanya's back to gently massage her buttocks.

Damn me, thought Tanya, this girl's tongue is magnificent. Her blood pressure was rising fast and she was tingling all over. She'd had a couple of trysts with girlfriends before, and always enjoyed them. Hell, Harry would have to wait. This was a right here, right now moment. Let's take a walk on the wild side, girl. She took her mouth away from Debbie's, ran a hand onto her breast and squeezed gently. 'Let's do it,' she breathed.

Debbie's face lit up with a broad smile. Tanya didn't think Debbie could ever look so happy. She let go of Tanya and held out her hand. 'Come with me.'

Debbie took Tanya's hand and led her to the bedroom. Within seconds they were naked and climbing onto the bed, caressing and kissing.

Tanya looked at an array of toys and lube set out on a bedside table. 'You were ready for me, then?' she smiled.

'I was certainly hoping I wasn't going to have to use them all on myself, as I usually do.'

A couple of minutes later, they were in the sixty-niner position, avidly devouring each other. Tanya, face awash in Debbie's wetness, heard a buzz start, then felt the vibrator ease its way inside her as Debbie's expert tongue concentrated on her clitoris.

Shit, that feels so good, she thought, as she reached for an implement herself, twisted it on, and slid it past her nose and into Debbie's vagina. Her friend moaned loudly, still lapping in Tanya's crotch.

A minute later, Tanya felt the coolness of lube being applied to her anus. Debbie's finger delicately probed up her arse.

Tanya was producing the louder groans now. God, this was heaven on sheets; she would have to make this a bit more regular. She knew Debbie deserved every bit of ecstasy she was getting. Tanya reached for the lube and eased three fingers together into Debbie's derrière. Leaving the existing toy vibrating in Debbie's vagina, Tanya reached for another dildo.

An hour later, a showered and smiling Tanya stepped out of Debbie's apartment. They kissed.

'Will you come again?' asked her host.

'You bet, sister.' She grinned. 'In more ways than one.'

Debbie smiled and hugged her. 'Good. I feel safe with you. I can't feel that way with men. As a girl I always wanted to have a hubby and kids. Not now, though.'

'I hear you.' Tanya stroked her face. 'See you soon.'

They were still kissing when the taxi beeped its horn. Tanya went quickly down the stairs and got into the cab, waving Debbie goodbye. She gave the cabbie the address for Harry's apartment block.

Fuck, I feel on fire tonight, thought Tanya, as she sat in the back of the taxi, savouring the fresh memories of Debbie. I could go all night on this adrenalin.

It was nearly eleven thirty as Tanya let herself into Harry's apartment. He'd given her a key on the basis that the only other woman he might conceivably be entertaining at his place would be Tessa. His exact words had been, 'Frankly, my dear, you'd be welcome to join in.'

She closed the door behind her, seeing light coming from Harry's bedroom. Looked as if he was reading. She certainly couldn't smell Tessa's perfume.

'Hi, Mr PI, surprise! And I'm as horny as hell.' She walked into his room.

He was reading Ken Bruen's *The Killing of the Tinkers*. 'Well, well, you've come to exactly the right place.'

Tanya thought of the three orgasms a short while ago courtesy of Deb, and decided that at least the same were required here. 'You make me cum at least three times, or you're on rations for the next month.'

'Babe, harsh measures. So, get naked and get on my face.' Harry threw down his book, and slid himself horizontal, pulling back the sheet to reveal his already hardening member.

Tanya teased it with her fingers as she straddled Harry's face with her thighs.

'God, I love this,' murmured Harry as his voice was swallowed by Tanya's crotch and his tongue got to work.

Tanya rode him hard. Orgasm number one was on its way.

By the time she woke up the next morning, and looked at Harry bringing her a coffee in bed, she recalled four orgasms. She could have gone on for more, but Harry was protesting a sore cock and lockjaw by that stage. She couldn't immediately come up with any connection, other than sheer adrenalin, between murder and orgasms, but that had been the best night of sex in her life. And despite her young years, she wasn't exactly inexperienced. But more than the sex, she couldn't ever remember feeling such complete and utter vibrancy inside her. Damn it, girl, you'd better stick to the sex alone, or you could end up a gun-toting vigilante. She grinned at her reflection in the mirror. She sipped her coffee and let the warmth of her inner blaze radiate through her.

— 3 —

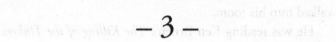

H arry was whistling, none too melodically, as he walked towards his office on late Monday afternoon. He'd been having coffee with Carla and Lauren and had finalized arrangements for the job in Victoria: lasciviously distract the prison guard whilst Harry and Trev extracted Herbert Farr for his one-way trip to hell. He left out the latter part from the briefing. Carla had laughed and said it was the first time she'd been asked to screw a screw. Both the girls knew better than to ask Harry why he was engaging them to do this bizarre job. But for the money offered, Carla said they would be happy to screw a whole prison of guards all day long. Lauren added that they'd make sure it was a shift the screw would never forget.

Harry stepped through the door of the office and into the tail end of a conversation.

'It'd be like Harry being let loose in a room full of Romy Schneider lookalikes,' Tanya was saying.

'Yeah, absolute carnage,' replied Trev. 'Floor covered with ravished Romys.'

Harry closed the door and walked over to his desk, opening the bottom drawer. 'Just one Romy and I'd be beside myself,' he grinned, pouring two glasses of Jameson.

'Is that right, Mr PI?' challenged Tanya. 'I agree she was stunning, though. I've seen enough bloody photos of her at your place.' She blew him a kiss.

'At least I wouldn't have any competition from you, Trev,' said Harry, passing him a whiskey.

Trev laughed. 'No worries there, mate. Her one-time lover, Alain Delon, however. I'd do him in a heartbeat.'

'Who?' asked Tanya.

'Oh, Tan, you are missing out. Come and have a look here,' said Trev, beckoning her over to the couch. He tapped his laptop keyboard and brought up a picture of Delon.

'Oh, yummy!' said Tanya. 'I'd do him, too. He's a complete dish.'

'Too bad he's straight,' lamented Trev.

Harry made a vodka soda for Tanya and took it over to her. Then he flicked the radio on and sat down at his desk with his drink. He opened up a gallery of Romy photos on his computer. He needed to compete with Trev and Tanya, who were sighing longingly over images of Alain Delon. Damn, Romy was beautiful, he thought, as he gazed at the photos.

'Right, Romy adulation done for the day,' said Harry, turning away from his screen and towards his team. 'Trev, the girls are good for the Victoria job.'

'Excellent. It'll be great to finally get down there. They give you their sizes for the nurse uniforms?'

'Oh, yeah, nearly forgot.' Harry pulled out his notebook. 'Both a size eight.'

'I could have told you that,' said Tanya. 'And anyway, why the hell aren't I working on this job with you?' She glared at Harry.

'Babe, two reasons, and don't get all bolshie about it. First is that you need a break from the hands-on operational work …'

'Why the hell, Harry?' interrupted Tanya. 'I'm good at it.'

'Yes, you certainly are. But you've had far too much on your mind for any reasonable person to deal with, and in our line of work, a momentary lapse can be catastrophic. I don't think I need to labour that point, do I?'

'Look, they didn't rape me and I got out okay. Plus, it's a month ago now.'

She was still on the couch with Trev, who put his hand on her shoulder. 'Tan, it was a close call, too bloody close,' he said.

Tanya looked crestfallen. She looked back at Harry, then to Trev, and then back to Harry. They both seemed pretty resolute. She also thought it was probably best not to try to bolster her argument by saying anything about her family visit on Friday night. 'And the second reason?' she asked Harry.

'This one's just as important in our considerations, although of a somewhat different flavour,' he replied.

Trev chuckled.

Harry continued. 'Babe, it's highly likely that actual sex with the prison guard will be required. This is not like the harbour cruise. It's not just a tease-and-entice job.'

'More like a full head job,' added Trev, smiling at her. 'Minimum.'

'Oh, I see,' she replied, her miffed expression evaporating. 'Okay, that's not my scene then. My full-service days are definitely over.'

Trev gave her a hug.

She took a mouthful of her vodka. 'But don't you guys sideline me. I *will* get back on track.'

'Absolutely, babe, but you do need more recuperation time,' said Harry.

'We're only interested in looking out for you,' added Trev.

She kissed Trev on the cheek and blew one at Harry. 'Thank you, my knights in tarnished armour.'

She was about to continue with more lip when the news bulletin came on the radio. The lead story was the discovery of two bodies with gunshot wounds in a house in Panania.

Tanya listened to the details. The police spokesperson was saying that the bodies of a man and woman were found when police were called to the address after a door-knocker reported strange smells. Police had now established a crime scene and forensic officers were in attendance. The homicide detectives were also at the scene. Police believed the victims were a married couple, Roger and Megan Allen. Anyone with information was asked to call Crime Stoppers. The next news item came on.

Tanya looked at Harry out of the corner of her eye. He'd gone back to his screen. Perhaps he hadn't taken much notice of her mother's new surname when Megan had hired him to find Tanya a couple of years ago. He probably only connected her surname, Roberts, to the case in his mind. She turned back to Trev and poked him in the ribs. Time to make sure nobody started thinking about the news story.

'So, find us some more silver-screen hunks we'd both like to shag.'

Trev laughed. 'You're on.'

The news bulletin droned on with the inanities of federal politics.

Trev was scrolling through images of male actors with Tanya murmuring approval every now and then. They agreed on George Clooney and Brad Pitt, but were divided on Daniel Craig and Clive Owen.

'Oh, for fuck's sake!' yelled Harry, a few minutes later.

Tanya and Trev looked up with the sudden outburst.

'What's up, mate?' asked Trev.

'I'm looking at *The Age* website for the Victorian news. Get this. A convicted paedophile has escaped from custody. The prisoner was in Ararat hospital under guard by Corrective Services. It identifies Herbert Farr, forty years of age, as being a previously convicted child sex offender from New South Wales. There's a description and the usual request to call Crime Stoppers with any information. What are the fucking chances?'

'You wouldn't fucking read about it,' added Trev.

'Useless Corrective Services bastards,' continued Harry, thumping his desk. 'Well, that shoots our little operation up the arse.'

'He'll probably head this way. It is his home state,' said Trev.

'Yeah, especially with sick old mum. If she is terminal, as Schwarz said, then Farr will be wanting to see her pronto. We got an address on her?'

'Yep. One Doris Farr, in Salamander Bay next to Port Stephens. And the family owns an old beach house a bit along the coast from there, up near Seal Rocks.'

Harry pondered, drumming his fingers on his blotter.

'Tell you what, why don't we pay Carla and Lauren to spend a few days up there, snooping around the beach house? We were going to pay them a packet for the prison guard gig anyway, so may as well use the money for this.'

'Agreed,' said Trev. 'I do love the way Dieter and Bernhard are just such generous donors to our cause.'

'Are you guys still milking that bank account?' asked Tanya.

'Only to finance ped-hunting activities,' replied Harry.

'And what better cause could he give to?' said Trev, smiling.

'Nice,' laughed Tanya.

'Anyway,' said Harry, 'the two girls can be our eyes on the ground. We're not going to be able to sit up there for days.'

'True. I like the idea. Farr might just decide to use that place, since the cops will cotton on to his mum's address some time soon and are sure to go visiting.'

'We won't reveal the target to them. On balance that's an unnecessary risk. We'll just get them to report if there's any human movement or a car at the beach house.'

'Yeah, I agree. Not knowing your target is far from perfect surveillance methodology, but the best option in the circumstances.'

'Exactly,' said Harry. 'Plus those girls will just look like a couple of backpackers having a beach-bum holiday, nothing to raise any suspicion even if Farr was to see them around.'

'Good plan, brother, let's get them up there,' said Trev.

'But what about me?' protested Tanya.

'No!' said Harry and Trev in unison.

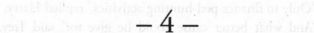

– 4 –

Connor O'Reilly put his phone in his pocket. He turned to Owen Driscoll next to him in the rented Ford Transit van parked in quiet Cavendish Street in Stanmore. 'Okay, our contact says she's on her way. Let's go.'

The pair got out of the van and walked quickly down the side path of a house. They were dressed in workmen's clothes and carrying tool bags. They'd cased the joint previously, so wasted no time. The old lock on a side door gave way easily as O'Reilly deftly manipulated his picklocks. The two Irishmen slid inside to wait.

Porcia Savage was feeling particularly conceited as she drove home on Friday afternoon. She'd had a pretty full week: successfully burying two more child-protection scandals, completely obfuscating a state ombudsman enquiry, promoting one of her rising sycophant stars, and shafting two departmental managers who'd dared to question her strategy. Yes, it had been a productive couple of weeks at the Office of Community Cohesion and Social Progress. And to top it off, she'd had another public accolade from her best friend, Gloria Steele. Savage was especially upbeat since Minister Steele's husband was away on business for the weekend and beyond, so she'd be able to visit the Minister for some overdue action between the sheets. She understood, of course, that the Minister needed to keep their relationship covert. Steele's sham marriage was politically vital, given the moral stances of certain significant donors to the Party. But Savage so wished it could be more committed: she wanted to eat that ministerial pussy a lot more often. And then, of course, there was the Minister's penchant for fisting. God, she loved that bit every time. Oh, well, at least she could look forward to tomorrow night.

Tonight, however, was a working evening at home with a bottle of chardonnay, polishing her submission to the Minister recommending that her previous protégé, Susannah Alexis, at the Department of Human Services, be appointed the new Director-General of the Department. Oh, such fond memories of mentoring young Susannah, she reminisced. She'd taught that impressionable, highly ambitious young thing a lot. She'd even got her used to fisting, impressing upon her that it was the ultimate power trip in the sexual arena. And lovely young Susannah had been so utterly loyal during that difficult time last year with the death of that druggy whore's kid. She'd proved incredibly proactive and effective in informing on that insufferable ex-cop on the staff who prattled on about ethics and evidence. Well, she'd sorted that precious wanker Stavros McMahon out, well and truly. The weak prick had hung himself: obviously not one destined to survive with the fittest. The world was better off without the likes of him, and the likes of that prostitute Lara Jacobs. Even her little son, when one came to think about it: he would have ended up being a welfare bludger as well, and probably a career criminal. Yep, she'd done a great job running the Department.

She was on a high, tripping on her thoughts of power and mastery, as she opened her front door in Stanmore and went inside. A chilled bottle of her favourite awaited her in the fridge. She closed the door behind her and walked purposefully towards the kitchen, dropping her briefcase on a hall-stand.

As she stepped into the kitchen, she detected an unusual smell: male body odour. Before she could react any further, a man stepped out in front of her. Christ, what was this? she thought, fear germinating in her brain. She turned, but another man now stood in front of her. She turned back. She reflexively went for her usual bullying authority. 'Who the hell are you and what the hell are you doing in my house? Get out now!' she yelled.

The first man laughed. An Irish accent followed. 'Don't give me that fucking power speech, bitch!'

O'Reilly punched Savage in the gut, doubling her over and dropping her onto her knees.

Savage tried to remain focused, but the pain was excruciating. The man grabbed her hair and pulled her over to the fridge, resting the back of her head against the metal door. He belted her in the face, breaking her nose. As she started to moan, the other man stuck a length of gaffer tape over her mouth. The first man leant down into her face. He was smiling.

Connor O'Reilly was enjoying himself. It was like the old days in Belfast, getting some cocky British soldier as a hostage. And they'd done none better than that Scottish wanker, Jock McPhail. But he simply loved turning the power tables around on these Establishment wankers. He'd thought long and hard about exactly which part satisfied him the most. As a more innocent and much younger man, he'd studied philosophy at Trinity College in Dublin, and the enquiring mind he'd developed had never left him.

And the result of his introspection? He'd decided, after much analysis, that it was the wiping off of the arrogant, condescending smiles that did it for him above all else. Apart, of course, from dispensing the ultimate justice.

He was going to enjoy doing this evil woman. This was more personal than anything prior: she'd orchestrated the cover-up of fault in his only grandson's murder. He'd never have the chance to meet little Beau now, and so she was going to suffer more than any arsehole he'd done before. And from reading the original departmental report that Kenmare had given him, it was also clear that Beau's death could have been prevented if her Department had done its job properly. Plus, of course, she was high up in the Establishment, always a prized target in his books. So, for both Lara and Beau, this was going to be a particularly special kind of revenge. He slapped Savage across the face. 'Look at me when I'm talking to you, bitch.'

Savage looked up despite the pain. Blood was running out of her nose, over the gaffer tape, and then dripping off her chin. A pair of cold, piercing green eyes looked at her.

'So, we're going to watch the next news bulletin on TV here, 'cos I think there's a story that will be especially close to home for you. Carnally close, if I'm well informed. And I think I am.'

Savage looked confused.

'After the news,' he continued, 'we're taking you somewhere nice and secluded. It'd be a lot easier for us to do you here, but I do so love to hear the screams of my chosen targets. And, of course, here in comfortable suburbia, that's not really the done thing.'

Savage wondered what the hell the arsehole was talking about. She looked at him, and then his friend, standing behind his shoulder. Oh, God, they're going to gang rape me, she thought, the panic gripping her more tightly still.

The man in front of her leant in again and slapped her. 'You don't know who I am, do you?'

She shook her head. He peeled back the gaffer tape a bit. She sucked in some air.

'Remember Lara Jacobs and her son, Beau?'

Savage looked at the man, her mind racing. What the hell could be the connection between this Irish thug and that little druggy slut? She said nothing.

He slapped her again. 'You covered up Beau's needless death. Your department was responsible. And he was my only grandchild.' He spat in her face. His eyes got a bit watery, which was the closest O'Reilly ever came to crying. 'You!' He jabbed his fingers into her chest. 'You stole my fucking heritage, you cunt!' he roared.

Savage tried to focus on herself, usually a strong suit for her, in order to sharpen her thoughts. Changing the topic was always a useful tactic. She looked back at the man.

'Please, please don't rape me.'

O'Reilly and Driscoll laughed loudly together.

'Rape you? Mary Mother of Christ, I wouldn't touch you if you were the last human orifice on Earth.'

Both men laughed more.

O'Reilly continued. 'My friend here, his hairy arsehole is way above you on the screwing list, and I sure don't find him attractive in the slightest. Rape you? Hell no!'

He leant in even closer. Savage tried to recoil, but the fridge behind her may as well have been a mountain. 'No, nothing sexual at all, bitch. What I am going to do is to butcher you. Slowly. And the whole time I'm doing it, you're going to think of Beau and Lara. And I'm going to constantly remind you what a corrupt government bitch you are. Are we clear?'

Savage was, for once in her life, utterly speechless.

He slapped her again. 'Good. Now let's watch the news. I do like to stay informed on current affairs.' He put the gaffer tape back over her mouth. Then he dragged her by the hair out of the kitchen and into the lounge room.

Driscoll turned on the TV.

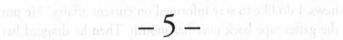

– 5 –

The same late afternoon hour saw an unusually agitated Harry at his desk, but with a glass of Jameson and a rapidly filling ashtray in front of him rather than any paperwork.

'For fuck's sake, it's been four days now and absolutely nothing on Farr. Where the hell is the prick?'

Trev, sitting in Tanya's chair, lit another smoke. 'Mate, I know it's bloody frustrating, but there's nothing else we can really do at the moment. We just gotta be patient. Let's see how long we can keep the girls up at the beach house.'

Harry sighed. 'Yeah, I know. But, I want this prick. Badly!'

'And we will get him. And then we'll go after the third one. I'm with you all the way on this, brother.'

'Thanks, Trev, you are a true mate. I really appreciate it. And then I'll help you with Father Barwick.'

Trev grinned. 'With this team on the case, the old padre is stuffed. It's good to have real friends, Harry.'

'Cheers to that.' Harry took a swig.

'I was thinking of Stavros McMahon a bit earlier.' Trev had stopped smiling.

'Yeah, poor bastard.'

'I know the reality is that true friends are very few in life, but it must be awful to get to that low, dark point where you feel there is absolutely no one you can reach out to.'

'The black dog, mate. I had to face plenty of depression after Orla, but fortunately something always kept the spark going somewhere inside. Mind you, I did a pretty good job at trying to drown myself in a bottle.'

'Know that feeling. I was a wreck for months after Jean-Louis, but like you, something kept me going. You hear people say that suicide is the coward's choice, but I just think it's tragic for everyone, including the deceased.'

'Yeah. Mate, I reckon those who want to pass judgement about suicide are those who've never had to deal with depression.'

'Yep. Self-righteousness is so bloody easy when you've never had to fight inside yourself. And the more I thought about Stavros, the more I felt that I wanted O'Reilly to really hurt that bitch Savage.'

'Couldn't agree more. It's letting the jungle take over, but in this case I've no problem whatsoever with that. Besides, we're cutting a swathe through a jungle ourselves.'

'Drink to that.' Trev drained his glass. 'Let's have a quick look at the news, and then run for the pub, I reckon.'

'I'll race you there. Last one to the bar shouts.'

'You're on,' said Trev, grinning and flicking on the television.

The adverts finished and the news bulletin came on.

'Fuck me drunk!' yelled Harry.

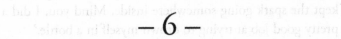

— 6 —

Gloria Steele, Minister for Human Communities and Youth Welfare, was looking smug as she made her way out of the cabinet meeting on Friday afternoon at the Park Royal Hotel in Parramatta. Her malignant expertise in covering up scandals in her crisis-ridden portfolio had earned her a stream of acclamations from her government colleagues. But today had been the climax she was looking for. Well, at least until her husband went away in the morning and she got to have dear Porcy over for a quiet, civilized Saturday night at her place: Thai takeaway, chardonnay, cunnilingus and fisting.

Yes, this afternoon she'd succeeded in rolling the Deputy-Premier and her ascent would be on the six o'clock news. A couple of years of apparently loyal service in the new role, then she'd shaft the Premier for the big chair. God how she loved politics, she thought. Fucking people over was even better than merely fucking them. Not that she minded it both ways, of course. And both ways, the higher up the ladder the fucking occurred, the bigger the rush.

She smiled to herself as she left the meeting suite and headed for the underground car park. Porcy was tomorrow's treat, for the full sleep-over. However, tonight, the prospective new department head, Susannah Alexis, had been told discreetly to expect a visit from the Minister, and to be alone. Steele had given her designated ministerial driver the afternoon off to free up her illicit movements. Ah, yes, thought Steele, young Susannah, ambitious Susannah, is going to learn to eat power pussy tonight. And I might even have to introduce her to my slippery fist. Was that too much for a first fuck? What the hell, she was the Minister after all.

Padraic Finnegan and Mickey O'Rourke had been surveilling the Minister for the whole week, waiting for the perfect opportunity. Connor O'Reilly had made it clear that this had to be completely clinical, absolutely no collateral victims. So, whilst opportunities had arisen to get to her car most days, there had always been the ministerial driver to contend with. By Thursday, Finnegan was getting fed up and called O'Reilly. 'For fuck's sake, Connor. We could be waiting weeks for the driver to piss off.'

'Padraic, he's just an ordinary guy working for a crust. He doesn't deserve to die when we take the Minister out. So, we wait until she's on her own. Is that clear?'

'Yes, Connor,' replied Finnegan.

'Anyway, it'll happen. All these respectable government scum have little secrets they don't want their staff to know about.'

Then Friday after lunch, it seemed to Finnegan and O'Rourke that O'Reilly had been quite prescient. Minister Steele left her office in the city in the early afternoon under her own steam and headed for Parramatta, no driver in sight.

Once her car was under the hotel, it was child's play for the two Irishmen, both expert bombmakers, to access the car park, fit the device, and leave. They sat themselves on a brick wall on the corner of Erby Place, with newspapers and soft drinks, and waited. It was a little street garden, nice and shady, about fifty metres from the hotel entrance. Their hire-car was parked at the end of the side street.

It was two hours later that the Minister's car came out of the car park entrance onto Phillip Street. A number of journos and photographers were around the hotel entrance, and they took a cursory interest in Steele leaving.

'Not yet, Mickey,' said Finnegan. 'We don't want any bystanders hurt. Let her car get well clear.'

The Minister's black BMW 7-series started to move east on Phillip Street, picking up speed. Finnegan could see she was the only person in the car. As soon as the pavements either side were clear of pedestrians, Finnegan, watching the receding car, said, 'Now, Mickey!'

O'Rourke pressed the detonator switch.

They felt the concussion blast wave as Steele's BMW exploded and careened into a row of parked cars. There were shattered windows everywhere, both cars and buildings.

The two men walked briskly away down Erby Place, got into their car, and pulled up to the main road, O'Rourke driving.

Finnegan got out a pair of binoculars and focused on the burning wreck. 'Yeah, that fucking politician is cooking nicely. Our job is done. Let's go, Mickey.'

They turned into Phillip Street and drove away.

Porcia Savage sat on the couch, bound and gagged, with one Irishman, the one who did the talking, sitting next to her. The other one, who'd turned on the TV with a flourish like a game-show host, was sitting in an armchair. He lit a cigarette and sat back in the cushioned comfort.

Savage absolutely abhorred smokers and she made a muffled noise of protest. This was her bloody house, after all, even in the current circumstances. Her loathing was such that it rose above her fear.

O'Reilly turned to Savage as she grunted. 'You got a problem with him smoking, have you?'

Savage made a noise and nodded her head.

'Owen, I think the queen bee here wants you to put your smoke out.' He turned back to Savage. 'Is that right?'

She nodded again.

'Oh, no problems, your ladyship,' said Driscoll. He stood up, walked over taking a long drag on his cigarette, and bent down in front of Savage. Then he jammed the burning butt into Savage's cheek. There was a hissing sound and instant smell of burning flesh as Savage convulsed in her seat.

O'Reilly laughed. 'I really don't think Owen liked being told what to do by a corrupt Establishment whore.

401

He's a bit strange like that, you know, a bit sensitive. Funny, isn't it?'

Driscoll sat back down and lit another cigarette.

O'Reilly jabbed his hand into her ribs. Tears were streaming down her face now. 'Do you remember Lara and Beau yet? Remember what you did to cover up their deaths?'

She looked at him coldly, through wet eyes.

'You think an apology might be in order?'

Savage never apologized, ever, for anything. Unless it was to her darling Minister. But these scum? She shook her head. Her natural arrogance was struggling to regain its pride of place, despite her pain.

'Oh, really? "No" is your answer? Is that what you're telling me?' he continued.

She nodded, and did her best to glare hatred at him.

O'Reilly pulled out a flick-knife from his pocket and opened it. He twisted around on the couch and put one knee into Savage's gut. He leant on her with all his weight, grinning, and then slowly hacked off her right ear.

Despite the gaffer tape, her screaming was still audible. But it was not loud enough to seep out of the house to any neighbours.

O'Reilly stood back from her, throwing her ear into her lap. It had felt like cutting through the gristle in a poor Irish stew, he thought. 'Personally, I think the occasional apology is good for the soul. But that's just my view of the world ...'

Driscoll interrupted. 'We've got a newsflash coming on, Connor.'

Savage looked at the TV screen in horror, tears streaming down her face. The newsflash carried vision of the burning ministerial car. Due to the cabinet meeting, the media had been heavily represented on site, so had captured the car bombing immediately after it occurred. The newsreader said that it was believed Minister Gloria Steele had been alone in her car at the time, having just left the meeting at the hotel. A photo of Steele appeared on the screen next to the news anchor. The footage then showed firemen dousing the last of the smouldering wreckage. The police hadn't had time to get a crime scene tent up to cover the charcoaled body in the driver's seat. The streetscape looked more like a news item from Baghdad or Kabul, not sleepy, suburban Sydney.

Savage thought of her powerful lover. The prospect of her life without Gloria in it was so ugly it was almost unimaginable. She started choking on tears and mucus as she reminisced about their secret life together.

O'Reilly leant across and ripped the tape off her mouth. 'Don't want you suffocating and leaving the party early, bitch.' He slapped her. 'But if you make any noise, the slightest sound, the other ear is coming off.'

Driscoll turned off the TV. 'Fine piece of work by the lads there,' he said. 'Shades of the old days back home.'

O'Reilly smiled. Then he turned to Savage, who had spat out a mouthful of phlegm and saliva, and put a fresh piece of gaffer tape over her mouth. 'Now, me little corrupt government slag. I've got good news and bad news for you.'

Savage glared at him. She tried to assume her best sneer of contempt, a look that usually came naturally to her. She thought to herself that she was going to beat this bastard. Because she never lost; she always prevailed.

O'Reilly read the arrogant look. 'Oh, my, my. Big tough boss lady, huh? I don't think so. No. The good news is that your friend, the Minister, died quickly. She wouldn't have known about it for more than a couple of seconds. You, on the other hand, are going to go very, very slowly, and very, very painfully. That's the bad news.'

He punched her twice in the face, which left her dazed. Then Driscoll put a pillowcase over her head. The pair of them lifted her off the couch and dumped her on the Persian rug that covered the expanse of red gum timber flooring in front of the TV and stereo unit. They lined her up with one end of the rug and then rolled her up loosely in it, making sure that her face was close enough to the end to get plenty of air.

'We'll leave her ear on the couch,' said O'Reilly. 'A little item to authenticate our story when we call this in.'

'A nice touch, Connor, pure style.' Driscoll grinned at him.

They picked the bundled Savage up and walked down the hallway to the front door.

'Back the van into the drive, close as you can get to the door,' said O'Reilly.

Driscoll went out.

He was back a minute later. They hefted the carpet roll into the back of the Transit van, closed Savage's front door, and got into the van.

They pulled out onto the street and headed off into the darkness.

– 8 –

Savage felt herself being tied to a chair. It seemed like a couple of hours since she'd been thrown in the vehicle, rolled up in the rug. She could smell the main Irishman close to her again. The other one was around, too, as she had heard the two of them talking before they pulled her out of the rug. She heard metallic sounds off to the side, and thuds as though heavy objects were being dumped on a hard surface.

Then the pillowcase came off. The two bastards were standing in front of her grinning. The light was subdued, emanating from a hurricane lamp on a table near her. It looked as if they were inside a small cabin. She looked at the men. You'll never get away with this, she thought. She tried to put that into words, but the gag meant she only uttered a muffled noise.

'Oh, the queen bee has got something she wants to say to us, Owen.'

Driscoll laughed. 'We'd better listen, then, Connor. She is a government bigwig after all.'

O'Reilly stepped forward and pulled the gag roughly off Savage's bloodied head. She drew a deep breath through her mouth.

'You arseholes! You'll pay for this! Do you know who I am?'

'Absolutely. And do we look bothered?' replied O'Reilly.

Savage turned her head towards a small window with broken glass panes. 'Help me!' she screamed at the top of her lungs.

The two Irishmen cracked up laughing. 'You know why we took the gag off, don't you?' said O'Reilly.

She looked at him, with loathing in her eyes.

'Give you a clue, you arrogant fuck. It wasn't so we could enjoy your dulcet tones,' said Driscoll.

'I like that, Owen,' said O'Reilly. He turned back to Savage. 'No, the reason we took the gag off is because out here may as well be outer space – no one can hear you scream.'

He smiled at her and spat in her face. 'We are seriously fucking miles from anywhere. So, go ahead, shout your lungs out. I can assure you that very shortly you'll be screaming without any choice in the matter.'

Savage glared at him, trying to hold down her growing fear. 'Fuck you!'

O'Reilly chuckled. He walked over to the small table on which sat a variety of tools. He picked up a pair of pliers. 'Always fancied a bit of dentistry,' he said, walking back to Savage. 'Hold her head, Owen.'

Driscoll stepped behind Savage and gripped her head with his arms.

'No!' screamed Savage.

'Feel like making that apology for Lara and Beau yet?'

Savage sneered at him.

O'Reilly grabbed her lower jaw and pulled her mouth open. The pliers loomed towards her. 'Sorry, bitch, government budget cuts. No anaesthetic.' He latched the pliers onto a premolar, wrenched them around as screams erupted from Savage's throat, and then jerked the tooth free, blood dripping from it. O'Reilly admired his work. 'However, it looks a bit uneven. Can't have that.'

Savage screamed again, sensing what was coming.

O'Reilly grabbed the opposite premolar with the pliers and viciously ripped it out. When the screaming had subsided, O'Reilly lowered his head, grabbed Savage's face by her chin, and looked into her eyes. He stared for several moments.

Then he spoke. 'All I see in there is darkness. I see a soul comprised entirely of pustulous dog turds. Now, what pain would you like next?'

Savage didn't reply.

'Of course, you can take the short cut and put an end to all this right now. You just need to apologize.'

Savage made a wet sucking sound as she inhaled rapidly through the blood and saliva. 'You're both fucking animals!' she croaked.

Driscoll spoke up. 'Well, Connor, if we're "fucking animals", as the almighty government whore has decreed, we may as well go hard-core with the blowtorch. What do you reckon?'

'Inspired choice, Owen.'

O'Reilly ripped Savage's blouse open, pulled a knife out from his pocket, and cut her bra off.

Driscoll fired up a hand-held blowtorch.

Savage looked at them in horror.

'You people are fucking barbarians!' she screeched.

'Oh, really? And you people are so civilized? Sitting there in your ivory towers of power making life and death decisions, all to further your own mercenary agendas and corrupt lifestyles. You cause untold misery for innocent people and then use your positions to cover it all up. I reckon that's pretty up there on the barbaric scale. Just my view, anyway.'

'And mine, too,' added Driscoll, as he passed the blowtorch to O'Reilly.

The roaring blue flame mesmerized Savage. Her innate arrogance rose up as it got closer and bravado prevailed. '*We* are where *we* are in the Establishment because *we* deserve it. We're better than you scum. That's why *we* run society, not you. It's the proper order of things.'

Driscoll stepped forward and spat on her. 'Well, that was a pretty fucking stupid speech to give to two Irishmen.'

O'Reilly smiled at Savage. 'Too true. So, all-powerful bitch, your born-to-rule attitude doesn't seem quite so dominant now, does it?'

'Fuck you! And your daughter was just a druggy gutter prostitute.'

O'Reilly's smile vanished. 'Okay, that was a red line crossed. Your short cut option is not on the table any more. You've just ensured I'm going to enjoy this even more. Cop this, you cunt!' yelled O'Reilly.

The screams as O'Reilly barbecued Savage's left breast were ear-shattering. When he'd finished, she looked as if she was going to pass out, her head lolling backwards.

'Give her a shot, Owen. Unconscious arseholes don't feel any pain, and we can't have that.'

Driscoll picked up a syringe of amphetamine from the table, stepped back to Savage, and injected it into her arm.

A moment later, Savage jerked in her restraints as the drug kicked in.

'Okay, that ugly titty was for Lara,' said O'Reilly.

Savage, refocusing her vision, looked loathingly at him, the smell of burnt flesh filling the small cabin.

'And this one's for Beau.' O'Reilly swung the blowtorch back and incinerated her other breast.

The screams were every bit as loud as the first time, but the shot of speed meant that Savage wasn't going to pass out any time soon.

When she recovered enough to speak, she looked up defiantly at O'Reilly, and then at Driscoll. He was now standing next to O'Reilly holding a pair of bolt cutters. She spat out an evil-looking mixture of saliva, blood and mucus, which landed in her lap. 'Monsters!' she gasped.

'Is that right?' said O'Reilly. 'I don't think so. Sure, we're violent men. That's the way we are. The "proper order of things" I believe was your phrase. But we admit what we are. We don't pretend anything else.'

'Nope, we are the genuine deal, take us or leave us,' added Driscoll, opening and closing the bolt cutters.

O'Reilly continued. 'You, on the other hand, are nothing but a fraud, a typical self-serving government wanker. You hide behind your veneer of respectability, but, in fact, you're more of a monster than either of us ever will be. Sure, you don't actually get your hands dirty, you haven't got the balls for that. But your arrogant corruption has far more monstrous results for society than anything we could ever do. What do you reckon, Owen?'

'Yep, agreed. And, bitch, at least we only hurt people for good reason, not just because we can, unlike you lot.'

Savage stared at them, her hatred searing hot in her eyes. She tried to respond, but it seemed her spirit was draining rapidly. She stayed silent.

'So,' said O'Reilly, 'for the memory of my daughter and my grandson, fuck you.'

He turned to Driscoll. 'Give me those, Owen, and undo her right hand.'

Savage tried feebly to struggle as Driscoll undid one of the ropes securing her to the chair, but the other ropes held her tightly. Driscoll moved her arm upwards, holding it tightly with her hand outstretched.

O'Reilly stepped forward, opening the jaws of the hungry-looking tool. He slid its jaws over her thumb and rammed the two handles together.

Savage shrieked as the digit came off. She screeched four more times as O'Reilly cut off her remaining fingers, one by one.

He gave her a couple of minutes to stop screaming, then leant into her face. 'Yes, maybe in some ways I am a monster. But to borrow from Sartre, one of my favourite philosophers when I was at university, at least I'm authentic. I live an authentic life. You do me wrong, and I will fuck you over, authentically. Nothing devious or concealed. You, on the other hand, you're all lies, deceit and treachery. No wonder you've risen to such heights in the government service.'

Savage tapped into the very last dregs of her reserves of arrogance. 'That's how the game's played,' she hissed at him. 'And in that game, the only one that counts, I'm a winner. You're both fucking losers.'

Both Irishmen fell about laughing.

'We're fucking losers?' said O'Reilly through his mirth. 'You hear that, Owen? We're the losers here.'

'Damn me, Connor, I'd never have guessed. I obviously didn't pay enough attention at school. Stupid me.'

'Stupid both of us, apparently,' said O'Reilly. 'At least according to queen bee here.'

Driscoll picked up a glass bottle from the table of tricks. 'Do you mind if I contribute here, Connor?'

'Be my guest, Owen.'

O'Reilly turned back to Savage. 'The problem with your argument, your ladyship, is that right here, right now, we're not on the set of your game. We're on our playing field, with our rules. And given how you're looking there, and the fact that you're going to die here tonight, I'd say *we* are looking like real winners.'

'Authentic winners,' chipped in Driscoll.

O'Reilly chuckled. 'Like that, Owen. Yes, authentic winners.' He continued to talk to Savage. 'You see, with all you wankers, once we step back into nature, you're all fucked. You only prosper because of the self-serving elitist structure you've perpetuated. Didn't save you today, though, did it?'

He spat in her face. 'Over to you, Owen.'

Driscoll pulled the glass stopper out of the bottle he was holding. 'A little drop of something special for you: sulphuric acid.' He poured the clear liquid over Savage's head.

She started screaming almost instantly.

Ten minutes later, not even the stimulant shot had much currency left. The barely conscious Savage looked at O'Reilly through one half-closed eye. The other one was fused completely shut by the acid, which had melted the skin and flesh down one side of her face.

O'Reilly was grinning at her. 'Still think you're a winner do you, *Director-General?*'

Just a grunt came from Savage.

'Well, it's been a pleasure, for us anyway. But the time for final justice is here. If I thought you had enough nerve function left to still feel much pain, then we'd continue. But you're now at that point where the brain has switched off the pain receptors. I've seen this before: a couple of British Army hostages back home. They just went blank, like you are now.'

He looked over at Driscoll. 'Owen, please?'

Driscoll passed him a machete. O'Reilly looked back at Savage.

'Time to die, O powerful one.' He laughed contemptuously. 'This is for my Lara, her Beau, and everyone else you've fucked over or fucked up. Even that ex-copper we heard about, Stavros McMahon, and believe me, I don't usually have any respect for the police. *Hasta la vista*, bitch! See you in hell.'

O'Reilly swung the machete in a sideways arc. It took Savage's mangled head clean off at the neck. Her head thudded to the floor, and rolled about a metre, leaving a trail of blood. It stopped, its ravaged face pointing towards the two men. The mouth had a distinct sneer to it.

'Jesus, Owen, even in death she's an arrogant cunt.'

'True, but you know what they say, Connor?'

'What do they say?'

'The only good arrogant cunt is a dead one.'

'I'll pay that, Owen. Now let's get the fuck out of here.'

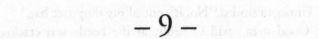

– 9 –

On Sunday afternoon, Singapore Airlines flight SQ222 was boarding at Sydney's Kingsford Smith Airport.

O'Reilly put his holdall in the overhead locker and sat down. He pulled his wallet out and opened it, revealing a photo of Lara with Beau as a tiny baby. He looked at them, then raised the photo to his face and kissed it. I wasn't much of a father or grandfather to you both, he thought, but at least I've avenged your deaths. He put the wallet away. He didn't dwell for too long: many years as an active operative in the IRA meant that compartmentalization came more easily to him than most people.

He looked over to the other side of the half-empty plane where Driscoll was seated. A scattering of other passengers were settling themselves in. Finnegan and O'Rourke were seated separately further up the plane. O'Reilly nodded at Driscoll, got up and headed for the toilets at the back. Driscoll headed in the same direction.

A minute later, they were joined by the other two.

'Well, lads, here we are. Heading home to the Emerald Isle. Been a long time for me. Thanks for your work, and for coming when I needed you,' said O'Reilly.

Finnegan responded. 'Always there for you, Connor. Always. Never forgotten what you did for us in Belfast.

And we liked getting into some action. It was like the old days.' He smiled and produced a half bottle of Bushmills.

'You get that through the security screening?' asked Driscoll.

Finnegan smiled. 'No, it's out of my duty-free bag.'

'Good man,' said O'Reilly, as the bottle was cracked open. They all drank in turn, passing the bottle for a couple of minutes.

'Padraic, you got that phone for me?' asked O'Reilly.

Finnegan handed him an old-style Nokia mobile. 'Completely untraceable and with an Irish SIM card, also untraceable.'

'Thanks, Padraic.'

'It'll work as long as the plane is within reach of a cell tower, so you could call as we're taking off and before we get too high up, but you'll be stuck in your seat until the seat belts can come off. In the shitter back here now would be the go if you want more privacy.'

'Indeed I will. Let's drink and then I'll make the call.'

The four of them spent a couple of minutes finishing off the bottle.

O'Reilly went to step into one of the toilets. 'See you lads in Singapore then.' He closed the toilet door behind him.

The others returned to their seats.

In the cubicle, O'Reilly took a piss. Then he closed the toilet seat and sat on it. He pulled a folded piece of paper out of his wallet and opened it up. He dialled a number. It connected. He didn't bother to disguise his voice. 'Is that Crime Stoppers? Okay, good. Listen carefully to what I have to say, I'm only going to say it once. No, don't interrupt me and I'm not giving you my fucking name. Listen to me! You'll find the body of a senior government official in a cabin near the Hawkesbury River. Her name is Porcia Savage, or should I say was.' He laughed. 'Now take down these map coordinates.' He read them from his piece of paper. 'And so you know I'm genuine, here's her home address we took her from. Just to prove my story, you'll find one of her ears on the couch. I cut it off and left it there. Oh, and I've let the newspapers and TV know.' He hung up before the operator could say anything further to him.

Just before boarding the flight, he'd sent an email to various media outlets using a bogus account he'd set up courtesy of the public computers in the departures terminal. The unsigned message detailed Savage's corrupt misdeeds and cited them as the reason for her execution.

He looked back at his piece of paper. There was a mobile number on it. He typed it into the phone and sent a message to Harry.

> Thanks for your help Harry. Watch the news.
> All the best. Connor.

Then he took the SIM out of the phone, wiped it clean of prints, and flushed it down the toilet. He rubbed the phone clean, wrapped it in paper towelling, and dropped it in the rubbish chute. He put the piece of paper from his wallet into his mouth, chewed and swallowed.

He walked back to his seat with a smile of unadulterated satisfaction on his face. Time to settle back and relax with a couple of movies and several more drinks. O'Reilly grinned as he felt the thrust of the four Rolls-Royce engines propel the Airbus A380 down the runway. And then they were airborne, climbing fast into the sky above Sydney, eight hours away from Singapore.

– 10 –

At the same time as flight SQ222 was climbing out of Sydney's airspace, at a secluded house at Treachery Beach north of Port Stephens, Herbert Farr was masturbating furiously as he watched a video on his laptop. It was one of his favourites in his collection, *Seven Sunday School Sluts*. He'd warmed up his libido with *Kindergarten Caretakers,* but had saved his serious manual relief for his main choice. Damn, he wished he were the guy playing the priest, what a plum job that would have been. He grunted loudly as he ejaculated.

He sighed, then wiped the semen off his laptop screen and keyboard. Ah, life was getting back on track, he considered. All in all, his escape from custody had gone swimmingly. Now he simply needed to keep a low profile until the heat died down. This old family beach shack was out of the way, and he could safely hang out here indefinitely, he thought. Then, in a post-ejaculatory mood of self-congratulation, he mused over his recent accomplishments.

By the time last Monday arrived, Herbie Farr had been in Ararat Hospital for several weeks, and was feeling well recuperated. As his strength returned, he decided he had to get out so he could see his dying mum. She wasn't long for this world, as she'd told him in her letters, and the custodial authorities were dragging their heels with his interstate transfer to a prison nearer Salamander Bay, where old Mrs Farr resided. At least if he were incarcerated either at Cessnock or St Heliers, she could come and visit him, but travelling to Victoria, over a thousand kilometres away, was out of the question.

No, not good enough, he considered, he absolutely needed to get out. Even if I get recaptured eventually, at least I will have spent time with Mum before she goes, he thought. And if he were still on the loose after she passed on, he'd find a way to get out of Australia and join Reggie in Laos. He worshipped Reggie, as if he were the patron saint of paedophiles. And from what his great friend had relayed, working at the orphanage over there was a pure smorgasbord of young carnal delicacies.

No, he was definitely over the restrictive prison life. Plus, after a couple of years inside, he was suffering serious withdrawal from indulging his own young-flesh proclivities. You could, to his surprise, get quite a wide range of illicit items in prison, but kiddie porn wasn't one of them. Not even the bent screws would go that far.

Over the whole of last weekend in his hospital bed, he had complained to the medical staff about the handcuffs securing his right hand to the bed rail being way too tight and that he was starting to get nerve pains along his arm. He even put on regular convincing spasms and twitching in his hand and arm.

The prison guards on their successive shifts had been distinctly unsympathetic. One even said if it were up to him the handcuffs would be around Herbie's throat. Fucking fascist prick. However, the doctor, a wonderful social-justice type (Herbie simply loved the bleeding-hearts brigade), instructed the guards to loosen off the metal bracelet. The second part of Herbie's charade was to develop an acute germ phobia, and so he got a full dispenser bottle of liquid hand cleanser gel within continual easy reach.

Just after lunch last Monday, the guard said he was going to the toilet. He checked the handcuffs were in place, and wandered off. The beauty of being a convict in hospital was that, as well as having a break from the prison, you got a room to yourself. The second the guard closed the door, Herbie slathered the slimy cleanser all over his shackled hand and wrist. With a degree of discomfort and pain, he scrunched up his hand enough to slide it out of the metal restraint. He hurriedly got his prison clothes from the cupboard next to the bed and slipped into them. Then he grabbed the screw's jacket hanging on the back of the chair and put it on. He picked up the officer's cap and stuck it on his head. He allowed himself a quick glance in the mirror, smiled, and then headed out the door. As he walked past an unattended nurse's trolley in the corridor, he grabbed a hypodermic in a sealed packet. He walked briskly out to the car park. Two nurses coming the other way took no notice of him.

He went out the double doors and walked over to a parked linen-delivery van. There was no one in it. He ducked behind the van, pulled up his left sleeve tensing his arm, and eased the needle into a vein protruding on the inside of his forearm. He watched as his blood slowly filled the hypodermic, chasing the withdrawing plunger. He pulled the sleeve back down and waited.

He'd seen the linen-service guy enter the hospital on a daily basis during the week. He was a scrawny, pimply boy of about nineteen. Herbie reckoned he could deal with him no problem. And blood-filled syringes commanded a certain respect. He'd learnt that trick from Reggie, who'd held one against a young mother's neck in her home in Sydney years earlier. It had been one of those great hunting trips for him, Reggie and Bernhard. The syringe had kept the mother compliant and quiet, although sobbing endlessly, whilst the three of them took turns on her ten-year-old daughter. So, Herbie knew the sheer power of the threatening needle. Laundry boy wouldn't put up any resistance at all.

Just then a nurse, a petite woman in her late twenties, came out of the building putting on a cardigan and heading for a line of parked cars.

Herbie moved quickly, ducking behind another row of cars. The nurse, not one he'd ever seen in his wing of the hospital, got into an old Toyota Camry. Herbie came up from the rear of the car, just as the engine started. He opened the front passenger door and jumped in, slamming the door behind him.

'What the hell?' yelled the startled woman.

Herbie held the blood-filled syringe in front of her. 'I'm that prisoner from room nineteen. Heard about me?'

She nodded nervously.

'I'm HIV positive. You do exactly what I say, or this gets injected into you. Understand?'

She started to shake and cry.

He moved the needle closer. 'Understand?' he said more firmly.

She nodded. 'Please … please don't hurt me. I've got a young child to look after.'

Herbie's interest was piqued. It was so, so long since he'd had any sexual playmates. He had to know more. 'Boy or girl?'

'Girl, Shelley. She's eight.'

That got Herbie's scrotum tingling. Right gender and delicious age. 'No hubby?'

'No, he left me.'

'Got a photo of her?'

With shaking hands the nurse opened her handbag and pulled out her purse. She opened it to reveal a picture of a little girl, big toothy grin and auburn hair in pigtails. The small photo wavered as her hands trembled. 'Please, just tell me what you want me to do,' she sobbed.

Herbie felt movement in his loins. Shit, he thought, this was a dilemma. He could go back to her place and keep her hostage whilst he unleashed his pent-up libido on little Shelley. But that would mean sticking around the area, and the cops would be hunting for him imminently.

What to do? He looked again at Shelley's big grin, picturing her without that little school uniform on. Damn it! No, as tempting as it was, there'd be time for fresh meat later. Bernhard was up in Sydney, and he'd be sure to have some young playthings accessible.

As the hospital doors opened for an orderly to enter the building, Herbie heard shouting. Okay, his decision was made. He had to get out of Ararat fast and head for Melbourne, before journeying north of the border to home in NSW.

'Drive, now!' he commanded the sobbing nurse.

She put the car into gear and drove out of the car park.

Herbie picked up her purse from the centre console. 'How much money you got in here?'

'Take it all, please. Just don't hurt me.'

Herbie pulled out the banknotes and counted $135. Not enough. 'Okay, we're going to an ATM and you're going to get me some more. Head for a bank.'

She drove slowly and tearfully along the main road.

As they approached a shopping centre, Herbie pointed to a cash machine. 'Over there. Let's go.'

She pulled into the closest parking space she could find.

Herbie took her driver's licence out of her purse. He read the name and address out loud. He waved it in front of the distraught nurse's face. 'Now, I know where you live. Any tricks from you, and I'm going over to your house to fuck your little girl. Got me?'

'Yes … please … I'll do whatever you say.'

'So, go over to the ATM and come back with as much as you can get out. And if I don't think it's the maximum, then it's back to your place for little Shelley to start sex-ed classes. Go!'

She scurried off to the cash machine, did a transaction, and returned to the car. Her hands were shaking again as she handed Herbie a wad of notes. 'That's eight hundred and fifty. It's all I've got in my card account. If you want more, I can go into the branch and withdraw from a different savings account.'

Herbie thought about it, but that option added too many unknowns to the equation. No point in taking needless risks. He had almost a thousand in cash. That was ample to see him through to his mum's house in Salamander Bay. He had money stashed there, and Mum was always good for a loan.

He looked at the distraught woman beside him. 'That's fine. You've done well. We won't be going to your place after all. Now get driving out of town, head for Melbourne.'

'But please, I've done what you asked. Can't you just take the car and leave me here?'

'What? So you can raise the alarm? Do I look fucking stupid?' He pulled the syringe into sight again. 'Drive, now!'

She restarted the engine.

'I'll let you go later, when you're nowhere near anyone else or any phones.'

Fresh tears started flowing down her cheeks as she put the car into gear and headed for the exit.

Thirty kilometres out of town, Herbie directed the nurse to turn down a side road. They drove for about another ten kilometres, until he told her to pull over in bushland. 'This is where you get out, nursey.' He ratted through her handbag and took out her mobile phone, slipping it into his pocket. 'And don't forget,' he added, waving her licence in the air, 'I know where you live. Any hiccups for me, and I'll be around later for a taste of little Shelley.' He smiled and wagged his tongue lasciviously. 'Are we clear?'

She nodded, lips trembling and her face pale. There were mascara streaks on her cheeks from her tears.

Of course, any hiccups would mean he'd got arrested, so visiting her little girl would be impossible, sadly, he thought, but she wasn't to know that. Fear was his principal weapon right now, and he was wielding it masterfully. 'Out you get, nursey.'

She did as she was told and closed the door behind her.

Yes, he thought as he drove away, it should be a couple of hours before she reaches anywhere to find passing traffic. He went back up the narrow road along which they'd entered the bushland. Yep, he'd be in Melbourne, having ditched the car, by the time she raised the alarm. Sure, the CCTV at the hospital might have captured him getting into her car, but probably no one would check that, or at least not put two and two together, until her car was reported missing. And that wouldn't happen until she spoke to someone.

Melbourne, here I come, thought Herbie. He happily noted the fuel gauge was showing over half a tank, and he settled in for the drive. He came back out onto the main road and turned east towards the Victorian capital. Despite his desire to get to the city and offload the stolen car, he kept to a sensible speed and drove carefully. He didn't need to raise the interest of any police patrol cars.

Just under two hours later, he parked in a multistorey car park near the Spencer Street coach terminal in central Melbourne. And so far, so good: nothing on the radio news yet about his escape.

He was tempted to keep the nurse's phone, which he had turned off. It was an older model that didn't need an access code. He thought about it. But he'd heard about the cops tracking people by their phones – prison conversation frequently related to law enforcement techniques, like a live-in college for criminals, really – so that probably wasn't a sensible option. He'd have to do without until he got to his mum's place, where all his own stuff was stashed.

He locked up the car, leaving the phone and driver's licence in the glove box. He threw the keys underneath it. He walked out of the parking station and into a nearby garment outlet centre. He bought clothes and a small travel bag, then went into the public toilets. Inside a cubicle, he dressed in a new shirt and pants, packing his other purchases in the travel bag. He rolled up the prison clothes and guard's jacket and cap and pushed them into a plastic carry bag from the shop, tying it tightly closed with its handles. He walked out of the centre, a new man. As he passed a bin, he dropped the plastic bag in it. Then, travel bag in hand, he headed for the coach terminal.

He walked into the terminal and looked for the Greyhound office. As he was about to step through the door, he caught sight of a wall-mounted TV screen in the passenger hall. He couldn't hear the story, but the picture of Ararat Prison was clear enough. Even clearer was his mug shot. Shit, he thought.

He stepped back from the door, exited the terminal, and walked up the footpath. Damn it, he'd had a good run so far, but it was getting risky now. What to do? As he ambled along, pondering his next move, he heard a voice.

'Any spare change, mate?'

He looked around and saw a skinny young man sitting on his haunches, holding out an upturned baseball cap. There were a few silver coins in it. A mangy bull-terrier was asleep next to him.

Herbie smiled to himself. Then he smiled at the beggar. 'Hey, mate,' he said. 'Tell you what, you do me a favour and I'll give you a hundred bucks.'

The tramp's eyes lit up, as much as such defeated eyes could. 'I don't do head jobs, but.'

'Nothing like that, don't worry.'

'Okay, what then?'

'I need you to walk into the Greyhound office over there and buy a single ticket to Sydney on the next bus. Then bring it back here, and I'll give you the hundred to keep.'

'That easy?'

'Yep, that easy. I'm guessing it'd take you a long time sitting here to earn a hundred.'

The young guy was on his feet. 'Damned right, bro. A very bloody long time.'

Herbie gave him $200 in fifties. 'That'll cover the ticket. And you keep the change, along with the hundred waiting out here for you.' Herbie waved two more fifties in his hand. 'I'll stay here and look after your dog and your stuff.' He looked down at the beggar's paltry possessions: an old suitcase on wheels, one broken; a small transistor radio; a plastic bag with half a dozen paperback books in it. The terrier lifted its head, but settled back when the tramp patted him.

'Okay,' said the young man, limping off towards the ticket office.

Ten minutes later, he was back. He handed the ticket to Herbie, and took the $100 from him. 'Gee, thanks mate. My lucky day.'

'Yours and mine both,' said Herbie. 'You've no idea. See you.'

Herbie headed off to lie low until the coach's departure in three hours' time. It was the overnight service to Sydney.

As dawn broke on Tuesday, the Greyhound coach was barrelling its way along the last stretch of the Hume Highway into Sydney.

When Herbie got off at Central Station, he bought both the Sydney daily newspapers and headed for McDonald's to get a late breakfast. As he wolfed down two egg and bacon muffins and a large black coffee, he flicked through the papers. He felt himself relaxing as he got to the end of the news section of the second paper and still no mention of him. Clearly it had remained Victorian local news thus far. Suited him perfectly. He finished his breakfast, used the restaurant's toilets, then walked back to the station complex. He found the office for Port Stephens Coaches, and got himself a ticket to his hometown, three hours north of Sydney.

By early evening, Herbie was sitting on a log fence next to a bus stop down the road from his mother's house in Salamander Bay, a suburb of Port Stephens. He knew from her letters that a home carer came every afternoon to help her. And she had an emergency button that summoned a nurse, or an ambulance, if she got desperate. She had told Herbie, several times, that she'd been born in the house, raised her family there, and by God, she was going to die there as well.

Just on six o'clock, a car driven by a youngish woman pulled out of the driveway and cruised off down Foreshore Drive.

Herbie walked the short distance to the house. He was hoping his spare key was still hidden under the garden gnome next to the front porch. Given the peremptory nature of his checking out of custody, he hadn't got any of his possessions, including his keys, back from the prison authorities.

The key was there. He opened the front door and stepped inside, putting his travel bag down and closing the door behind him.

'What did you forget, Cheryl?' called his mother.

'No, Mama, it's me, Herbie. I'm here.'

'Herbie? Herbie?!'

He went up the hallway and stepped into the doorway of her bedroom. She was propped up with a soap opera droning away on a television on a stand at the end of the bed.

Herbie beamed at her. He loved his mother so much. 'I got out early for good behaviour and came straight here to see you, Mama.'

'Oh, Herbie, Herbie. Oh, this has made my day. My year, in fact. Come and give your mama a big kiss.'

She held out her arms and Herbie bounced over, almost asphyxiating her with his hugs and kisses. 'How are you, Mama?'

'Not so good, my love, but it comes to us all. Doctor reckons it's not long now.'

Herbie felt as if he was going to cry. 'I don't want you to go, Mama. I love you. I need you.'

She touched his face. 'I love you, too, Herbie. But I've had a decent, long life. My only complaint in recent years is those two little sluts making up those awful, vile stories about you, and then those sodding retards on the jury believing them. There's no bloody justice any more.'

'No, there isn't. Bloody kids these days, make up all sorts of shit. But I'm here now, Mama.'

'Ooh, dinner with my Herbie tonight then?'

'Absolutely. I can go to the shops and get something to cook. What about roast chicken, your favourite?'

'Oh, Herbie, would you? I'd love that. The food that Cheryl brings is okay, but I haven't had a home-cooked roast since last year.'

Herbie winced inside as he thought back to not being there when his mum had had her stroke last year, and she really needed him.

'You take my car,' she said. 'It's in the garage. Your cousin, Timmy, who comes to do the garden each week for me, takes it out for a spin every now and then. So, it still keeps running just fine.'

Excellent, thought Herbie. Wheels into the bargain, which Mum wouldn't miss. He'd stay as long as he could with dear old Mum, but it was probably only a matter of days before the cops expanded their search for him beyond the borders of Victoria. Then he'd have to move on to the beach house, which the cops likely wouldn't know about, since as far as he knew, no one in the family had ever been listed as living there. He didn't stop to reflect on the matter more deeply, or he might have considered utility connections and other paper trails.

'Okay, Mama, I'll be back soon. Keys on the hall-stand as usual?'

'Yes, dear. And get some white wine, Herbie. Cheryl's lovely, but she strictly follows the doctor's instructions of no booze. And I'm damned if I'm not going to enjoy a drink now. Nothing to lose, really.' She gave a weak laugh.

'Riesling, I recall?'

'Yes, love. Need some cash?'

Herbie thought about that. Better to have options. He reckoned his mum would have a stash. She'd always mistrusted banks. 'That'd be good, Mama. I didn't really get to save any in prison.'

'Of course, love. Those slutty little minxes have a lot to answer for.' She paused. 'You remember that box of private things in the back of the hall cupboard?'

'Yes.'

'Well, it's my savings account now. You help yourself, Herbie. I sure can't take it with me when I go.'

'Mama, please don't talk like that,' Herbie pleaded.

'Herbie, my darling boy, it's just the way it is.' Her ashen face smiled lovingly at him.

Before he could start crying, he turned and went out into the hall to look for the private box. He opened the cupboard and sucked in the dusty smell that brought back childhood memories of playing hidey. He slid the wooden box out and opened it. It was about the size of a shoebox and it was stuffed with money and other valuables. Oh, this was going to make things rather easier, Herbie thought. He smiled to himself as he pocketed two large wads of twenty-dollar notes. At least five grand there, he mused. He put the box back and closed the cupboard. Next stop, his room at the back of the house.

It was exactly as he'd left it, except for an envelope on the pillow of the bed. He opened the envelope and smiled as he saw the 'Welcome Home!' card from his mum. How long had that been there? She had obviously known he'd come back at some stage. So, so sweet, he thought. How he loved his dear mama.

He pulled open the top drawer of a chest and took out a mobile phone, a laptop, and two chargers. He plugged everything in to start getting power back into the devices. His mum had been paying the monthly accounts before he even went to prison.

He walked out of his room holding the card. As he went back up the hallway, he ducked into his mum's room, kissed her, thanking her for the card, and went out of the house, collecting the car keys from the stand near the front door.

Herbie opened the garage and walked in. His mum's Holden Astra was clean as a whistle. He opened the driver's door, leant in and put the key into the ignition. Then a sudden thought came to him. He stepped back, went to the rear of the garage and knelt down in front of a workbench. He reached under it and retrieved a slim plastic box.

He smiled. Out of the box he pulled two small pairs of knickers. He raised them to his face and inhaled deeply. Ah, yes, he could still smell her, that delightful nine-year-old he'd befriended at the shopping centre all those years ago. There was a lot to be said for the inattention and neediness of single mothers with drug habits. It'd been the easiest babysitting assignment he'd ever had. And did it pay off. He buried his face in the panties. Oh, the memories.

Well, he'd be hunting again soon enough. He replaced his trophies and got into the car. He headed for the shops.

It was four days later when he saw the first news mention in New South Wales of his prison escape, and his photo was published with the story. It was time to head for the house at Treachery Beach to lie low for a while. It wouldn't be long before one of the neighbours put two and two together and called the cops. A couple of them had waved to him since his return, but he'd avoided any chats and they wouldn't have known his recent prison status.

Damn it, he thought. He'd started grooming a girl at the local park when he went on his afternoon walk, carefully timed to be exactly after school hours. But he had to stay free: he was not going back to prison, ever. The prepubescent carnal delights of South-East Asia with Reggie were on the cards big time. So was catching up with Bernhard for some young local meat in the very near future, just as soon as the heat died down. Yes, the next little girl he got in his clutches, he'd have to harden up and kill her afterwards so she couldn't talk. His prison sojourn attested to the mistake of leaving your victims alive to tell the tale. And it couldn't be too hard. He'd watched the great Reggie do in that copper's daughter all those years ago. And they never got caught for that one. Still, for now the priority was to hide. Child porn on his laptop would have to suffice.

So, Saturday afternoon saw Herbie getting his stuff together, telling his mum he'd be back soon and not to believe anything on the TV about him.

She smiled at him. 'Herbie, my love, I wouldn't believe a bad word about you, even if it came from the parish priest himself.'

Well, thought Herbie, there wouldn't likely be a bad word from Father Charles. He'd first slid up Herbie's arse when he was an eleven-year-old altar boy. Yes, Father Charles would only sing Herbie's praises. The clergy weren't exactly the place you went for an honest account. Still, he'd also learnt valuable moves and tricks from the pederast, arse-fucking priest, so he wasn't all bad.

Herbie told his mum he'd be back in a few days. Then he tootled off in her car, up the coast to the beach house.

As he turned off the main road onto the smaller, unpaved one down to Treachery Beach, he was distracted by his thoughts and he nearly collided with a car containing two young women.

Shit, he chided himself, he needed to be more careful. A car accident, even a minor bingle, could mean the cops. Strange, he thought, there's nothing much down here, aside from his family's shack, and a little beach very few people except the locals knew about. Oh, well, maybe those girls had just discovered the idyllic, secluded beach. They looked like beach-bum girls. One blonde and one brunette, both with large breasts in bikini tops from what he could see. Way too old for his tastes, though. No, once breasts started, it was all over. He thought nothing more of the car and the girls, and drove the short distance to the shack.

And so it was on the Sunday, after a great night's sleep with the sound of the waves roaring in, that Herbie was beating his meat over his laptop. It got his juices well and truly flowing, which was immensely enjoyable, but it was also a problem. He needed action, real action: real of the young, in-the-flesh variety. Well, he had wheels now, and a bucket-load of cash.

Maybe a foray down to Sydney? His old mate Bernhard was bound to be into plenty of action; he usually was. Something about that German work ethic. Bernie was always hard at it, getting results. Or maybe Bernie could bring some young morsels up here: the perfect spot for a very private orgy. They'd done it before, many years ago.

He picked up his mobile and dialled Bernhard's number. He got voicemail. 'Hey, big Bernie! It's Herbie. I'm out. Wanna see you. Need some chicken. Up at the beach house. Call me.'

He put the phone down and went to get a beer from the fridge, before returning to make another selection from his child porn video collection.

– 11 –

Sunday afternoon also saw Harry and Trev at the office. With Carla and Lauren having left the Treachery Beach and Seal Rocks area the previous day, the sleuths needed to do rapid work on a new plan to hunt down Herbert Farr, who was proving as elusive as a compassionate banker.

The two girls, Harry's temporary surveillance team, had hung around being well-paid beach bums for the last few days. However, they'd seen no human movement at the house for the whole time, and their escort agency needed them back in Sydney for a Japanese trade delegation. Even with the good money they'd got from Harry, high-class hooking paid a shitload better than being stand-ins for Harry and Trev. So, two of the best-looking surveillance operatives in the history of the private investigation industry pulled up stumps and headed south back to Sydney.

Harry was tapping his fingers on his desk in frustration. 'Surely Farr wouldn't be at his mother's place. A visit, sure, but too bloody obvious to actually stay there when you're on the run. The cops would have to get around to checking next of kin's addresses.'

'Yeah, I agree, and probably sooner rather than later,' replied Trev.

'Well, if he hasn't already, he'll definitely visit mummy dear at some point, though. Given his failed efforts to get the interstate transfer, his dying mother would've been top of his mind when he decided to do a runner.'

'True. But we can ill afford to sit up there for days ourselves. Plus we don't exactly look like a couple of surfer dudes. We'd stick out like pork chops at a bar mitzvah.'

'We might not have much choice, brother. We can't hire any associates to do it, 'cos they'd naturally want to know the target, just like we would. And we cannot afford to be linked to Farr in any bloody way.' Harry paused and lit a smoke. 'At least not in any way we can remotely avoid,' he continued. 'And that's the beauty, in more ways than one, of using amateur stand-ins like the girls. We get eyes in the field, but no awkward questions.'

'Yep, precisely. When are they likely to be free again?' asked Trev. 'We could get them to go back up for a few more days.'

'Yeah, possibly. But wouldn't be until the week after next, Carla said. That trade delegation is in town all week long.'

Trev chuckled. 'Serious economic hot air during the day, serious economic boost to the local sex trade at night.'

Harry smiled. 'Spot on, mate. It's sex that makes the world go round, certainly not free fucking trade agreements.' He exhaled a cloud of smoke. 'Trev, I am getting so desperate to catch this fucker. Now that he's out on the loose, my blood pressure is running high.'

'Chill, Harry, we'll get him. We're better than him, so we'll win.'

'Yeah, I keep telling myself that. I'm just impatient, mate.'

'Understandable.'

Just then Harry's phoned bleeped with a message. He picked it up off his desk and frowned. 'It's from O'Reilly. He says thanks, and to watch the news.'

'Well, this could be huge. We'd better take the man's suggestion,' said Trev, flicking on the TV.

'Maybe we'll hear about something other than the car bombing of Steele.'

'Here's hoping.'

A few minutes later, the early news bulletin came on and, for the first time in forty-eight hours, the assassination of Minister Steele wasn't top bill. Rather, pride of place went to the discovery of a decapitated and mutilated body of a woman in a deserted shack north of Sydney. There was aerial footage from a news chopper, then the reporter at the scene came on camera with her latest report:

> 'Well, Tara, police have confirmed that they've found the body of an adult female. They say the body is decapitated and shows sign of extensive mutilation, but they're not giving any details. I asked them if this meant the woman was tortured, but they refused to be drawn on that.'
> 'And any news on the identity?' asked the newscaster.
> 'Nothing from the police, Tara, but we did receive an anonymous email a short while ago claiming that the body was Porcia Savage, the Director-General of the Office of Community Cohesion and Social Progress. That email described a location just like this one, and so the speculation is that this body is that of Ms Savage. I'll bring you more information as it comes to hand.'
> 'Thanks, Melanie.'

The newscaster in the studio took over the screen again:

> 'The email we received was simultaneously sent
> to multiple media outlets. It goes into explicit
> detail, with allegations of Porcia Savage being
> involved in the cover-up of child deaths in her
> time at the Department of Human Services.
> The email also ties in the car-bomb killing
> of Minister Gloria Steele two days ago. The
> Premier has refused to comment on any aspect
> of the email.'

The news bulletin moved on to the next item.

Trev killed the screen with the remote. 'Well fucking well. Looks as though O'Reilly achieved his vengeful objectives.'

'And how,' said Harry. 'Mate, I bet the message I got was sent either from the air or just before boarding.'

'Oh, yes. He'll be long gone, along with any compatriots. I'd put money on him having needed a team for this. That car bombing was so Northern Ireland,' said Trev.

'Definitely. Well, mate, refreshing to see that once in a while the old saying "every dog has its day" actually comes true. A bit of bloody karma.'

'Yep, I'll drink to that, Harry. These so-called respectable people can still be utter scum.'

'All too often, I agree. Think I'll pour us a drink.' Harry pulled out the Jameson bottle and put generous slugs into two glasses.

As Trev walked over and picked up his whiskey, a message alert came from a phone sitting on top of the office safe.

Harry looked at Trev. 'That's not yours, is it?'

'No, mate, that's Bernhard's. I charged it up after we heard Farr was on the run, just on the off chance.'

'Good thinking.'

'We won't be able to answer the phone, but we can play the message game.'

'Fingers crossed,' said Harry.

Trev picked the phone up. 'You fucking beauty!'

'Is it Farr?' said Harry, as eagerly as a kid asking to go into a toyshop.

'It's coming up as his number in the contact list.' He listened to the message, then looked back at Harry, smiling. 'Think we're on a live one, brother.' He repeated the message. 'And we need to message back shortly, show Bernie's enthusiasm.'

'Yeah, absolutely,' said Harry keenly. 'How soon can we get there, fully equipped, you reckon?'

'Well, brother, a couple of things to organize now we know where he is. Especially if we're going to do the whole job up there, and do it properly.'

'Cool. But we don't want to delay our trip, mate. It'll only be a matter of time before some cop digs deep enough and figures out that Farr's mother owns that beach house. You managed it, so they will, too, eventually.'

'Probably, if they're putting the effort in. And it wasn't hard to do with the publicly available land records, so chances are it won't be long,' replied Trev.

'Okay, so when can we get going?'

Trev thought quickly, his fingers counting off things from a mental list. He looked over at Harry. 'I reckon we can get everything we need tomorrow, and hit him first thing Tuesday morning, just as the sun comes up.'

'Ah, the old dawn raid,' said Harry, a dreamy grin on his face. 'Hell, that brings back some memories, brother.'

Trev smiled. 'Sure does. I'll text back then.' He read his message out to Harry.

> Herbie! So good to hear from you. Will come
> up Tuesday. Busy tomorrow with Dieter. Will
> bring you juicy young surprise!

Harry laughed. 'Nice touch, mate.'
Trev pressed 'Send'.
The phone beeped again.
'Ah, he's taken the bait.' Trev showed Harry the phone.

> Great Bernie, can't wait to c u. Need the surprise!
> LOL

'Sure going to be a fucking surprise,' said Harry, refilling the glasses.

Trev laughed. 'Mate, it'll be the biggest surprise since Adolf Hitler stepped into a joint in Munich called Boots and Belts for a couple of quick steins and found himself in a Jewish gay bar.'

– 12 –

It was dark and moistly warm at 5.30 a.m. on Tuesday morning. Harry and Trev grabbed their weapons and a backpack each. They left the VW van in the empty gravel car park at the beach. They'd placed a fake 'Road Closed' barrier at the start of the track after they'd turned off the main road: didn't need any locals coming down for an early surf. Out of the van, they began the short trek to the Farr holiday house.

Harry was half sternly focused and half exuberant: that wild mixture of nerves, anticipation, and sheer avenging bloodlust. Every day he thought of Orla, what she must have gone through. She would always be in his mind, but he hoped that as time went on, the memories would become sweeter and less tainted.

The air was as heavy as lead and as still as a grave. At this time, pre-dawn, even the wildlife was silent. The pair moved stealthily towards their quarry. The sandy dirt was damp underfoot. The humidity overnight, combined with a downpour, had dampened everything, but without lowering the temperature.

Harry peered through the shrubs in front of the house. He closed his eyes momentarily to picture Orla and to reinforce his violent resolve. He saw her; told her he loved her.

He opened his eyes. The young eucalypt beside him gleamed in the first sunrays breaching the eastern horizon over the Pacific Ocean behind them. Droplets of water collected at the tips of its grey-green leaves, and then fell earthwards like the tears of dawn. It was as if Mother Nature were weeping at the prospect of imminent violence.

'Ready?' he whispered to Trev.

'Always.'

The pair slipped on balaclavas, dashed over the sandy open ground in front of the house, and silently moved onto the narrow verandah. Harry tried the door handle and found it locked. 'He must have got used to locked doors,' he whispered to Trev.

'Do it old school, then,' Trev murmured.

Harry stood back and launched his foot into the door. His force took it clean off its hinges as it crashed inwards.

Herbie was sleeping the sleep of the righteous, to the soothing noise of the waves rolling onto the beach. The enveloping darkness outside was only tempered by the faint glow of the moon, and by his nightlight illuminated on the bedside stand. An earlier stretch in prison many years ago had left him petrified of the dark: one black night he'd found himself pinned down to his bunk as barbed wire was rammed up his anus. A supposed administrative error in the prison admissions office had landed him in mainstream rather than in the segregation wing. Turned out the mainstream population had a spectacularly special welcome for child molesters.

Now, he had dreamy images of the little girls from the last video he'd watched floating around in his depraved mind.

He started from his sound sleep at a loud noise. He opened his eyes, noticing the faint beginnings of daylight seeping through the gaps in the blind. Then there were footsteps. Suddenly the bedroom door burst open and two men with masked faces rushed in, and they had guns. Surely he was still dreaming, he thought. He was sure he had PTSD from his prison experiences. He half sat up.

The stockier of the two men reached him on the bed and smashed his hand across Herbie's face in a vicious backhander.

No, he wasn't dreaming, he reconsidered as he fell back onto the bed in serious pain. Blood started to run out of his nose. What the hell was going on? Who were these monsters? What were they going to do to him? Would he get to see his dear mum again? Oh, shit, everything had been going so well, too.

Harry put his .38 barrel against Farr's head and pulled back the hammer.

'No, please don't hurt me,' whimpered Farr.

'Okay, fucker, the passwords and codes for your phone there and laptop out in the lounge.'

'They're open, no … no codes.'

'Fuck off, dipshit, everyone has codes,' said Harry, pushing the gun barrel into Farr's cheek.

'No, honestly. I've just got out of prison and haven't set things up properly yet.'

'We'll see. But if you're lying, I'm going to put you in some serious bloody pain,' growled Harry.

'Please, I'm telling you the truth,' replied Farr, starting to cry.

Trev exited the bedroom, returning a moment later carrying the laptop. 'Well, believe it or not, he was telling the truth. I'm in.'

Harry passed Trev the mobile phone from the bedside table. Trev pushed a button. 'Yep, no code here, either.'

'Sweet,' said Harry, pulling off his balaclava. Trev did likewise.

Harry smiled down at the cowering Farr. He holstered his .38. 'Know what it means when the intruders take off their masks?'

'No ... no, I don't.'

'Means we don't give a toss if you see our faces,' added Trev.

'I don't get it,' said Farr.

Harry looked at Trev. 'This prick doesn't watch enough crime dramas.'

Trev laughed. 'Too true. Far too busy drooling over kiddie porn.' He looked down at Farr. 'Fuckstain, the fact that we don't give a flying rat's arse about you seeing our ugly mugs means that we're not remotely worried about you identifying us to the cops.'

'But, please, sir, I won't say anything to the cops. I hate the cops.'

Both the sleuths laughed.

'No, you won't say anything,' said Harry, leaning down into his face. 'Because you're going to be fucking dead and, as they say, dead men don't talk.'

'And they don't fuck any more kids,' added Trev.

Farr started whimpering like a whining cat. 'But why? Why me?'

'Ah, such a great existential question, don't you think, Mr Kenmare?' said Trev in a mocking tone.

'Truly philosophical, Mr Matson.' Harry smiled, then punched Farr in the face. The whimpering turned into snotty blubbering as Farr's nose bled even more onto the pillow.

'I'll tell you why, fucktard,' growled Harry, leaning over him again. 'Remember that little girl you animals butchered in the Royal National Park?'

The blubbing slowed as Farr turned his eyes to look up at Harry.

'Yes, arsehole, you should be looking terrified right now. That little girl's name was Orla.'

'Orla?' moaned Farr.

'Orla was my daughter. I was a cop back then.'

'I ... I didn't know she was a cop's daughter.'

'Don't fucking lie to me!' shouted Harry in Farr's face, making him recoil as far as possible into the now blood-spattered pillow.

'But ... but I didn't, honest.'

'Listen, cunty,' said Trev, pulling a phone out of his bag. 'Bernhard told us everything. Before he died, that is.'

'Bernhard? Dead? No, I don't believe you.' Farr lifted his head slightly, in the merest hint of defiance. 'I had a message from him on Sunday. He's coming to visit me here. Today, in fact. He'll be here soon.'

Trev chuckled and put the phone in front of Farr's face. 'Recognize the message?'

Farr looked lost. 'But ...'

'Yeah, this is Bernhard's phone. How the fuck do you think we knew where to find you?' said Trev.

Fear again gripped Farr's face, the bravado evaporating.

'So, Herbie, you little piece of cockroach shit, you're going to tell us all about what you did to my Orla, exactly where Reggie Wheeler is, and about all the other deviant crimes against kids you haven't been caught for.'

Harry paused and took a deep breath before continuing. 'And I want all the details about my little girl, arsehole. So I know exactly what was done to her and who did what. And don't forget we've already got Bernhard's story.'

Farr looked at him. 'I'm sorry about your daughter, I am really. It was Reggie's idea to kill her.'

'Yeah, we've heard that before. And I tend to believe you,' said Harry.

Farr looked relieved, but not for long.

Harry bent back down. 'You just wanted to … screw her, didn't you?!' he yelled, having difficulty getting the coital verb out.

Farr merely whimpered in response.

Trev, meanwhile, had set up a camcorder on a tripod and pulled out from his backpack a pair of pliers, bolt cutters, a soldering iron, and a hair-curling iron. The latter two were now plugged in.

'But … but …' continued the increasingly desperate Farr. 'I've got connections, you know!' The vain bravado resurfaced.

'Oh, really?' mocked Harry. 'Fat fucking lot of good they're going to be to you now.'

'I know senior police!'

Trev shook his head. For a different human on the bed, it might have been a look of pity. But not for this specimen. 'A minute ago you hated cops,' said Trev. 'Now they're your mates.'

'There are ones who like what I like,' said Farr, sticking his chin forward defiantly. 'They'll get you two, you'll be fucked!' He was becoming more daring. At least until Harry punched him in the face again.

'There's only one person here who's fucked, idiot!' Harry grabbed him by the throat. 'So who are these so-called senior police connections?'

'And where's Reggie?' chipped in Trev, pressing the record button on the camera.

'I'm not telling you anything!' screamed Farr, blood and saliva spraying out with the words.

Harry punched him again. 'We'll see about that.'

Trev was now concentrating on Farr's laptop.

'Brother, there's not much here, aside from the usual kiddie porn videos. But there is a separate folder that is password protected. I think Herbie lied to us.'

'Ooh, naughty Herbie. Well, we can't have that, can we, Mr Matson?'

'No, Mr Kenmare, we certainly cannot. Time for the tools?'

'Maybe.' Harry turned back to Farr. He grabbed his face by his jaw. 'Password, arsehole. Now!'

'No!' yelled Farr.

'Now time for the tools?' asked Trev.

'Absolutely. Open the hardware store, Mr Matson.'

'All yours, Mr Kenmare,' said Trev, waving with a flourish at the paraphernalia set out.

Harry assessed the situation. Farr was lying on a flat wooden bed, so there was nothing to tie him to. 'Okay, Trev, you hold him down and I'll do first honours.'

'Roger that.' Trev moved in behind the pillow end of the bed and held Farr down in an ugly looking full nelson. Farr struggled, thrashing his legs and yelling for help.

Harry pulled the blanket off Farr, picked up two socks from the floor and rammed them in Farr's mouth. The shouting became muffled. Then Harry pulled Farr's shorts down. Farr squealed.

'Okay, Herbie, you have no idea what we've got in store for you,' said Harry, with a smile.

Farr had broken out in a sweat, but his moving had diminished as he failed to contest Trev's strength.

'So, Herbie,' continued Harry, 'we're going to show you some real pain, and I mean pain in capital fucking letters. Then you'll tell us everything we want to know. If you don't, even worse pain will follow. Now, after the first dose, you'll probably think nothing could be more painful. But, believe me, Herbie, the pain can *always* be increased. Is that clear enough, cunty?'

There was a sudden fountain of urine in the air as Farr pissed himself.

Harry moved quickly to avoid it hitting him. 'Ah, Herbie. Well might you be scared, 'cos this is really going to hurt unbelievably.'

Farr resumed struggling, but Trev had him pinned down firmly.

Harry came back with the soldering iron on an extension lead. He put the iron down on the bed, close enough to Farr's leg for the captive to feel the radiating heat. He pulled on a latex glove, then picked up the iron with his other hand. He looked at Farr, who was dumbstruck with fear.

'This is going to be agony and you deserve every bit of it. And as the pain invades every nerve cell in your disgusting body, I want you to think of my Orla, and remember this is the vengeance that scum like you warrant.'

Harry sat down across Farr's legs. He grabbed Farr's flaccid penis in his gloved hand, tensed his arm muscles to steady it, and then slowly moved the soldering iron towards Farr. He prolonged the coming together of the two objects, ironically both phallic, for dramatic effect.

Farr's body bucked like a rodeo bull as Harry inserted the tip of the soldering iron into the eye of Farr's dick. It sizzled, as flesh burned, and the pungent smell of cauterizing human meat drifted into the room's atmosphere. After the searingly hot metal shaft had gone five centimetres into Farr's penis, Harry withdrew it.

The pain was so severe that Farr had stopped convulsing and was close to passing out.

Trev released his grip and slapped Farr twice across the face. That brought back a bit of life. He pulled the socks out of Farr's mouth.

Farr gasped and drooled saliva mixed with mucus. 'Please … please … no more.' He was sobbing uncontrollably.

'Well, Herbie,' said Harry, 'start talking. First, the password for the protected file on your computer.'

'It's … it's chickenhawk sixty-nine, all lowercase. I promise you. Please, no more pain. Please!' he begged.

Trev let go of Farr, walked over to the table and picked up the laptop. He tapped at the keyboard. 'Good boy, Herbie,' he said. He turned to Harry. 'I'm in, mate.'

'What's it look like?' asked Harry.

'Well, there's a file called "Reggie", and one called "Police". What do you know?'

'Open that police one up, mate.'

Trev did a few keystrokes. Then he whistled. 'Well, there are emails, photos, videos. Oh, look, even a file called "Lowe". We should have bought a Lotto ticket on the way up here, brother.'

Harry thought back to his nemesis, Commander Mervyn Lowe, and then allowed himself a slight smile as he thought of Lowe having his head hacked off in the remand prison exercise yard last year.

Harry's face hardened again. He turned back to Farr. 'What's your connection with Lowe? And any other cops? And, again, remember Bernie told us everything before he died.'

'I can't … can't tell you.' Farr retreated to his resistant persona.

'Oh, yes, you will,' said Harry, standing up and returning with the curling iron.

Trev walked back over and grabbed Farr again.

Farr's eyes almost popped out, but he couldn't find any words. Not really surprising: when you're naked, pinned down, with an already scorched urethra, and now with a roastingly hot curling iron coming your way, what is there to say?

Trev turned Farr over and pinned him down to the bed again. Harry sat back on Farr's legs and went to work with the hot curling iron. He teased Farr by lightly jabbing his scrotum with the hot metal. That brought on a screech. Trev pushed Farr's head into the bed. Then Harry rammed the curling iron up Farr's rectum. The mattress stifled Farr's screams. The two sleuths grimaced as a stench of burnt flesh and human shit flooded the room.

Harry and Trev stood back as Farr groaned and sobbed into the bedding.

'We can edit the video to remove our interview assistance,' said Trev.

'Good. But we might need to offer more help before the session is done. There's a treasure trove of intel here, just waiting inside this wanker's mouth.' Harry stepped over to the bed and leant down towards Farr's buried head. 'Want some more pain, cunty?'

'Noooo!' Farr wailed. He slowly lifted his face, his eyes swollen with tears and saliva hanging off his chin like a slobbering Labrador.

'Now, did Lowe ever go near my Orla?'

'No, no. It was just the three of us.'

'How did Lowe come to have a video of Orla then?'

'I used to supply him with porn.'

'You give copies to anyone else?'

'No, never. I promise.' Farr burst out crying again.

'All right, Herbie. You ready to be a good boy for us, or are you enjoying the pain, maybe like some more?'

'Please, please, no. I'll do whatever you want.'

'Okay, easy option for you then. Sit up, and look at the camera at the end of the bed. Then tell us, in this order, everything we want to know. Number one, what you did to my Orla; two, where Reggie is, and don't just say Laos, because we know that much; three, who your police connections are; and lastly, we want to hear about any other child sex offences, the ones you haven't been caught for. Especially any dead kids. We could solve a few cases and give peace to some poor families, perhaps. You got it?'

Farr nodded slowly, the trail of dribble swaying in the fetid, shitty, burnt air.

Harry joined Trev behind the camera.

Farr hesitated.

Harry picked up the soldering iron. 'You want more, fucktard?' he yelled.

'No ... no ... please, no.' Farr hauled himself up into a sitting position and looked into the camera.

'Remember, Herbie, it's Orla one, Reggie two, police connections three, and other kiddie victims four, in that order. Now fucking get on with it,' hissed Harry. He waved the soldering iron encouragingly.

Farr nodded desperately, and spat a mouthful of saliva, phlegm and blood onto the yellowed sheet in front of him. He opened his mouth and started.

Harry closed his eyes, his knuckles straining white, as Farr's description of the rape and murder of Orla mirrored Schwarz's: how they'd grabbed her in the street; taken her back to Reggie's den and raped her on video; the girl saying her dad was a cop; Reggie saying they needed to get rid of her; the drive to the national park; raping her again; the shallow grave; Reggie killing her with a shovel. When he included the part where Reggie urinated on Orla in the grave, Harry knew that Farr had given them it all.

Harry took several deep breaths and then opened his eyes. 'Enough. Move on to Reggie,' he said between gritted teeth.

'Reggie … Reggie's working at an orphanage in Laos, in Luang Prabang. He's also got an apartment in the capital, Vientiane. There are emails on my computer with details.'

Trev tapped away on the laptop. 'Can't see any with Reggie's name,' said Trev. 'You might need to do a bit more soldering, Harry.'

'No!' shrieked Farr. 'No, his email name is Santa Claus.'

'Sick bastard,' said Harry.

'Okay, found him,' said Trev. He clicked open a few emails. 'Oh, very good indeed. Addresses, photos, and, oh, shit, kids …'

Harry looked back at Farr. 'Okay, Herbie, that's your part one and part two done. Now for part three, the cops.'

Farr half choked as he tried to continue talking.

'Get on with it, Herbie,' said Harry, raising the soldering iron back into view.

Farr sniffed wetly and noisily swallowed some phlegm. 'Well, there was Mr Lowe, but he's dead. I read that in the newspaper. I only met one other, Mr Hayes. I know there were others, but I didn't meet them.'

'Do you mean Assistant Commissioner Hayes?' asked Harry.

'I don't know what title he has, I just know he's very senior. His name's Bevan, I think.'

Harry whistled. 'Yep, AC Bevan Hayes. Rising star in the fight against terrorism, now seconded to Canberra.'

'Fucking beauty,' said Trev. 'How do you know there are others, Herbie, if you haven't met them?'

'Because Mr Lowe used to tell me how many of them would destroy my life if I didn't keep getting them kids and porn.'

'You have any direct contact with Hayes?' asked Harry. 'Emails, phone calls, anything?'

'No. My contact was Mr Lowe. I only met Mr Hayes once, about three years ago, just before I went to prison.'

'Where did you meet him?'

'I had this kid, a girl. Mother lived next door to where I was staying. She was a druggy and had gone away for a few days, left the kid with me. So, I told Mr Lowe. He told me to stay put with the kid. Then he turned up with this other guy.'

'Hayes?'

'Yeah. I only know that because I checked his pockets when him and Lowe were taking their turns with the girl. And ...' Farr stopped himself.

'What, Herbie? Don't stop now, because there is no limit to the pain I can inflict on you,' said Harry.

Farr looked uneasily at Harry.

'I got a video, it was my insurance.'

'What for?'

'In case I got busted in Sydney or New South Wales. I was going to use it to force them to get any charges dropped.'

'And instead you got caught with your filthy dick up some poor kid in Melbourne, so your insurance was pretty useless,' said Trev. 'Not quite as corrupt down in Victoria.'

'Yeah, I guess. So, I went to prison. But the video's on there.' He pointed at the laptop.

'What's the file name?'

'It's "Piggies Porking",' he sighed.

Harry shook his head. 'You really are a sick prick.'

'Found it,' said Trev, after a few keystrokes. He pressed 'Play'.

He and Harry watched the first twenty seconds of two men raping a young girl.

'Well, there's Lowe,' said Trev.

'And the other one sure as hell looks like Bevan Hayes,' added Harry. 'We need to go through this machine like a dose of salts.'

'Mate, by the time I've finished, this machine will feel like the ladies' college in ancient Rome after the barbarians had finished.'

Harry turned back to Farr. 'Okay, Herbie, tell us about the other kids.'

'I can't remember all of them,' moaned Farr.

'No doubt, you sick piece of shit, but do your best. Or it's more pain for Herbie, another close encounter with Mr Soldering Iron.'

'Okay, okay, I'll do my best.'

And so Farr proceeded, with an occasional spurring on from Harry waving his hot iron, to vomit up episode after episode of paedophilic depravity. Harry and Trev stood back behind the camera and listened. Farr petered out eventually and flopped back against the wall behind the bed.

'That it, Herbie?' asked Harry.

Farr nodded with an exhausted look in his eyes.

Harry turned to Trev. 'You need anything else, brother?'

'Nope, all good, mate.' He nodded at Harry.

'So, all done, Herbie. Time to say your goodbyes.' Harry pulled out his .38 and walked towards Farr.

'But, no, no … I told you everything,' he whined.

'Maybe, maybe not. That's not the point. You raped and murdered my little girl, Orla. The price is death.'

Harry wasn't interested in any more talking. He stood next to the bed, raised his revolver to Farr's forehead and pulled the trigger.

One loud bang, one hollow-point .38 bullet, and Herbert Farr, accomplished paedophile, prison escapee, and utter waste of oxygen, renounced his citizenship of Planet Earth.

'Okay,' said Trev, packing up the camera and tripod. 'Let's get cleaned up and get the hell out of here.'

'Roger that,' said Harry.

'How you feeling, brother?'

Harry smiled grimly. 'Satisfied. Just the big fish to catch now.'

It took fifteen minutes for the sleuths to dig a shallow grave in the sandy soil near the house. They carried out Farr's naked body, wrapped in the yellowed sheet, and dropped him in the trench. Harry peeled back the sheet. Trev then poured two large buckets of liquid caustic soda over Farr's corpse.

'We'll let him sizzle a bit in the air before we fill it in,' said Trev.

'No worries. Let's pack up everything else then.'

Twenty minutes later, Farr's meagre possessions were in the VW van: his computer, phone and wallet all collected for further examination or exploitation, and his clothing and bedding bagged for disposal. Anyone who went into the house later would need to look for hairs on the floor for a DNA analysis or dust for prints on door handles and light switches to find any evidence that Farr had ever been there at all.

Harry and Trev shovelled the sandy soil back into the hole that was Farr's final resting place. His body was already chemically burned beyond recognition.

As the sleuths drove away from the beach house, the van was filled with the morning sun rising gloriously over the vast Pacific Ocean, the honey-coloured sunrise providing the sunset on another phase in Harry's quest to avenge his little Orla.

– 13 –

Harry had showered twice since getting back to the city from his and Trev's beachside butchery. The first had been a long, hot sojourn to wash away the pungent pong of their early-morning exploits. In close proximity to a crime scene, blood and other bodily fluids and excretions had a pervasive and lingering odour. A second shower had followed an early-afternoon nap to freshen up for an evening out at the Emerald Bar, a quiet celebration of the second milestone in his three-part hunt for vengeance and justice.

Before any celebrating, however, Harry had a visit to make. And so late afternoon saw him again standing in front of Orla's grave at Rookwood. Trev was standing a few metres away.

Harry placed a bunch of pink carnations in the vase embedded in the ground. He filled it from a water bottle. Then he knelt with his hand on the headstone. 'My little Orla, the second monster is dead. The last one might take us a while, but I'll be back to let you know. I love you, Orla.' Harry kissed the marble and stood up, walking back to Trev.

Trev hugged him. 'All good, mate?'

'Yeah, thanks.'

'And since we know you are the most unlikely floral expert on the planet, were carnations particular favourites of Orla's or do they mean something particular?'

'Pink carnations stand for "I will never forget you".'

'Beautiful touch, Harry. You've got a decent heart. And a pretty fair right hook, too, as Herbie Farr found out.'

'Good riddance to another fucking oxygen thief. And talking of bottom feeders, any news on your Father Barwick? Seems ages since you've mentioned him.'

'Yeah, nothing major to report, that's why. But my man over in Perth called a little while ago and said he had a promising lead. He was hoping to be able to give me something concrete within the next month or so.'

'Sweet. Looking forward to joining you on your hunt, too.'

'Good man. But for now, time to celebrate your success.'

Sydney was at its sweltering summer worst that Tuesday evening. The air was so heavy and close it felt as though Mother Nature were trying to suffocate the planet, punish it for its sins.

The pair of PIs walked into the pub shortly before six, the front bar almost deserted. Tanya had beaten them there, and was sitting at a table with Liam. Harry ambled over, whilst Trev ordered three pints of Guinness and a vodka lime at the bar.

'I thought you'd be out the back having a smoke, Your Eminence,' said Harry.

'Too bloody hot,' said Liam. 'It's out for a quick ciggie every so often, but then back in here for the cool air. We'll go out again when you two have had a bit of a drink.'

Trev put the vodka down in front of Tanya. 'There you go, Tan.'

'Cheers, Trev.'

'The Guinness, gentlemen, is on its way.'

A moment later a barmaid brought the three creamy pints over on a tray. They all chinked glasses.

'I detect an aura about you two this evening,' said Liam. 'Just like I do about this angel recently.' He lightly brushed Tanya's blonde hair. 'Pray tell?'

Harry grinned at him and took a long draw on his pint, as did Trev.

'Come on, man,' said Liam.

'Let's just say it's two down, one to go. The big one,' said Harry quietly, looking straight into Liam's eyes.

The old Irishman broke into a grin. 'You two are good, very good.' He raised his glass. 'To Orla.'

'To Orla,' they all repeated.

'And what's with you this last week or so, young lady?' Liam asked Tanya. Before she could reply, the news bulletin started on the big screen.

'Hold tight, Your Eminence, we want to see the news,' said Trev, winking at him.

Tanya looked into her drink.

The newscast started, as most had since Friday, with a live cross to police headquarters for the latest on the car-bomb murder of Minister Gloria Steele, as well as its links to the killing of Porcia Savage. The reporter at the scene came on screen:

> Police are maintaining that both killings were professional hits, particularly given the sophistication of the bomb used on Minister Steele's car and the well-established links between her and Porcia Savage. However, the Police Commissioner was again tight-lipped

this afternoon about any leads they may have.
And this is despite the announcement by the
Premier yesterday of a five hundred thousand
dollar reward for information on these crimes.

'Bloody amazing how quickly a large reward is thrown out
there when the victim is one of the Establishment,' said
Harry, shaking his head.

'The bastards look after themselves, without fail,' said
Trev.

'Too true,' smiled Liam. 'But, reward or not, they
won't solve them. O'Reilly and his men will never see the
inside of a court for these.'

'Ironic,' said Trev. 'Justice chasing justice, one could
say, with ethics questionable all round.'

Tanya joined in. 'If there's one thing I've learnt from
working with you two, it's that justice and ethics don't
seem to have much in common a lot of the time.'

'Amen to that,' said Trev. 'And I use the word in a
totally atheist way.' He smiled at them.

'Well,' said Harry, 'as far as I'm concerned, the
departure of these two utterly evil bitches from the planet
is karma at its very best. So, I say, here's to karma.' He
raised his glass.

'To karma,' rejoined the others.

'And I'll even let you get away with calling them
bitches, not my favourite term for women,' said Tanya,
poking Harry in the ribs.

'Well, generally I agree with you, Tan,' said Trev, 'but
this pair certainly deserve the name. A pair of evil, mongrel
dogs, I reckon, who got what they deserved.'

'Agreed,' said Harry. He smiled at Tanya. 'Babe, as you
well know, I both love and respect women. Shit, I'd happily

get on my knees in front of you and start worshipping right now, and it'd be genuine bloody worship.'

Liam and Trev both burst out laughing.

'We want to see that,' teased Trev.

'Bring it on!' added Liam loudly.

Before Harry could continue, Tanya leant towards him, putting on a stern face. She paused a moment, then smiled. 'If you were on your knees in front of me, big boy, there's only one thing you'd be doing, and it wouldn't be bloody worship!' She smiled again, and downed the rest of her vodka.

All three guys roared with laughter.

'Touché,' said Harry. 'I'll pay that one.'

'I'll get you another drink, young lady,' said Liam.

'Thank you,' she smiled at him.

As Liam hauled himself up to go to the bar, another news story grabbed their attention. The newscaster started talking:

> And staying with the current spate of violent killings rocking Sydney, police say they still haven't established a motive for the execution-style killings of a husband and wife couple in Panania ten days ago. Roger and Megan Allen were both shot in the head at point-blank range with a nine-millimetre handgun. The detective leading the investigation said the lack of witnesses hearing any gunshots indicated a silencer was probably used, again pointing to a professional killing. He added that this was consistent with underworld-style executions. We're now crossing live to our reporter on the scene in Panania. What's the latest, Katrina?

Thanks, Louise. The house behind me is still closed off as a crime scene. But we have learned that police combing through the house found a large amount of child pornography, including photos of the dead man, Roger Allen, in what they described as compromising positions with children.

'Sounds like good riddance to another bloody rock spider,' said Harry.

'Yep,' said Trev.

It's also now known that the dead woman, Megan Allen, was previously married and went by the surname of Roberts. Enquiries are continuing, but with very few leads.

Harry frowned. 'For some reason, that house looks familiar.'

'Really?' said Trev. 'A lot of those old suburban houses look alike, mate.'

Harry looked at Tanya, who was staring into her glass again. 'Babe, the name Roberts. Where did you grow up?'

Tanya looked at him, then at Trev, then back at Harry. 'Looks like more justice, doesn't it?' She spoke quietly and grinned. 'It's absolutely raining karma.'

'What the fuck?' said Trev.

'I knew it. I've been to that house, when you were supposedly missing and your mother hired me.'

Tanya held Harry's stare.

'Did you?' whispered Harry.

Tanya winked at them.

'Tan,' said Trev, looking aghast, 'where the fuck did you get a nine millimetre with a silencer?'

She leant into them. 'Archie Longman,' she whispered.

'Bloody hell,' exclaimed Harry.

'Don't worry. You guys have taught me well, so no traces. And Archie certainly won't be saying anything.'

'Too true, no leads in him for the cops,' said Harry. 'Divine One, you never cease to amaze me.'

'Not bloody wrong,' added Trev.

Tanya simply smiled with a mixture of mischief and pride on her beautiful face, her blue eyes blazing with life, and her expression accentuating the classic lines of her high cheek-bones.

Harry looked into the remains of his drink. Then he raised his eyes. Liam was still at the bar. 'Team, I think it's time for us to go on a holiday. Get away from Sydney for a timely absence from the local scene.'

Trev smiled. 'Yeah, that might be quite prudent for a while.'

Harry continued. 'I reckon a trek around South-East Asia is in order. My birthday next month, so drinks somewhere tropical, I feel.'

'That's right, February eighth, isn't it?' said Trev.

'Yeah, our Harry's one of those independent-thinking Aquarians,' said Tanya, touching his hand.

'That he is. So, the tropics with a particular emphasis on Laos, I'd venture,' said Trev.

'Bang on, brother,' replied Harry.

'Cool!' said Tanya. 'I've never been anywhere like that. And don't even think of leaving me behind. I need to get away.'

'Babe,' said Harry, touching her hand, 'you're part of the team, so you're coming.'

'Sweet. And at least this won't be a bloody three-day train trip.'

461

The two guys laughed.

'Oh, and talking of team, so to speak,' said Harry. 'I had a little idea in the shower this afternoon.'

'Of course,' said Trev. 'Where else does one have the best ideas?'

'Exactly. So, my idea is along these lines. We got a shitload of filthy bonus money from the rapists' house in Punchbowl. I've been doing some research and found that there is effective, albeit expensive, surgery available in the US that could rebuild Zanza's tongue and let him speak again. What say we give the big fella a present?'

'Harry Kenmare, you are a lovely man,' said Tanya. She leant over and kissed him.

Trev slapped Harry on the shoulder. 'That's your Aquarian altruism coming out. I couldn't think of a more decent use for the money, brother.'

'Thank you, team. I'll talk to Zanza and Mama then, get things organized.'

Liam returned with Tanya's fresh drink.

'Let's go for a smoke,' said Harry.

They all went out to the beer garden.

Harry gazed up at the evening sky, with its hint of waning sunshine. He pictured a humid jungle clearing, and his meeting with Reggie Wheeler. His hunt had gone well over the five months since he'd got hold of that police file with the details of the three mongrels who needed to be put down.

Bernhard Schwarz had been relatively straightforward, despite the collateral death of Dieter. Still, no great loss to humanity.

Herbert Farr had looked as if it was going to be bloody difficult with him being in prison. But then Herbie's desire for freedom to visit his dying old mum had had the ironic side-effect of delivering the molester to his own fate.

So, for Harry's hunt, only Reggie Wheeler remained. But he was the trophy mongrel: the one who murdered Orla. It was going to be challenging on a whole different level from the first two kills. It was overseas, without ready access to all the resources Harry and Trev were used to. Plus Wheeler, the ringleader, would have a level of cunning and viciousness that Schwarz and Farr, whatever their own evil attributes, had lacked. And it was those two qualities that would make Wheeler a far more dangerous foe.

And when the final showdown arrived, Harry knew that to properly avenge Orla, he'd need to do Reggie with his bare hands. It would have to be up close, intimately personal, and hideously violent. Nothing less would sate him.

After all, this was Harry's quest.

* * * * *

Epigraph Sources

PART 1 – Page 1:

1. Ross Macdonald © 1950.
   The Drowning Pool, p.7. (Edition – Penguin 2012).

2. Charles Bukowski © 1971.
   Post Office, p.112. (Edition – Virgin 2009).

PART 2 – Page 117:

3. William Ard © 1957.
   Deadly Beloved, p.49. (Edition – Dell Publishing 1958).

4. Gustave Flaubert [as cited by Robert Baldick © 1971.]
   Dinner at Magny's, p.104. (Edition – Penguin 1973).

PART 3 – Page 213:

5. Raymond Chandler © 1940.
   Farewell My Lovely, p.97. (Edition – Penguin 2005).

6. John Updike © 2000.
   'The Women Who Got Away', in *The Women Who Got Away,* p.58. (Edition – Penguin 2007).

PART 4 – Page 301:

7. Mickey Spillane © 1947.
    I, The Jury, p.162.   (Edition – Orion Books 2015).

8. Gabriel García Márquez © 1994.
    Of Love and Other Demons, p.6.   (Edition – Penguin 1996).

PART 5 – Page 371:

9. Christa Faust © 2008.
    Money Shot, p.200.   (Edition – Hard Case Crime 2008).

10. Georges Simenon © 1961.
    The Train, p.130.   (Edition – Pocket Books 1968).

Glossary

For all my readers who are not familiar with the local vernacular and law enforcement jargon, here is a helpful list of the acronyms and abbreviations, as well as the Australian slang and colloquialisms, used throughout the text. Some non-Australian ones are also included.

Acronyms/Abbreviations:

AC	Assistant Commissioner (senior police rank)
AFP	Australian Federal Police
ATM	automated teller machine (cashpoint machine)
CBD	central business district (city centre, downtown)
CEO	Chief Executive Officer (corporate President)
CFO	Chief Financial Officer (corporate VP Finance)

D (demon)	slang for 'detective'
DPP	Director of Public Prosecutions (like the District Attorney)
GDs	general duties (uniformed police)
ICAC	Independent Commission Against Corruption (NSW)
IRA	Irish Republican Army
MO	*modus operandi* (method of operation)
NGV	National Gallery of Victoria
NSW	New South Wales (the State of)
PTSD	post-traumatic stress disorder
RUC	Royal Ulster Constabulary
SMH	*Sydney Morning Herald*
TAB	Totalisator Agency Board (betting outlet chain)
TAFE	Technical and Further Education (Australian tertiary college system)
WA	Western Australia (the State of)

Colloquialisms (in the sense they are used in this text):

'Allahu akbar'	'Allah is the greatest' (Arabic chant)
arvo	afternoon
Baygon	brand of insecticide
bewdy	a beautiful thing
binos	binoculars
Brizzie	Brisbane (capital of Queensland, an Australian state)
brumby	wild horse
bush (the)	the Australian countryside
chicken	child victim (paedophile slang)
circle work	doing 360 degree burn-outs in a car
CommBank	Commonwealth Bank (Australia's biggest bank)
demon (D)	police detective
dero	tramp, itinerant
dinkum	the real thing, genuine

doona	duvet, Continental quilt
doughnuts	see 'circle work'
drum	information
dunny	toilet
Feds	Australian Federal Police
gat	handgun
good sort	attractive girl or woman
grog	alcohol
hammer	heroin
Indian Pacific	Australian train service from east coast to west coast
job (in the)	in the police force
kaffir	black African (derogatory white African slang)
klicks	kilometres
Malachi Crunch	sexual position sandwiching a female between two males
moolah	money, cash

ped	paedophile
pineapples	Australian $50 notes (yellow in colour)
piss	alcohol
pom	English person
Port Jackson	the first historic name of Sydney
P-plate	the "P" sign provisional drivers must attach to their cars
Provo	member of the Provisional IRA (Irish & British slang)
recce	reconnaissance
rego plate	vehicle registration plate
rock spider	paedophile, child molester
'roger' (in dialogue)	police jargon for 'affirmative', usually used over the police radio
roger (to)	to have sexual intercourse (English slang)
root	sexual intercourse

rubbernecking	bystander watching behaviour at a scene
shadowing	following, as in surveillance
sharmouta	whore (Arabic slang)
sheila	girl, woman
shout	a round of drinks at a bar / to buy a shout
skippy	slang term used by immigrants to Australia to refer to Australians (from the TV show about a kangaroo called "Skippy")
sledging	throwing insults
Special Constable	armed officer with limited police powers assigned to protection duties
stubby	a 375 ml bottle of beer
town bike	promiscuous girl or woman
tradie	tradesman
true blue	genuine

Acknowledgements

They say the second novel is hardest. Personally, I respectfully disagree.

I've loved writing *Harry's Quest*, the sequel to *Harry's World*. Yes, of course writing is hard work, but then so is everything worthwhile. I've loved growing my characters, expanding the arc of action with them, and driving along the story and their lives, hopefully taking you, the reader, with them.

It's a special feeling, being creative. And there is more to come. Harry and friends are not finished yet, but if you've got here then you're at the end of the novel, and so you've already worked that out for yourself.

My promise is that I won't keep you waiting as long for the next one. I think I'm getting the hang of it! Thank you for reading.

For everything it takes to write and publish a novel, I've got plenty of people I wish to thank:

To my partner Ruth for her support, endless encouragement, and reading all the drafts. And especially for putting up with my writing stuff spread over most available surfaces in the apartment. Ah, living with an author!